The Lazaretto

a novel by

Jason Phillip Reeser

Other books by Jason Phillip Reeser

<u>Fiction</u>
Jury Rig

Cities of the Dead

Lady in the Lazaretto
(coming Summer of 2013)

<u>Non-Fiction</u>
Room with Paris View

Praise for Jason Phillip Reeser's

Lazaretto Trilogy

"The Lazaretto is more than just a place of exile, it is a state of mind. Part psychological thriller, part murder mystery, part bitter-sweet romance, the *Lady in the Lazaretto* is always science fiction at its best." — A.C. Flory, author of *Vohktah*

"Noir literature is uncompromising, and this is an uncompromising science fiction murder mystery by a writer with a mature voice that is sustained throughout the book." — Marc S., *GoodReads* reviewer

"I've been a fan of this series from book one. The combination of noir detective story and high-concept science fiction, while not totally unique, is exceptionally well done. Read the book description. Read the sample. But start with book one in the series, because you will want to follow Gregor, Lilly, McNally and Russell from the beginning of their shared journey through the Lazaretto. Highly recommended for readers of mysteries and hard science fiction. " -S.J. Hunter, author of the *Longevity Law Enforcement* series.

"Reeser does a great job of creating a solid *Whodunnit* in a believable future non-Earth setting." — Jessica F., *Amazon* reviewer

Trilogy Edition, September, 2014
Copyright ©2012 by Jason Phillip Reeser
Cover Art Copyright ©2013 by Jason Phillip Reeser
First Printing June, 2012

ISBN: 978-0615778518

Rocket Fire Books
Westlake, Louisiana
rocketfirebooks.com

For Kathryn.
Your encouragement
is as limitless
as the heavens.

"Society knows perfectly well how to kill a man
and has methods more subtle than death."
--André Gide

"One of the greatest diseases is
to be nobody to anybody."
--Mother Teresa

The people of Earth had never given the Lazaretto system serious thought. The quarantine moon was not hidden from public view, though it did suffer from a collective ennui in society which had grown so bored with anything remotely connected to bureaucracy that all government functions were virtually ignored. Those aware of the Lazaretto took the usual, cynical view of government programs and assumed that it was either an excessive budgetary drain or inefficient and inept process worthy only of disdain and a certain macabre derision.

The inception of the Lazaretto controls had become necessary in the wake of rampant interplanetary epidemics. By the time the Lazaretto system had brought a measured control over the migration of interplanetary diseases, the great interplanetary travel age had ended. No longer did the average man seek to fulfill his wanderlust by booking a flight to the outer planets. Colonists found fewer reasons to visit the home world. Technology had stepped in where angels and tourists had feared to tread. Virtual Vacations replaced actual off-planet larks and there were even segments of the population who had rediscovered the joy of reading about far-off lands. Travel writers like Gloria Dempsey and Pete Nguyen risked the dangerous trip to the stars and wrote poetically of Phasis, Dnepr and the other exotic planets in the Euxine system. The Lazaretto came too late to save the massive travel needs of the early, heady days of space travel.

Interplanetary travel, however, was far from dead. The business of trade was far too lucrative and necessary to die from fear. Death and disease could not stop men from plying their trades in the dark recesses of the universe. The dangers only served to decrease supply and increase demand. Profits soared. The implementation of the Lazaretto built and toppled empires in a matter of months. Old bastions of finance came crashing down while enterprising young upstarts built upon their ruins.

It was this association with massive trade empires that ensured the Lazaretto's corrupt and distant reputation with the general population. And if the corrupting influences of business were not enough to keep one away, the second dominant presence in the Lazaretto was equally distasteful: the government.

The Lazaretto was a throughway for government diplomats, military leadership and personnel, and a myriad assortment of lesser members of the massive central governing institution. Although there were fewer government employees traveling through the Lazaretto than employees of the trade conglomerates, their penchant for corruption was on an equal scale.

It had been the needs of both business and government that had finally convinced the government to spend the money to establish the Lazaretto. At first, small lazarettos had been built on as many planets as possible. They were small facilities, designed for minimum traffic. There had been too many sites to build to allow for any sizable Planet Lazarettos. Before they had been built they were outdated, run down, and in dire need of upgrades. All of them were too small to handle the regular flux of travelers. It took two years of crippling logjams at the lazarettos before the central Lazaretto was given the green light.

Built in the center of the Euxine system, on the largest of Sinop's moons, the Lazaretto was a gateway. All traffic into and out of the system came through the gateway. Any traffic headed back into Earth's Solar System had to leave through the gateway. Any traffic connecting a planet to another planet within the Euxine System—Bukovina, Dnepr, Phasis, Arcobia, and Sinop—had to pass through the gateway without exception.

Once the government had issued the directive to build a central lazaretto, there was a surprising lack of conflict over where it should be based. Sinop's moon, Aegean, was an optimum choice that found nearly universal favor.

Aegean was an anomalous moon that had surprised early space explorers. Though clearly a moon of Sinop, it was found to have its own atmosphere. Moreover, nearly 98% of its surface was covered in water. Its one continent, nothing more than an island, was originally named Far Britain by its founder, British astroexplorer Sir Edward Brown. Though smaller than his homeland, Brown was astounded at how identical the weather patterns reminded him of home.

Far Britain was never settled due to the overabundance of good land available on Sinop. A gentler climate and less hostile environment made the colonists on Sinop forget all about their odd little moon. The decision to build the Lazaretto on Aegean changed all of that. Suddenly, that odd little moon was the center of attention. Despite its rainy atmosphere, it gained a population as workers descended on its wet island to build the interstellar quarantine port.

The Lazaretto was built as two separate ports: one for travelers, one for shipping. Both ports had profoundly different procedures for controlling the spread of contagions.

No human was allowed to enter the shipping port. This restriction also applied to animals, although by this time most of the planets had adopted a ban on the transshipment of livestock between planets. The entire operation was controlled and operated by machines.

As freighters arrived at the quarantine port, all crewmembers were required to disembark and transported to a ship that was leaving quarantine and destined for their planet of origin. In this way, the crew avoided quarantine.

The freighters that entered the shipping port were sprayed down with a toxic biocide that could guarantee the eradication of all known contagions. The toxin was lethal to all living beings. This toxin, once applied, remained on the freighter for twenty-four hours, after which it was deactivated with a heat wash. Nine days were set aside as a safety measure to ensure the toxin was no longer a threat. Although this method of decontamination was expensive, it had a valuable benefit: all freighters were allowed to leave quarantine after this ten day period—one-fourth the time required for humans in quarantine.

Human travelers were required to participate in a more passive quarantine system. Upon arrival at the Lazaretto, all travelers were processed and placed into one of four quadrants. Each quadrant was on a fifty-day cycle. Each quadrant was open for ten days to allow travelers to arrive. Once that quadrant shut its doors, it remained sealed for forty days. No one was allowed in or out.

The travelers who were in quarantine were not treated with any vaccinations. A careful study of the contagions known to be found on the various Euxine planets had determined that any contagion already infecting an individual would manifest itself within ten days. But travelers were forced to wait another thirty days. This was the most important precaution taken by the Lazaretto protocols to make certain that no passengers carried the Euxine Spirare.

The Euxine Spirare was an influenza strain that had once nearly wiped out one-quarter of the populations of the Euxine System and was the final factor in the decision to build the lazarettos. The Plague, so named by a fearful populace, was deadly to nearly eighty per cent of those infected with the virus. The virus had one predictable trait; it could not live beyond four weeks. IHS added two days to the four-week period and required the thirty days of quarantine.

There were no treatments used on sick travelers. IHS had recommended that treatments and vaccinations be avoided as cost-prohibitive. While shipping must be expedited, travelers could wait. The time wasted in quarantine meant nothing to IHS.

Book One

Missing Person

Gregor Lepov tapped an unopened pack of cigarettes on the ticket counter like an ancient telegraph operator. A ticket agent with a cream-filled face focused his attention on the cigarette pack. Lepov stopped.

"Smoking is not allowed on interplanetary flights."

"Really?" Lepov stuffed the pack inside his overcoat. "If I see anyone who smokes I'll pass on your little rule."

The agent glared at the pocket that hid the offending contraband. "Sir."

"I don't smoke, if that's what you're worried about." Lepov slid his PDT over the ticket agent's scanner. Somewhere in the city, money was transferred from Lepov's meager account into AirGlobal's overflowing account. "Don't look so upset. You've outlawed smoking and I'm all for it. But surely you don't object to cigarettes on principle, only when they're on fire."

He boarded the *Bradbury*, a cold, efficient ship. Nothing about her inspired a traveler to consider the great adventure that lay beyond the atmosphere. Her flawless metallic skin gave no hint of the vast void through which she would slip. Its blunt nose seemed out of place; this was no needle-point threading the stars. It was nothing more than a common freighter bearing people as her cargo. Lepov could afford nothing better.

The *Bradbury* was adequately comfortable and safe enough. Accidents in space had ceased to occur more than a hundred years ago. Lepov had never been off planet before but he knew that even the most expensive flights wouldn't spare him the one aspect of the flight he wished he could avoid: stasis.

It was a testament to his need for a client that he boarded the *Bradbury* that day. He had been put in stasis once before and he'd nearly died from the experience. A malfunction in a diagnostic cabinet had triggered the shutdown of his stasis purge during the last stage of reanimation. It had left him with a bad taste for long distance travel.

"Mr. Lepov?"

He'd heard of the famed beauty one found on an interplanetary flight. It was a widely held belief that Flightresses were only a step below the angels. His Flightress was proof that widely held beliefs and fame could be overrated. Her name badge announced her name as "Belle." There had to be a story to explain that one, Lepov mused. His criticism notwithstanding, he warmed to Belle's smiling face and smiled in turn.

"Do you require anything?" she asked as she stored his bag

overhead.

"No, thank you," Lepov took his seat, "unless you know how to make stasis an option on this flight."

"No such luck," she whispered.

Closing his eyes, he thought of his client, Eudia Layne. She had appeared at his door clutching a framed photograph of her son as if he were still a newborn. He wasn't. And Eudia Layne was no young mother.

He pulled a copy of that photograph from the inside pocket of his jacket. So Mrs. Layne was worried about her little boy Ethan. How sweet. A little finger work was all it took to learn that Ethan Layne was no kid. He was twenty-four. Lepov had found no criminal record. Little Ethan was probably just hiding from his mother. Easy money for Lepov.

"Prepare for stasis."

Lepov grabbed hold of his chair, bracing himself.

He opened his eyes and took in a deep breath. It seemed as if he could not satisfy his need to fill his lungs. With one protracted gasp he sucked at the air as if he would never need to exhale again. His only wish: to draw breath deeper into his being. His chest began to tremble, pain swept his heart. Lepov drank in more air, sure he was drowning himself. He could feel his back arching, crushing himself into the seat. The Flightress Belle stood over him, disinterest on that unsightly face. He was dying and she didn't give a damn.

Long after he was sure his chest should have split open he lurched forward and silently screamed as a flood of pain and tangible relief gushed from his wide-open mouth, purging the great breath he had devoured.

It was over. His breathing returned to normal though his chest hurt. Belle placed a soft hand on his arm and bent to examine him. She smiled as he fixed his eyes on her and tried to focus his thoughts.

"Did you see a truck run over me?" He was only half-joking.

"Welcome to the Lazaretto. Do you feel alright?"

"I'll let you know as soon as I find my teeth." Lepov put a hand to his mouth. "All there. I guess I'm alright."

She handed him a glass of water that he only noticed after she had put it in his hand. "Drink this slowly. Your throat will be dry and very sore."

Lepov did as he was told. She mothered him some more, making sure he drank the whole glass and could stand on his own two feet without assistance. This took time and he leaned on the seat in front of him in a vain effort to appear strong. When she asked him to take a step he made a grand effort that almost left him on his face. Belle's strong grip and solid stance kept him upright.

"You're okay now, I think." She let go of him and reached up for his bag. He took the black strap and slung it over his shoulder. The weight of it acted as a counterbalance and he was able to take three consecutive steps without losing his balance.

"Have you ever been to the Lazaretto?"

"No, but I hear the golf courses are out of this world."

"You watch yourself in there." Her smile could not hide her concern.

Lepov had completely forgotten about the Lazaretto, though he was only moments away from setting foot into it. A chill swept over him as if he'd been caught in a sudden downpour. He'd heard unpleasant tales of the quarantine moon since he was a kid. The kind of tales you didn't like to hear in the dark. His disorientation from the stasis was passing and he steadied himself at the *Bradbury's* exit. It was time to find out which stories were real and which ones were lies. He stepped into the terminal.

2

On the twenty-second floor of a steel and concrete office building, the Collector stood looking out over the lights of Lazaretto's Center City shortly after midnight. Heavy traffic on the main streets told him it was a weekend. The permanent residents were seeking diversions. A great pool of lights and activity far out by Delta Quadrant indicated the late arrival of a transport; Delta was about to roll into its incubation and these last arrivals would consider themselves lucky that they would be quarantined the minimum number of days. At the extreme right of his view, a cargo shipment was rolling onto a flight lane for departure.

"Come in." The Collector lifted a glass to his lips as he waved in his associate with his free hand. He had known unquestionably that the Agent would arrive on time. "Pour yourself a drink."

"What do you want?"

"Civilized as always." The Collector poured the drink and held it out.

"You called me as if I work for you. I don't."

"You work at my discretion," the Collector reminded the Agent.

"And what work do you require?"

"You had intended to move into Delta before lock down. Do not."

The Collector set down the glass and crossed from the windows to the center of the room. Etched into the floor below his feet was a circular image of the Lazaretto as seen from space. As a ring of sparkling metal matching the size of the seal began to drop from the ceiling, the Collector began to remove each piece of his clothing. With great care he laid them on the floor outside the seal.

"I have business on Bukovina," the Agent said defiantly, ignoring the Collector's nudity.

"This is not a discussion. I can suspend your travel status."

"No, you won't do that."

The Collector's eyes focused intensely on his visitor.

"And why won't I do that?"

"It draws a straight line from you to me. You don't want that."

"There are other ways to keep you here." The ring now hovered one meter off the floor. A second ring descended, stopping two meters above the floor. The Collector stood in the center of the rings. He stretched out his arms; he was only inches away from touching the lower ring with his fingertips.

"You have a funny way of asking for my cooperation." The Agent watched the Collector inside the rings with a hint of disgust then turned towards the elevator. "I'll stay, for now. Call me."

"Yes," the Collector nodded. "You'll stay."

With a last push of his hands, he touched the ring with the tips of his fingers. Twice the rings flashed yellow before flashing red. A high-pitched howling roared within the circumference of the rings. The Collector's body shook, his hair smashed against his forehead. The high-pressure wave of sonic pulses scoured at his naked body, scraping the skin with shuddering violence. After two minutes of buffeting, the sonic pulses faded. Before the howling ceased, the Collector's hair swirled in a cyclonic burst of final energy.

As the rings ascended, the Collector twitched as if struck with palsy. He bent forward, his upper body suddenly too heavy. It required a great deal of effort for him to regain his balance. A door opened in the back of the room and a stainless-steel automated butler rolled into view. The Collector snatched a clean white towel from its silver tray.

"Can you feel it?" The question hissed through the empty room. "I am clean. *I am clean.*"

Flecks of blood from his scoured body smeared into the white towel as the Collector brushed down the surface of his pathogen free body.

3

"All passengers must enter Lazaretto Registration. All passengers must enter Lazaretto Registration."

The detached voice spoke softly over and over again. Lepov could not hear his own shoes on the gleaming white floor of the terminal as hundreds of other travelers rushed past him in every direction. Yet over the tumultuous mix of voices and baggage carts and video screens he could still hear that one disembodied voice.

"*All passengers must enter Lazaretto Registration.*"

He glanced up at the spotless arched ceiling, trying to spy the source of the droning voice.

"Like the call of the Sirens. Stick wax in your ears, it makes no difference." A man dressed in a black suit laughed at Lepov. "I don't know how they do it. Like a bug inside your head. Look all you want. I've never found a speaker anywhere. But there it is."

"*All passengers must...*"

"...enter Lazaretto Registration. Someday, I'll find the wench who recorded that and tie her down so she'll have to listen to herself for forty straight days of insanity. I'm Silas."

"*All passengers must enter Lazaretto Registration.*"

Lepov stuck out his hand. Silas backed off and didn't offer his own.

"You aren't suggesting we hear that for forty days, are you?"

"No, no. Just on arrivals. Once you clear through *Lazaretto Registration* you don't hear the voice."

A surge of passengers pushed them apart as they approached a wall of glass doors. The words *Lazaretto Quarantine* were etched in stone above them. The flux of the crowd steered them through the doors and under the words and into a crowded passage.

The passage was made entirely of glass. It was solid enough to bear the weight of the moving crowd. An air gap sealed off a second passage in which Lepov could see a less crowded passage. He knew these were lazars, men and women who spent most of their time in transit, and therefore never mixed with the Lazaretto general population. They were allowed to leave for other planets as long as they stayed in the system. The older, first lazarettos that were still on the colony planets were used in this way. It was an express lane system that allowed one the illusion of traveling to a planet without actually being allowed into it.

Lepov's group entered a vast hall. Funneled into three lines, they approached a row of counters. They were in for a long wait. Above him, the ceiling was forty feet away. To his right the hall stretched out like an enormous indoor stadium. Lines of people were visible farther away. He began to wonder just how many of them were arriving in the Lazaretto. There must have been several thousand. The general din of conversations echoed through the great hall as if a massive party were underway.

"Tag."

Lepov handed his Personal Data Tag to a man behind one of the chrome and glass counters.

"Place of departure non-quarantine?" The man passed the metal tag over his reader and gave Lepov a once over. Jowls hung low, he reminded Lepov of a dog that had lived near his boyhood home. When Lepov nodded, the man nodded back. Lepov tried not to stare at his jiggling skin. "You are aware that you are registering with unknown pathogen levels?"

"Yes," Lepov said without nodding.

"First-timer's are allowed a handheld guide. Don't bother upgrading to the Cerebral Guide. You do not want one of those stuck in your head. They never shut up. Stick with the Digital Guide. Twenty-four hours. Make use of it."

"I will."

"Pick up your guide at the main doors. Your PDT will activate the service. Go that way." He pointed towards a set of doors behind him.

A wide stairwell lay beyond the doors. Lepov descended it and entered a corridor where people were lined up waiting to pass through a security checkpoint. Ahead of him and to his right, he could hear a woman speaking with her young daughter. The girl sounded as if she could not have been more than ten years old.

"What will we do for forty days?" she asked.

"Oh, I don't know, Susan. Let's not think about it right now. I'm not sure this is the right line." The mother was clearly irritated.

"But forty days is forever. Won't daddy miss us?"

"Hardly," the mother spat contemptuously. To cover her rash response, she added: "He'll be fine. It's our turn to travel."

Lepov directed his attention to a young couple standing next to him. They were holding hands and brushing gently against each other.

"This is great!" The young man was giddy. "I've got you all to myself. Dave King wouldn't dare follow us here. He'd never willingly submit to forty days of quarantine. Not even to chase you, babe."

"Charlie," the girl pulled away from him and rolled her eyes, "leave Dave alone. He can't chase me, he's got appointments scheduled for at least the next few months. I thought you weren't going to start that paranoid act again. Dave King is married and loves his wife. And I love you. Did you already forget that little wedding ceremony yesterday?"

"No, of course not." The giddiness became nervousness. "One heck of a honeymoon, huh? Cooped up in the Lazaretto. This job better be worth it. Last time I passed through here I nearly went out of my mind."

"Now wait a minute," the girl shook her head with an easy laugh. "Weren't you saying a minute ago how great it will be to be trapped with me in our private room? *Without* Dave King?"

"I didn't have a private room before. I swore I'd never stay in a dormitory again. No matter how cheap they are."

That was more than Lepov needed to hear. A dormitory was all he could afford. He glanced down at his tag, wishing there was some way to change his reservation. There wasn't. Private rooms were both cost-prohibitive and hard to get without advanced reservations.

4

Joey Cho stepped out of the *Blue Forty's* bright lights and dug around in his pockets. He could not find his PDT. He really didn't want to walk back to his hotel. There was enough rain falling to collect on his eyelashes and blur with his vision. It would be a long, wet walk. The effects of the cheap alcohol he'd been drinking wouldn't help either.

Masthead Avenue was still lit up at that time of night. The streetlights didn't power down to fifty percent until three o'clock. Cho should have gone back into the club to find his PDT but he was three drinks beyond the ability to think clearly.

He began walking along Masthead. He could see the hotel from where he was. It was nine blocks away but it stood twenty stories higher than any building near it. Nine blocks was going to take forever.

As he crossed the first intersection, the lights powered down, disorienting him. He stood in the middle of the intersection trying to guess the significance of this event.

Three o'clock.

"Oh, my God," Cho rubbed his temples and tried to picture three o'clock in his mind. "How'd it get this late?"

He never saw the TransitCar as it approached Masthead from the side street in which he was standing. The first thing he heard was the car engine whine as the driver jammed the throttle into a negative position. A howl rose out of the engine that nearly shattered Cho's eardrums. He threw himself forward as the driver slung the TransitCar to the right. It was a lucky guess for both of them. Like a freight train tearing past him, Cho felt the suction of the passing car as he landed hands-first on the street, ripping bits of bloody skin from his palms.

The TransitCar's driver had lost control and the car's momentum spun it back around towards Cho on the wet surface. Despite the burning in his hands he pushed himself off the street and lunged for the shadow of an open doorway facing the adjoining street. Cho fell hard onto a large bundle that was piled in one of the corners. A heavy odor of blood and decay overwhelmed his senses as the heavy car smashed into the building meters from where he lay. It took a few seconds to realize he was lying on top of a body. A swollen, purpled face was smashed against his own. A thick, sticky substance wet his mouth. Instinct reacted more quickly than reason. He wiped and licked at his mouth even as he pushed himself off the corpse. Air moaned through the dead man's vocal chords. Joey Cho screamed.

5

"You have to see this." Detective Arturo Fenelli stood behind the damaged TransitCar as if it were a shield.

"Show me." Lieutenant Ed MacNally had arrived.

"It's right on the other side of this wreck," Fenelli said with a shake of his head. "You look. I've seen it already."

MacNally lowered his head and gave Fenelli a look that clearly meant *you gotta be kidding*. He disappeared around the car.

"You got a light?"

"Oh, fine." Fenelli walked around to the other side of the wreck in resignation. "Right here."

"Huh," MacNally grunted after he shined the light on the body. "Ain't that disgusting?" MacNally's tone made it clear he obviously did *not* find it disgusting.

MacNally was a large man, with chiseled features that made his face look like granite. He did not move gracefully; rather, he made short predetermined moves that always had a purpose. He was overweight, but carried most of it above the belt. This enabled him to move without appearing sluggish.

Fenelli was no Stanly Laurel to MacNally's Oliver Hardy. He carried ten to twenty pounds more than he should, but few people knew it. His body spread his excess evenly making it difficult to detect. But Fenelli knew it, and it slowed him down. He was past forty now and he felt tired far more than he used to.

"Health Services pulled in right behind you. Davis is suiting up. They told us not to get too close."

"You wanna get close to that?" MacNally showed no intention of advancing, though he showed no desire to back off either.

"I wanted to stay back over there." Fenelli jerked a thumb back towards the TransitCar.

"What's his PDT tell us?"

"Says his name is Jack Ford. A lazar from Phasis."

"That's gotta be biological, this ain't no murder."

"You don't think he was beaten to death?"

"Do you?" MacNally asked.

Fenelli forced himself to look at the body again. The body's position made visual examination difficult. From what he could see, the upper torso, including the upper arms and most of the head, were deeply bruised and grossly swollen. The body—the man—had been wearing a business suit. Where the flesh was swollen, it stretched the fabric, giving Fenelli the impression that the suit was a balloon filled with air. From about the waist down, the suit pants were lying as they should be, suggesting that the damage did not extend below the beltline.

"Could have been beaten to death," Fenelli decided. "But that would be one unbelievable beating."

"Forget it," MacNally shook his head. "That's gotta be bacteriological, viral, or what's the other one I said already?"

"Biological."

"Yeah, one of those."

"You a Doctor now, Mac?" Davis, the IHS Technician, pushed past the detectives and stood over the body. He was a little, bearded man with white, matted hair that looked as if it belonged on the back of a stray dog.

"Wait a minute, Davis. Fenelli, did they get all the visuals?"

"Yeah, they finished up before you got here." Two camera technicians had captured moving and still shots from every angle possible.

"It's all yours, Davis." MacNally backed away from the body.

Lazaretto protocol was unique at a crime scene. All bodies had to be sampled and removed for testing. The threat of disease—whether from virus, pathogen, or biological origin—had to be assessed and identified immediately. The only exception being murder.

If a detective declared a death to be homicide, the on-site IHS representative sampled the body then released it into police custody.

"All mine, huh? This is disgusting." Davis knelt beside the corpse stuffed in its suit, pulled off a pair of glasses, and cleaned them on his jacket. He spoke to the detectives as if they were children. "This does not smell right."

"What's it supposed to smell like?" Fenelli asked.

"Not this, that's for sure. Well, time to lick 'em and bag 'em."

No matter how many times Fenelli heard Davis make crass comments like that he couldn't help but wonder if there was something wrong with the man.

Lick 'em and bag 'em was not a technical term, though it was accurate in its description. Davis first laid an adhesive strip on the neck of the body. He counted to fifteen before peeling it back off.

After carefully sealing the strip in a plastic envelope, he stuck a hypodermic needle into the same area of the flesh and extracted two vials of blood. As he worked, two IHS techs rolled a gurney near the body. A clear plastic body bag lay open on it. Protected by full BIO suits, the two men carefully lifted the body into the bag. The swollen flesh burst in several places as they handled it. They did not react to the mess, clearly expecting it.

"That's enough for me," Fenelli turned away before the body bag was sealed. MacNally watched the procedure until the bag was both sealed and tagged.

"You write the report, Fenelli. I'm going back to bed."

That was fine with Fenelli. There was little chance he could have gone back to sleep any time soon. He wouldn't be eating breakfast either.

6

Maria Duvalls sat alone in the white-tiled cafeteria of the *Terminal Clinique de Lazaretto* at four-thirty in the morning. The harsh glare of the fluorescent lights kept her eyes cast down as if she were praying.

She was wearing a soft green nurse's uniform. The uniform pants and top looked more like scrubs than the usual nurse's garb, but the clinic's dress code was relaxed for its employees. Her hair, shoulder length, was held back in a faded blue bandanna. She kept her tired eyes hidden under bangs sticking out from the bandanna. She had seen many unpleasant things in the clinic and it showed.

Startled when a door opened at the end of the cafeteria closest to her, she twisted in her seat to see who was entering.

"Maria, you're still here?" A man with a heavy French accent leaned through the doorway. He was close to fifty, with thick black hair and a delicately trimmed Van Dyke beard.

She smiled, tired but happy to see her husband.

"Georges, I'll be going soon. I promise." She swept her bangs to one side with the back of her hand. She did not hide her eyes from Georges.

"Wait a little longer and I can take you home. It is late." He lifted his watch and corrected himself. "No, no. It is early now. You really mustn't be out alone this late."

"I'll be fine. You can't leave for another two hours. You're the only doctor on the floor tonight." Maria seemed to gain strength from speaking with him. No longer hunched over, she pulled herself straight and even managed to pull her shoulders back a little.

"I could leave early." Georges sat next to her and pulled her close with one arm. "I'm the boss, remember? I can leave any time I like."

"No," she placed a finger over his lips, "I will be fine. Trust me. You know, we are very blessed."

Georges did not miss the sadness in her voice.

"Is it your friend you are thinking of?"

"He had a bad night. It's why I'm still here." Maria rested her head on his shoulder.

"What's his name? It always escapes me."

"Kjarsta. Kjarsta Zoltis." She listened as Georges tried to pronounce the first name. She said it slowly. "*Share-stah.*"

He repeated it.

"Yes, that's close." Maria smiled at his attempt. "He doesn't sleep much now. He is in great pain."

"And refuses the morphine?"

"He hates it more than the pain. He has a sharp mind. He does not want to lose it." Maria sat up and looked at Georges with the eyes of a child. "I'm afraid he will be in pain now until the end."

"That is possible. I am not familiar with his case but I understand little is known about the pathogen killing him. I cannot say what the end will be like for him. It will be hard to watch. Hard for you." As Georges spoke, Maria tightened her grip on his hand. "This Kjarsta means a lot to you. I'm sorry."

"He is a special person. But, they are all special, and all abandoned."

"He has you," Georges squeezed her hand and kissed her forehead.

"And I must go." Maria pulled away from him and rose.

Georges stood as well, gently taking her in his arms. He was shorter than Maria though he stood eye to eye with her. His natural poise ensured he stood fully erect, head up and eyes forward. Maria kept her head down. Georges was forever lifting her chin with one finger.

"Look at me, Maria." He smiled at her as her eyes met his. "I am serious. You must be careful. I could call your brother. I'm certain he will be going to work soon. He could pick you up."

"No," she insisted. "And you only lifted my chin to steal a kiss from me."

"I only remind you to hold your head up and be proud of who you are," Georges protested. "But you may be too smart for your own good."

Georges' beard darted forward with a quick kiss.

"Thief!" she scolded him.

"I take what is rightfully mine," he said with mock solemnity.

Maria left the cafeteria, her spirits uplifted by her husband's foolishness. The stolen kiss routine had been played out by Georges and her since they had been young newlyweds in France. That had been over thirty years ago. She had once heard a doctor's wife say that she tired of the repetition of marriage. Maria could not understand that. She found comfort in the familiar patterns of interaction. She had no desire for new, fascinating conversations. Georges was a man of habit. She liked that.

Georges' concern for her safety was one of those deeply ingrained habits. He always fussed over her and worried that some evil would befall her in the city. Maria, though a shy woman by nature, had always held the strongest belief that God watched after her. She believed that if she were kind to those around her, God would see to it that those around her would be kind in return.

That kind of thinking drove her brother Arturo crazy. He was a homicide detective and he never ceased to support Georges in his attempts to shelter her. She did not mind it really. Arturo and Georges were good men and she deeply loved them both.

She rode an elevator down to the lower lobby then headed down a brightly lit hallway. A set of doors stood impassively at the end of the hall. Moments before she placed her hand on one of the doors it swung away from her. A young security guard, dressed in a green uniform with stiff shoulder boards and a matching hat, towered over her.

"Mrs. Duvalls, what a pleasant surprise."

"Good morning, Karl." Maria had expected him. She knew Georges had called Karl as soon as she had left the cafeteria. Another habit.

"Heading home?"

"Yes, I am."

"I could call a TransitCar for you."

"No thank you, Karl. I'll walk to the SubTransit station." She always did. And she knew Karl would offer to walk with her.

"I'm about to go on break. I could escort you. Just to be safe."

"That would be nice. I'm sorry to be a bother." It was no use trying to dissuade him. No doubt Georges had ordered Karl to escort her. She did not want him in trouble with her husband. Georges was a kind man but he could become angry if he felt his wife had been neglected.

"No bother, Mrs. Duvalls." Karl opened a door and they stepped out of the clinic and into the early morning darkness of the Lazaretto.

7

Arturo Fenelli hitched a ride back to the precinct with a patrol officer. He was tired. Calls at 3:30 in the morning were inconvenient on the best of nights. His definition of the best of nights included getting to sleep around nine o'clock—ten at the latest. He had not had the best of nights. A headache had kept him awake till well past one. Two and a half hours of sleep. That was only enough to make a man mad.

Fenelli laughed at himself when he thought about that. It was a phrase his father had repeated all through his life. If he remembered correctly, it was something his father had said shortly before he died. He'd been talking about the pain relief he received from a prescribed drug. *It only kills the pain enough to make a man mad.*

Fenelli closed his eyes for a few seconds. The buoyant motion of the PoliceTransit dulled his senses. He thought he might have said the words aloud: *it's only enough to make a man mad.* The headache made him mad. His head was splitting. *It's splitting enough to make a man mad.* The patrolman steered them into a right turn. Fenelli felt himself lean to the left. *It's enough to turn a man to the right.*

A close-up image of swollen, putrid skin filled his vision. Someone turned the bruised head to the right. The puffed up body was sick to its stomach. Nauseous.

The PoliceTransit glided to a stop and Fenelli's head dipped down as inertia released him from its grip.

The swollen head dipped down at the same time. Body fluids spilled from a rip that appeared in the back of the neck.

"You okay, sir?"

Fenelli stared at the patrol officer for three counts of reality. He felt like he might vomit as the graphic images lingered in his head.

"I'm good," he lied. He held the palm of his right hand over his clammy forehead. "I'm not sure I ever really woke up."

"I understand, sir."

"You're Ken Oland's kid, aren't ya?" Fenelli gave the patrolman a solid look under the dome light.

"Yes sir."

"Your dad and I went through cadet school together. Damn near thirty years ago, I guess." Cadet school rarely crossed his mind anymore.

"Yes sir. He's spoken of you often, sir."

"Really?" Fenelli climbed out of the passenger compartment and stretched his legs. He didn't know what else to say to the kid. It was disconcerting to hear that Ken Oland had often spoken of him. Fenelli hadn't even spoken to Ken in years. They'd been close the first year on the force. But disparate assignments pushed them onto separate career paths. As far as Fenelli knew, Ken was a desk Sergeant in one of the quadrants. Maybe in Alpha, but he couldn't remember.

More troubling to Fenelli was the knowledge that he had *never* spoken of Ken Oland to anyone in his family. Work was something he never brought home. He had determined as a young patrol officer that he would never allow the dirt and grime of police work to soil his family's life, going so far as to promise that he wouldn't even speak of his coworkers to his wife or kids.

On his worst days, he had kept his work on the force walled off from his family. The department shrink had told him once that such silence was unhealthy. Fenelli readily answered that he was willing to take that risk. His own health came second to that of his family's.

The current incident was a prime example. He would never tell his family about that body. Why introduce such evil into their world?

"I'll tell dad I saw you. He's always asking how you're doing."

"Yeah." Should he defend himself for not having sought out the kid's father over the years? Maybe there was no defense. "Tell him I said to look me up. I don't get much time off, but I can usually get away for lunch."

Patrol Officer Oland shot off a final *yessir*. Fenelli had no idea if he'd ever hear from the kid's father, and tried to forget about it. At least he had been able to quit thinking about that awful body for a few minutes.

8

The SubTransit station was across the street and one block down. The walkway should have been well lit but several overhead lights were not working and had been inoperative for many months. Maria was silently pleased at Karl's presence. Although she had not lied when she told Georges she did not worry over her safety, she did wish that all of the lighting would be repaired. Georges had made a call to the Lazaretto Administration on two separate occasions but there had been no repairs. She had been tickled by his bombastic manner on the phone but at the same time she had been flattered at his efforts on her behalf.

Karl, his large frame stuffed with muscles, walked between Maria and the street. The young man's protective manner reminded her of her childhood back in Rome. Back then it had been Arturo walking beside her. He had never been as tall or muscular as Karl had, but Arturo had appeared as big to her when she had been so young.

Arturo had never bullied her as she had seen other older brothers treat their sisters. Arturo had always been tender with her. He could be hard when he had to be; their neighborhood had not been the safest place to grow up. But he had only been as hard as he had to be, and only when he had to be. It had been about survival for him, not a chosen lifestyle.

Thinking about her brother made her realize she had not called him for many weeks. She would call him. They tried to make a habit of eating lunch together but more often than not time slipped away from them both and the lunch dates went unscheduled.

As Maria and Karl descended the stairway into the station, Maria took hold of Karl's arm. He patiently allowed her to set the pace.

"Look at that, a train is just arriving." Karl led her onto the loading platform and stepped inside the train after the doors split open. He made sure she stepped over the gap between the platform and the train before pulling his arm free from her hold. With a quick glance around the train—Maria knew he was scanning the car for signs of danger—the security guard tipped his hat and stepped out of the doorframe as the doors slid shut.

Maria chose a bench in the empty car. Her feet were beginning to ache. She was glad the car was empty; she could remove her shoes and let her feet breath. Most of the trains heading out to the residential neighborhoods were empty at that time of morning. The ones heading into Center City would have a few early commuters on them. In an hour the incoming trains would be full. If there had been other riders in the car she would never have taken off her shoes.

Leaning back, she closed her eyes. Pushing a button in the armrest of her seat, she spoke after a bell chimed.

"Trireme Station," she said aloud. Her seat would vibrate and a bell would chime when the train arrived at her station.

"Trireme?"

Maria was startled by a man's voice coming from the back of the car. She watched a fair-haired young man sit up. He'd been lying on the last bench. His wrinkled clothing pointed to a night spent in the car.

"Yes," Maria answered him. "Trireme Station."

"I'm getting off at Trireme too."

The young man slid off the bench and walked the length of the car while keeping his eyes on Maria. As if he had been invited, he walked directly to Maria and sat beside her.

"You came from the hospital." He examined her green scrubs.

"Yes," she felt a trace of apprehension as she lowered her head, hiding behind her hair.

"Do I know you?" He pulled back to get a full look at her.

"I don't believe so," Maria kept her head down. Arturo had schooled her well and she did not offer her name.

She turned her gaze to the doors. Above them she could see the station map. There were six stations left before Trireme. As they rode in silence, Maria became uncomfortable under the man's constant scrutiny. Should she leave the car at the next station? Would he let her? There was no reason for her to think like that, save his indelicate decision to sit so close to her, yet her apprehension grew.

The train slowed as it approached the next station. As the car came to a stop the doors slid open. The platform was empty.

Maria tried to breathe normally, hoping other passengers would arrive. The station beyond the platform remained deserted.

"I'm sure I've seen you before," he finally said.

The doors remained open allowing Maria to examine the view of the station. It was as silent and still as a painting.

"You ride the late train home often, don't you?"

"Yes, I suppose I do."

A bell tone sounded above them.

"Your husband doesn't mind?"

"My husband?" Maria couldn't resist looking fully at him.

"You are married, aren't you?" He pointed at the ring on her finger.

"Yes. And yes, he minds."

"I'm sure he does."

The doors closed and Maria and the man remained alone.

9

A man entered the IHS office wearing a spotless black suit. A drab grey tie hung from a white collar with its top button fastened. With measured and deliberate steps he approached a woman at the first desk and stood ramrod straight.

"Dr. Gerhardt Haupt to see Dr. Fisher." His accent was German.

"One moment, please." Helen Segal had the distinct feeling that someone was in trouble. She tapped a command into her deskscreen.

"You're to go right in, Dr. Haupt." There was relief in her tone. The problem had been handed over to others. She turned and arched one eyebrow at Julia, a woman sitting at the desk beside her.

"That man looks like he wants to fire someone," Julia quipped.

"Don't get too excited, dear. The only thing I know is he's from Earth." Helen did not want to start rumors about people losing their jobs. The Lazaretto was a lousy place to be stranded without a job.

Helen and Julia had come to the Lazaretto together. It had all seemed like so much fun then. *Opportunities Abound at IHS! Lazaretto Workers Save Extra Money!* Helen thought about all the money that she had been able to save. There was indeed extra money in the bank. And why not? What could one spend money on in the Lazaretto?

Helen spent the next thirty minutes watching Dr. Fisher's door. The visitor had not come out. As she answered the phone, keyed in schedules and tried not to look at the door, an ominous silence hung over it. It was common to hear Dr. Fisher's anxious voice through the door as he met with visitors, but since Dr. Haupt had entered the office and closed the door, Helen had heard nothing.

She was tempted to interrupt them and give Dr. Fisher an excuse to end the meeting: incoming call, personnel emergency, something requiring his attention down in the lab. Helen was convinced, however, that the German would see right through her. She had no desire to be the recipient of his retribution. Let Dr. Fisher get himself out of there, she decided. Self-preservation made for clear thinking.

Helen Segal had been a clear thinker all of her life. Though her decision to seek employment in the Lazaretto had been a mistake—she had not had all of the pertinent facts when she decided to leave Sinop for the Lazaretto—she had wisely taken an office position over a laboratory position, removing her from what had promised to be a dangerous job that risked exposure to many different pathogens.

Helen's red hair was still dark and full at forty-one. Her figure had begun to show those accumulated years around her thirty-sixth birthday as it had become harder to keep her weight down. She took particular care to hide the effects of age with makeup knowing full well that she was fooling no one.

At night, when she lay in bed surrounded by the shadows and doubts of a single woman's sleepless nights, she would wonder why she bothered to keep up her appearance. She was no less beautiful than the girls with whom she'd grown up but she had never found favor with the opposite sex. At first glance, the fact was a curiosity. If she began to consider it, the fact was troubling. Dwelling on it was an invitation to depression. Men seemed to like her but they always kept their distance. She had once convinced herself that men were intimidated by her overwhelming beauty. This had only been a chimera: a weak use of bravado that fell to pieces as easily as a broken heart. She had taught herself not to dwell on it.

She could not help but dwell on that silent door of Dr. Fisher's. The visitor from Earth could only be trouble.

"Stop worrying," Julia's lowered voice scolded playfully.

"I'm not worrying."

"You've been staring at that door like it's going to break free and attack you. You think that Doctor might be looking for a good time?"

"You mean looking for a young, perky, receptionist from accounting who's recently thrown out her boyfriend?" Helen waved her away with a feigned dismissive snap of her wrist.

"Ouch," Julia bit at her lower lip. "Do I really fit that description? You know, the boyfriend deserved to be thrown out. But I don't deserve to be alone—I was made for love."

"That's true, honey. If any woman were made for love it'd be you. And God protect any man you try to love. But I seriously doubt this Dr. Haupt's the man for you."

"Doctor or no Doctor, I won't be lonely for long." Julia flashed a mischievous smile. "Care to join me this evening?"

"I'd rather not," said Helen. She had gone to a club with Julia one night and regretted it ever since. It had dawned on her fairly early in the evening that she was no longer a kid at heart looking for a night of fireworks and fun. She had stayed long enough not to offend her younger friend and then excused herself. The nightlife was not for her.

Lost in thought over that disastrous night, she had not noticed Dr. Fisher's door open. She did notice, however, when the stiff German stopped at her desk and spoke.

"You are Miss Segal?"

"Y-yes—" Helen managed to say.

"Good. Be in my assigned office in one hour."

Helen could not respond to the German's rapidly delivered command before he turned and strode from the office.

"Helen!" Dr. Fisher called from his open door.

Helen hurried into his office as she pondered the German's words.

"Helen, I'm really sorry about this. Did he speak with you already?" Dr. Fisher indicated an upholstered seat and waited as she took the proffered seat.

Dr. Albert Fisher had a head full of tight, curly hair and a face that was soft and friendly. His brow was often creased with an anxious furrow. His facial expression often suggested that he was having difficulty thinking of the right words to say.

"This really came at me out of the blue." Dr. Fisher held his hands out with both palms up in supplication. "I didn't realize...I was aware he was coming. You remember I mentioned this guy Haupt was coming? Maybe two or three weeks ago. Oh, I really should have spoken with you first, of course. Very rude of me, I know."

"Spoken with me about what?" Helen interrupted him. She knew he would have endlessly fumbled around with an apology if she had let him.

"Oh, I hope you don't mind. I was fully aware of the Official Review. But I should have remembered their request. I can't imagine what I was thinking. I had intended to deal with this last week, but we had that meeting with the Chief Administrator—"

"Request?" Helen was picking out the important bits of his ramblings.

"Yes, like I said, the request. Of course I didn't think you would mind, you've always provided such professional work and I was sure you could handle the job with diplomacy."

"Dr. Fisher?" Helen made eye contact with him.

"This Dr. Haupt," he said after some hesitation, "is here to conduct a review of our office. He has requested that we provide him with a clerk who is familiar with our procedures and personnel. I was going to suggest a clerk from Sam's department when he caught me off guard. He asked that you be assigned to work with him. I have no idea why."

The German had asked for her?

"You told him he could have me?" she finally asked. She already knew the answer to that.

"I really don't think I could have refused him. He comes straight from IHS in Baltimore. *The* Baltimore, as in *Earth*. I really hope you don't mind. I've given him an office on the floor below us. Helen, could you do this for me? Give it a shot?"

"Do I have a choice?" she asked. It was not a sarcastic question. She could plainly see Dr. Fisher's helplessness matched her own.

"You can choose to be cooperative or uncooperative." The doctor clearly worried that she might choose the latter option.

"Judging by Dr. Haupt's demeanor, I had better be a good little girl and cooperate. I doubt he suffers uncooperative females for long."

Doctor Fisher plied her with gratitude and repeated apologies. Helen smiled politely in an attempt to ignore the chill that had come over her.

10

Detective Fenelli sat quietly at his desk wishing he were back home. His report on the body had been filed and he was momentarily free. MacNally had not yet come in.

The office was an open room fifteen meters wide by thirty meters deep. Most of the perimeter was crowded with computer cabinets, bookshelves, and filing cabinets. More cabinets stood in the center of the room with boxes of old paperwork stacked on and around them in no particular order. Desks were arranged around this island of dead files with the same lack of organization. Near one end of the room, a smaller office was separated from the main room by a wall of glazed glass. Against this wall a table had been loaded down with two older coffee machines and an even older model of a wastewater purifier.

With a room-shaking slam, the main office door crashed shut. MacNally pulled off his long coat and threw it on a corner of Fenelli's desk.

"You got that report yet?" asked MacNally.

"I haven't turned it in yet. But it's all under here." Fenelli gestured at the coat covering his deskscreen. MacNally pushed the coat aside to read the displayed report. "You didn't think I would send it off without you, did you?"

MacNally only shot Fenelli a funny look as he scanned the report.

"What would I need to see this for? Some dumb guy gets sick and swells up on a public street? I really don't care. Send the damn thing."

Fenelli leaned forward and tapped a red icon. The file disappeared in a wink of light. Fenelli knew from experience that if he hadn't waited for MacNally, he would never have heard the end of it. However, Fenelli had been partnered with MacNally long enough to ignore his petulant ways.

"We got anything else?" asked MacNally, picking through the papers on Fenelli's desk.

Although most of civilization had become a paperless society, paper was still in use in the Lazaretto. Built with a meager budget, the Lazaretto had been supplied with obsolete computer systems that were unreliable when they were actually working. Data storage was even less reliable. Paper records were used to back up the erratic data storage. No money was available for computer upgrades but a loophole had allowed officials to be able to order as much paper as they wanted. It cost more money to import the paper but no mid-level administrator cared to correct this. Paper records became common again. The great stack of papers in the center of the office was the result of this snafu.

"As a matter of fact, we really don't have anything," Fenelli looked up as he spoke. "I was thinking I could head back home for some sleep."

"What about Trahan? Ain't he gotta be put on this morning's transport to Conde Sur?" The prison transports could take prisoners who had not waited out the forty-day quarantine. No one cared what contagions were spread amongst the inhabitants of the prison barges.

"That's not until the morning after next." Fenelli felt hopeful. "So I guess I'll get out of here. Get some sleep and be back after lunch."

"What's that?"

A document flashed on Fenelli's screen. At roughly the same time, a young clerk with an improbable mustache approached MacNally and handed him a folder. As Fenelli opened his electronic document, MacNally spread his folder out on his arm and bent over its contents.

"What the hell is this?" MacNally lifted the first page from the folder and flipped it over, then back again.

"You reading the same thing I'm reading?" asked Fenelli.

"This says it's the IHS results on our body from this morning. But that can't be right," MacNally kept flipping the page over as if its text would eventually transform into something more logical.

Fenelli had to agree. The guys at IHS never sent results back this quickly. Fenelli tried to think of an exception to that statement, but he realized it was no exaggeration. IHS *never* sent results this quickly.

"They must have mixed up their results with some other data."

"No," MacNally examined the page. "Everything here points to our Masthead body. Swelling, bruising of the tissue. You're kidding..."

Fenelli had seen it too, at nearly the same time. Neither man spoke.

They both read the report from beginning to end. They skipped nothing. Only after reading every line did MacNally finally speak.

"I don't believe it."

"It's hard to believe."

"No, Fenelli, I mean it. I do not believe this. First of all, since when does IHS even run these tests this fast? And when have they ever been that quick to send us results?"

"Never," Fenelli stood up and stuck his finger into MacNally's paper report. "And that's not something I've ever seen. IHS has never stamped a death as *non-contagion/pathogen* without running secondary tests."

"I'm going in to talk to Jenkins. This can't be right." MacNally hesitated. "Otherwise..."

"Yeah, I know. Otherwise, this was one hellacious, brutal murder."

MacNally nodded softly and walked over to the wall of glazed glass. A door appeared under the pressure of his hand. After he passed through it, the door closed and the outline of the door vanished.

11

Maria lay with her eyes closed, afraid to open them. Only two hours had passed. She should have slept for at least four hours, if not six. But something had been bothering her. Something had invaded her sleep.

The man in the SubTransit car. Shame had awakened her.

With a flush she remembered it all: the anxious ride to Trireme Station. It had taken longer as each minute slipped by. The young man had seemed to slide closer with each sway of the car. She had actually begun to wonder if the seats were drawing together.

And then they had arrived at Trireme. She shook her head and sat up, physically attempting to shake off the weight of her guilt. Doors sliding open—she had been too afraid to move—her body frozen to that seat—there had come the sudden conviction that her legs would not work. She dared not leave the train. No matter how afraid she had felt next to the man in the car, she feared him all the more out in the station.

Unable to relax her visible features, she had waited, watching the man with fear. He had stood, that disturbing smile on his face, and he had waited as well. He had hovered over her as if he were attempting to manipulate her by the sheer power of his presence.

And then he had gone; vanished. She had forced herself to stand and exit the car but she could find no courage to walk home. In the advanced stages of a panic attack, she had fled home, rushing nightmarishly against the flow of morning commuters.

She could have laughed at herself if she had not known how terrified she had become. The door. Code in. Lock it twice. Stumble to a chair. Sink into it. Cry. Shake and try to breathe. Pray.

Maria stood up from the bed and pulled a heavy robe around her. She felt chilled despite the controlled temperature of the apartment. For once, it was working fine, but she held herself tight all the same.

She made it all the way to the vanity mirror over a white metallic sink before she could articulate her shame.

Pray. It had been the last thing she had done.

There had never been any reason to believe she had been in danger. The young man had been attentive, forward, but surely that had not made him dangerous? Surely she could have found a way to show him kindness and not fear. Hadn't she insisted to Georges that God would watch over her? Why had she so quickly abandoned her faith?

Georges' and Karl's concerns had heightened her fears. It would be easy to blame them and their good intentions. But she knew how hollow that blame would be. She delicately ran her fingers through her hair and watched it fall back into place. No, she had allowed her fears to cloud her view of the young man. It was most certain she had offended him.

She had lived her life trying to appease those around her. She could not remember a time when she had not been afraid of offending people. As a child she had learned to keep her head down and never make eye contact. It was a challenge to most people. It set them on edge; left them uneasy. It had always angered her father.

He had been an angry man. Maria and her family had come to accept that. None of them had known why he was angry. Her mother took the brunt of his temper, but Maria had known there were no boundaries with him. He could strike out at any of them and for any reason.

It had not taken long to discover that looking her father in the eye was like flipping the switch on an explosives detonator. Her brother had learned it as well, but had never backed down. Arturo never looked away from their father. When their father beat him, Arturo never fought back. But Maria could still see her brother holding his head up and staring into the infuriated eyes of their father.

Maria had never dared such defiance. She had lowered her head and her spirit and tried to escape her father's rage. It had been her way of surviving.

Maria had not thought about her father for a long time; maybe years. Neither had she conjured up images of Arturo taking his beatings with such passive defiance since she was a young woman. She had almost forgotten about it.

Yet now, as bits and pieces of that past ran through her mind, she marveled at a completely new idea. Was it possible Arturo had defied their father *for her*? Had he merely been attempting to keep their father's attention away from her? Why had she never thought of that before?

Maybe she had. Maybe she had known it once. It was possible she had forced herself to forget it. Even now, as she considered what Arturo had done all those years ago, guilt blindsided her. Had he taken that abuse for her? It upset her to think about it; a burden too heavy to bear.

12

If he tried, Lepov could forget he was in the Lazaretto. Once past registration, he was simply living on a new world. A restricted world, to be sure. But there were few worlds left that allowed unrestricted travel. As long as you didn't want to go too far, you felt free enough. And for the moment, Lepov only wanted to get out and have a drink.

He left the dormitory after locking his bags in a metal footlocker under his bed. The dormitory stood on a busy street like any other in his hometown — neon-lit, crowded, and in need of a strong antiseptic rinse. Bars and cafés lined the street with balconied apartments over them. Above those, flat pale rectangles stretched into the shadows as far as he could see. A seemingly infinite number of windows stared down at him.

Ignoring the first two bars he passed, he stepped into one that was well-lit, more of a luncheonette than a bar. The sparse, after lunch crowd ignored him. Lepov sat at the bar. The bartender sat hunched over a book at the far end of the bar.

"Hey." Lepov tapped the counter twice with the tip of a finger.

The bartender furrowed his brow and kept reading. He brought his hand up as a guide and began to follow the words, then stuck his thick index finger at the end of a paragraph and looked up.

"Can I get a beer?"

"Sure." The bartender didn't move.

"Is it good?"

"It's only beer, pal."

"No, I meant the book." Lepov nodded at the paperback.

"It's just a book." The man dog-eared his page and slipped the book under the counter. He was young. Hardly old enough to drink. He looked every bit like a student to Lepov; working his way through school.

"Are you a student?" No sooner had Lepov asked the question before he knew the answer. Student where? No one enrolled in Lazaretto University. It didn't exist. He smiled and tried to laugh at his own question, as if the crack had been on purpose.

"Are you a cop?" He set a beer down in front of Lepov.

Two women were sitting behind him at a booth. Lepov heard one of them break the rhythm of their conversation with a snicker.

He drank the beer quickly, not enjoying any of it. The bartender went back to his book, the women to their chatter. The others in the room made sure never to make eye contact with him. Lepov could hear his own breathing; swallowing was noisy to him. He stood up and left.

It was a pathetic attempt at getting to know the locals, like trying to make a friend in a backwoods village on Bukovina. He tried the next bar with a determination to be more relaxed and natural.

13

Fenelli had gone home to sleep. He hadn't asked MacNally for permission, and he hadn't really cared. He'd needed sleep.

Technically, Lieutenant MacNally was senior to Fenelli. As such, he had to do what MacNally told him — technically. What had always surprised Fenelli was his senior partner's disinterest in pulling rank. He'd much rather bully Fenelli into listening than give a direct order. Maybe MacNally liked the tug-o-war; a way to keep his edge. Maybe it had to do with Fenelli never tugging too hard from his end of the rope.

Going home had made sense. MacNally was still in Jenkins's office. He'd been there for two hours. Whatever was going on would continue without him. It was a good time for MacNally to be the senior detective. Fenelli rarely got involved with the higher-ups.

"Can I get you something? You hungry?"

Fenelli's wife, Lynne, stood over him. She pulled off his shoes and placed them at the end of the couch.

"No, thanks, hon. I had something back at the office. I gotta sleep. My head still hurts. Did I wake you this morning?"

She shook her head. Dark hair and wide-set eyes were the first things any man noticed about Lynne Fenelli. She was heavier than most women, but she refused to take the usual diet aids. She swore they made her cranky and Fenelli assured her he'd rather she be curvy than cranky.

"I can't guarantee it's going to be quiet around here. Lee was coming over for some soup. She wants to talk." Lynne made a face that Fenelli had expected. Their neighbor, a retiree from the Lazaretto Food Services, lived right across the hall and never missed a chance to stop by and talk. She was sweet enough, but by God, she could talk.

"I don't wanna sleep in the bedroom. I'll sleep too much. Let her come in and jabber in the kitchen. She won't bother me."

"You kind of look handsome there, in a worn-out way." Lynne ruffled his thin hair and chuckled as she headed towards the kitchen.

"Just your average, handsome, middle-aged guy with too much weight and too little hair. I'll bet I drive you crazy."

"Oh, that's about right," she spoke loud enough to be heard from the other room. "You certainly drive me crazy. Go to sleep!"

"That's what I was doing," he muttered.

He immediately felt a hand on his shoulder. His eyes popped open and Lynne was back in the room.

"It's Mac."

"What?" Fenelli sat up and looked around. "I never heard the door."

"On the phone," she corrected him.

"I never heard that either," he took the slim silver phone from her and held his hand over the input. "Did I sleep any?"

"Only about a half hour." The sympathetic look on her face said she knew he'd never get the sleep he wanted after he spoke to MacNally.

"Where'd you go?" MacNally asked as soon as Fenelli spoke.

"You're some detective. You call me at home to ask where I am?"

"That's hysterical, Fenelli. Get back here. We've got work to do."

"Hand me my shoes, Lynne. Ed's crackin' the whip." Fenelli spoke to his wife, but MacNally could hear him too.

"Really? You went home to fool around with the old lady?" MacNally followed his joke with a grunt that was supposed to be a laugh.

"Your shoes," Lynne handed her husband his shoes and took the phone from him. She had heard MacNally. "Lt. MacNally, I will reluctantly allow you to order my husband back to the office. But you should know I'm angry with you for interrupting. Shame on you, Ed."

Fenelli rolled his eyes at her innuendo as she ended the transmission.

"You know he gets jealous."

"I'm in competition with a grouchy old man. That can really crush a girl's vanity."

"You'll live." Fenelli kissed her cheek and headed out the door.

If MacNally wanted him back at the office, then Jenkins had backed up the lab report. This was now a murder investigation.

The damage to the body had been bad enough when he thought of it as the results of a natural death. As an image, natural death was a lousy term. But if it had been the result of a pathogen it would still have been a form of natural death, no matter how unpleasant.

But matching the image of the distorted body with the label murder was enough to unsettle Fenelli's stomach. It did a job on his psyche as well. Who could have done something that violent? If only they could have hung this on an age-old boogeyman: space aliens. It was a departmental joke that was really more of a wish. The more space exploration confirmed the absence of aliens, the less chance wild and violent crimes could be blamed on the fantastic creatures that the early colonists had always believed existed. No such luck, they'd discovered. The scariest thing in outer space was still man.

Judging by the condition of that body, the man they'd be looking for might be the scariest one Fenelli had ever heard of.

The elevator doors had not even opened before Fenelli's personal phone whistled.

"Change of plans." It was MacNally. "Come out to Fourth Street. 1800 block. You should get there before me. We got another one."

Fenelli read the address sent to his screen. It shocked Fenelli to realize it was no more than a few block from his own home.

Another what? Body? Fenelli felt sick at the thought. He could have asked MacNally for details but he didn't want to know any. He'd be there soon enough. And if his guess was right, there was no reason in the world he would need to know sooner rather than later.

14

Helen Segal hesitated in front of a plain office door. If she hadn't been so unsettled at the coming encounter she would have laughed at herself. Of what was she afraid? If anything, she told herself, she ought to look forward to this. It was a chance to break away from the boredom of her daily routine.

A chill ran through her. If only the German had not been so cold. She knocked.

"Come." The command carried easily through the door.

Helen obeyed. She stepped into the office and closed the door with a precision she rarely used. She even felt she was standing more erect than usual. The German's disciplined demeanor was contagious.

The small room had only a desk and chair.

"You are a few minutes late," Dr. Haupt stated. "That is acceptable. I only ask that it not become a habit. Follow me."

Turning on his heel, he disappeared through a second doorway. Helen followed.

"Sit down."

She did. This room was only slightly bigger. He took a seat behind a desk, looked up at Helen, and spoke without preamble.

"I have been sent here to conduct a review of IHS in the Lazaretto. I requested that you be assigned to assist me in this review. I will not allow this review to become entangled in politics. Nor will I allow personal feelings to become a factor. This investigation is about the ability of the IHS to fulfill its purpose here at the Lazaretto. If it is efficiently doing so, then I will report as much and leave as quickly as possible. If it is not, then I will report as much, give my recommendations to Earth, and await further instructions. Do you understand?"

Helen understood too well. The German was not there to cut anyone slack. And she was now caught in the middle. How had this happened?

"Yes," she nodded. She'd fought the urge to add *yes sir.*

"Excellent. We will begin immediately. I have already listed the documentation that I require. You will find the list here." He pulled a data tag from his breast pocket and handed it to her. "Forward this to the appropriate departments. See that I have the required system passes so that I can view all documentation at their original electronic storage sites, as well as any required passes necessary to print out hard copies."

Helen took the data tag and left the room. Outside his office, she sat at what was now her desk. Spartan as the room was, the desk contained everything she would need. At least all the components were installed. It was even more outdated than normal.

The deskscreen actually had a keypad for data input. She spoke a few simple commands and confirmed what she had suspected: the system had no vocal input. Even the data tag was not picked up by a proximity reader. She had to set it in a data port before the desk could read it.

This office was no accident. Dr. Fisher had assigned this office to the German to obstruct the review. If they had given Dr. Haupt an obsolete office system to hinder him, what did that say about her role as his assistant? It clarified her situation. She had been baffled that she had been asked to help in the review. She was, after all, only a secretary. Now she understood. She was also an outdated secretary that was expected to slow things down.

"I'm not only going to be caught in the middle of a bureaucratic battle," she murmured, "but I'm going to be used as a shield as well. Tough luck, old girl."

Of course, she might be reading too much into her situation. It was possible that Dr. Fisher had merely assigned this particular office because there were no others available. And hadn't Dr. Haupt *requested* her? Didn't that negate her theory that she had been assigned for nefarious reasons?

"Stop fussing," she ordered herself.

The list from the data tag displayed on her deskscreen and Helen scanned its contents for anything out of the ordinary.

Archived Annual Reports and Audits were near the top of the list. She had expected those. The same went for his request of daily reports, fiscal reviews and many other documents that would present him with an overall view of the IHS facility. All of those were administrative records that would require little authorization.

As she had also expected, he requested lab data relating to the numbers of healthy travelers and contaminated travelers. Such numbers were not as straightforward as they might seem. Few records were kept on healthy travelers. Assumptions were made on the number of travelers leaving the planet as opposed to those same travelers arriving. This was an educated guess that suggested travelers who entered the Lazaretto *and* left it were predominantly healthy and in no way contaminated. According to one study from many years ago, it was determined that ten to fifteen per cent of these travelers had in fact arrived with some sort of contaminant that had run its course during the forty-day quarantine. She would have to explain that if he were not already aware of the fact.

The list also contained requests for more specific lab data: types of contaminants, treatments, outbreaks and containments. She also saw documentation requests from areas with which she was unfamiliar. She would have to get someone to help on determining what authorizations she would need for those.

Helen was surprised to realize she had personally seen many of these reports over the last year. Working for Dr. Fisher, she received and annotated all types of reports and reviews she then passed on to Dr. Fisher as the IHS Administrator. Was that why Dr. Haupt had requested her? How could that be to his advantage? Surely he wanted someone who had no personal involvement in the life cycle of these documents. An opportunity to interfere—to protect herself and those she knew—would be too tempting, at least from Dr. Haupt's point of view. It was hard to imagine he would not realize this. Why take the risk?

She was fussing again. She decided she didn't want to know what the German was thinking. She knew she had better tread carefully.

15

Lilly Stewart sipped at a cup of the worst coffee she had ever tasted. She had known it would be when she ordered it. Comic Joe's always had the worst coffee and the highest prices. Bad-tasting, expensive coffee was the price she paid for the quiet, placid atmosphere of the coffee house. More important than the atmosphere was the clientele. Compared to other bars and coffee shops in that sector, the patrons of Comic Joe's were absolutely cultivated.

She sat in a booth made of dark red leather and mahogany wood. She doubted whether the leather and mahogany were real, although she'd seen stranger things in her travels. Both materials, real or not, were heavily polished, glistening in the overhead can lighting. She held a book with her left hand.

If she had refocused from the page in front of her to the room around her, she would have seen eight more booths in an L shape opposite a dark and scarred bar. This too was mahogany, and the cushions on the barstools were the same red leather. Behind the bar, reflecting the entire length of booths as well as the bar, hung a monstrous mirror over twenty feet long. From her viewpoint Lilly would have been able to see not only the bartender rubbing down the glossy surface of the bar, but she would have been able to see the complete view of his back in the mirror from his belt on up. But her eyes remained on her book.

She knew the bartender was looking at her, however, even as he swirled his cotton bar towel over the same spot. Lilly was easy to look at, he had once told her. He had made fun of her hair, though it was obvious he was actually quite taken with it. Her white hair was long, and held high at the back of her head with a ponytail. Her jet-black eyebrows tapered down over a roman nose and dark chocolate eyes. Her mouth was small, the lower lip protruding in the middle, a glossy dark red that matched the seats of her booth. Her slim body held her head impossibly steady. Long graceful fingers curled around the book with one hand while the second hand cradled the cup of coffee.

She was aware of the bartender's scrutiny and it made her uncomfortable. She disliked attention, yet her strong, graceful presence drew others to her. At one point, while reading, she stopped and looked up. Her eyes fixed on nothing in particular. The bartender stopped wiping at the bar, expecting her to call him, to ask for more coffee. Instead, she merely ran a finger over the top of her cup while lost in thought. She lowered her head and resumed reading.

In the space of the next silent moment, the door to Comic Joe's swung inward. An old bell attached to the top tried to ring, announcing the arrival of a customer, but it only managed a dull clank. A man stepped inside and watched the bell with suspicion as the door slowly closed. He raised a brow at its odd sound and walked to the bar.

Lilly was facing the door. Even as she read she could see the man enter. His hesitant arrival caught her attention. There was something in his stature that suggested humility — a firm yet unassuming nature. She could almost believe he was a lost little boy searching for a familiar face.

He ordered a drink. She liked his voice immediately. It sounded like the voice of an old friend; a kind friend. He pulled a flat black rectangle from his jacket pocket and held it up, scrutinizing it as if he were an archeologist examining a shard of pottery freshly dug from an ancient ruin. It was the size of a cigarette box. After holding it both close to his face as well as at arm's length, he shook it. With an indifferent resignation, he tossed it on the bar.

Lilly laid down her book, not bothering to mark the page. She slid from the booth and crossed to the bar until she stood beside the man. Her long fingers reached out and closed over the black object.

"Squeeze it," she said as he turned and examined her. She held the box up and softly squeezed its edges. A digital display of color flashed on the small screen.

"Hey, thanks. I think my digital guide should have come with instructions. I've been carrying that thing around for most of the day. I've only got a few hours left on the rental."

The bartender set the man's drink down on a square white napkin.

"Can I offer you a drink in gratitude?"

Lilly smiled and nodded towards her booth. "I'd take another bad cup of coffee."

"Coffee for the lady." He motioned to the bartender. "Matter of fact, coffee sounds better than this." He pushed the drink back towards the bartender.

"It won't be," Lilly warned him. "Come sit down." She led him to the booth and they both slid sideways onto the red leather seats.

"You're reading a book," he said.

"Are you surprised? Women illiterate on your home world?"

"Bukovina? No, nothing like that. I saw a bartender reading a book a few minutes ago. That's kind of odd; real paper-bound books."

"A labor of love that actually made it to fruition." Although she was sitting in the booth, she managed to lean forward enough to bow at her waist with one firm nod of her pony-tailed head. "I'm Lilly Stewart."

"Gregor Lepov," Lepov held out his hand. "A pleasure meeting you, Miss Stewart."

"Lilly," she prompted. She looked down at his rough hand but made no move to extend her own for a handshake.

"Lilly. Whose labor? What labor?"

"Some ridiculously rich man—so rich his name doesn't matter— had a funny idea. He collected thousands of old books, like this one. And after collecting these books, he shipped them to the Lazaretto. He seemed to think that all these people sitting around in quarantine would enjoy reading a real, live book." Lilly was enjoying herself. She loved the story of the rich man and his books and warmed to the subject. "He collected books of every kind: classic novels, torrid paperbacks, whiz-bang science fiction, dark mysteries. But he also sent poetry, philosophy—man's greatest and deepest minds. And then he threw in everything else he could find: cookbooks, gardening books, textbooks, almanacs."

The bartender set two cups of coffee in front of them and removed Lilly's empty cup.

"So he ships them all here, and distributes them all over. You know, after a few days here, the idea of reading a book on concrete engineering begins to make sense."

"You're reading poetry, not concrete engineering." Lepov raised the coffee to his lips and drank. "Oh, my—that *is* bad."

"I warned you," Lilly laughed.

"You said bad coffee...I didn't know." Lepov began to laugh even as he lifted the cup to drink again. "What is this?"

"It's coffee. Nothing but bad coffee."

"You know," Lepov set the coffee down and pushed it aside, "you're the friendliest person I've met since I started this trip. Well, except maybe one other lady; a Flightress by the name of Belle."

"How lucky for you, Gregor Lepov. A Flightress, no less?"

"No, not that friendly." He nearly blushed. "I meant that people here aren't exactly neighborly. They're rather cautious."

"This isn't a normal world, Gregor. You'll get use to that." She moved from using his full name to his first name with seamless grace. She liked his name; liked hearing herself say it. It was a strong name and she already believed it fit him.

"And how is this world abnormal?"

"Idle people, suspicions and fears of contagions—helpless frustrations. The moneyman with the books was right. Escape helps." She sat across from him and began to wonder who this man was. He was a big man who looked as if he could do anything he put his mind to. But it was the little-boy-lost act that intrigued her. From what she could see, it was no act. "It's your first time. You'll understand after awhile. You'll learn that people are unwilling to shake your hand—a possible path for contagions. What brings you to the Lazaretto for the first time?"

"Passing through," he tried another sip of the coffee and grimaced. "No handshakes. Noted."

Lilly could see him catalog the fact with a tilt of his head as if he were writing notations on a pad. She had a feeling he did that with all information. She knew this man's questions were never trivial.

"No," Lilly considered his response and rejected it, "you're not passing through."

He said nothing in reply.

"So you have secrets? That's okay. We all have those." She was sorry to discover it. A thin but perceptible wall had been instantly raised between them. She suppressed the urge to withdraw from him and looked him in the eye. "Well, Gregor, if, after your Digital Guide has ceased to offer its services, I can be of assistance to you in any way—" she paused to take a breath, "—count on me. I'll be your corporeal guide."

He nodded in gratitude. She could not tell if he had sensed the change in this early stage of their friendship, but she was sure that boundaries had clearly been set.

He reached inside his coat and pulled out a box of cigarettes, setting them down in front of him. She noticed the box was still sealed in plastic as he played with it, flipping it over and over on the table. It was a nervous gesture; he did not appear to be aware he was doing it.

"My lucky charm," he said after he noticed her watching the box.

"How's that?"

"I quit smoking these damn things two years, three months, and a handful of days ago. I bought this last pack as a way to remember how much I was hooked on 'em."

"Or maybe as proof that you're in control?" she suggested. His smile told her she had made a pretty accurate guess.

"This place have a bad lunch, too?" He slipped the pack back in his pocket.

"Actually," she admitted, "it's not all that bad."

16

Fenelli made it to the 1800 block before MacNally. An IHS MedicalTransit hovered silently near the entrance with red lights spinning in unison from each corner of the van. Three PoliceTransits were lined up on one side of the street. Fenelli parked his own vehicle half a block away and jaywalked across the street. He did not see any IHS personnel on the street and asked a patrol officer at the entrance about them.

"IHS? He just got here. Walked inside maybe two minutes ago."

"Thanks, officer." Fenelli always tried to show the street guys some respect. He well remembered the poor treatment detectives had given him back when he had worn the uniform. "Were you first on the scene?"

"No, that's Fritsch. I haven't been in there. From what I hear, I don't want to."

"Yeah, that's what I was thinking." Fenelli unbuttoned his coat and stepped through the door.

The building was made up of apartments much like his own. An officer in the lobby directed him to the fifth floor. The elevator was operational. Leaving the elevator, he walked towards a group of men standing at the far end of the hallway beside a door to a stairwell.

"Fenelli, where's your gorilla?" asked an older man bearing a Sergeant's rank on his sleeve. The other officers with him snickered.

"I taught him how to park the car this week, Maggie."

Sergeant McGee scowled at the nickname. His friends called him Maggie but he had never considered a detective to be a friend.

"You should have tethered him to it. If MacNally insults one of my boys again I ain't gonna let it pass. You tell him that, Fenelli."

"You tell him," Fenelli walked by without slowing. His empathy for street cops never extended to McGee. "The body's on the stairs?"

"The kid? Yeah, on the landing. Have fun."

Kid? Fenelli hesitated at the door before giving it a push.

"Fenelli's gonna lose his lunch," Sergeant McGee said to the others. He knew Fenelli could still hear him. There was a perverted sense of humor in his tone. "He's got kids of his own. No doubt. He'll come back outa there white as a comet. Fast as one, too."

Fenelli entered the stairwell angered. Not at McGee. He was

used to his tasteless humor. More to the point, McGee had been right. Fenelli did have kids, though they were grown, and if the body was a young kid and looked anything like the body from last night then it was possible he would get sick and have to get back out of there.

"Fenelli?" The IHS man was not Davis this time. It was a younger man with the rather comical name of Bibbly.

"What's going on?" Fenelli saw immediately that Bibbly was packing up his equipment and preparing to leave. He wondered that equipment had even had time to be unpacked.

"It's all yours. I don't envy you."

A small bundle of bloody clothes lay on the middle landing between the fifth and fourth floors. Fenelli could not see much of it until the IHS man climbed up to the fifth floor landing and freed up his line of sight.

"You've already taken your lab samples?" he asked skeptically.

"Oh, I didn't need to. This kid's an exact replica of the victim from last night. We have orders to let you have it." Bibbly sounded relieved that he did not have to *lick 'em and bag 'em.*

"I don't get it."

"Nothing about it to get, Fenelli. We're labeling this one same as the last. It's all yours."

Bibbly hurried from the stairwell as if he were afraid someone back at the office might change their mind. The door slammed shut and the resulting *boom* echoed down the bare walls and scuffed concrete stairs.

Somewhere in the back of his mind, Fenelli could see Sergeant McGee waiting expectantly in the hall, ready to laugh as Fenelli bolted from the stairwell. But that was the least of his worries. He was far more concerned with what he was about to see on the landing.

It was indeed a child. The small boy could not have been seven years old. He was dressed in loose play clothes, hand-me-downs that were too big for him. Because of this, the swelling on the body did not appear as grotesque as it had on the man in the suit. But Fenelli knew it was only an optical illusion. As far as he could estimate, the boy's bruises were indicative of a similar attack. From his face to the lower end of his torso, the boy had been bludgeoned. Viciously assaulted.

McGee had been right. Bile threatened to rise up his throat. The boy's distorted face reminded him of his own kids.

God in Heaven, he wanted to cry out, *why had this happened*?

"What in God's name happened?" MacNally asked from behind. Fenelli was surprised to hear his partner asking a nearly identical question, albeit in a less reverential tone.

"I didn't hear you come in," Fenelli said. The trivial was easier to talk about at times like this.

"Watch out," MacNally pushed past his partner and approached the body. "IHS already tested and cleared this, right?"

"Sort of," he answered.

"What does that mean?" MacNally squatted beside the small body and studied it as if he did not even notice the disturbing violence and its stench. "Can't be maybe ten years old, huh?"

"I doubt he's eight." Another trivial matter on which to concentrate. Fenelli had been a father of young kids and could estimate a child's age far more accurately than the childless MacNally.

"What did *sort of* mean — about IHS?" MacNally hadn't taken his eyes off the child.

"IHS got here maybe five minutes before me, but when I came in, he was already leaving. Said he had orders to turn it over to us." He winced at calling the child *it*. "If I understood correctly, he said he didn't run tests. The visible damage confirmed the kid was a victim like the body last night. I've never seen them not test a body. They don't do that."

"Yeah, that's weird." MacNally stood up and scanned the stairwell with a sweep of his head. "Not much to go on, is there?"

"We'll look at the visuals that were taken. See if anything shows up with the filters." It was getting easier for Fenelli the more they conducted their business.

Did MacNally understand how difficult this was for him? Was that why he was being less caustic in his comments and more businesslike in his actions? Or did this kid's death bother MacNally as much as it had Fenelli? Was it possible MacNally's tough shell had been cracked?

"I want to talk to the first officer on the scene."

"Hold on," Fenelli pulled open the door and leaned into the fifth floor hall. The officers around Sergeant McGee spoke in quiet tones but stopped when Fenelli yelled "Fritsch!"

A young pimple-faced officer who might as well have had *rookie* stamped across his forehead looked up. After a glance at McGee — looking for permission to assist the detectives, Fenelli guessed — he followed Fenelli into the stairwell.

"Give me the story," MacNally said with manufactured patience.

"Well, uh, I got the call, about 11:00. I think…I think his mother found him." It appeared that young Fritsch was going to give them the whole story as slowly as he could without actually stuttering. MacNally rolled his eyes when the rookie said *I think*. "I'm sorry. It was definitely his mother. She'd been looking for him since this morning. I think… he was there for breakfast but shortly after that he was supposed to go to a store and come right back."

"Did he?"

"No, uh, no. I checked with the store. He never showed up." Fritsch kept his eyes on MacNally and it was obvious he was intent on not looking down at the child.

"Is this the position he was in when you found him?" Fenelli asked.

"Yeah. That's it."

"Don't look at me, Officer Fritsch." MacNally read the name from his badge. "Look at the victim. Detective Fenelli asked you if this was the position you found him in. You won't know that until you look at him. You have not been in here for a while, right? IHS came in here, the visual artists came in, and two detectives have been in here. Do not presume that the body has not been moved. Look before you answer."

Fritsch swallowed hard and then looked down at the middle landing. It looked as if he were having trouble exhaling. He was taking in one long breath that went on forever.

"Same position?"

"Yes." He finally figured out how to exhale.

"Okay, that was easy, wasn't it?" MacNally climbed the steps to the fifth floor landing and edged his large bulk past Fenelli and the rookie. "Let's go talk to the mother."

17

Maria sat at a small table in her kitchen and watched Georges finish eating the soup she had made for him. Maria had already finished eating her plate of garden vegetables with sliced almonds sprinkled over them. Garden vegetables were difficult to purchase in the Lazaretto and these were the only sign that pointed to her husband's high income.

As Directing Physician for the clinic, he had been forced to accept a salary the Board insisted he be paid. The money was credited to an account back in Paris. Georges withdrew a sufficient amount to ensure a comfortable living.

But the vegetables had been a gift from Georges. He had ordered them from Dnepr and they arrived every month. Maria knew he was concerned for her health. She had never been sick, but she had lost her energy as each year passed. She did not think of herself as frail, but she was well aware that she was not nearly as strong as she ought to be.

And so she ate her vegetables as the doctor ordered. It pleased Georges to see her eat them, though he declined to eat them with her. She had tried to insist he eat them but he did not listen.

He was content to eat soup.

"Are you okay?" Georges asked her. It was a routine question for him but she could hear more concern in his voice than she usually did.

"I'm tired. I did not sleep much before you came home. Why, don't I look well?"

"It's nothing, only I thought you seemed upset when I came in." He looked into his soup and thought quietly for a moment before looking back at her. "Did you see Karl when you left the clinic?"

"Yes, he was very sweet. He walked with me until I stepped onto the SubTransit. I'm fine. You might be worrying too much about me again. Finish your soup."

She had not told him about the young man on the SubTransit. She knew it would worry him. And the more she thought about it, the less she believed there was anything about which to worry. The young man had been overly friendly but he had been polite. Georges had the suspicious and wary mind of a husband and he would certainly see the actions of the young man as threatening—ominous even. Poor Karl might be forced to escort her all the way home, next time.

No, she decided, she would keep silent about the incident. She would probably never see the young man again.

But clearly Georges had detected something in her manner. She had to be careful about that. Once Georges scented a problem he never gave up until he had rooted it out. And Georges was in need of sleep as badly as she. Perhaps even more.

"I will clean up. You need sleep." Maria took his soup bowl and did her best to appear happy. "Will you stay on the late shift much longer?"

"Maybe another week. I have nearly seen all that is necessary."

Georges had been working the late shift for the past week. It was something he did periodically so as to observe the doctors and nurses with whom he did not normally work. As Directing Physician, he felt it was vital to interact with all personnel at the clinic.

"You look tired," Maria brushed his thick hair and tried to force it to lie down. "You do not handle night work as well as you once did."

"I was thirty years old then. I am happy I only do this occasionally. I'll leave the dark of night for the young men." Georges reached up and took her hand, pulling it from his head down to his lips. "You are not quite as young either, Maria. You should stop working nights as well."

"It is his worst time of the day. I told him I would be there for him." She was speaking of Kjarsta.

"I know," Georges' voice was tired and the words came out as a whisper. "I know. But I still don't like it."

"He could not hide it last night. The pain is getting worse. He is so proud, and tries so hard to make us believe he can handle it. He said that to me once. He told me never to pity him because he can handle the pain. He said he could take it all in and make it go away. Perhaps he believes in the gods of his people."

"Who are his people? He's from Phasis, isn't he?"

"Yes, but I don't know who they are. I know so little about Phasis. But no matter his beliefs, he cannot override the pain. I have watched him when he sleeps. It eats at him. As if a shadow is draining him of light, a little at a time. He always smiles when he awakes to find me sitting with him. But I know better. The pain is etched too deeply in his face."

Maria's eyes watered. She did not like to speak of such things. A tear slipped from one eye and she quickly brushed it away.

"You need to sleep more than I," Georges ran his own finger over her cheek to dry a second tear. "I will clean up. Give me the bowl. It will take no time. Go. Lie down. I'll join you in a minute."

Maria nodded. She needed to sleep, to quit thinking about Kjarsta, to forget the young man in the SubTransit, to shut down for more than a few hours. Georges gently pushed her towards their bedroom.

18

"Tell me everything, come on." Julia patted the table and shifted excitedly in her chair. "I want to hear it all. I want to know about him, what he wants with you — all the details."

Helen settled into her chair at the small lunch table and smoothed down her long skirt. She had known lunch would be like this and she didn't mind in the least. It was rather flattering to know that for once, she had excitement of her own to share.

"Well?" Julia demanded.

"I suppose it's safe to tell you that I won't be back in the office any time soon. I'm temporarily assigned to Dr. Haupt."

"Doing what? I can't imagine working with him. He's a cadaver."

"Julia, be kind. He is a little stiff, but..." Helen was having trouble coming up with a suitable compliment.

"Well," Julia fussed with one half of her sandwich, "what does he talk about? Did he ask about me?"

"He doesn't talk about anything. He could barely speak enough words to tell me what he wants me to do. I have to fill in the gaps. Sort of extrapolate what he wants from the few cryptic words he speaks."

Helen felt guilty exaggerating like that. Regardless of how short a time she'd known the German, she did not like to speak ill of him. Of course, his strict demeanor and short manner made it easy for her to dislike him. She recognized how natural it was to feel reprimanded in his presence regardless of what he said.

"Poor Helen—stuck with a weirdo."

"No, he's not so bad." Helen looked for a way to atone for her previous comment. "He's polite. There will be less of a strain between us over time and become familiar with each other."

"Well, polite can be another word for *cold*," Julia brushed off the idea. "Polite men have always been a nuisance to me."

Both women sought refuge from the conversation by turning their attention to their lunches. The next few minutes were occupied with complimentary utterances about their food, as if they were taste-testers at an amateur cooking contest.

"Did I tell you," Julia suddenly lost interest in her food as her mind shifted gears, "about tonight?"

"You asked if I wanted to join you. Out to another club?"

"Not just any club, Helen dearest. I've been invited to the *Blue Forty*." Julia opened her eyes wide as if Helen should recognize the name. "Don't act like you don't know what the *Forty* is! I showed you that article about it, remember? That tight little place on Masthead. Invitation only? I know you remember."

"I think so," Helen lied.

"Right, that's the one. Only big-money Lazars get in there, especially tonight. Delta's about to close down, so they're having a Delta send-off. You have to come with me!"

"No, I'd better not. I'm worn out. I'd rather get some rest."

Helen wanted to admit her nerves were shot from trying to figure out what was really going on with her job and Dr. Haupt.

"You won't come?" Julia made big eyes at Helen and tilted her head to one side. She held that pose for only a few seconds, then stopped posing and shook her head.

"You're messing everything up. I wanted to surprise you."

"With what?" Helen asked.

"I was going to introduce you to Billy." Julia rolled her eyes off to one side in her best imitation of coy.

"Okay, I'll bite. Who's Billy?" Helen had no interest in Billy, but Julia would never stop until the question was asked.

"Only the greatest guy I've met in a really, really, long time."

The look in Julia's eyes told Helen this was going to be another one of Julia's mistakes. She'd seen that look on three separate occasions and each of the three guys had given Julia nothing but pain and regret. Helen knew Julia would never learn.

"Relax," Julia tried to soothe her, "this guy's wonderful. He's employed. Isn't that a nice change?"

"Employed doing what?" Helen asked skeptically.

"He wouldn't say. But I think it's a pretty good job. Now, don't roll your eyes, Helen. I may not know what it is he does, but I know he works for Laz Administration. Or at least, that's who signed his checks."

"Signed? Past tense?" Helen sighed and shook her head for good measure.

"He's got some kind of difficulty, right now. Some kind of disagreement with his boss. It's not as bad as you think, dearie. He'll get it straightened out. And I really don't care anyway. This way, he's always got plenty of time to spend with me. He's an absolute taste of Earth!"

"Sure, plenty of time to spend with you." Helen had heard Julia say that about the last two men. Only, Julia had eventually tired of them always hanging around her apartment with nothing to do. "Julia, you haven't let him move in, have you?"

"Of course, why wouldn't I? Trust me, Helen. When you meet this guy you'll know I've made the right choice. I wouldn't care if he'd dropped out of the sky; I want him home with me. All for me."

Somehow, lunch had lost its flavor. Between Julia's new boyfriend and Helen's new boss, she felt lightheaded. Neither new development could end well.

"Come to the *Blue Forty* with me tonight, please?" Julia was overzealous in her begging.

"I'm sorry, Julia. I simply can't. I'd better get home tonight. I get the feeling I'm going to need my rest on this new job. Don't take offense."

"You're gonna miss a lot."

Julia ate the last bite of her sandwich and scooped up her trash from the table, flashing a disappointed smile at Helen as she headed back to work. Helen sat alone for a few moments, looking at her half-eaten sandwich. Her usual practice was to save whatever she hadn't eaten for dinner. But for the time being, she found it difficult to care at all about the sandwich, her supper, or anything else for that matter.

She decided it made no difference to her why she'd been chosen to work with Dr. Haupt. From that moment on she would no longer ponder the consequences of being placed in an awkward position between Dr. Fisher and Dr. Haupt. She determined to do whatever job had been given her to the best of her abilities and damn the end results.

She briefly considered joining Julia at the club that night but decided that her reckless frame of mind was not a good starting point for a night in a club. She was going to go straight home. But first, she had to make it through the rest of her first day working for the German.

19

Gregor Lepov liked the woman's company far more than the coffee. His mind and body were still trying to synch up after his shuttle flight. The coffee helped, but chatting with Lilly was the better therapy. It gave him a chance to get his feet more firmly planted on the ground. And he decided that he didn't give a damn about Ethan Layne. He'd start looking for him later. For now, he'd concentrate on Lilly.

It wasn't that he was playing hooky from work. He could simply tell he was in no shape to do his job. Stasis had left him far more addled than he had expected. His mind was definitely not as sharp as it should have been. Lepov was not the type of man to admit to weakness but he was forced to admit he was not ready to go looking for that kid.

He let the sour taste of the coffee work its way through him while he sat listening to Lilly. It didn't hurt that she was pleasant to watch. Her white hair was unusual and distracting. He decided he liked white hair.

One of the men who had been standing at the far end of the bar began to walk in their direction. He walked with a rhythm in his step that suggested he could hear music that no one else could hear. He slowed down as he approached Lilly's table. Lepov had seen him coming and watched the man with distrust. The man put a hand on the back of Lilly's booth and leaned over her.

"A sexy woman like you needs a real man like me. Move over."

Lilly slid over without hesitation.

"I never pass up the chance to be with a real man." She reached over and picked up her cup of coffee. With the same gesture she managed to point in Lepov's direction. "Gregor Lepov, a new acquaintance. Gregor, this is Carlos Montillo, a dear friend and obviously, a real man."

Lepov remembered handshakes were taboo. He nodded his head, mimicking Montillo's gesture.

"Nice to meet you, Mr. Montillo. Lilly has taken a virgin traveler under her wings and has been tutoring me on the finer points of the Lazaretto."

"How lucky for you. Miss Stewart, I am certain, will be a most excellent tutor." Montillo swung his gaze around to Lilly with an exaggerated wink. "I wish she would tutor me. This would be an exquisite thing. Though I am not a virgin…anything."

Lepov had met dozens of guys like Carlos Montillo during his years both as a cop and as a private detective. Women almost always found such obvious playacting charming. Lepov had always found it impossible to endure. The sweet-talker appeared to be of Spanish descent. Most likely he came from one of the more distant colonies near the far edges of the Euxine system. Many Spanish colonies had chosen to set themselves up where they could govern themselves with a certain sense of isolation.

"You will be coming tonight, Lilly?" Montillo asked. His tone was confident though his face expressed playful concern.

"Never miss it, Carlos." She smiled at the Spaniard as if he were her favorite pet. She explained to Lepov: "a few of us hard-working types are getting together to let our hair down for the night. We tend to let business overtake our personal lives so we fight back every now and then. Would you be interested in coming along? I can't promise you much beyond a few good drinks and moderately interesting conversation."

"I shouldn't intrude—" Lepov politely declined.

"That's not the point. You'll be an important addition to the evening." Montillo was adamant. "Come with Lilly. She'll make sure everyone loves you."

"It's only for a few hours. It won't be that bad," Lilly promised.

"And who are these hard-working-types? Co-workers? Do you work here, in the Laz?"

"Oh, no." Lilly smiled pleasantly. With the shake of her head she was able to suggest the question was silly without making Lepov feel that he was silly for asking it. "We're Lazars."

"I see," Lepov said.

"He's never heard the term," Montillo's smile was less pleasant. "I'll bet he has no idea what a Lazar is."

"I've heard the term," Lepov added.

"I do my business in the Laz," Lilly explained. "You might say I live here. Off and on."

"Business?"

"I'm a dealer in art. Antiques."

"Lilly is more than a broker in rare art," Montillo added with flair, "She personally escorts the piece from its point of origin to the collector. And everything must pass through the Lazaretto. And so too, must Lilly. And we are all the better for it. She is a flower, our Lilly."

"That's rather thick, Carlos," Lilly scolded.

"Wouldn't a piece of art move through the Lazaretto faster if you did not accompany it? I understood cargo has only a ten day layover."

"That's true, Gregor. Escorting the art multiplies the length of its quarantine by four. My personal attention is not for expediency. It is to ensure the authenticity of the piece. I must see the piece when I purchase it for a collector, and I must be there to make sure the same piece is put in the hands of a collector. My personal attention is a guarantee."

"And a pretty price tag as well," Montillo added with his approval. "But don't think she only moves one piece at a time, Lepov. Lilly is a shrewd businesswoman. She manages to double up her transit charges. Sometimes even triple them."

"That must work out nicely for you," Lepov said. "If I ever become wealthy and begin to collect art from the far reaches of the Euxine, I'll look you up. Now what about you, Mr. Montillo?" Lepov asked.

"I'm a broker, of sorts. Nothing as romantic as Lilly's antiques. At the moment, I am representing two separate companies in a joint shipment of raw materials."

Lepov recognized the evasive answer for what it was. He was prying where he had no business. Wouldn't he have done the same if they had been asking the questions? He changed the subject.

His best bet was to stop investigating and enjoy the evening.

20

Dounia Rodyakov sat on a metal kitchen chair. At forty-five years old she would never have another son like her Misha. The boy had come to her late. There were those who'd said she was too old to bear him. But she had defied them all. She had stubbornly given birth to a strong little boy who should have been the light of her later years.

She sat upright in the metal chair as if her body were made of that same metal. If she had wanted to lean back, if she had wanted to relax, she would have been unable to do it. Occasionally, she trembled, much like a steel rod trembles when struck with force. It was obvious to Fenelli that the truth was hitting her with enough force to slowly break down her rigid defenses. Each time it hammered at her she shook with the blow.

"Mrs. Rodyakov," MacNally sat on a matching chair on the opposite side of the table. He had softened his manner more than Fenelli had ever seen, "I don't want to take up more of your time than is necessary. And the sooner we get this finished, the sooner we can leave you alone."

She shook at the word *alone*. MacNally cleared his throat and looked to Fenelli leaning in the doorway.

"Mrs. Rodyakov? The Lieutenant is going to ask you a few questions, is that alright?" Fenelli asked in a firm, loud voice.

The woman sat with her knees together and her hands clasped over them. She had been staring at the center of the table but turned her head when Fenelli spoke. She wore a look of surprise, as if she had no idea why these two men were in her kitchen.

"Was Mikhail spending time with anyone lately?" MacNally asked gently.

Mrs. Rodyakov sat perfectly still and Fenelli wondered if she had even heard the question. He was about to suggest they call for medical help when the woman shook her head almost imperceptibly.

"Okay," MacNally smiled encouragingly at her. "Did you hear anything outside your door this morning?"

She shook her head again.

"How did you find him?" MacNally watched her expression and realized too late he'd made a mistake.

"Dead." She trembled all over.

"I'm sorry, Mrs. Rodyakov. What I meant to ask was why did you look for him in the stairwell?" The big detective glanced back at Fenelli with a look of helplessness on his face. He was better suited to working-over suspects, not nurturing emotionally damaged mothers.

"He hides there, sometimes." Her sudden words caught both detectives off guard.

"In the stairwell? Did he meet friends there?"

"No." Tears formed a glaze across her eyes.

Fenelli understood her. He was leaning on the doorframe because he too was having trouble coping with what he had seen. If the little Russian boy had been his, he was confident he would not have been able to cope with a bunch of questions, regardless of the detective's discretion.

"Do you have a husband, Mrs. Rodyakov?" Although the detectives knew the answer to that question, they preferred to ask as if they were unaware of her marriage status. Many times, despite official court records, the man listed on the certificate was not always around.

"Of course." She seemed surprised at the question.

"Where can we contact him, is he at work?"

"I'm not sure." She answered MacNally with a puzzled look. "He should be there, but I called him. He was not there."

Fenelli slipped out of the room and went back out into the hallway.

"Hey, McGee." He waved the Sergeant over to him. "Has anyone been able to contact the father?"

"No," McGee answered promptly. Something in Fenelli's tone must have convinced the Sergeant that the time for droll wit had passed. "He's employed at some bar in Center City. He's a dishwasher. He doesn't report into work until this evening. But no one can find him."

Fenelli rejoined MacNally in the kitchen. Mrs. Rodyakov was still sitting upright and finding it difficult to answer questions. MacNally looked up at Fenelli.

Fenelli leaned close to his partner. "No one can find him."

"Did your husband see Mikhail last night?" MacNally asked her. She nodded. "Did he see Mikhail this morning?" She shook her head.

When MacNally asked her if her husband had been drunk when he came home last night, she vigorously shook her head.

Fenelli touched MacNally on the arm and indicated with a tilt of his head that they back off. MacNally seemed relieved at the suggestion.

"You're not getting much out of her right now," Fenelli said once they were in the front room. "Let's see what the visuals give us and we can come back if we need to."

"I'll tell her we'll get back to her. Hate to just leave her like this. But I don't like the idea of taking her down to Homicide, either."

"We don't have to," Fenelli pulled open the front door. "Go sit with her for a few minutes. I'll be back."

He hadn't seen any female officers in the building but Fenelli had a better idea. He walked back down the hall and spoke with McGee and the others. If he could find a neighbor who was well known to Mrs. Rodyakov, they could make sure she had someone to stay with her. She was in no condition to be alone. Where was her husband? More than likely he was sleeping off last night's alcohol with someone he shouldn't. It was a cynical presumption, but Fenelli rarely found absentee husband's to be devoted.

A neighbor was found who knew the Rodyakovs. She only knew them in passing but she had information that proved to be useful.

"I think they have family upstairs. Maybe two floors up. A brother or a sister. Something like that." The neighbor apologized for her inability to be more specific.

"No, that's helpful." Fenelli sent one of the officers to find the relative. "Did you hear anything this morning? Did you see anyone up here that didn't belong?"

"No," the neighbor looked up at Fenelli, half hidden by her door. "Is it really the boy? He's been murdered?"

"He's dead." It was an abstract word in relation to what was lying on the landing between the fourth and fifth floors.

Mr. Rodyakov's brother was found on the seventh floor. He'd

been unaware of what was going on two floors below him. Nearly sixty years old, he could hardly hear anything the officers tried to tell him. No, he had not known Mikhail was dead. No, he had not seen his brother all morning. Yes, he would look after his sister-in-law.

Mrs. Rodyakov continued to sit in a semi-catatonic state. Her brother-in-law, once he understood what was happening, knew what to do. He began making tea and shooed the police out of the apartment.

A police MedTech unit arrived to recover the body in the stairwell. Fenelli and MacNally watched as they wheeled the small body bag into the elevator. Thomas, the lead tech was livid and directed his anger at the detectives.

"Those damn IHS guys are reckless. What are we doing picking up a body like this? If they weren't sure he was contaminant free, they should have taken him and done their own lab work on him."

"Bibbly said he was sure. Though I can't see how he could be." Fenelli thought about what Thomas was trying to say. "What makes you think they weren't sure?"

"They coated this kid. They could have warned us. We would have worn protection anyway, but that's sloppy. And it's a cheap way to handle it. Makes me mad to see it. Kid's parents got no money so they think no one cares about him."

"What are you talking about?" Fenelli asked.

"They sprayed him with Shipper's Formula."

"The biocide?"

"Yeah, kills certain contagions within minutes. Of course, it kills the host as well. But I've seen them do it to a corpse before. It's a cheaper way to handle the possibility of contagions. You never know what the corpse had, but whatever it was is neutralized. It's an older safety measure that is rarely used anymore."

"You must be wrong about that, Thomas. Bibbly told me there was no contagion threat at all."

"Well I'm sure there wasn't. That's why I hate to see them coat him. It's an overly cautious way to handle this. This IHS guy is probably afraid of his own shadow. But even so, I'd like to knock his teeth in."

"Why?" Fenelli didn't understand.

"That stuff is toxic. If my guys hadn't been wearing complete protection, it might have gotten into their skin. And like I said, it kills the host. It doesn't take a lot of it."

That's all we need, Fenelli thought. One of our own dying from someone's incompetence. There had been enough death in the last twenty-four hours.

21

Georges was still asleep when Maria left their apartment and would remain so for many hours. Maria had been awakened by wind buffeting their windows. She knew she would never get back to sleep. She had learned long ago not to fight it. Better to get out of bed and find something to do.

Getting out of the apartment was something she enjoyed. She missed the open spaces of Italy. Although she had been raised in the crowded neighborhoods of Rome, she had spent many summers in Villa Santa Lucia at the base of the northern slope of Monte Cassino. Wandering about the wooded slopes alone, she had found that the insular daydreams of youth could shelter her, however briefly, from her father's dominance. The unspoiled landscapes provided escape from the impure world of man.

Georges had been able to supply that in her life. He was gentle with her, and never sought to dominate her, recognizing the soft spirit in her that shied away from cruelty, sarcasm, and the profane.

Her brother Arturo had also been able to protect her from such things for a time, but then he had left home and she had needed someone like Georges. But even Georges could not be all that she would need.

She still craved that isolation she had known in Villa Santa Lucia. She had been lucky enough, even in the crowded, sullied atmosphere of the Lazaretto, to find it.

Terran Park had been designed by the Lazaretto Administrators to be a tribute to Earth. It was meant to provide the confined crowds of travelers a last chance to enjoy grass between their toes before a quadrant locked down. But Lazaretto travelers had their own ideas, and meeting in the parochial setting of a lush park was not one of them. Most people facing forty days of quarantine embraced a *carpe diem* posture and reveled their nights away in Center City clubs. Terran Park was largely ignored.

Maria loved it; a twenty-acre park set between Center City and its residential zone.

Along the northern edge of the park, Bosporus Avenue was crowded with tax-free shops where travelers could buy nearly everything from the Euxine System. A majority of the items were tacky replicas of Phasian Living Jewels, Dneprish perfumes, Bukovinan knives, and many other items that Lazaretto travelers discovered — much too late, of course — were not only worthless, but had no practical value during their extended layover. A few of the shops did handle quality items, including a wine shop that sold authentic Sinopese wine. Wine was highly valuable during the forty-day quarantine for those who could afford it.

The southern edge of the park was lined with apartment buildings, the tallest in the Lazaretto. Six soaring sentinels built in the Futurist architecture of the mid-twentieth century stood like robotic fingers of glass, steel and concrete. Their designer had expected them to glow like the pillars of a great and shining city. Instead, the persistent gray overcast of this moon's atmosphere rendered them something more menacing, like the six fingers of a robot clawing desperately for sunlight at the shroud of sky overhead.

Maria and Georges lived in One Terran Towers, the first tower built. Their apartment was on the backside of the tower, facing Trireme Avenue. Maria had longed to obtain an apartment on the park side, but none had been available when they moved in, and she had come to think of their place as home, no longer wishing to move again. She did not mind that the home she shared with Georges did not look out over her private haven. That might have been too invasive.

Not having a view of the park from their rooms also gave the park a more mysterious aura. She might have lost her desire for its trees and waterways had they become familiar to her. As it was, she always felt a sense of wonder as she entered her sanctuary.

So now, as Georges slept, she made her way down the tower and out into the park. A stone walkway led from the tower into the shadows of a thick grove of hardwood trees. The weather was clear, the midday sun almost visible through the light cloud cover. The trees and grass were damp from the morning mist; the paving stones discolored and still slick. It was a beautiful day, Maria thought. Exactly what she needed to shed her troubled thoughts of Kjarsta.

After walking through the grove, she crossed a glade carpeted with a feathery grass that held millions of jeweled droplets left from the mist. They did not shine as they would have in sunlight, but Maria could catch pale reflections all around her. She had always thought of them as sad diamonds. She enjoyed such ideas. Surely sad diamonds were used to make fairy jewelry.

It was silly to have such fancies. Georges did not disapprove of such things but he never understood them either. It was harmless, she knew. Beneficial, even. Those kinds of ideas kept her going in a world as harsh as the Lazaretto. Terran Park served the same purpose.

Beyond the glade, she approached a fountain. The fountain was made up of four gentle streams that poured forth from the mouths of four pitchers being held by as many stone fauns. The fauns stood in a square with their backs to each other, each one with a different facial expression. One had the face of happiness, the second a melancholy face. The third face was peaceful and contented. The fourth face was full of anger and rage.

Maria sat on a bench that faced the melancholy faun. From there, she could see the happy and content fauns in profile, but more importantly the face of the angry faun was turned away from her. She never liked to sit where she could see it. She detested its harshness and could only feel fear and despair when looking upon it.

The melancholy faun never conveyed this feeling of despair. She knew sadness; it had been a part of her since she was a young child. She found comfort in that. Georges had shown her a way not to revel in it; he had in fact given her a reason not to revel in it.

But rage was a beast she had known as well, although it had never been one that had found a home in her. She had fled from its terrifying presence into her private world, and she wanted never to allow it into her sanctuary. She often wondered who had sculpted the fauns, and why he had allowed such anger in the park.

If only the fairies would turn it to dust. At the least, Georges could arrange to have it removed for her birthday. More fancy she knew would never happen. She avoided mentioning the park to Georges. It was something of which they rarely spoke. The faun, for all his rage, had to stay. But she did not have to look at him.

"Maria!" a small voice shouted her name.

Any other voice would have broken the spell of the fountain and the park. Maria would have pulled away from it, maybe even have tried to hide from it. But not this voice.

"Maria!" a second voice called. It was smaller than the first.

Maria smiled at two children who appeared from out of the woods. The bigger child was a boy of ten years named Jack. He had a heavy frame and broad shoulders. Despite his size, he seemed to move everywhere on tiptoe. The second child was seven years of age. Her name was Beth. She was a round-faced girl with plump arms and legs. Her cheeks glowed bright red and she often brushed back her long yellow hair with both hands at the same time.

The children's father was a doctor at the clinic: Dr. David Edgars, a virologist on loan from Dnepr's Becker University. David and Cathy Edgars were a breath of fresh air for the clinic. Full of youth and energy, their most precious commodity that they had smuggled into the Lazaretto was hope. It had been concealed in Dr. Edgar's medical education and early intern work at Becker. Though younger than the doctors who had been laboring at the Lazaretto for innumerable years, his education was far more up-to-date and incorporated techniques about which the clinic doctors had only read. But hope had also secreted itself with the Edgars' arrival in the spirits of their two children.

With the gray backdrop of the constantly damp Lazaretto, Jack and Beth Edgars spread sunshine wherever they ran. And running was their primary mode of transport. To them, the wet dark moon they discovered was full of adventure and mystery. They had found nothing dreary or despairing about it. It was a one hundred and eighty degree twist from their home on Dnepr and they couldn't get enough of it.

Jack and Beth delighted in the murkiness of the Lazaretto. Terran Park had become their private wonderland.

When Maria had first met them, it had been at a welcoming party for the Edgars held in her and Georges' apartment. The Edgars had moved into Three Terran Towers, and the little party had been designed as a simple meet and greet. The children had been reserved, in awe of all the new faces. There were no other children present that evening and the Edgars kids had been disappointed and sulky.

But the first day she had met them in the park she discovered two different little people. It was as if two woodland fairies had sprung from her imagination. Jack and Beth were the most wonder-struck children with whom she had ever interacted. It was the one interruption she ever hoped for in her private time at the park.

"You can't beat me!" Jack seemed to leap as his speed increased, as if adding height to his run would make him that much faster.

Beth's only response was a soft but impassioned growl as she strained to win the impromptu race.

Maria turned sideways on the bench and watched them streak towards her. This, she told herself, was exactly what she needed. Sleep could erase her fatigue but these children could eradicate her silly fears and her despair for Kjarsta. She and Georges had never been able to have children, but for this time of her life, she had been given a taste of what it would have been like.

For now, the taste brought her joy. Somewhere in her heart, she knew one day they may be taken from her, but she chose to leave that bitterness for another day.

"Told her I'd win." Jack gasped for breath in between the words as he slowed before reaching the bench.

"I almost did!" Beth was still a short distance away, her bare legs pumping as fast as she could make them while she tried to keep her skirt from flying up too high.

"I'll let her next time." Jack made a face at the sharp pain of a side stitch.

"You're quite gallant." Maria winked at him and they both smiled; Jack's chivalry had been duly noted.

"We came to see you." Beth had been forced to run harder to keep up with her brother, but she was breathing far less raggedly than he.

"Well, I had an idea." Maria answered solemnly.

"But ask us why."

"Why?"

"Because..." Beth made a silly face, "...we like you."

"And mom made us go outside," Jack added.

"Well, anyway, who cares why we're here? The best part is—we get to see you!" Beth had obviously put a great deal of thought into that.

"It makes me very happy," Maria stroked Beth's soft hair.

As the children played around her, Maria felt as if there could be no painful nights for Kjarsta. She could believe there had been no young man on the SubTransit. It even seemed as if she had never been tired.

Glancing up at the faun in front of her, Maria felt as if that downhearted creature had begun to look more like its contented brother. What was the angry faun doing surrounded by all this joy? Did it still rage at the world around it? Could it possibly continue to project its malice in the presence of these innocent babes?

No, she warned herself. She dare not circle the fountain to look. She refused to allow wickedness into her private world.

22

MacNally had not been idle on the way back to Homicide. As soon as he walked through the doors, he was giving out orders.

"I want a full autopsy on the kid. Soon. And who has the visuals?"

"We're cleaning them up right now." A young VTech with a nametag that read *Wojawski* held up his hand. "Should have the full spectrum up for you in ten more minutes."

"Well, don't rush it, huh? I need the cleanest set of layers possible."

Crime scene visuals were taken with a multistage camera that recorded six aspects of the crime scene. Aspects one and two were simply a range of physical surface images that allowed investigators to view all images at their original aspect or magnified up to 48 times their original size. The clarity of the magnification depended on the HD rate used in the recording. The remaining four aspects recorded thermal images, chemical scans, CT scans, and radiation scans.

"What do you have so far?" MacNally asked the VTech.

"I went ahead and processed levels four and six. Mass spectrometer was calibrated yesterday so it should be near perfect. Carbon dating will give us time of death and chronological sequence of the attack. I have computer analysis cooking them right now. If anything is there we'll know in a few minutes. Anything you looking for in particular?"

"Maybe, but let it run on its own. I don't want to generate suggestions that might confuse it." This had been a problem with the script that searched the visuals for anomalies. If factors were added to aid the search, it often misinterpreted data simply to meet those factors.

"No in-house recordings at that building?" MacNally asked Fenelli.

"There's a partial video of the lobby, but it only takes intermittent shots. The other cameras haven't worked in years." That was to be expected in that neighborhood. Most building owners wouldn't spend the money on repairs, and most tenants never complained about the lack of visual oversight. Most people did not like being watched.

"So what's the tally?"

"Well, everyone seen on the screen was identifiable. We'll have to talk with all of them and establish who has alibis and who doesn't. As far as the coverage gaps, they're big enough that anyone could have slipped in or out of the building unseen. There's a pretty decent security lock on the lobby doors and service entrances. So the chance some stargazer walked in off the street and killed him is pretty slim."

"Basically, we got a lot to do." MacNally sighed. Fenelli wondered if MacNally was frustrated with the amount of work ahead of them or if he was still thinking about the savageness of the boy's death.

"There's something else." Fenelli had not been sure he was going to bring it up, but he did not want to miss anything for the boy's sake. "Something that didn't make sense to me."

"What's that?" MacNally dropped into a chair and loosened his tie.

"One of the Medical Officers said something to me that I can't get a hold of." Fenelli began to tell MacNally about Thomas and his anger over the Shipper's Formula.

"This biocide ought to show up on the chemical analysis, right?"

"No," Fenelli said, "visuals were taken before Bibbly got on site."

"Well, it's only a safety precaution, right? Maybe he's just a paranoid kid. Besides, what do we know about IHS procedure? They change their procedures all the time."

Fenelli knew MacNally was right. They rarely ever checked up on the latest procedural changes down at IHS. It was always easier to let them remember their own complex way of doing things. But that wasn't the only thing that was eating him.

"It's not only that, Ed. I can't stop thinking about how IHS handled that Masthead body. That was unreal."

"I've been thinking about that." MacNally nodded slowly as if he were answering a question that only he could hear. "Now this whatsisname—"

"Bibbly."

"—Bibbly, he essentially ignores this dead boy and gives him to us."

"I wouldn't say he ignored him. More like he was scared of him. Won't touch him, coats him. I got the feeling he wanted to flee."

"I think we ought to let everyone else chase down alibis." MacNally sat up and flipped on his deskscreen.

"You want to talk to Jenkins about this first?" Fenelli realized MacNally had never explained the phone call to his apartment. "Hey, why'd you want me back at the station?"

"When?"

"When you called me at home. You'd been talking to Jenkins all morning, and were all fired up about something. What did Jenkins say?"

"He didn't like the IHS report either. But after he made a few calls, he hit a brick wall. So as far as he was concerned, we had to pursue Jack Ford's death as a murder."

"So you don't want to talk to Jenkins anymore."

"Yeah." MacNally pulled up a file and scanned it. He used a finger to mark his place as he read, slowly following the text by swiveling his head back and forth. It was the only time Fenelli would have suggested Ed MacNally could look like a schoolboy.

"Well?" Fenelli interrupted him.

"Let me do some reading first. In fact, you go read up on this Shipper's stuff. We need to know more before we go talk to IHS. Unless you'd rather read these IHS procedures."

Fenelli would have preferred to read algebra equations over government procedures. He was more than willing to research the biocide spray. He wasn't sure if he wanted to be right and find out IHS was hiding something, or be wrong while making a false accusation against the most powerful government agency in the Lazaretto.

"I hope you don't get us in trouble," MacNally muttered. Apparently, his partner had been thinking the same thing.

23

Helen Segal fought to keep her balance in the crowded SubTransit car. It was the German's fault she had come late to the station. If she had been able to leave early with Julia, as was her usual schedule, she would have missed the heavier crowds going home and found a seat. IHS was the largest employer in the Laz and it was never more evident than in the commuter cars.

The German—Dr. Haupt, she corrected herself—had shown no indication of finishing up by four o'clock. As it was her first day with him, Helen had not wanted to upset him by suggesting she leave with the early commuters. She continued to work on his list of documentation and access authorizations without comment.

Julia had stopped by, of course, to draw her away. She had also tried to get another look at Dr. Haupt and tried to make Helen commit to coming to the *Blue Forty*. She had not succeeded at either task.

Standing in the SubTransit car would have been more bearable if the handrail above her had been usable. However, when she had stepped inside the car, she had reached out and felt something wet on the handrail. She had decided she would take her chances without holding on. With a widened stance, she concentrated on staying upright.

The SubTransit slid to a stop and the doors seemed to part under the pressure of the commuters flowing out of it. Helen waited for the majority of them to wash out before she left the car. Now that she was in the middle of the commuter rush, she was in no hurry to get home.

No one was waiting for her. She had no plans. All she really wanted to do was get inside her apartment and soak in a hot bath. She wasn't even sure she wanted to eat. If only she hadn't thrown away the second half of her sandwich. Making supper was the last thing she wanted to do.

Entering her security code, Helen closed herself in her apartment. The noise of the rushing crowds still seemed to whirl around in her head. She dropped down in a soft chair and bowed her head. She needed silence. She hadn't realized how uptight she had been—how nerve-racking it had been to be in the same room with the doctor. It was as if she had been holding her breath all day while standing at attention.

Would every day be like this? How could she stand it?

After slipping off her shoes, she decided against supper and went straight towards her bedroom. The small bathroom across from her bedroom had enough room for a full-sized tub. She was glad she had insisted on that. Many smaller apartments had only standup showers.

She had the hot water running when her phone rang. It was Julia.

"Helen, there's still time." As Helen had expected, Julia made a last ditch effort to get her out of the apartment.

"Too late, I'm already in a bath that feels too good to leave." It wasn't exactly the truth, but it was close enough. The sight of the hot, steaming water hardened her resolve to stay at home.

"You could always come later. And speaking of later, how late did you have to stay today?" Julia sounded as if staying late was the same as catching a fatal disease.

"Late enough that I only made it home a few minutes ago."

"Well, don't make a habit of that. I don't think I like your Dr. Haupt. Should I talk to Dr. Fisher for you?"

"It's not as bad as all that," Helen said.

"Well, we're about to go." Julia's mind shifted into a more festive gear and she forgot any concern that she might have had for Helen. "Come, come, *come*. Okay? Don't make tonight sad for me!"

Helen felt much better as she slipped out of her clothes and into the water. The thought that Julia's night could be ruined because Helen failed to show up was comical. Helen knew that once Julia entered that club, she wouldn't give Helen another thought. In her own way, Helen was being just as self-centered. There wasn't anything she wanted to do more than soak in the water and focus on forgetting about Dr. Gerhard Haupt.

24

Lilly was not sure why she had insisted Gregor Lepov come to that night's gathering. It was not like her to allow a stranger to get to know her beyond a casual introduction. It created complications. It was, in fact, one of her trademarks in her business. She kept to herself.

There were few people who could honestly say they knew Lilly Stewart. None of them ever spent time in the Lazaretto. And of those few, only one had ever loved her: her ex-husband Shay.

She rarely thought about Shay Stewart. It was true she had once loved him but that was merely a fact from her past. If Shay ever thought about her, or if he even continued to love her, she knew nothing about it. She could believe he still thought about her, but she doubted he still loved her. The prison holds orbiting Sinop provided a man all the time in silent space to consider whoever had betrayed him to the government. She could almost guarantee Shay was thinking of her.

The pain of that betrayal had led her to believe she would never allow herself to come that close to a man again. No matter how deeply she had loved Shay, she had found it impossible to do anything but turn him in to save her own skin. It mattered little that he had in fact been trying to double-cross her. The end result was a logical satisfaction that she had beaten him at his own game. At the same time she had become haunted with a regret that could still be painful.

So why this desire to see Gregor again? It's true the gathering was only a meaningless party but she knew that on some second or third level, it meant more to her. It was ridiculous, of course. She did not know this man. She knew nothing of what he was.

What little she knew of him she had learned only by listening to him. Believing what someone said was unheard of in her behavior. If it had been anyone else, she would have made a few calls, and asked a great deal more questions. What was she doing? She was, she realized, acting like a schoolgirl.

As if to confirm her assessment, she felt her heart skip as Gregor appeared in the doorway of the apartment and took two hesitant steps into the room. He was scanning the room, most likely searching for her, and she held back for a moment. She recognized that lost-boy look and fell for it all over again.

"Easy, girl," Carlos Montillo cautioned sub-rosa. He had easily read her reaction to the stranger's entrance.

"Thanks for the advice," Lilly handed Carlos the empty glass she'd been holding and crossed the room.

The party was being held in a large apartment owned by a Lazar named Cam Raley. Raley was a wine merchant with the singular eccentricity of basing his business in the middle of the Lazaretto. Instead of keeping an office on Sinop, the Euxine System's preeminent maker of fine wines, and shipping the wines through the cargo quarantine—which consisted of chemical treatment with the shorter ten-day incubation—Cam Raley actually warehoused his stock of wines in the Lazaretto.

Lilly understood his strategy as it was close to her own. He set himself up within the quarantine city to make it more difficult for buyers to purchase his product. The obstacle was irresistible. Customers were convinced his superior wines beat anything readily available in the planetary shops. Like Lilly, he had learned to harness the power of the forty-day incubation period.

His shrewdness had paid off and the evidence was in his apartment. The two-hundred-square-meters of his penthouse gave testimony to his wealth by its sheer size; living space being prohibitively costly in the Lazaretto. The apartment was not stuffed with expensive furniture and décor. It was stylishly Spartan, with only a few well-spaced pieces of art hung on the walls. His real display of affluence could be seen in the material used from the floor to the ceiling.

The flooring was made of true Earth mined marble. It had not been recycled from older buildings from the Industrial Age of the Twentieth Century. That would have been too easy to acquire. This was Virgin Marble from the dwindling quarries of Monte Altissima; carved from the depths of a mountain that once supplied the ancient sculptor Michelangelo. The interior walls were made from a giant sequoia that had once stood on the Californian north coast for nearly two thousand years. But the walls were overshadowed by the trim that outlined them. The wood that comprised the molding and baseboards, though made from a tree of an even greater age than the sequoia, was not what impressed visitors. When visitors were told of how much wood from a Bristlecone Pine of the Sierra Nevadas was wasted to cut and shape the trim — a tree twice as old as the giant sequoias — they were justifiably awed.

The large living space that opened up from the entrance doors was crowded with nearly fifty people. Lilly had to thread her way carefully through the mixed groups being careful not to make physical contact if at all possible. As she worked her way across the room, she occasionally looked up to keep her eye on Gregor.

He really did intrigue her. He was no young buck; he must have been over forty. His square jaw was edged with creases that already suggested a long and rough life. Black, bristle hair held a dusting of gray around his ears, as if it had been sprinkled on with a saltshaker. Once-broad shoulders were noticeably beginning to hunch forward and his waistline was already expanding beyond the beltline of his cheap suit. When he raised a hand in greeting, she spied large, rough hands.

Nothing about him, she concluded, gave the impression that he was young. But even after noting these details, she could not shake the belief that he looked like a little boy who had lost his way. As if to confirm it, his face brightened when he saw her, although there was a certain intimation of embarrassment on his face as well. The little boy was happy to have been found but was self-conscious at ever having been lost.

"This is a small get-together?" he grimaced as he scanned the room.

"It is only a few of Cam's associates."

"Cam?"

"Our host, Cam Raley. Come with me and I'll introduce you." Lilly reached out a hand and guided him with a light hold on his upper arm.

Cam Raley stood near a bank of windows that formed the entire north wall of the apartment. The dim overhead lighting along the wall cut down on the light reflected from the inside. Beyond the glass — real sand-based glass — a grand view of the Lazaretto night lay below them.

Raley was a large man, with the well-defined physique that was readily recognized as chemically sculpted. No matter that the muscled shape was his natural body; a chemically sculpted body *looked* artificial because it was inherently perfect. This anatomical perfection eventually brought the chemical sculpture fad to an end, but not before hundreds of thousands learned that there was no process that could undo the results of the sculpting chemicals. Fortunately for Raley, he had avoided the bulky Competition formula and was stuck with only the less obvious Rigid formula. Bright blonde color accentuated his perfectly sculpted hair. Neither the color nor the hair's thickness looked anywhere near natural. Somehow, when it was all added together, he was less irritating to the eyes than one might expect for a man who looked exactly like a mannequin.

"Lilly, you look lovely." Cam Raley nodded to her and then turned his attention to Gregor. "I'm Cam Raley. Welcome to my home."

"Thank you," Gregor nodded in return.

Lilly watched the two men examine each other. She knew Raley, and expected him to inspect someone new cautiously. But as Gregor returned the scrutiny with a similar gaze, she realized she should have expected that. Maybe he wasn't as lost as he appeared.

Gregor had made a comment about the view of the Lazaretto as Lilly had been thinking to herself. She had not heard exactly what he had said but she caught Raley's reply.

"Yes, it may well be the only beautiful view of the Lazaretto — an overhead view at night. I am hesitant to say it, being a loyal member of this odd city, but a daylight view of the Laz, high or low, is not exactly enticing. It is preferable to gloss us over with a coat of the blackened night before gazing upon us from a distance. Getting a closer look with any level of illumination will often reveal things we Lazars would rather keep to ourselves."

"Such civic pride, Cam."

"Mine is a fair observation, Lilly." Raley shook a finger at her with the air of a professor scolding his favorite student. "I do have civic pride. But I am only too aware of how worn down our home has become. The Lazaretto was established over fifty years ago. We have received so few funds since then to modernize and freshen up our world. Even with this view of the city lights, I have to say my guests would do better to turn around and enjoy my small but rare collection of ancient oils."

Raley cocked his head and abruptly spoke to Gregor.

"Do you know much about the painting masters of Ancient Europe?"

"Very little."

"That's quite alright; I have never been able to find many people who can appreciate what I have collected here on my walls. But it matters little. I know their history and I know their worth. It is enough for me."

"If I'm not mistaken," Gregor looked to Lilly as if he were mentally flipping back through that invisible notepad of his, "Miss Stewart should know something about them."

"Oh, my good Mr. Lepov. Lilly knows far more about my collection than anyone. There is no doubt about that."

Lilly raised her glass at Raley and nodded. Raley's comment was an understatement. Lilly had brokered all but two of the oils in his collection. He was one of her most steady costumers.

Carlos Montillo and another man approached the windows and nodded to the group centered on Cam Raley. Gregor had already met the fast-talking Montillo. He nodded in recognition then turned and gave his attention to a tall man Lilly introduced as Shaw Parks.

"Any friend of Lilly's is a lost cause." Parks bowed curtly. Gregor suppressed the urge to offer his hand and bowed stiffly in return.

"He might be right," Lilly admitted.

Parks rudely looked over Gregor from head to foot. "By your cheap suit I can tell you aren't a Lazar. And you're alone, so you're no tourist. If I didn't know any better I'd say you were a cop."

Gregor shrugged off the idea with a smile and a quick-witted comment. But he hadn't been quick enough to evade Lilly's scrutiny. She could see the logic of Parks' observation and it surprised her. She thought of the way he seemed to make notations of everything that was said and it fit the mold. Was he a cop? She filed the thought in the back of her mind for later consideration.

Lilly could see that Gregor did not like Parks. Most people didn't, but Gregor did not make much of an effort to conceal the fact. He kept a wary watch on Parks. There was a part of her that admired Gregor for that. Parks was no good, even if no one had the nerve to mention it in public. She was pleased to see Gregor had no problem recognizing the fact. She wondered again if he really was a cop.

"Gregor is simply in the wrong place at the wrong time, Shaw. He was looking for a good cup of coffee at Comic Joe's."

"Oh, that's a bad move." Montillo downed a small glass of bourbon. It wasn't his first and it sure wasn't going to be his last. "One goes to Comic Joe's for good coffee as much as one comes to the Lazaretto for their health."

"We aren't all here for our health?" Gregor cast a dry look at Lilly. "But seriously, Lilly forewarned me about the bad coffee. I think she thought I would spit it out if I hadn't been warned."

"And did you?" Raley asked politely. It was obvious he was

uncomfortable with trivial comments about good and bad coffee.

"Oh, no. It was all right. It was bad, but not that bad. It tasted like coffee used to taste when I smoked cigarettes."

Lilly tried to focus on the conversation but was once again surprised she could do little but watch Gregor in fascination. Montillo had said it best. *Easy, girl.*

25

"Is this a joke?" Fenelli stood looking over the edge of the roof of the Beta Three Hotel. "Who's making this stuff up? *I* wouldn't climb down there. Certainly not because of a few LazarCops like us. Would *you* climb down there?"

"Nope."

"Well alright, then. So why do we think this guy did?"

"He's not on the roof, and he's not spread out on the street below."

"You're brilliant, Ed." Fenelli leaned out and frowned at the black iron pipe that snaked down the face of the twelve-story cinderblock building. "So where is he?"

MacNally stood with the outside of his right foot on the extreme edge of the roof. He turned his head and stared down to the street over 40 meters away.

"He's about three stories down, holed up in one of those window insets. They're not a meter deep. Maybe one meter high by half that wide. The windows don't open, and I doubt he can break them. By my calculations, this idiot is seriously wishing he hadn't climbed down there."

Fenelli risked leaning out farther. "You can actually see him?"

"No, I didn't say that." MacNally unholstered his service weapon and aimed it with both hands cradling its black grips.

"What—what are you doing, Ed?"

MacNally squeezed the trigger. The pistol spit a bullet. Below them, the barely visible ledge of one of the insets spat out a cloud of masonry chips and dust.

After waiting for a count of five, MacNally adjusted his aim and fired into another inset.

"Hey! Cut it out!" Two hands showed themselves from inside an inset to the left of where MacNally had been firing. The hands were shaking. "You're gonna kill me!"

"He's in that one," MacNally nodded at the hands matter-of-factly. He raised his voice as he said, "Quit whining!"

"Ed," Fenelli looked doubtfully over the edge of the roof. "How are we supposed to get that guy out of there?"

"I'll stop shooting when you climb back up here!"

"When I what?" The voice from the inset shrilled.

Another bullet chipped away at the visible edge of the window inset.

"Hold it! Hold it! Hold it!" The two hands came back out and began to feel around for the pipe.

"Should we throw him a rope?" Fenelli asked.

"You got a rope?"

"No."

"Then don't ask questions like that."

The two detectives watched their fugitive firmly grasp the iron pipe and swing his body into view. His motions were shaky, and Fenelli felt sure the man would fall to his death. MacNally watched with less interest, as if he didn't care about the climber's chances of success or failure. More than likely, Fenelli guessed, MacNally was already thinking over their next step after getting some information out of this kid.

The young man was breathing heavily with a mixture of fear and exertion. He kept glancing upwards, judging the distance remaining. He did a good job of not looking down. In between his staggered and labored breathing, he talked to himself, as well as the cops waiting for him on the roof.

"What am I doing? Crazy cops! This is—oh jeez—I can't do this."

"Just a little further." Fenelli knelt down and offered a word of encouragement. He expected a rebuff from MacNally but the big man remained silent. "Pull yourself up a few more times and I'll be able to grab your collar."

"Are you crazy?" The climber winced at the offer. "My jacket's unbuttoned. You'll pull it right off me."

"Okay, forget I offered." Fenelli stood up and shrugged his shoulders at MacNally. "I know. He's not worth the trouble, right?"

"Oh he's worth the trouble. We need him."

"What if he falls?"

"He's not gonna fall," MacNally spit over the side, narrowly missing their quarry. "This guys not as helpless as he's letting on."

"Well maybe I'm not, but you don't have to spit on me!" The man's hand slapped the edge of the roof and felt around for anything to grab. "Hey! Come on! Grab my hand!"

MacNally grabbed the hand. His quickness was surpassed only by his strength. He jerked the climber up and over the edge of the roof, dumping him onto its solid surface in an undignified sprawl. MacNally's shoe settled on the man's belt buckle.

"You'd better explain yourself, Murphy."

"Whatd'ya talkin' about?" Murphy lay still. He was well aware of MacNally's willingness to violate his rights.

"You might be stupid, but don't think I am. We run you down every week and you expect it. You're our most productive snitch, and you always will be. Now, why did you run tonight? You knew we'd catch you. There was no question of that, was there? So why the big scene?"

"Maybe I'm tired of being your snitch." Murphy made the smart remark before MacNally's shoe knocked the breath out of him.

"And maybe you're tired of your freedom. You're not real bright."

"Maybe I'm tired of my what? Freedom? You're kidding me!" Murphy's mouth was ahead of his reason. He could not keep it shut. "I'm stuck in this loony bin for the rest of my life and you call it freedom? We're both stuck here like rats. Neither one of us got any freedom. Hey, Fenelli, ain't being stuck with this pig everyday worse than prison?"

MacNally lifted his foot to kick Murphy hard when Fenelli intervened. He waved MacNally off and squatted down to answer the question. "MacNally is one of the rooms in Purgatory set up for me, I'll grant you that. But at least he's not dating *my* sister."

"Oh, that's funny, Fenelli. He'd better stay away from my sister."

"So if you go to jail for whatever charge I want to make up, who takes care of your dear, sick, sister?" MacNally asked.

"Oh, just tell me what you want to know this time." Murphy sat up and rubbed his hands.

"The body on Masthead Street. From last night." MacNally waited.

"The Lazar? What's that got to do with me? What would I know about a suit kickin' off?"

"I wanta know where he had his suits altered, you Neanderthal. What do you think I wanta know? Who's responsible?"

"What?" Murphy, still sitting down, scooted away from MacNally, a look of true bewilderment on his face. "What does that mean? Responsible? Nobody did him! The guy died from something."

"Like a heavy beating?" MacNally leaned over Murphy.

"What? No!"

"Murphy," Fenelli was supposed to be playing good cop, but his patience was as thin as MacNally's, "the guy was a punching bag. If we hadn't found his PDT, we might not have known he was human. Now you've had to have heard something."

"Absolutely not," Murphy said emphatically. "Hey, look. No one's even talking about this guy. I only know about him 'cause I read it in the paper. He was a crummy Lazar, for Pete's sake. The paper said he sold for some Interplanetary Meat company or something. What would anyone kill him for? You got a cigarette?"

"I had no idea you could read, Murphy." MacNally pulled a cigarette from a pack and lit it. He ignored Murphy's outstretched hand. "So that's it? You're refusing to talk?" He let out a lungful of smoke and put the cigarette back to his lips.

"I ain't refusing nothing!" Murphy stood up, turning to Fenelli for a sympathetic ear. "Tell him, Fenelli, I'm cooperating. I'd love to tell him something. You know me, I give what I know. What's the deal with this dead Lazar, huh? You guys gotta have something better to do."

"He's not the only one, Murphy." Fenelli handed the snitch a cigarette. Murphy snatched it and lit it in a hurry as if MacNally might take it away from him before he could get a good drag on it.

"Not the only one who what?" With his hands still shaking from the climb, he dropped the cigarette and stooped down to pick it back up.

"Someone died in nearly the same manner. This morning. This one was only a kid. Seven years old." Fenelli took a step towards Murphy and backed him to the edge of the roof.

"Hadn't heard about that."

"You haven't heard about much." MacNally boxed Murphy in. Murphy's heels hit the lip of the roof.

"Now just wait a minute! Hold on!" Murphy's voice rose in fear. "You think I'd lie to you? When have I ever lied to you guys? I know how this works. You guys catch me lying or workin' the passengers again and Kitty gets run out of that fancy hospital. I *know* this. And I wouldn't do nothin' to hurt her."

"You haven't heard anything. That's it?"

"Man, *nobody's* talking about this." Murphy slipped between the detectives and took a few steps towards the stairs. When it became apparent they weren't going to stop him, Murphy took off.

"I don't want to believe it, but I think he may be telling the truth."

"You'd better hope he is, Fenelli. You're the one who let him go."

Fenelli hoped he was right as well. He was having trouble keeping the image of the dead boy out of his head. Fenelli had seen many corpses in his day, but the boy's body had shaken him. Fenelli had raised four kids, and he was sure the victim had looked something like his youngest boy Federico. Of course he couldn't be too sure. The boy's features were too distorted for that. And Federico was nearly thirty now. But Fenelli could not shake the thought. He could not help but put Federico's face on that swollen body.

Maybe they would catch a break at the IHS offices in the

morning. Maybe they would discover this was all a mistake.

Otherwise, a real psychopath was loose in the Lazaretto.

26

"So what is your business here? No one comes to the Lazaretto on a whim," Cam Raley asked.

"I may have lost my mind," Lepov said without hesitation. Lepov allowed himself a weak, embarrassed smile. "Well, this Doctor, he tries to make me see that my inability to sleep, my bum knee, as well as several internal difficulties, all stem from stress. So I book a flight to some resort called Sky Globe, or something—"

"Global Sky," Montillo corrected him. "I've been there. Expensive."

"Right, Global Sky. No one, not the agent who sold me the ticket, not the classy little brochure they sent to my house, not even the government people who issued me my traveling papers—no one told me I'd have to sit in quarantine in a Lazaretto for forty days. What does anybody think this is gonna do to my stress?"

It wasn't that Lepov needed to lie. He instinctively avoided mentioning his job. Most people had something to hide, and the discovery of a Private Investigator was a definite mood killer.

"You don't get out much, do you?" Parks' didn't like him.

"Well," Lepov couldn't ignore his condescension, "Traveling's overrated, you know? You're just shuttled around like school children."

"Traveling can be dangerous around here," added Montillo.

"Traveling is merely business," Lilly added. Lepov noticed she was more detached than she'd been in the coffee shop. More cautious. He wanted to get away from this crowd and get her back to that coffee shop.

As Montillo and Parks bantered back and forth, Lepov's mind lost track of their conversation. Out of the corner of his eye he could see that Lilly was not paying any attention to them either. It looked as if she were watching him. Maybe she was thinking about coffee too.

Cam Raley began to disengage from their conversation. There were many other guests with whom he needed to mingle.

"Mr. Lepov, it has been a pleasure meeting you. And Lilly, my dear, I'm relieved to hear you're not leaving us. I hope you linger here as long as possible. You are a balm for those of us stuck in the Lazaretto."

Lilly shook her head as she said: "No, Cam. I won't be staying for any extended period of time. But it's true I won't be leaving yet. There are a few things I must do that will prevent me from slipping out through Delta."

"I thought you were going," Montillo sounded pleased to be wrong.

"Not just yet." She spoke to Montillo, but her eyes were locked on Lepov.

Lepov was ready to get out of there. He told Lilly he was leaving and she rode in the elevator with him and walked with him to the street.

"I'm glad you came, Gregor Lepov." She took an impish delight in saying his full name. "It's a long way back to Delta."

"Well, I'm actually staying in a dormitory here in Center City."

"You're not staying in Delta? Don't you plan to leave through Delta? It closes in a couple of days. You'll have to move in soon. You don't want to miss that Global Sky reservation."

"I'll slip into Delta before it closes."

Lilly waved at a TransitCar lurking in the shadows and it slid out of the shadow and stopped next to them.

"Don't wait too long," Lilly stood close to him. "I have something going on tomorrow, and I don't know how much of the day it will take. But I don't have any plans tomorrow night."

"I'll be busy tomorrow as well," Lepov said. "I could call you if you tell me where to call."

"No, I won't do that." She watched him climb into the TransitCar and leaned down to finish speaking. "And don't tell me where you're staying. I'll find you anyway. It's a gift I have."

"The only gift I ever got was a bicycle from an old uncle who wore his hair like a woman's. I don't have the bicycle anymore, but I can never get the image of that hair out of my head."

"Good night, Gregor." She watched the TransitCar pull away.

Lepov gave his address to the driver and sat back in thought. It was time to start thinking about Ethan Layne. Time to forget Lilly Stewart. For all he knew, Lilly might not even contact him again. Maybe, in fact, he had downed one too many drinks and he shouldn't trust anything going through his mind for the rest of the night.

The driver had to wake him once they arrived at his building.

27

The Terminal Clinique de Lazaretto was a private clinic whose mission was to care for the terminally ill travelers who found themselves trapped by the Lazaretto's bureaucratic policies. The Clinic provided compassion after the Lazaretto Administration declared a traveler *nullus exitus*. Literally, the sick traveler was told they could never exit Aegean.

Funded by donations, the Clinic had been operating in the Lazaretto for over thirty years. Many of those stuck in the Lazaretto were able to care for themselves and lived independently in Center City. Some who required care were allowed to live in the Clinic. Patients in the Clinic were given as much care as possible, and the doctors and nurses made extraordinary efforts to bring dignity to the last days of these dying souls who had been left by their government to die.

Cures were still sought by the clinic's doctors, but when a cure could be found, it had no liberating effect on the patient cured. Lazaretto Administration policy was ironclad: no traveler who had been declared *nullus exitus* could ever leave the Lazaretto. It mattered little if that patient had been cured by a new medical procedure or drug. The Administrators would not allow anyone to threaten the health of the billions of humans inhabiting the planets of the Euxine System.

Maria was not officially employed by the Clinic. She volunteered alongside a handful of others who had been drawn to the service of the condemned patients. She had done so since the first day Georges had arrived at the Clinic. From the moment she had toured the Clinic with her husband, she had seen how much the patients needed human interaction, and had begun immediately fulfilling that need.

Georges was against her getting involved. He understood the dangers of contamination and was aware there were no guarantees working with patients whose terminal status had developed from a contagion. But Georges had become a doctor for the same reason Maria volunteered: he too saw a need that demanded action. He could not find it in his heart to force her to remain uninvolved.

Maria sat on a hard plastic chair in a darkened room with her head propped against a wall. She held a closed book in her hand. Her finger had been holding her place earlier but it had slipped out from between the pages. Maria was not asleep, but she knew she was close to being so. She needed to get up and get some coffee—Della, the night nurse, would have a pot brewed and waiting for her—but the movement might wake the man who lay asleep on the bed in front of her.

Kjarsta Zoltis lay under a thin sheet breathing unevenly as he slept. He was obviously a big man: broad-chested, long arms and legs, and a face that seemed to be bigger than the rest of his head. He was closing in on his seventieth year. White tufts of hair stood out at odd angles from the crown of his head. Even in the darkness, Maria could see the strength evident from his brow line to his jaw.

It was easy to see how strong a man he had once been. That made it all the more tragic to see how much his demon had gnawed away at him from the inside out. He now had the appearance of a man who, though he still had the size of a large and hardened fighter, was dry and brittle, as if he had already died and were all too aware of it.

She would wait for the coffee. Kjarsta was stirring and she always tried to be there if and when he awoke. It was her primary reason for being there. There were nurses who could care for him during the day; clean him, feed him, and change his clothes and bedding. But the night duty nurses were too busy to be there when he awoke in pain or confusion. He could not always ring for their help and they could not always get to him if he did. Maria made sure to be there.

A string of curses gurgled from Kjarsta's throat. Maria set the book down and leaned forward. He did not always awake at times like this. She would say nothing unless she could be sure he was no longer asleep.

More curses. He looked as if he were going to sit up, his barrel-shaped chest heaving at the effort. It was involuntary. He was no longer strong enough to raise his great frame, no matter how hollow it had become. The curses became whimpers.

Maria approached the bed. His hand was shaking and she reached out, placing her own hand over his. She felt the large hand react to her touch; heard him whimper and whisper furtively. A spasm shook his legs.

"Hey, lady." Kjarsta's deep voice rattled and guttered like a great overworked engine that sucked in too much air. Each word required effort. "I must still be quite a man to wake up next to a doll like you."

Maria never took offense at Kjarsta's profanities. In truth, she never noticed them. She was only aware of how much it hurt him to speak, and how much he tried to hide it. She never let him know she could see through his bravado. It would have hurt him more than his physical pain.

"Can you drink?" She picked up a cup and turned up the light so he could see it.

"Like a rocket ship drinks fuel." He coughed as he tried to laugh. "God's teeth! I drank a lot of weird things worse than rocket fuel."

Maria made sure he could see her smile. Making her laugh and smile was a job he took seriously.

He spilled as much as he swallowed. Maria had expected this and caught most of it with a soft cloth. A hard cough brought up phlegm and she wiped that away as well. She had been doing this long enough that embarrassment no longer showed in his eyes. It was a measure of the inner strength that was still stored in his spirit. When he could, he hid his weaknesses. When he could not, he accepted them without despair.

"I saw the children today," Maria's voice, always gentle, was softer than normal. "They were racing."

Kjarsta listened but made no effort to reply. He enjoyed hearing about the Edgars' children. He had never met them; he never would. Yet, he demanded to be kept informed anytime she saw them.

"She can be a real shooting star, you know. Streaking everywhere as fast as..." Maria's voice softened to a whisper and then faded to silence.

Kjarsta was sleeping again. That was unusual. Most nights, if he awoke, the pain was intense enough to keep him awake the rest of the night. Maria waited to ensure he was actually asleep. After several minutes she reached over, reduced the lights, and left in search of coffee.

28

The Agent entered the Collector's office, standing only a few feet inside the room. The Collector lay on a table covered in pale blue light. The edges of the light did not extend beyond the Collector's body. During this treatment, the Collector's clothes remained in place.

"I have a job for you." This job had come up suddenly. The Collector had no intention of telling the Agent this. It would make him look impulsive. It would make the Collector appear to be unable to predict what steps came next. That would not be to his advantage. The Agent had to believe that the Collector was the prime mover of the pieces on the chessboard. He must appear to be in control at all times. It was his primary path to controlling the Agent.

"Well?" The Agent asked, skeptically eyeing the blue light.

"This man could be a problem. Unlike the Doctor, who is a public figure, this man is here with unofficial status. That will be an advantage."

A visual image of the man appeared on a deskscreen near the Agent. Information on the man ran in a column to the left of the image.

"His purpose here?"

"There is every indication he is working in concert with the Doctor. This information on him was given to me today." The Collector reached out a hand to indicate a line from the data that was highlighted in red. The blue light followed his hand, keeping it totally encapsulated. "He is a licensed investigator."

The Agent scanned the image without changing expression.

"Government?"

"No. Independent. That leaves him unprotected." The Collector winced in obvious pain as the blue light deepened its hue.

"Kill him?"

"Be serious. Remove him, but do so without harm. And however you do this, make it appear to be his fault. We must stay above reproach on this. The Doctor must not take interest in the fate of his colleague."

"And the Doctor?" The Agent wanted clear orders.

"Be patient. For now, the Doctor is off limits."

The Collector said nothing, giving the Agent time to think. As the silence grew, the Collector grew disappointed with his agent. He was well aware that the Agent had already met the man whose face was displayed on the screen. And although there was no definitive reason for the Agent to mention this, he had hoped the Agent would not have hesitated to speak of it. The Collector did not like complications. He expected the Agent to complete the assignment without any complications.

"Is there anything else?" asked the Agent. The Agent wanted out of the room. The blue light had begun to flicker and there was a faint smell of burnt hair.

"Apparently not. I will contact you in a few days."

The Collector watched the Agent leave with only the slightest of reservations.

He had no more time to consider the Agent's silence about the investigator. The light had darkened to a rich purple and the Collector could feel the heat penetrating deep inside. Breathing became difficult. He fought off the nausea by focusing on one word: *clean.*

Clean.

29

Whether he was in the Lazaretto or back on his home planet, to Lepov, the job was the same: force yourself out of bed, dress, and get out the door no matter how disinterested you feel. The cold and brooding world of the Lazaretto did not change his perspective. Legwork was the same no matter which retched corner of the Euxine System you were in.

He left his dormitory late in the morning. The pneumatic elevators were not working and he descended the four flights of stairs with a sour expression on his face. His left knee was acting up again. Every time he dropped his weight on it he winced, if not in pain each time, at least in anticipation of pain. It was a helluva way to begin a day of legwork.

Outside, Lepov made it down the seven steps of the stoop and leaned on a stone newel post in order to take the pressure off his knee. At times like this he knew that if he'd had a wife she'd have nagged at him until he went to a doctor. She might have had a point.

A small bakery around the corner provided him with a perfunctory sweet roll and he washed it down with an indispensable cup of coffee. The coffee was much better than the cup he'd had with Lilly Stewart. The caffeine seemed to mollify the pain in his knee. He wasn't sure if that was wishful thinking but either way he was able to walk with more confidence.

Hailing a TransitCar, he gave the driver an address, settled back, and closed his eyes, content to rest his knee for a few minutes.

"Happens every time," the driver said aloud.

Lepov opened his eyes and watched the back of the driver's head.

"I said it happens every time," the driver had evidently been hoping for his fare to ask *what* happens every time. After saying it the second time he kept right on talking. "Two days before a quadrant closes up, Center City gets as empty as a cold can of beer in a fat man's hand. No one wants to get stuck in here when the doors are closed. That's ten more days they'd have to stay in this lousy place. Now you take today; Delta closes day after tomorrow. By lunchtime, I won't be able to find a fare until Alpha opens up three days later. I ain't complainin'. Cause when it opens up—I'll be busier than a soldier in his first whorehouse."

Lepov watched the empty street and had to admit the town looked deserted. He grunted enough to assure the driver he was listening. If he hadn't, the driver would have gone to even greater lengths to get his attention. Lepov tried to avoid that while making sure he didn't encourage the guy at the same time.

"I had a fare—oh, I'd say a year, maybe two years ago—anyway, this guy hails me down in the middle of the street, wavin' his arms. I thought he was sick or something. Turns out, he was in real trouble. He'd met some girl, went to her place in Center City, right down Third there maybe two blocks away. Anyway, they fool around, he's drunk and sleeps it off. Only he was s'pose to be in Beta. Wham! The doors shut, he's still asleep at her place. So now, he's gonna be ten days late if he can't get into Beta. More importantly, he's gonna miss his *wife's* birthday!"

The driver laughed too much. Lepov had known the punch line well before the driver had delivered it. Such anecdotes weren't that funny to a private detective who made a living off of infidelity.

"The relief on his face when I reminded him about the Grace Period was priceless. He'd looked like a poor man who'd just won the lottery."

"How does that work?" Lepov was curious enough to be drawn in.

"What, the Grace Period? Oh, that's stuff you really need to know. Up to two days after the doors close, you can get in for a fee." The driver let out a low chuckle. "A big fat fee. It's an escape clause for the wealthy. Don't think of using it unless you got money layin' around waitin' to burn. And judging by the neighborhood I picked you up from, you ain't got that kinda money."

"Yeah," Lepov sighed, "well I ain't got a wife with a birthday either."

Somewhere in the course of the conversation he had started to think about Lilly Stewart. It irritated him to think she had come to mind simply because the driver had been talking about wives. He had never been the kind of man who sized up every woman he ever met as a possible wife. He left that to the romantics. He liked to believe he could meet a woman and be as objective about her as he was about men. That was his job: evaluate people for what they were, not for what they looked like.

Lepov understood the Lazaretto was much like a prison, and he knew that even the most average of women seemed far above average within the Lazaretto's confining environment. It was possible Lilly Stewart benefited from this phenomenon. If not, it would mean that after successfully keeping himself emotionally unattached to a woman since his divorce, he was falling for a woman he knew nothing about.

Maybe the answer was simple: maybe there was something in the water. Maybe she was something special. Was that so impossible?

30

Rain tried to fall outside the precinct building and Fenelli was sure it would finally succeed as they headed out the back entrance. After living on Aegean long enough, he had come to accept the weather for what it was: a mean-spirited old cuss. It reminded him a lot of his father.

"Hey, Lieutenant!" The VTech from yesterday who had taken charge of the Rodyakov visuals waved from across the room. MacNally and Fenelli stood with their coats in one hand and their hats in another and waited while he circled around the great stack of files.

"I've got it all set up in room 6. You can see everything we've got."

"Any glitches?" MacNally always expected glitches.

"No, sir." Wojawski took offense at the question.

"That's a nice change. We'll want to look at it when we get back."

"I don't like what you're saying," Wojawski pulled back his shoulders and lifted his chin. The youngster had eaten a heavy dose of his oats that morning. "I know how to follow procedures. We made no mistakes."

MacNally stared at Wojawski for a time, then turned towards Fenelli with a curious look. Without saying a word he shook his head and walked away. Fenelli held back a moment as MacNally made for the door. Once his partner was out of earshot he turned to the young VTech.

"He doesn't mean to sound like he expected you to screw it all up. It's just his way." Fenelli put a hand on the young officer's shoulder. "Let me ask you something, Wojawski. You ever seen a little dog? You know, little thing maybe this big? Do you know what happens when a little dog barks at a big dog?"

Wojawski tried to look like he didn't care.

"The stupid little dog gets transferred to escorting prison shuttles."

"That answer that has nothing to do with dogs. That doesn't make any sense," Wojawski rolled his eyes.

"Neither do you when you try to upset my partner. Discreet is a powerful word. Look it up."

Fenelli walked away from the VTech, barely concealing a smile. It wasn't that he meant to be harsh with the kid. And he certainly wasn't going to run around defending MacNally. He simply hated hearing MacNally whine about young cops on the force. It was a hobby of MacNally's, and he never passed up a free chance to gripe on the subject.

MacNally stood outside the back entrance. A driveway ramp led up to street level. The big Lieutenant was halfway up the ramp. The rain had finally succeeded in falling and it was getting better at it by the minute. MacNally's coat was soaked before he could climb to the top of the ramp.

"Hey, Ed! Why don't you come back down here with the car and get me?" Fenelli's voice bounced up the concrete ramp.

"Come on," MacNally said as if he hadn't heard his partner. Fenelli couldn't be sure if he had or not. "I want to be there when IHS unlocks their doors."

"Great," Fenelli groused aloud, "that dumb VTech screwed up a good morning. Ed's gonna be impossible. And all because some kid's new enough to remember his procedures." To Fenelli, the worst part about newbies was their maddening habit of reciting procedures and regulations.

Walking through the rain, it occurred to Fenelli that this was precisely why Bibbly's behavior had been bothering him. Bibbly was new enough to know IHS procedure. And after MacNally gave him a rundown of what those procedures were, Fenelli did not have to guess something was wrong anymore.

MacNally scowled when Fenelli got into their car.

"He's just a young kid. Don't let him get to you like that."

"Oh, he don't bother me. I'm grouchy about something else." MacNally stared out the rain-covered window beside him.

Fenelli pulled the car onto the street. The rain shield was working properly for once and he had a clear field of vision across his driving lane. There was little traffic on the streets.

"What bothers me, Fenelli, is why we have to waste time at IHS. If the two of us can tell something is wrong with the way they're handling this, why can't anyone else? If this turns out to be some computer glitch, I'm not only gonna bark about this. I'm gonna bite somebody."

"Yeah, well be friendly until we find out what's going on, okay? I don't want to have to go bail you out of IHS jail." Fenelli tried to sound lighthearted about it, but he was worried MacNally would make a scene.

He hadn't even wanted to go to IHS. He had proposed they send over a written request for more information on Jack Ford and work things out from the precinct. MacNally wouldn't hear of it. He wanted to stand in front of someone's desk and make them nervous. But Fenelli had a funny feeling that no one makes the IHS nervous. Not even the police.

But that wouldn't stop MacNally. IHS might be the biggest dog on the block, but MacNally was going to bark at them anyway. It was pointless to ask MacNally to look up the word *discreet*.

31

Maria left the clinic after sharing breakfast with Georges in the cafeteria. By the time she left for home, the SubTransit station was filling with early commuters. Even the outward-bound cars had more riders than usual. Rain had been falling on the clinic's side of Center City. Its wet energy increased the general commuter's need to hurry.

For Maria, the rain was welcome. It reminded her of how blessed she was to be able to be out in the middle of it. Even with her umbrella, she could feel cold fingers of rain running down her neck and under her collar as the wind blew rhythmic blasts of wet chill against her back.

The rain had fallen heavily on the park. The storm had blown in from the south and while it was still growling over Center City, the tail end of the storm was already passing over Maria.

Cold clean air filled Maria's lungs. Her shoes scraped crisply over the wet walkways. Despite the long night at Kjarsta's side, she felt recharged. A few eggs and a strawberry biscuit had boosted her energy. And Georges had gone out of his way to cheer her. He always knew when she needed that. The cool morning storm had completed her rejuvenation.

When she reached her apartment, she had no desire to sleep. That could come later. She changed out of her wet clothes and slid on a pair of warm cotton pants and an old sweater of Georges'. It hung on her like an oversized coat and smelled strongly of pipe tobacco; Georges called his pipe his one civilized vice. Its aroma was a double comfort for her; it reminded her of Georges, it also reminded her of an Uncle back in Rome.

Dressed for the cold, she slipped out of the apartment and into Terran Park. The wet woodland was special to her, as if it had recently been cleansed. She remembered once how she had convinced Georges to come with her after a storm. He had complained at how wet and dirty everything looked. She had marveled at their disparate viewpoints.

She had no idea if Kjarsta would have enjoyed the park before he had been sick. Kjarsta never spoke about his life before he had fallen ill save for his usual comments about his hard drinking and womanizing. Maria believed most of them were only attempts to shock or amuse her. It was certain he had not been a saint as evidenced by his many strange and unusual tattoos. But she had never pried into his past; it was none of her business. More importantly, it made no difference what he had been. It only mattered what he was now: a sick and lonely man.

The brisk air of the park lifted her spirits, even as she wondered if there really was much she could do for Kjarsta. The clinic was doing nothing to cure him. His malady had control of him; slowly and painfully killing him. Many times after a night of watching over him she could not combat the doubt that assailed her. What good were her efforts? Did she really believe that being there when he awoke meant anything to him?

But such uncertainties had no place on such a fresh day.

Before long, she approached the faun fountain again. Still wet from the rain, the fauns looked darker and harder. To Maria, they appeared stronger, as if they were no longer made of stone but of a living and breathing strength. She liked that. She had never been strong, not like Kjarsta with his physically impressive stature — before he was sick, not as he was now — or like Georges with his quiet and solid resolve.

Maria was glad she could not see the angry faun. If it could become stronger and harder could it grow strong enough to destroy its three brothers? Rage had a strength that terrified her. As always, she stayed well clear of that side of the fountain.

It was an absolute shock, then, when a voice called from the angry faun's side of the fountain.

"Hello."

She recognized the voice. Before she could remember where she had heard it, the young man from the SubTransit car came around the fountain towards her. Maria felt the chill in the air deepen. She stepped back and hit her leg on one of the stone benches. She nodded at the young man and sank onto the cold, wet bench.

What was he doing here? This was, after all, her personal sanctuary. He had no right to intrude. She flushed as these thoughts flashed through her mind. It was unkind of her to think like that. He was harmless and as free to use the park as anyone. She tried to smile, to hide the selfish thoughts that lingered in her mind.

"Trireme station." He said this as if he were supplying the answer to a puzzling question. "I remember you."

Maria watched him as he continued to come closer. As he had done in the SubTransit car, he came straight to her and sat down. There was a smile on his face as he turned to look back at the fountain.

"It's cold," he said. He inhaled deeply and loosely shook his shoulders. He was wearing a long-sleeved shirt but it was obviously too thin for the temperature. A pair of black canvas pants matched his black shoes. Without a hat, the breeze messed his hair with each gust.

Maria nodded again, pushing a strand of her shoulder length hair away from her eyes. She was not frightened of the young man but she was tempted to fear him. His familiarity with her disturbed her, as did his ability to startle her as if he were an apparition appearing out of thin air. She could not help but wonder if he had followed her. Despite how prudent it was for her to be cautious, she made an effort to ignore these warning signs. She well remembered the regret she'd felt after their first meeting. It had been wrong to assume the young man was a threat that first time they'd met, and it was wrong to do so now.

Or was it? She couldn't make up her mind. She was too tired to make good decisions. It appeared as if he had every intention of staying right there beside her, as he had in the SubTransit car.

Did she dare get up and leave? Would he follow her? There was no reason to believe such a thing but she could not shake the feeling. The combination of her growing unease and her unjust imagination disturbed her. She blamed it on her fatigue and resolved to be polite.

"Do you like the fauns?" she asked him. The question surprised her even as she asked it. She was merely attempting to make small talk in the hopes it would diffuse her fears.

"Yes, of course." The young man rose and walked to the edge of the fountain, tilting his head as he studied the detail on the nearest stone figure. "They're whimsical, fragile things. Is there one you like the most? I'm not sure which one I'd choose."

He began to circle the fountain, examining each faun, one at a time.

Fragile? Maria could not imagine he saw them as fragile. If that were the case, how fragile must she appear? Fear washed over her. It shook her to know she was with a man who thought her so fragile and defenseless. She wanted to leave, to rush back to the safety of her home.

The young man—and that was the only label she could think of for him—had made his way to the other side of the fountain. He was with the angry, rage-filled faun. It did not surprise her that he stopped there. Was he thinking it was his favorite? Was he feeding off its vile spirit?

Fear won the day and she forced herself off the bench and into the open glade. She willed herself to keep moving without looking back. She focused on the grove of trees in front of her.

Georges' sweater no longer kept out the bight of the morning chill. She dared not look back to confirm her fear that she was being followed.

32

"You have done well," Dr. Haupt sat rigidly at his desk looking down at his deskscreen. With deliberate jerks of his hand, he paged through the various screens of documents. "Thank you, Helen."

Helen had not expected both a compliment and a thank you. She was unprepared to respond. All she really felt was relief, as if much needed breathing space had been created for her in that small office.

Standing inside Dr. Haupt's doorway, the temptation to retreat to her desk was strong but she decided it was wiser to remain where she was. With men like Dr. Haupt, leaving without permission would be viewed as the greater mistake rather than staying too long.

"Before we begin to analyze all of this, we need to speak with Dr. Fisher. There are a few things I want to clear up with him."

Helen caught his use of the word *we*. Was he expecting her to help him analyze all those documents? And why would she need to go with him to Dr. Fisher's office?

"We shall go immediately." Dr. Haupt stood and pulled at the hem of his jacket. "Come."

"Shall I call ahead?" Helen asked.

"No. I never call ahead. It is unnecessary."

Heels clicking with determined rhythm, Dr. Haupt moved through the halls of the IHS offices like a battle tank. No man could have stopped him.

Helen was surprised to discover she already felt like an outsider as they entered Dr. Fisher's outer office. A replacement sat at her old desk, a blond perky girl who looked like she wasn't a day over sixteen. At least Julia's was a familiar face.

"We will see Dr. Fisher," Dr. Haupt announced.

"Oh, well I don't know." The perky one looked startled at his announcement. She gave Helen and Dr. Haupt a look as if they were unwanted salesmen. "I'll have to check with him."

"No, you won't." Dr. Haupt ceased to notice the secretary and headed for Dr. Fisher's door. For the first time, Helen felt glad to be in the German's company. She resisted the temptation to smile in triumph at the perky girl. It had not been easy to resist.

They walked into Dr. Fisher's office without knocking and Helen shut the door. Dr. Fisher had been seated behind his desk but stumbled to his feet at the sight of Dr. Haupt.

"Doctor, I wasn't told to expect you. Good morning, I… I hope everything is in order. Helen. Helen, good morning." He would have gone on tripping over words and searching for something meaningful to say if Dr. Haupt had not stopped him.

"Dr. Fisher, I will not take up your time. I want first to request a larger office. I will need more space, both for myself and Ms. Segal. Please see to it. I want to be in the new office before lunch. Secondly, I must tell you I am displeased with the obsolete equipment you have provided for Ms. Segal. Make sure she is given the most updated system available. I will not allow my assistant to be treated in this manner."

"Oh, well most certainly. I had no idea — space you say? They put you in a small office? I hope you… that's really unacceptable. I'm terribly sorry. Please, forgive me. I'll make sure… Helen's system? I can't imagine why…Helen, are you doing okay?"

Dr. Fisher had nervously turned his attention away from the menacing Doctor and fixed his eyes on his secretary — his former secretary — as if she were a safety line.

"We do not need to discuss the why. It is only necessary that you correct this immediately." Dr. Haupt would not be distracted.

Helen couldn't be sure but she thought she caught a glimpse of a mischievous wink from Dr. Haupt. If she had interpreted the look correctly it would have been the first sign that he had a sense of humor.

It took Helen a moment to realize she had never mentioned the outdated system she had been given. Yet here stood Dr. Haupt, demanding she be given better equipment. If she had even considered complaining about it, she would have felt certain he would have scolded her and demanded she do her job regardless of the office system.

This cold, hard German might not be the automaton she had imagined him to be. Was it possible working for him might not be as bad as she had imagined?

The door to Dr. Fisher's office swung open unexpectedly and two large men in wet raincoats crowded into the office.

"Dr. Fisher?" the bigger of the two men spoke first.

"What's this about?" Dr. Fisher stammered.

"I'm Lieutenant MacNally, from Center City Homicide. We have several questions you need to answer."

The second man had an honest face. His features were not as rough as Lieutenant MacNally's. She liked him immediately.

"Now wait a minute. You are out of line, bursting in here like this. I'm the Chief of the Medical staff here, and you have no right..."

"I don't have time for that." The big detective gave Helen and Dr. Haupt a quick inspection. "I need to ask you some questions and I need the answers right now. The public health is in question here."

Dr. Fisher was not used to being handled in such a way. And after Dr. Haupt had strong-armed him in the same manner, he was trying to regain control of his own office. But before he could demand that his intruders get out, he glanced over at the German.

Dr. Haupt watched with intense scrutiny. How the IHS cooperated with the local police, especially in regards to a possible public health threat, was the kind of thing he was there to observe. Dr. Fisher hesitated. Helen knew he was cornered; she had seen that look on his face before. It hadn't happened often, but she knew when he was beaten.

"Well, I don't want to endanger the public. How can I help you?"

"We want to know about Jack Ford. The report we received on his body sent up some red flags in our department."

"Jack Ford? I'm not familiar with that name."

Helen knew Dr. Fisher was not telling the truth.

"A body your boys picked up two nights ago. The cause of death was unknown, and IHS brought him here for testing. We received an NCP ruling on him. And there was no secondary set of tests run."

"We got the report only hours after he'd been picked up," the second man added.

Helen could see Dr. Fisher growing more agitated. He spoke quickly in an attempt to silence the detectives.

"Oh, yes. That was Jack Ford. I remember now. Terrible, just awful. We made every effort to expedite that report. Chief Administrator Reno himself called me and asked that we make every effort to find out if the man had been murdered. He was determined that we not lose any time in the pursuit of the murderer. The secondary tests will be run, of course. That goes without saying. Only, the results were so conclusive, we felt we could send them to you with absolute confidence in their accuracy."

The two officers were silent for a moment. Helen watched Dr. Fisher wipe his face with a handkerchief. Dr. Haupt had not moved nor had he said one word since the other men had entered.

"One of your men labeled a second body this morning as a non-contagion/pathogen. He never ran the first test. How can that happen?"

"A decision like that is made at the technician's discretion. It does not happen often, but it is perfectly...well, as you can see, it was done. Such a decision is always reviewed by the medical board, and we will certainly look at this one. However, everything I've seen on that... there is no discrepancy that I can see. Mr. Bibbly was merely doing his job."

Lieutenant MacNally looked as if he were ready to continue his attack. His partner stopped him with a hand on his arm. They exchanged looks and the second detective won out.

"I can expect those changes I require by lunchtime, Dr. Fisher?" Dr. Haupt had finally decided to interrupt. "Helen, we will leave these gentlemen alone."

She barely had time to wave at Julia before she rushed to keep up with Dr. Haupt as he left the office in quick time. She caught up to him at the elevator.

"Come straight into my office," he said as they left the elevator. Helen hurried after him.

"Tell me what you did not like back there." Dr. Haupt stopped at his desk and turned to face Helen.

"Sir?" She did not know what he meant.

"When Dr. Fisher was answering those men, you showed obvious disapproval. Was he not telling them the truth?"

"That's not really for me to say. Maybe Dr. Fisher could answer..."

"Dr. Fisher might answer my question?" Dr. Haupt's voice grew louder at the suggestion. "Do you think he would volunteer to tell me he had lied to the local police? You had better tell me what you know. And do not say it is not for you to say. That is precisely why you are here. You are here to tell me what these thousands of documents cannot tell me. You are here to tell me the truth."

Helen was startled at the German's insistence. But at the same time, she finally understood what her role was going to be. She took a deep breath, needing time to think. She was going to have to choose sides in what could easily turn into a nasty political war. And from what she could see, her new boss was the most formidable opponent on the field of battle.

33

The driver talked nonstop until Lepov paid him and stepped in front of Ethan Layne's building. There was nothing about it that made it stand out from any other building on that street. Only the worn black numbers on the battered door told him he was at the right place. He climbed the steps of the covered entrance testing his knee on each step. He was pleasantly surprised to discover the pain had gone.

The small foyer and first level hallway were dimly lit. There was enough light for him to see this place looked worse than his dormitory. One look at the elevator was enough to make him seek out the stairwell. Even if the old lift did work, he wasn't about to trust it with his life. It looked rotten, as if a river had run down that elevator shaft over the years and soaked all the wood until it was warped and soft to the touch.

Lepov grabbed hold of the stairwell's handrail and pulled himself up the first step. He did not hurry. He rested two separate times before he reached the eighth floor where Layne's door stood opposite the stairwell.

Lepov knocked in case someone was actually there. He expected no one and grabbed the door knob. To his surprise, someone inside pulled the door open a few inches.

"What do you want?" A young woman stared at him with steely eyes from within a shadow.

"I'm looking for Ethan Layne. Do I have the wrong door?"

"It's the right door. Ethan is not here. What do you want?"

"I'm here on behalf of—a friend of Ethan's. May I come in?" Lepov caught the smell of cigarette smoke and although there were days he couldn't stand to smell it anymore, this day it smelled good.

"Hold on," the woman said, and quickly closed the door.

The hallway had only one working light in it, and that was thirty feet down to his right. Pale light from a window at one end of the hall was the only other illumination. Lepov began to wonder if he'd been a fool to allow the door to close on him. No one should have been at Ethan's apartment. His mother had said nothing about a roommate.

More than likely, he thought, the mother was unaware that her son was shacked up with a woman. That might explain everything.

He was hoping that would be the case. He wanted to get out of the Lazaretto as soon as possible.

"Alright," the woman said as the door opened, "you may come in. I was just leaving."

She was about twenty, with brown hair cut like a little boy's. She was terribly thin. Her dark brown eyes were hidden behind a worried brow. Her small mouth looked even smaller as she chewed on her bottom lip. She carried two packs, one slung over each shoulder. She tried not to make eye contact as she attempted to get past Lepov.

"Hold on a minute, Miss." He stood his ground and blocked her exit. He had a good idea she was doing more than leaving. It looked like she was *fleeing*.

"I have to go! I haven't time to talk."

"You'd better do some talking," Lepov put a hand on one of the packs and firmly guided her back into Layne's apartment. He decided not to waste time with this girl. "In fact, you better do a lot of talking."

"Who are you?" she asked, jerking away from his touch. "Who are you to touch me? Huh?"

Lepov stepped back as she angrily dropped onto a couch with hard black cushions. The packs slid down her arms and she pulled one of them onto her lap. Still angry, she rammed a hand into its main compartment and fished around in it. Lepov didn't wait to see why. He swiped a big hand down and snatched the pack away from her. She called out as if she'd been stung by a wasp. It took Lepov a moment to realize the hand she yanked from the pack was holding a small caliber gun. She aimed it at him.

"Don't." His tone was enough to make her hesitate. In one easy move he tossed the pack back towards the still open door and snatched the gun from her hand. At the same time he moved forward and pinned her to the couch with the other hand.

"Damn you!" She squirmed with nowhere to go.

"Now hold on. I'm not the one pulling guns on strangers."

The woman kicked him. It was a lucky shot. She hit his knee. Pain washed over him in distinct waves. He staggered back two steps, biting back a mouthful of curses. The woman recognized what had happened and smiled, quite pleased with herself.

"We better start over," Lepov tensed as another wave of pain rolled through his leg. "I'm simply looking for Ethan Layne."

"Does he owe you money? Or was he screwing your wife?" An impish smile came out even as he could still see anger in her eyes.

"No and no. I take it you wouldn't approve of that last item, huh?"

"I didn't care about the other women." The set of her jaw said otherwise. "He owed me money. And he's been gone a long time now."

"So you thought you'd liquidate a few of his things?" Lepov looked around the apartment. It was a small two-room affair. There was a bedroom in the back. The main room was kitchen, living and storage all wrapped up in one. As far as he could tell, most of Layne's things were gone. The woman had been there before.

"I'm taking what I can. Do you care? I paid for most of it over the last two years. I can't prove it, but what do you care?"

Lepov admitted he didn't care in the least. He only wanted Layne.

"So where is he?" Lepov removed the bullets from her gun. When he had finished, he dropped them into the front pocket of his pants.

"Why do you want to know?" She brushed her hair back in a nervous gesture. As short as it was, it was still long enough to conceal a bruise high up on her forehead.

"I doubt that's Ethan's doing, unless you've seen him in the past couple of days." Lepov leaned forward and pushed the hair back more to see the extent of the damage. "This is maybe 24 or 48 hours old."

"You know so much about bruises, huh? I'm not surprised. You probably beat your woman."

"I don't have a woman, but if I did, and she was anything like you, I'd sure as hell beat her."

The woman glared at him, shocked by his frankness before she understood he was putting her on. She smiled wickedly.

"I'm Greta Becker. I've been living with Ethan for two years." She pulled out a cigarette and lit it, blowing a cloud of smoke around her face. "Are you a cop?"

"No. My name is Lepov. Ethan's mother was getting worried." That cigarette didn't just smell good to him, it made him think about opening the pack in his coat pocket. He fought off the impulse though he could not take his eyes off the cigarette.

"A private detective?" She pronounced each word with extra care then shrugged off the revelation with a laugh.

"Who did that to you?" Lepov pointed at her injury.

"What do you care? I live in a rough neighborhood."

"That why you carry the gun?"

"Not that it helped. The gun is useless against bastards like you."

"Sometimes." Lepov tossed her the gun. "Unless you know what to do with it, it only causes more trouble. Someone's going to start asking uncomfortable questions about your gun. Like why are you carrying one and emptying out a missing man's apartment. That looks bad."

If she understood the implication, she didn't let on.

"I'm trying to say that with the police asking questions about Ethan's disappearance, they're bound to think it's strange—you stealing all this and having a gun in your possession."

"They haven't." She challenged Lepov with a hard stare.

"Haven't what?"

"Been asking questions. They haven't been asking questions."

"I'd been told Ethan had been missing for three weeks now." Lepov tried to work the timing out in his head. "When did you last see him?"

"I'll tell you, but it does you no good. I hadn't seen him in nearly two months. I'd left him."

"That other woman you didn't mind so much?" Lepov's question was colder than his tone.

"Yes," she nodded. Some of her hard exterior began to soften. "I came back a week ago. When I saw he wasn't here, I figured he got out of the Laz. Maybe he had jumped into a closing quadrant without time to pack. As far as I knew, he was never coming back."

It wasn't her conjectures about Ethan's disappearance that grabbed his attention. He was still focused on what she'd said about the police.

"Greta, you said the police aren't asking questions?"

"No. I know a few of the neighbors here, and they say no one has been around looking for him. As far as I know, you're the first."

"He did work for the Lazaretto Administrative Unit, didn't he?" She nodded firmly. "Wouldn't they wonder where he was?"

"It's why I thought he took off."

"No," Lepov shook his head while trying to puzzle out what he was hearing. "I checked all of that out before I flew out here. According to official records, he's still within the Lazaretto."

It took only a cursory glance around the room for Lepov to realize he had lost any chance of finding information in the apartment. The woman had taken too much. She had nearly stripped the place bare.

"You sure did a job on this place," Lepov shook his head. "I don't suppose you happened to notice anything unusual before you began to dismantle everything?"

"I don't think so." Her answer was both guarded and petulant.

"Sorry if the question offends you, but I have to say you haven't exactly done me a favor here. You said it looked like he hadn't packed, is that right?"

"Maybe a little. Some clothes but nothing else."

"Forgive the implication, but did it look as if someone else had been living with him?"

The implication was apparently not going to be forgiven, or even acknowledged. Greta Becker stood up and snatched up the pack on the couch. Keeping one eye on Lepov, she moved to the door and retrieved the second pack, clutching both of them as if she were hugging lost children who'd just been found.

"You can't keep me here. And I don't have to answer your questions. For all I know you did something to Ethan. I should call the cops."

"Right," Lepov allowed a mocking smile on his lips. There wasn't a chance in hell she'd call the cops. She didn't realize he was now practically forced to contact them. Once someone official did begin to look for Layne, they would quickly discover the looting of his rooms. And once they discovered that, anyone associated with Layne would come under suspicion. And he was sure it would eventually become known he was there for the sole purpose of tracking down Layne. The longer he kept in the shadows the more suspicious he would look to the authorities.

"I think it's only fair to warn you that I'll be calling them." Lepov stood at the top of the stairs and watched her descend. "I won't call them until tomorrow. That gives you a day to decide what you're gonna do, and how you're gonna answer their questions."

Her sharp curse echoed up the cavernous stairwell.

34

"Do you believe him?" Fenelli stood outside the main entrance of the IHS building. Rain still fell.

"We don't have much choice," MacNally answered.

"That bit about Reno doesn't make any sense. Why would the Chief Administrator care about this case? Why demand they hurry this thing?"

"You can't want me to question the highest government nitwit in the Laz, do ya?" MacNally asked. "Aren't you the one that's supposed to keep me from making mistakes like that? I'm the one that's supposed to *make* dumb suggestions like that."

Fenelli was surprised at his partner's mood. He had not expected MacNally to walk out of the IHS with his tail between his legs.

"You want to tell me what's going on?" It wasn't like MacNally to hold out on Fenelli.

MacNally waved at Fenelli to follow him and headed towards the car. The rain was only a nuisance now but there were several deep puddles of muddy water they had to sidestep. The streets were pockmarked with holes and patches; bad enough in some stretches to make Fenelli think of the surface of an unprotected moon. Most people in the Lazaretto never thought of it as a moon. Of course, these small depressions and craters weren't the result of space debris, merely the result of years and years of non-existent maintenance budgets.

"Fisher didn't tell me anything I hadn't already heard." MacNally started talking as soon as they closed the doors of the car. "Jenkins told me the same thing. I couldn't get a solid answer from him about why Reno was involved in this. I don't think Jenkins really knew. What I do know is that we took a chance coming here. We spent time on this instead of starting this investigation. Well, we verified what Jenkins was told. That's all we can do."

"And you know what that means?" Fenelli asked.

"That we've got a sadistic bastard out there who we'd better catch. And we'd better do it soon. You might want to iron the wrinkles out of your suit, Fenelli, 'cause it looks like everyone's watching us." MacNally laid his head back on his seat and let out a long breath. "I'm already getting a headache."

"So let's start with the Visuals." Fenelli pulled out into the street. He'd only made it a hundred meters when a call came through on his personal phone. He read the name. "I wonder what she wants."

Fenelli opened the line and heard a shaky voice call his name.

"Maria? What's the matter?"

"It might be nothing…" Maria's voice broke. "I might have imagined it, I don't know. Maybe he's not a threat."

"Slow down, Maria. Who are you talking about?" Fenelli pushed the phone to his ear to hear her more clearly.

"I think a man's following me. I saw him the other day — and now at the park. What does he want?"

"Maria, where are you?"

"I'm in Terran Park. Somewhere. A call box."

"Are you in danger right now? Let me meet you."

"No. I'm tired, and not making any sense." She spoke quickly, as if she were afraid she'd change her mind if she allowed herself time to think. "Don't come. I'll be fine. I never should have called you. I'm making something out of nothing. You're too busy to come running down here to calm down your silly little sister. But thank you, Arturo."

"I haven't done anything, Maria."

"Yes, you have. You've helped me think more clearly. Hearing your voice and knowing I could reach you helps more than you know."

Fenelli told her to call if she saw the man again.

"That's what cops are for. Bug me whenever you want."

"Thank you, Arturo." The transmission ended.

Fenelli slid his phone back into his jacket pocket. It was not unlike Maria to panic over something that turned out to be nothing. But Fenelli felt uneasy. Maybe it was the recent murders; it was a stretch to suggest the man she spoke of had anything to do with the murders, but Fenelli's radar was more sensitive at the moment.

"Why are you wasting time?" MacNally reached out and punched a button on the center console. "I'll have a patrol car swing by the park and look around. It's not gonna hurt anything."

Fenelli agreed. Taking care of Maria had been a tough job growing up. She was so small and easy to terrify. If it wasn't their father bullying her, it was a kid down the street. Arturo had given several boys a message they would never forget in the shadows of an alleyway. Not exactly lawful procedure, but at that age law had never been his first consideration.

"You want to call her husband?"

Arturo had not even thought about his brother-in-law. Maria's troubled voice had sent him back to their days in Rome before either one of them had ever met Georges. It had been easy to slip back into the role of her protector. He had never completely given up that role.

"Yeah, I'll call him."

"Then," MacNally added as if it were only an afterthought, "we better find this murderer."

35

Lepov spent hours in Ethan Layne's apartment sifting through the flotsam and jetsam of what had been left of Layne's world: Greta Becker had erased a large chunk of that world.

But what was left over was enough to get Lepov started. He had found several drawers and a small bookshelf stuffed with utility bills, pay stubs, receipts, and all kinds of paper records. It looked as if Layne had never thrown anything away. None of it was organized; things weren't going to be that simple for Lepov. But he had somewhere to begin.

Layne had indeed been employed by the Lazaretto Administration. He was a technician who performed maintenance on air control systems. His work included preventative maintenance as well as making service calls on malfunctioning air controllers. He worked on government equipment not only in Lazaretto Administration buildings, but also in buildings used by IHS and other government facilities.

What Lepov had not been able to find was any evidence that Layne had been involved in private work on the side. As he looked through the stacks of paper records, he kept an eye out for any such evidence. Privately contracted work was often a source of trouble. Had Layne worked for someone who was involved in criminal activity? Had he quarreled with a private client?

Piecing as much together as he could, Lepov guessed that Layne had not been back to his apartment for six weeks at the most. Several receipts were lying on the table in the main room with a date that was one day shy of six weeks ago. An unpaid power bill lay opened, and Lepov had also seen an unopened envelope from the same company with the word *overdue* stamped on it in red.

All that paper made him curious. Back on Bukovina, and any other planet, paper was no longer used. Everything was kept on electronic data systems. Yet, it was obvious that nearly everything here in the Lazaretto used paper records. He would have to ask Lilly about that.

If Layne's girlfriend had been right—if he had actually grabbed a few things and taken off in a hurry—there was little evidence to support her theory. Layne's closets were still full of clothes. Lepov had also found a particular item jammed under one of the stacks of papers that made him doubt Layne had ever considered leaving the Lazaretto: Layne's personal data tag. How was he able to get by without that? It couldn't be a duplicate. Losing one was a major administrative disaster, and Lepov would have found a record of it before this.

Lepov sat at Layne's kitchen table and looked around. The fact of the matter was the girlfriend had taken too much from the room. The desksystem was gone, which in itself was the biggest loss. How had she taken something that large? With it Lepov could have reconstructed phone records, messages, possibly even a door log. He might have built a list of people whom he could interview.

Stupid girl. Would it do any good to track her down? Even if he found her, would she still have the desk? Or would she have sold it? She could have kept it, but she probably erased anything on it connecting her to Layne. He decided he'd forget her for now. If he ran completely out of options, he would look her up.

He copied down most of the information he'd found on the various bills and records regarding Layne's financial accounts. There was a good chance he could break down the account numbers and get a peek inside them. His computer had a few programs that could do that sort of thing. Most of the more advanced systems were impossible to crack but Lepov was beginning to realize that the Lazaretto was crawling with out-dated technologies.

That would be his first step, he decided. After which, he'd try to talk with someone where Layne worked. There should be enough time left before the Layne's shop closed for the day.

The TransitCar ride to his dormitory hadn't taken near as long as it had taken Lepov to descend the stairs in Layne's building. His knee had started throbbing, a result of the kick from Layne's girlfriend. If he never saw that girl again he'd die a happy man.

The pain was worse climbing up to his dormitory and he thought of a few reasons why he ought to see that girl again. Most of them involved kicking *her* in the knee. But as he took his last step onto his floor he realized he'd have trouble kicking anything for the time being.

When he found Lilly Stewart sitting on his bed waiting for him, he forgot all about the girl. The other beds were empty. They were alone.

"That's a nice gift you've got. I might have to hire you if I lose my dog." Lepov was impressed. She had told him she'd find him. "I thought you were going to be busy today."

"My plans changed," she said with a shrug.

"That's becoming a habit with you. I hope I'm not interfering in your business in any way." It was flattering to think she was changing her plans because of him.

"No," she laughed softly, "It's nothing like that. I hope I'm not interfering with you. You did say something about your own schedule."

Good lord, Lepov thought, we sound like two teenagers playing coy. He limped towards a window and looked out over the street. Those few steps reminded him he was no teenager. His knee was on fire. Lilly had obviously seen him favor his left leg.

"Are you alright?"

"Sure, that bum knee I mentioned last night, remember? Maybe it's all this rain and cold makes it kinda grouchy." That and a bitter girlfriend who kicks like a mule, he wanted to add.

"So much for my idea." Lilly stood up, suddenly uncomfortable.

"What did you have in mind?"

"Lunch, that's all. But I doubt you feel like climbing back down those stairs with your knee bothering you that much. You probably already ate, anyway. It's a little late for lunch."

"I'm starving." Lepov looked back out the window. "Would it be ungentlemanly of me to suggest you run down and pick something up for us? It wouldn't be the greatest setting for a picnic, but as long as they don't throw us out of here I think it would do."

"You get off that knee, and I'll be right back." Lilly's face brightened up. She turned to go, her ponytail swinging freely behind her. Snatching up her coat she had laid on Lepov's bed, she rushed out the door.

Lepov didn't sit down right away. He stayed at the window and waited until he saw Lilly come out on the street. She crossed over to the other side, closing her coat against the chill wind blowing between the buildings, and headed off to Lepov's left until he could no longer see her.

He had not expected to find her here. Quite to the contrary, he had not even thought about her since the morning ride in the TransitCar. To be more honest with himself, he knew he really had no business taking the time to eat with her. He had to try to get into Layne's accounts as well as get out to Layne's worksite. He was wasting time. But there was one fact that he couldn't deny: he was hungry.

About to step away from the window and get off his knee, he watched a PoliceTransit brake in front of his building. Another car, this one without identification on it, was right behind it. Lepov had been around enough to recognize what was happening. Two uniformed patrolmen left their car and two men in civilian clothes climbed out of the unmarked car. All four men dashed up the steps and through the doors directly below Lepov's window.

"Oh, nuts," Lepov muttered aloud. His knee wasn't the only thing that was giving off a bad feeling. He turned and looked over the room and saw his bed with the footlocker underneath it. The use of the footlocker came with the charge for the bed. He had the code to it, and it was filled with his travel bags.

He had a peculiar feeling that there was something else in that locker that hadn't been there before. What exactly it was, he wasn't sure of. But he had a pretty good idea he was about to find out.

The four men climbing the stairs sounded like a crew of carpenters hammering away like madmen. They shoved open his door and crowded into the room shouting and pointing guns directly at Lepov.

They weren't going to be subtle about it. No one asked him his name. And one of the cops in civilian clothes made straight for his footlocker.

Lepov put both hands in the air and shook his head. One of the uniforms grabbed Lepov's right wrist and pulled it down and behind his back.

"Gregor Lepov," the second man in civilian clothes walked up and held out a badge. He was a black man with gray hair and an ugly scar that ran across his forehead. "I'm Detective David Khalid. You are being arrested for having in your possession a cache of fraudulent personal data tags."

"You haven't even got the footlocker open yet, would you like the code?"

"No, we won't need the code." Khalid stepped aside as the uniformed officer pushed Lepov towards the door.

"Oh, Lilly," Lepov whispered so softly even he couldn't hear himself. "What are you up to?"

His knee hurt like hell on every step of that stairwell.

36

The Collector lay on a stainless steel table with his eyes closed; a man in a white smock slowly inserted a large needle into his chest cavity a few inches under the pit of his right arm. The pain was evident by his clenched jaw though he worked to ignore it. Instead, he concentrated on an image in his head. He imagined the occupant of his elevator. He was absolutely certain the man in the elevator was nervous, even sweating profusely. The coming interview would be stressful for the man. The Collector took in deep draughts of air and expelled them slowly.

He would not allow stress to have control over him.

The elevator opened and its occupant stepped out hesitantly, as if he lacked the courage to face the Collector.

"Come in."

The man nodded vigorously and stutter-stepped forward into a small arc of light. He rubbed his hands together, as if he were a surgeon scrubbing before an operation. He was alarmed at the site of the Collector stretched out on the table. The Collector's shirt had been removed and his powerful chest was an odd background for the image of the needle slowly being extracted.

"Say nothing. He is almost finished." The Collector managed to say through clenched teeth.

The man in the smock finished withdrawing the needle and carefully proceeded to wrap the syringe in plastic. A pulse of blood drained from the needle mark, pooling on the cold silver table. When the medical technician turned towards the Collector with a swab to stop the bleeding the Collector waved him away.

"Leave it. Take the sample and inform me as soon as you have results. Don't waste time." The Collector sat up, the side of his ribs smeared with the blood pooling beside him. Grabbing a small towel, the Collector wiped gently at the needle mark. With each stroke, the bloody skin turned pasty white. Each time, the needle mark became free of blood for one or two seconds. And each time, blood would begin to flow again from the small wound.

The visitor stared at the issue of blood in fascination.

"I don't have to tell you it's nothing serious, do I?" The Collector, tired of wiping at the blood, rammed the towel hard against his ribs and held it there. "I imagine you're surprised to find I had blood running in my veins at all, am I right?"

The medical technician was gone now. He had taken a back exit, not coming anywhere near the visitor or the front entrance elevator.

"All right, then. Don't waste time. You requested this meeting," the Collector said with a strong tone of disapproval, "now let's get it over with. Why have you come?"

"Well, it's...okay, this might not seem important enough to you for us to meet. I understand that. But just give me a... I'll be plain. Two detectives showed up today asking... questions, a lot of questions. Not a lot, really. They only had a few."

"Make your point."

"I am...that's what I'm...so they asked about the bodies. It doesn't matter, really. Here's the point." He held out a hand. "I'm getting to the point. These detectives are asking...they're decidedly good questions. You see?"

"And what do you want?" The Collector was determined to keep the conversation simple.

"What do I want? Nothing. Nothing at all. I just want you to know what's happening. I'm not the one to say what I want. That's for you to decide."

"I will take care of this. Do not come here again." The Collector's words were cold and final.

The man understood that. He took a few halting steps towards the elevator and then nearly ran the rest of the way.

The Collector considered what would have to be done. The Agent, already busy, was about to become even more so.

37

The eyes of the German never looked away from Helen. He would not allow her to avoid his question.

"More than likely he forgot that he had seen the report."

"I am not asking for your opinion." Dr. Haupt's voice was sharper than usual. "Tell me again. You had given him the report on Jack Ford early that morning?"

"Yes," Helen, feeling as if she were being cross-examined by a fierce prosecutor, decided to keep her answers short.

"Are you certain he would have read it between now and then?"

"Yes."

"There is something else, yes?" Dr. Haupt cocked his head, his attention drawn to the look on her face.

"When I brought him the report—" Helen stopped. She was not sure what she should say. Dr. Fisher had always been kind to her.

She had no desire to hand him over to the German. His answers to the detectives, however, had truly puzzled her. Was she obligated now to lie to this man as cover for Dr. Fisher?

"Helen?" Dr. Haupt drew her eyes to his. "We must come to an understanding. I will make myself perfectly clear. After I have done so, you will have to make a decision. Do you understand?"

She did.

"Good. First, understand that I am here to do a job. I am not here to make friends. I am also not here to remove people from their jobs. I am here to make a report on the efficiency of this IHS operation as it pertains to the mission set out by the administrators back on Earth.

"That mission is a simple and clear directive: the IHS is entrusted with the health of the Euxine system. As such, they must oversee the quarantine process of the Lazaretto in a manner that eliminates the spread of contagions from one world to another. That is the only reason for the existence of the IHS. Anything that threatens the failure of that mission will come, in time, to my attention. That is my mission: to search out factors that might inhibit the IHS from performing their mission.

"I do not care who holds on to their position and who loses their position. It is no concern of mine. My concern is the safety of the billions of inhabitants of both the populations of Earth and her colonies in the Euxine System.

"It was my intention to use your knowledge of this operation to supplement the data I would be reviewing. As Dr. Fisher's secretary, you not only have a solid understanding of IHS protocol, but the personnel here as well. In order for your knowledge to be of use to me, however, you will have to be completely open with me. There will be no half measures. If you cannot do so, I will return you to Dr. Fisher's office and I will still find out what I need. It will simply take longer. But be assured that I will find all that I require for this report."

Dr. Haupt paused and Helen wondered if he were finished. Did he expect a response to that? Was he expecting some kind of oath of allegiance? She would not have been shocked if he had asked her to swear on the seal of the IHS that she would commit herself to seeking out every dirty little secret hidden within the walls of the IHS. Was that what he wanted?

Perhaps she was being too reactionary. Helen had always been a more practical woman, even as a young woman raised on Sinop by her undisciplined parents. They had constantly encouraged her to get out and sow wild oats before the obligations of life dragged her away from the freedom of youth. But Helen had never embraced such ideas. Life had always been a series of choices and consequences. And wasn't that what Dr. Haupt was talking about?

The choice before her was clear enough. She could hold on to the obligations of friendship and refuse to assist Dr. Haupt. Or she could rise above her personal considerations and assist him in making certain the IHS operated in the most proficient manner. Was there anything ignoble in that? Which was the greater shame? Her willingness to sever her loyalties? Or refusing to serve the greater good?

"So Helen, was there something else about Dr. Fisher's response that bothered you?"

It was no idle question. Helen knew he was asking a question that was not localized to Dr. Fisher's response to the detective's questions. Answering him honestly would be a signal to Dr. Haupt that she worked for him now, and not Dr. Fisher.

"When I brought him the report," she began, "he seemed to be expecting it. His exact words were 'It's about time.' He was, in fact, highly interested in the report. To suggest that he had forgotten Jack Ford's name is impossible. And once I had given him the report, he had me connect him to several different people with whom he had lengthy conversations. One of them was Chief Administrator Reno."

"Dr. Fisher stated Reno wanted the tests expedited. Is that true?"

"The request for expediting the tests had to come before then."

"The body was not found until early in the morning." Dr. Haupt sat at his desk but never relaxed his posture. "Are you saying someone could have known about this body earlier? Before it was dead?"

"No," Helen quickly corrected that idea, "I'm saying there might have been some kind of standing order for the technicians. The tests were nearly done before Dr. Fisher came into the office."

"He could have contacted the technicians from home?"

"No. There's no procedure for that. There are assistant doctors who oversee any calls that come during the night shift. I would have seen any reports from them if they had been required to wake Dr. Fisher at home."

"So perhaps the lab technicians were acting under some kind of protocol that was personally issued by whom? Fisher?"

"If so, there would have to be a record of that somewhere. I know that if there were such a protocol sent out, it wasn't done from the proper channels. I would have seen them go out from his office."

"This is something you could find?"

Here we go, thought Helen. This is a one-way trip. If she had been right about the obvious practical choice, why did she already feel guilty?

"If the lab had a revised protocol, there'll be a record of it somewhere. I'll find it."

"Tell me when you do." Dr. Haupt turned his attention to his deskscreen. Helen had been dismissed.

38

The image on the screen looked like an alien landscape. There were sharp ridges and shadowed valleys with a heavy red tint covering everything. The images panned slowly from left to right.

"At this magnification, we would have found anything like clothing fibers, hair, even food particles. After deleting the fibers and hairs that matched the boy's clothes and hair, we found nothing. We're looking at a section of his neck here."

Wojawski watched the detectives expectantly. He had stopped panning the image, his fingers poised over the controls, ready to bring up any image they might request.

"So, we can assume the killer wore gloves. Fully dressed." MacNally chewed on his lower lip.

"But dressed in some kind of soft polyplastic outfit. The gloves would be the same," Fenelli agreed. "At least that would explain the lack of foreign fibers. But even polyplastics ought to leave a residue. Anything from the chemical scan?"

"I didn't see anything like you're talking about," Wojawski tapped in a command and the far right side of the screen displayed an analysis document with a column of names on the left and numbers on the right.

"What are these?" MacNally paged through paper copies and held up the same analysis. He pointed to the last few listed compounds.

"I couldn't tell you what the symbols stand for, but those last few are engineered compounds. They're not something found in polyplastics, but they're more in line with cleaning chemicals. Could be as simple as body cleansers. Maybe even colognes."

MacNally stared hard at Wojawski. "Maybe? Tell me you can do better than that." He raised his hands in exasperation and appealed to Fenelli, as if his partner could make Wojawski more competent.

"Well, they generally list these things as engineered compounds. We'd have to break them down further if there was enough present at the time the visuals were taken. It takes time."

"And you didn't do that?"

"It's not standard, you know, unless you guys ask for it. Do you want us to do that?" Wojawski looked from one detective to the other. Their silent irritation spoke volumes. "We'll do that. That's fine. We'll try to break them down and identify them. No problem."

"You didn't do this on Ford's visuals?" Fenelli watched

MacNally try to contain his anger at the young VTech.

After a moment where it looked as if Wojawski was going to defend himself, he simply shrugged his shoulders. Maybe he had looked up the meaning of discreet after all, thought Fenelli.

"Time of death is definite?" MacNally skipped ahead in the report in what looked like an effort to diffuse his anger.

"Sure," Wojawski said, "I mean yes. We were able to get a solid reading on that. The time is a fact you can count on."

"Okay, so the kid died how long after he left?" Fenelli looked back at his notes. "The mother said he left—jeez, he didn't live long. He couldn't have gone anywhere. He might have had time to stop in at someone's apartment before heading down the stairs."

"Why the stairs?" MacNally looked up from the report. "The elevator was working."

"Could be as simple as the fact that he's a kid and kids often do things out of the ordinary."

"Or as simple as meeting someone in the stairwell."

"I need a break," MacNally still looked as if he were fighting off the urge to strangle Wojawski. "Do we have anyone running crossdata on Ford and Rodyakov?"

Fenelli shook his head. "Not yet."

"Well, get someone on that, okay? About the only break we've got right now is the fact that we've got two crimes and most likely one killer. So if even the slightest detail crosschecks with both crimes, we may have something. Hell, I'll take anything, right now."

"I'll set it up." Fenelli stood up from where he'd been viewing the visuals and grabbed his notebook.

"And don't run a script on it." MacNally shouted after him. "I want someone who can think to look at it."

Fenelli hadn't planned to ask a computer to check the crossdata. He had something better than a computer. He had Puzzle Pete.

Pete Landon was an underachieving beat cop who'd been pulled from the streets when it had been brought to his superiors' attention that he was a puzzle whiz. It wasn't old jigsaw puzzles that captured his attention. He was a word sleuth and a numbers wizard.

With the math skills of a professor, and the word skills of a linguistic genius, Pete had no desire to make a living from either one of his gifts. He enjoyed being a cop, and spent his off days solving meaningless puzzles. He had been forced to leave his patrolman's position by his captain. From Pete's point of view, the increased stress from a job with greater responsibility was never worth the increase in pay. It was a simple equation that Pete could see clearly in his head.

Fenelli found Pete down on the first floor of the precinct, in an office close to the duty sergeant's front desk. It was noisy here.

Patrolmen, suspects, and everybody came in and out of the main doors of the precinct at all hours of the day and night. The cold rainy weather only made it worse. It was Pete's way of staying close to his old job.

"You busy?" Fenelli asked.

"Go back upstairs and make shadow puppets for MacNally. Children get bored so easily." Pete was younger than Fenelli by maybe ten years. He had a head full of dark curly hair that fell down to his shoulders. Every time he moved his head, his hair shook like a lion's mane.

"And you get a haircut."

"Nobody said I had to work for Homicide." Pete abandoned his tough guy impersonation. "What are you doing down here?"

"I was serious," Fenelli said. "Are you busy?"

"No, not really. I'm supposed to be backcracking a bunch of fake Personal Data Tags. Do you know how boring that is? One time, I actually did it in my sleep purely to prove a point."

"I was hoping I could steal you away from the fraud division and see if you might—"

"Check the crossdata on the double murder you've got on your hands?" White teeth gleamed from Pete's exaggerated smile.

"Only if you don't mind."

Fenelli was not surprised Pete had anticipated his reasons for coming to see him. Pete was sharp. He would have made an outstanding homicide detective. There were times Fenelli really resented Pete's lazy streak. But most of the time, Fenelli admired Pete for knowing what he wanted and sticking to it.

"I would love to play with your crossdata. But I can't." Pete scratched at the side of his face. He looked genuinely sympathetic.

"Can't? Won't?"

"Can't. Look, Fenelli, I wasn't kidding about this PDT stuff. This doesn't come from *my* boss. This comes from *his* boss. Khalid has something going on right now and it must be big. They stuffed some guy in one of the interrogation rooms about a half hour ago. Threw these PDT's at me and demanded I backcrack 'em within the hour."

"You said that was easy. You're probably already done." Fenelli knew he wasn't going to convince Pete to change his answer.

"Come back this afternoon, maybe I'll be done."

At least Pete had modified his answer. That was something.

39

When he considered his position, Lepov decided things could have been worse. Sitting in the interrogation room, he was off his knee, at least for the time being. And when he'd told them he was hungry, they'd brought him a fairly decent sandwich. But the best thing going for him was the fact he'd been left alone long enough to think.

It hadn't taken long to work out the most likely scenario. Lilly, after all, had approached him at the coffee shop. She must have something to do with Ethan Layne's disappearance. And this juvenile prank was designed to get him out of the way. It didn't tell him much, but it proved that this was more than a simple missing person's case.

It would have been easy to blame himself for falling prey to her game, but Lepov was more annoyed at having thought she might be special. Of course, it made sense if he considered she had gone out of her way to get his attention.

There was no telling how much longer he was going to be left alone and he needed to quit thinking about her. The more important issue was how to get out of this jam. They would know by now he was a licensed investigator. But it wouldn't mean much to them. Lepov had known plenty of private detectives that were dirty; there were as many of them as there were dirty cops.

Of course he'd tell them about Layne. Eudia Layne had never said this had to remain confidential, and he sure wasn't going to jail for her even if she had wanted him to keep quiet. Besides, Lepov had always known he would eventually have to talk with the police.

But should he tell them about Lilly? If he could manage to get the charges dropped he might rather deal with her on his own. He would have to tell them about Greta Becker. Now that's a woman he wouldn't mind getting into trouble. She could kick all the patrolmen she wanted for all he cared.

A buzzer broke his concentration. It did not stop its irritating clamor until the door to the interrogation room opened and Detective Khalid entered the room and shut the door.

"Can I have another sandwich?" asked Lepov.

"No." Khalid held a folder and read from one of its pages. "How long have you been a licensed investigator?"

"I don't know, what's it say on that page you're holding?" Lepov hadn't meant to sound petulant but he didn't expect his behavior to be much of a factor in what was about to happen. These cops were either going to play Lilly's game out to the end, or they'd seen through it and would eventually release him.

"Bukovina?" Khalid read the word aloud as if it were a question.

"Home sweet home."

Khalid set down the folder and dropped into a chair. He rubbed the scar on his forehead before he spoke.

"Tell me the whole story and maybe we can work something out."

"Tell you the whole story?" Lepov looked Khalid in the eye and tried to gauge how much he knew. He had revealed precious little information with the few questions he'd asked. The trouble with telling half-truths was trying to guess what half of the truth the other man knew, if he knew any of it at all. Khalid was shrewder than Lepov had expected. By not asking too many questions, Lepov was left with no room to wiggle.

"Just tell me, between you and me."

Lepov would have been an idiot to think they were alone. He was sure there were at least two visual feeds providing images to any number of observers. In addition, there would be recorders transcribing every word, possibly even displaying them as convenient subtitles accompanying the visuals. Despite its worn down appearance, this precinct building couldn't have been that technologically out-of-date.

"I'll tell you whatever you want." Lepov made an impulsive decision to give the cops everything. So far, he hadn't seen anything in the Lazaretto worth losing his freedom over. "You want me to start with the data tags or why I'm here in this garbage dump?"

"The one is the reason for the other, right?" Khalid asked.

"No, why I'm here may only have an indirect link to the tags. Don't you want to know who hired me?"

"Okay, I'll bite. Who hired you?"

"I was hired by Eudia Layne to find her missing son Ethan Layne."

Khalid had obviously never heard of the Laynes.

The buzzer sounded again as the door swung open. An officer entered the room. The buzzer filled the room with its bawling and the officer spoke directly into Khalid's ear in order to be heard. The officer left, the door was closed and the room became silent again.

"I've been asked if you'll repeat what you just said."

"I was hired by Eudia Layne to find her missing son Ethan Layne."

"Spell the names." Lepov spelled them. Khalid wrote them down.

"Have you found him?"

"No." Lepov resisted the urge to make a caustic comment about his arrest hampering his search. He had no idea what that patrolman had said, but Khalid's expression and posture had changed rather pointedly. He seemed much more interested in what Lepov was saying.

"So you aren't really booked into Global Sky resort, is that right?"

"No, I'm not." Lepov watched Khalid scratch down more notes.

"I'll get you that sandwich." The detective grabbed his folder and stood up.

"Was it something I said?" Lepov asked.

Khalid ignored Lepov as he rapped on the door and left the room.

Now what? Lepov hadn't told them anything. All he had done was mention Ethan Layne. Did they know about Layne? From what that Becker girl had said, the police weren't looking for Layne. And as far as Lepov could tell, Khalid had not even recognized his name.

The officer sure hadn't jumpstarted that interest in Khalid. More than likely he had passed on a message for someone else.

Lepov looked up and tried to spot the cameras. Someone had been watching. Someone with an interest in Ethan Layne.

What had Ethan Layne done? And to whom had he done it? His simple case was more complicated than he had expected.

40

After waking, Maria had slipped back into Georges' sweater. She sat now on the corner of a couch with her knees drawn up to her chest, a light blanket made of actual cotton draped over them. The gray light of the late afternoon was the only light in the apartment.

She wished she could build a fire. It was one of the inconveniences of the Lazaretto. Few trees grew on Aegean; firewood was scarce. It was much too heavy and bulky to be shipped in from other planets. Only the wealthy bothered to incorporate a fireplace into their homes.

Although Maria knew there was little reason for her to worry over it, she had been sitting on the couch for nearly an hour wishing she had never called her brother. What had come over her? The young man had seemed pleasant enough, even friendly. He had done nothing to deserve her suspicions.

"Maria?" Georges called from their bedroom.

"I'm out here. Are you hungry?"

"Not really," Georges said. He stepped out of the bedroom and stood looking at her. He wore a dark red robe cinched at the waist, his hands stuck in its pockets.

She held out a hand and he crossed the room, sliding onto the couch beside her. She unfolded her legs and laid them across his lap.

"You look cold," Georges ran his hands over her legs, gently rubbing them. "I could turn up the heat."

"No, I'm fine. I like to bundle up, you know that."

"Hmm, I know. Don't you worry that I'm cold?" He was teasing her and she knew it.

"You don't get cold. Why don't you ever get cold?" Maria had never understood Georges' indifference to low temperatures.

"I don't think about it."

Georges was like that. He maintained his slim build because he never thought to eat. He paid so little attention to anything. It was why she felt so special around him. She was one of the few things he ever noticed.

"Maria, Arturo called me. Tell me what that was about."

Here was another of Georges' traits: he never bandied words about.

"It was nothing, I think I was over-tired. I don't know why I called him." She had not wanted to worry Georges, but understood why Arturo had called him. Arturo was being cautious.

"Tell me exactly what is going on. Let me decide if it is nothing."

She told him. She told him about the SubTransit ride and the park. Each time she had gone over it in her mind she had realized how childishly she had reacted to the young man. Now, as she heard herself describe the young man to Georges aloud, she was completely embarrassed at her behavior.

"What is the matter?" Georges reached out as she turned away from him, tears pooling in her eyes. "There's no need for that. You know, you may have done the right thing."

"What do you—?" Maria's voice faltered.

"Arturo tells me that two people have recently been murdered, and it would be wise to be more careful. So you see? According to your brother, you are right to be cautious."

An uneasy feeling came over Maria. She had already unfairly judged this young man. Was he now to be considered a murderer? Was that the best she could do? She had devoted so much of her time to caring for Kjarsta and others like him, showing love and compassion to those who so desperately needed her. In a world that had callously pushed these dying men and women to the margins of life, she had found a way to give them some small measure of dignity and pride. And yet, here was a young man who had done nothing to Maria save committing the sin of friendliness. Now, she had cast the pall of suspicion over him.

She could not blame Georges or Arturo for their caution. She had been the one to raise an unwarranted alarm. Her own mistrust had cast aspersions on a man who, for all she knew, may have the heart of a saint.

"Please be careful, Maria. If you see him again, and he shows any interest in you, I want you to call your brother or me right away."

To what purpose? Maria felt saddened by it all.

"Maria, promise me you will." Georges' tone had gone from

tender to serious. "I don't want you to take any chances. Tell me you won't."

Maria nodded. Tears threatened to return. She would not argue with Georges. He did not understand. She would make an effort to be careful though she was not sure she could be as careful as Georges wished.

"How about I take you down to our little diner?" A small diner sat on the other side of Trireme Avenue. It was an older restaurant that had once been a novelty diner. But now, after years of heavy use and little effort by the owners to keep it up, it had become rundown and its novelty atmosphere merely felt outdated. Georges and Maria liked it for reasons of their own. It reminded them of a favorite Parisian café back on Earth.

"Please, do. We haven't been there in two weeks." Maria visibly brightened up at the thought. Despite its dinginess, she loved it.

"We need to get dressed." Georges eyed the sweater Maria was wearing. "I'll need my sweater. It's cold out there."

Maria saw the playful look in his eyes and pulled away from him.

"Don't," she said, pulling away as he reached for her.

Georges backed off. He knew when he could tease her and when he couldn't. She had always been grateful that he understood her. Even after twenty plus years of marriage, she had never been able to put on the role of a playful lover. Georges never complained.

But he was willing to complain when she took too much time getting ready to go anywhere. And he hurried, and harassed, and chastised her until he managed to get her out the door.

His efforts paid off. Maria stood smiling in the center of the elevator. She was beginning to feel much like she had in the park earlier that morning. Only, it was clear Georges was much more effective as a tonic than the weather. As they headed across the street, Maria surprised both Georges and herself by laughing out loud.

How silly she had been. Why had she been so panicky about that young man? It was obvious she had overreacted. She should never have involved Arturo. Any homicide detective would have a suspicious attitude. It was natural that he would pass that on to her husband. Men were always quick to judge other men harshly. She did not wish to make that mistake. She would look for a way to undo what she had done.

The cold afternoon only made the diner that much more inviting.

41

Lepov ate his second sandwich alone. Khalid had not come back. The chair he was sitting in had begun to hurt his back. He would have stood up and walked around if not for the pain in his knee. Just thinking about standing hurt.

Some dumb woman steals most of Ethan Layne's belongings, pulls a gun on him, and kicks him in his knee. And which one of them is in jail? Lepov wasn't impressed with the skills of Lazaretto's Law Enforcement.

The buzzer again. Khalid returned. Lepov was too tired to be clever.

"Mr. Lepov," Khalid began, "I want to clarify your position here in the Lazaretto. You are a private detective, hired to find an employee of the Lazaretto Administration: Ethan Layne. Is that correct?"

"Didn't we already do this?"

Khalid glared at him.

"Correct." Lepov kept his response to a minimum.

"And your interest in Layne?"

"He's missing. A fact you guys don't seem to grasp. All I'm doing is the legwork for mama. She's not as blasé about her missing boy as you."

Khalid looked up, as if he were trying to decide what to say next. It took Lepov a moment before he realized Khalid was looking into one of the recorders. Was he waiting for instructions? Lepov wished he knew who was out there. It might be more effective to direct the rest of his answers to that unknown set of eyes watching his every move and the set of ears listening to his every word.

Come out of your hiding place, Lepov wanted to say aloud. Instead, he returned his attention to Khalid, who had asked a question.

"I'm sorry?" Lepov played stupid — a role he knew well.

"Can you explain the PDT's in your footlocker?"

"Even discounting the fact that the footlocker is in a non-private dormitory where anyone could have come along and stashed them, and ignoring the fact that the coded lock on the footlocker could be breached by most children nine years and older, I can tell you I have no proof I didn't put them there. But, do you really care either way? And, what the hell is taking so long? You could have finished hours ago."

Someone knocked hard on the outside of the door.

"That's what we're waiting for," Khalid pointed towards the door. As it opened, Khalid stood and shook the hand of the man who entered. Once the buzzer cut off, Khalid turned to introduce the newcomer.

"Lepov, meet the Lazaretto's Chief Administrator: Claude Reno."

Reno was a big man with well-muscled shoulders that were easy to see under his suit coat. He had thick hair and a deep voice. He also seemed eager to meet Lepov. He stepped forward immediately and offered to shake Lepov's hand. He instinctively stuck his own hand out and forgot that a handshake was no simple gesture in the Lazaretto.

"Mr. Lepov, I wanted to personally express my regrets at your treatment. Detective Khalid has filled me in on what has been happening with you and I am embarrassed at this department's behavior."

Lepov glanced over at Khalid as Reno spoke and saw the anger Khalid could not conceal. Reno was laying it on too thick in his detective's opinion. Khalid had obviously been following orders.

"It seems we were led astray by someone who was trying to use you as a decoy. I have been assured this miscreant will be apprehended soon. Is there anything I can do for you to prove the sincerity of my apology?"

"You could tell me why no one is looking for Ethan Layne." Lepov wasn't about to buy Reno's sincerity.

"I don't know. But I am going to find out. There is much going on here I am going to look into." Reno turned a cold eye to Khalid.

"We'll have Mr. Lepov's things ready for him in a minute."

"Of course you will. Gregor—may I call you Gregor?—let me know if anything has been misplaced." Reno put special emphasis on the word *misplaced* and aimed yet another hard stare at the detective.

Reno was trying too hard. As a matter of fact, Reno was fumbling around like an excited child. Something did not make sense. It looked for all the heavens as if Reno were making this up as he went along.

Could a man reach the top position of something as extensive as the Lazaretto with the skills and mind of a bumbler? Lepov doubted it. But if Reno were a man with power and a shrewd mind, what could possibly cause him to act this way?

"I want you to know, Gregor, we want to help you find Ethan Layne. I implore you to take advantage of the resources at our disposal as you search for him. We will keep you updated on anything we can find about him. We want to work with you on this— side by side."

Good Lord. Lepov smiled and thanked Reno even as he inwardly groaned. He had never heard of a police organization that wanted to share information with a private detective. It had never happened in the past, and Lepov was positive it would never happen; now or in the future. If Reno spoke of cooperating, it could only mean they were suddenly interested in finding Layne and had no idea where he was.

Lepov wasn't about to pass up the offer of assistance, though. He wanted to use their resources. Of course, an eager acceptance of their cooperation was out of the question. They might be acting like amateurs and underestimating him, but he wasn't about to do the same.

"I want to go back to my room and rest. It's been a bad day and your weather is laughing at my bad knee."

"I understand you are in one of the dormitories, is that right?" Reno shepherded him along a hallway towards the elevators. "You'll never get much rest there. Why don't you let me put you up in a proper hotel? It's the least we could do for you."

"That's a nice gesture, but I'll be okay." Lepov stopped at the elevator and watched Khalid shoo some uniformed men out of it. Before he knew it, Lepov was crammed in the elevator with Reno, Khalid, and several unidentified men.

Lepov had been rushed into the interrogation room as quickly as he was being rushed back out. These guys didn't do anything at a leisurely pace. It gave him precious little time to think straight.

Reno kept asking him about Layne, if he had discovered anything about him. Khalid hadn't mentioned the fraudulent PDT's since Reno had intervened. And now Reno wanted the Lazaretto police to be at his side as he searched for Layne. Reno kept coming back to making offers of assistance. He clearly wanted Lepov's search for Layne unimpeded.

His knee throbbed relentlessly as they signed out Lepov and his possessions at the front desk with dizzying alacrity. He wondered briefly if the police had sifted through his computer files. He filed that concern in the back of his mind and turned his attention to Reno.

Why was the Chief Administrator—a clinical title which was a poor substitute for the title of Mayor—rushing him out the door? Was he that worried about a lawsuit? He doubted that. He wasn't being cautious about liability. If anything, he was being reckless.

But he wasn't being completely forthright, either. The offer of a hotel room was more than a magnanimous gesture. It would have been a way to keep a detailed watch on Lepov. There was no way he would willingly set himself up in what could only be a surveillance fishbowl.

With a final effort, Reno and his detectives nearly launched Lepov through the front doors and down the steps of the precinct building. Before he could comment on their near manic behavior, Lepov stood alone on the stone steps.

Two things occurred to him simultaneously. He stood perfectly still and tried to focus on both items. The first item merely confirmed an earlier supposition of his. Khalid had mentioned Global Sky.

None of the police had been at that Lazar party. But Lilly had been. That might prove that she had turned him in. The bit about Global Sky had probably come out when they had questioned her. The second item did nothing but confuse this same supposition of his. Lilly sat on a bench a few yards from the bottom step; had she been expecting his release.

Lepov limped down the last few steps as Lilly stood to meet him. She looked relieved. What was going on? Lepov didn't have a clue.

42

Homicide was nearly empty. Most of the detectives were out conducting interviews in the Rodyakov building, as well as interviewing people in the buildings on Masthead where Jack Ford was found. They were casting a wide net because MacNally and Fenelli had yet to find any lead significant enough to follow.

With his feet propped on a desk, MacNally looked tired and irritated.

"The door log says Ford had never been to Rodyakov's building. And this little Rodyakov had never been *anywhere* on Masthead. In fact, these two had never crossed paths anywhere that we can find, right?"

"Yeah," Fenelli had been running the crossdata check himself after he'd failed to enlist Pete Landon for the job. "I can't find anyone that is even partially connected to them that has been to both crime sites. I had even hoped Ford had crossed paths with the boy's father, who works at a club called the *Blue Forty*. But Ford never crossed the front door of that joint. The only connection there was Joey Cho had been in the club. But when I ran his time on the door logs with the time of death for Ford — aw, hell, MacNally. I get a headache trying to sort out this nonsense."

"You realize that the most likely suspect is the senior Rodyakov?" MacNally ignored the various scenarios that Fenelli had been outlining. "Mashing data is all well and good, but we ought to be able to make some reasonable deductions on our own. I can't say I really believe the father did it, but his disappearance makes for a massive question mark.

"And the only logical connection between these two murders is that club. But I can't find a way to make it."

"You're both being impatient," Pete Landon said, approaching the detectives. "I asked you to come back this afternoon, you never came."

"I was about to go back down and beg for your help." Fenelli felt the first glimmer of hope at the sight of Puzzle Pete. "Can you go over our data?"

"I already have. You guys caught a break like you wouldn't believe." Pete grabbed a chair and pulled it towards MacNally's desk. Without asking, he grabbed a stack of papers and stuck them on top of an already overloaded filing cabinet, clearing a space on MacNally's desk large enough for him to sit on. He put his feet up in the chair he'd taken.

"What the hell do you think you're doing?" MacNally barked.

"I'm about to give you a possible suspect, if that's okay." Pete reached over and punched in a few commands on MacNally's deskscreen. He looked up and placidly waited for a reply.

"Okay," MacNally's anger was abated for the moment.

"As you guys probably know by now, nothing cross checks on your two victims as far as the computer is concerned. I won't even go into that. And you were right, MacNally, the only possible connection was this club on Masthead. But Ford had never been to the club. That didn't worry me. I needed a suspect, not the victim. So I took Ford's movements that night, and tried to find a match at any of those locations with anyone at this *Blue Forty* place. Unfortunately I hit a dozen names. Facial recon was solid enough to verify the names from the PDT's with the faces on record. Any one of them could have been a suspect.

"I tried something else. I ran the facial recon on all locations, and crossed it with the PDT logs."

"Looking for anyone with a fake ID." MacNally nodded. "But it never works. Anyone using fake data tags knows to keep his head down at the door. You never get a good look at him."

"Just wait." Pete held up a hand as if he hated to be rushed. "That's exactly what I was thinking. So I ran facial recon to list any shots that had been labeled unreadable. Again, I found too many. But when I ran the PDT's against them, one of them hit at the restaurant Jack Ford ate at and at the *Blue Forty*. This guy here mismatched his PDT by his hair color."

MacNally and Fenelli leaned over the pictures.

"The fact that his hair is blond is the only thing you can see of this guy." MacNally tried to brighten the image but the man's face was turned down enough to be in perpetual shadow.

"His tag says he should have red hair?" Fenelli shook his head. "For all we know he had it recently colored. And maybe this guy's too shy to look up for the camera. This is a little thin."

"I don't do thin." Pete tapped his feet on the seat of the chair. He was clearly pleased with himself. "I said you guys caught a break, and I meant it. I can prove this guy was using fake ID. You remember those PDT's I was backcracking for Fraud this morning?"

Fenelli nodded. He was quickly losing interest in Pete's story. If all he had was a guy with a fake ID, it was meaningless. He could have been an under-aged kid trying to get into the club, or he might simply have been using the ID so he wouldn't have to pay for a meal.

"This guy's number was in the same number series as the batch of fake PDT's I was working on. They were issued by the same forger."

"Wouldn't they be random?" Fenelli might have lost interest, but he couldn't help but ask the question. He knew he'd regret asking it as soon as he did. Pete launched into a lecture on his favorite subject.

"No, there's a problem with randomly generated numbers. First of all, you might end up duplicating a number already in circulation. Second, you might randomly generate an easily recognizable number; something that contains several groups of repeating numbers. Forgers never want anything that can be recognized. The beauty of a false ID in this system is the size of the number—the number of integers—which makes it impossible to recognize at a glance.

"So, the forger sets up a random number program that will actually generate numbers within a certain series that he is assured is not yet in circulation. At the same time, he'll lay in a few behavioral codes to purge that series of any recognizable patterns."

"But you recognized them." MacNally asked skeptically.

"The program will look for patterns in the numbers. Sequential declination, repetitious sets of integers, obvious things like that, none of which the program would allow in groups of four or possibly five integers at a time. It would be assumed the human eye couldn't keep track of more than that at one time. Unfortunately for the forger, to rule out larger groups of integers might drastically reduce the available numbers that could be manufactured."

"And you can spot these sequences?" Now Fenelli was skeptical.

"Maybe. But more importantly, I can see what the computer can't see. Remember, it's looking for numbered sequences. It's a mathematical analysis. Now, don't get me wrong, I can spot some of them like that. But I'm quicker at picking up the visual sequence. A computer doesn't look at it like a human does. But some of us can look at the numbers as a picture. Sort of like how we read. We never read every letter in a word. For example, we see the six letters of the word *genius* as one image, not as six individual images. So the substitution is made in our minds; like substituting an image of me for the image of those six letters."

Pete nearly took a bow, he was obviously proud of what he'd done.

"Okay, genius, so what does your PDT's have to do with this blond guy?"

"I identified the forger of the PDT's I was working on. Oddly enough, when I told Khalid that, he didn't care. I don't know why. It seems Claude Reno got involved and they lost all interest in the PDT's."

"Okay," Fenelli was not as impressed as Pete wanted them to be, "but there's still nothing to connect this blonde guy to the murders."

"Oh," Pete looked momentarily lost in thought. He allowed a sheepish grin before continuing. "My mistake. I forgot two little details. This PDT number showed up purchasing a drink at the restaurant bar at the same time Jack Ford was purchasing one. And it also showed up as an exit point for our guy leaving the *Blue Forty* through the kitchen. The dishwasher, Rodyakov, was there at the time."

"Are you serious?" MacNally pulled his feet from off his desk and sat up straight. "This blond guy met Ford at a bar, and met with the Rodyakov kid's father the same night?"

"No good pictures taken, were there?" Fenelli felt sure he knew the answer to that. Pete shook his mane of curly hair.

"But we've got the forger, right?" MacNally nearly jumped to his feet.

"Name and present location." Pete tapped one finger on the deskscreen, displaying the forger's picture and PDT readings.

43

It had taken an inordinate amount of time for Dr. Haupt's relocation to his larger office. Dr. Fisher had not failed to give Dr. Haupt what he wanted, but the poorly organized effort was Dr. Fisher's way of lodging a protest. Helen could see it and she knew Dr. Haupt could as well.

Her office equipment had been upgraded, as Dr. Haupt had demanded. Helen was still surprised at how he had handled that. She had never once suspected he was aware of her outdated equipment. He had never asked about it. He had never commented on it. Yet, he had not hesitated to confront Dr. Fisher about it and demand it be corrected.

She had decided against thanking him. Once the situation had been rectified, he would have seen little point in discussing it. Thanking him would have been unnecessary. He had merely done what was needed.

If she wasn't careful, Helen realized, she'd become as cold and pragmatic as her new boss.

The new office was larger, but the real addition to their workspace was a third room that contained a large conference table.

In this conference room they would have plenty of space to organize and analyze the great numbers of documents that they would be reviewing.

Dr. Haupt had decided to take advantage of the paper hard copies that had been printed and stored on site. He had seen the benefit in using paper copies right away. No one could make unauthorized changes to them as they could to electronic documents filed on the desksystems. It was a unique opportunity to be certain the data had not been tampered with. Furthermore, Dr. Haupt told Helen to retrieve most of the documents personally, decreasing the likelihood that someone would corrupt the paperwork.

When Helen understood what he wanted, she discovered she was getting bolder with him. "Dr. Haupt, I will never be able to retrieve the documents you require. You will have to get me some help."

The German turned away from his deskscreen and examined her. He was not angry. She wondered if he was actually amused at her brazenness.

"Well? Have you a suggestion?"

"I do." Helen had held little faith that he would allow her to suggest a name. Her luck was holding. She had to make that suggestion on a level with which he would relate. "I have a colleague in the front office that will not only do a good job for you, but will be trustworthy as well."

"Tell me her name, and I will arrange it."

Dr. Haupt's authority was something impressive to see. Within an hour, Julia had been transferred to their office.

"Helen, what is this all about?" Julia asked as soon as she entered.

"Sit down and I'll explain everything." Helen was a bit nervous at having Julia join her. She hoped her friend could understand the delicacy of their position working for Dr. Haupt. But despite her reservations, she knew Julia really was the one person at IHS she could trust.

Relying on her memory, Helen tried to impress Julia with the same sense of sobriety that Dr. Haupt had instilled in her with his short but succinct speeches. She needed Julia to understand the importance of what they were doing. But she did not want Julia to hear it from Dr. Haupt. Helen wanted to be able to warn Julia of the ramifications of what they were doing and how it might possibly conflict with their loyalties to Dr. Fisher and the IHS staff.

"I'm not a child, Helen. You don't have to spell it out for me." Julia rolled her eyes. "We're probably gonna shoot our jobs in the ass before this is all over. Thanks for the invitation to suicide."

Helen cringed at Julia's crass remark. But even as she did, she understood Julia was right. She really had dragged Julia into the frying pan with her. The guilt must have been plainly visible. Julia rolled her eyes again.

"Oh, don't cry about it. What are friends for, right? Besides, I was getting tired of this place anyway."

"I doubt it will come to that," Helen tried to sound positive.

"Who cares either way, huh?"

Julia was already helping a great deal. Her disdain for the seriousness of their position was a welcome change to Helen's concern. She wasn't sure Dr. Haupt would appreciate this younger assistant, but Helen would do what she could to smooth things out on that front.

"Well," Helen gave a half-hearted grin, "you might as well meet him."

"How's this?" Julia adopted a sour expression. "Will this work?"

"Don't start—" Helen wagged a finger at Julia.

Once they were in his office, Dr. Haupt gave Julia a long stare. He said nothing until he had examined her for almost a minute. Finally, he addressed Helen while continuing to stare at the newcomer.

"You have explained everything to her?"

"Yes."

"Do you require additional office equipment?"

"No," Helen answered. "Most of the time one of us will be out digging up documents. What we have will be fine."

"Very good, then." He turned to look at Helen. "What have you found out about the revised lab protocols?"

"I was in the middle of writing up a report on that when the men arrived to move us to this new office. I can finish it up now, if you like."

"Just summarize for me. It is getting late and I do not want to keep you after hours."

"I did find a request that specified the actions to be taken in the event a body was discovered with the physical symptoms similar to Jack Ford. It is hard to follow, but I was not able to read the actual protocol."

"If that is so, how do you know of it?" Dr. Haupt asked.

"I went down to the lab, and one of the technicians there was willing to show me a note that had been hand written reminding every shift of the request. The note only mentioned expediting the tests, and added they make sure the new protocol was followed to the letter. The file number and location of the new protocol was written on the note."

"But it was no longer in the system when you looked for it?"

"I couldn't get to it. But I think it's still there." Helen paused. "We will have to make an official request to get the authorization to look at it. It is accessible only by the laboratory through an elevated authorization."

"Do not do that, for now. I want you two ladies to go home for the day. We will look at this again."

Helen and Julia were not about to argue with their boss. They shut down the office system and left for home.

Helen could not help but feel better as she rode the SubTransit that evening. Just having Julia in the office with her relieved a great deal of the stress that had again begun to build up within her. Now all she needed was another long hot bath.

44

It had not taken Lilly long to make the connection between the police activity on the street and Gregor's disappearance. She had returned to the dormitory with a sack full of lunch. She'd left the dormitory with a head full of questions.

She remembered Shaw Parks' succinct observation at the previous night's party. Parks had asked Gregor if he was a cop.

Something about that question had captured her attention. There was that odd manner Gregor had of taking in information; the way he seemed to make a mental note of different things she had said. She had also noticed the way he always watched everything around him. That was his Little Boy Lost routine she had liked so much.

On a less tangible note, she knew that Montillo and Parks had been uneasy around him. They had both questioned her as to why she had invited him last night. If she hadn't been so attracted to him, would she have felt as uneasy?

But then he had been arrested. She had cursed her decision to leave in search of lunch. It was important that she know what had happened. Had he really been arrested? Could it possibly be a charade? He could have been an undercover cop; it would have made sense.

And if that was his role, what was he after? Was she suspected of making illegal sales? Or were the police simply fishing for anyone that might take the bait? Was Gregor there to pick up whoever he could for a star in the Fraud Department's crown?

With each question, she had eventually answered in Gregor's favor. It was irritating the way she was drawn to his defense. She was not acting like the Lilly Stewart most people knew. Lilly Stewart wouldn't have allowed Gregor Lepov to get anywhere near her. There were too many questions that needed answering before she would have allowed that. But she was having trouble playing the role of that Lilly.

She flushed as she realized she preferred to be the Lilly that Gregor was getting to know: a soft heart who didn't mind showing up at his room and nearly begging to eat lunch with him. If she hadn't liked the change as much as she had, she would have been embarrassed for herself. But she did like it. God help her if that clouded her judgment to the point of trouble. It made little sense to her, but she felt willing to risk it.

And with that settled in her mind, she had known she would have to go and find out what happened to him. She would have to go find out if he'd been arrested. What irony, she had thought, to meet someone for whom she was willing to change her life only to see him arrested.

No one at the precinct could tell her anything about Gregor. She had waited for hours before she had finally been told that he was being held on the vague charges of fraud. That had been the most she could learn. It hadn't told her much and she had been left wondering what to do.

Cam Raley had been her lifeline. Cam had a few friends on the force, and he had been able to get one of them to promise to call if he learned anything. It had shocked her when Cam's friend called her only an hour later to say Gregor was being freed. Lilly had barely had time to reach the station before she had seen Gregor descending its steps.

Her heart skipped a few beats when their eyes met—not from excitement or fear—she read suspicion and anger in his eyes. Something was wrong. Something was terribly wrong.

"Hello, Lilly." His voice was hard, as cold as the air around them.

She had wanted to say something kind to him; something that would let him know she'd been worried about him. His manner changed all that. She wasn't sure how she should react to him. All she could manage to do was pull the collar of her coat around her neck to ward off the sudden chill. Whether it was the chill of the late afternoon wind or Gregor's behavior made little difference to her. Either way, she needed to protect herself against both.

"Are you disappointed?" His wolfish smile unnerved her. She didn't understand his question. "I didn't expect to see you here. How bold."

"I was waiting for you. What's going on?" Her defenses were down. They had been all day. She'd been acting more like a worried lover than the shrewd Lazar she'd been for so long.

"You tell me. You're the one who wanted me in jail."

That hit her like a jab to the kidneys. She jerked back as if physically hit. Her defense systems began automatically engaging. She had to protect herself, and do it fast.

"You had me going for awhile. I thought we had a little something happening between us."

"What do you mean?" Lilly tried frantically to catch up. Gregor seemed to think she was disagreeing with him.

"I was sort of falling for you, Lilly. I guess that's what happens when a woman like you works so hard to put on a show. I'd be embarrassed at my behavior but frankly I think any guy would've fallen for you. And that's me, as dumb as the next guy."

Lilly had completely lost track of what he was saying. Had he just complimented her? Had he, in the same breath, just accused her of deceiving him?

"I hope you'll excuse me if I don't invite you back up to my place," Gregor took a few steps past her. "I've already been screwed once today. If I get the urge for more of the same I'll give you a call."

Lilly stood speechless as he walked away from her. Her defenses had nearly been back in place, but it had been too little too late. The cruelty of his attack had struck her deeply. Lilly wanted to cry. Lilly Stewart wouldn't let her.

45

Fenelli made no attempt to conceal his identity when he opened the door of Comic Joe's. He would never convince anyone that he wasn't a cop. The bartender probably knew who he was. Maybe even a few of the patrons would recognize him. His face occasionally showed up on news reports and it wasn't unusual to receive stares and hear whispers behind his back. MacNally was even more widely recognized. It's why Fenelli went through the front door and MacNally came in the back.

The bar wasn't crowded but it was getting there. It was almost five o'clock and office workers who didn't want to go home were beginning to fill up the stools at the long bar as well as the red booths along the wall. A few of the customers turned to stare at him. Two bartenders were in view: one of them ignored him, but the larger one stopped what he was doing and studied Fenelli as he walked towards the bar.

"Something we can get you, Captain?" the big bartender asked in a high-pitched saccharine voice. Fenelli wasn't sure if the guy was making that voice up or not.

Fenelli shook his head and stopped at the corner of the bar closest to the front door. He removed his hat and tossed it in front of him.

"You want me to fill that with beer?" This got the second bartender to look in Fenelli's direction and laugh at his coworker's little joke.

Fenelli shook his head again, and this time he smiled and sat on the stool in front of him. He left one foot touching the ground and rested the second one on the footrest of the stool next to him.

"Well, if you don't want anything, what are you doing?" The second bartender sounded like a tough guy.

"I'm waiting." Fenelli continued to smile.

"For what, cop?"

"For that." Fenelli pointed down the bar to the far end of the room.

The bartender turned in time to see MacNally appear at the back door. He stepped through it as if he hoped to start a fight.

MacNally focused on a booth that was only an arm's length away. A single occupant of the booth sat looking at him. He was a dark man with a small black mustache. He looked like he wanted to get the hell out of that booth but already MacNally blocked his retreat. Resignation darkened his eyes as MacNally slid into the man's seat.

Fenelli grabbed his hat and slipped off his stool. He walked slowly down the length of the bar and joined MacNally on the opposite bench.

"You mind if we join you, Romeo?" MacNally smiled.

"You got the wrong guy. My name is Carlos."

"You think we didn't know that?" Fenelli pulled out a notebook and flipped it open. "Carlos Montillo. Arrived in Lazaretto twenty-four days ago. Listed as a Memento Broker—whatever the hell that is— home planet Arcobia. Good so far?"

"Arcobia?" MacNally grunted his amusement. "That figures."

Carlos watched them but said nothing.

"What else? Oh yeah, says here you are a dealer in fine manufactured fake PDT's. What's that stand for?" Fenelli looked up at his partner.

"Personal Data Tags." MacNally supplied the answer almost before Fenelli could ask his question.

"Are you guys serious? Are you really coming in here to accuse me of this?" Carlos spread his arms in exasperation.

"We are," Fenelli nodded at MacNally for confirmation. MacNally nodded in return as he mumbled an affirmation.

"And then you add this comedy bit? What do you really want?"

"We want to find a killer." MacNally dropped his light banter and looked Carlos in the eye.

"Whoa, now I killed someone?" They had Carlos' full attention.

"There are two people dead. Are you admitting to something?"

Fenelli never had the slightest suspicion that this guy was the killer. But it didn't hurt to give him the impression that he was a suspect. It might encourage him to cooperate. No one ever wanted to go down for murder—not even to cover for a friend. Unless he was smart enough to know how the game was played.

"Go to hell. You don't have anything on me." This one was smart enough. "Are you even gonna take me in for questioning? Or don't you have enough to take me in?"

This one was more than smart enough. Fenelli hoped he and MacNally would prove to be smarter. The truth of the matter was, even though Pete's conclusion was logical, it was too fragile to do much with it. Carlos would be back on the street as soon as a lawyer showed up. Even a piss-ant lawyer who had cheated on his bar exams could have punched holes in the theory from which they were operating.

But that didn't mean they were wrong. There was a high probability that Carlos, going by the name of Romeo, had sold the murderer a fake PDT.

"My partner was a little overzealous to suggest you killed anyone." Fenelli hoped his lines didn't sound like they'd been written by a cheap novelist. That's what they sounded like to him. "He's talking about relativity. You know, how one thing relates to another, and another, and so forth? My partner thinks that if you're the one who sold a guy a fake PDT, and then he used that ID to get around town and kill two people—well he thinks that makes you responsible. That make any sense?"

"Hell, no!"

"We're not talking about some petty crime, Carlos." MacNally leaned over and crowded the Spaniard into the corner of the booth. "There're two people who have been violently murdered. And one of them was a kid. Just a little kid. So you can be offended all you want. I don't care. If you sold this guy his ID, and we catch him, I'm gonna make sure he points you out. And then you'll get a lesson in relativism."

"I don't know what you're talking about. Is there anything else you want with me?" Carlos had looked as if MacNally had shaken him, but he was quickly regaining control.

"No." MacNally took a drink from the cup that had been sitting in front of Carlos. He made a face and spit back into it. "Sorry, I thought that was coffee."

"It was." Carlos gestured angrily at both detectives.

Fenelli and MacNally were out on the street before they spoke.

"You think we got him?" MacNally asked.

"We'll wait and see. And MacNally?"

"What?"

"It's relativity." Fenelli corrected him.

"What did I say?"

"Relativism. That means like everything is true. You meant that everything is related."

"Hell, Fenelli, Romeo's too stupid to know the difference."

46

Impulsive decisions irritated the Collector. But this one was necessary to keep control of all the players in the game. He had already misjudged one of the players. And in doing so, he had nearly removed a vital player from his own team. That could not happen again.

"I was only acting on your orders." The Collector's Agent said dangerously. It was not an accusation per se, but it was an attempt to project the blame back onto the Collector.

"I didn't call you up here to discuss what has already transpired." The Collector had to let the Agent's impertinence go unpunished, though never forgotten. "What I require will be something more delicate. You will have to be more careful than ever. This must be done right."

"As I said: to date, my actions have been careful — and right."

"Then you will have no problem with these next tasks." The Collector allowed a little fire to show in his eyes. Not much. Just enough.

The Agent must have decided to be more careful. There were no more incautious comments.

A young woman came into the office from one of the back rooms. She was of mixed ethnicity — from a mixed pool of Asian and Indian blood the Collector surmised — and had black hair that seemed to shine from the glow of her glistening olive skin. She wore a sheer thigh-length robe of which neither the Collector nor the Agent took any notice. Two small cups sat in the center of a bamboo tray she carried.

"Just a moment," the Collector signaled to her and she approached with the tray. The Collector picked up the cup on his right and inspected its contents: three different sized capsules of three widely different colors. "The little tramp got it wrong once, ruined three weeks of treatments."

The Agent looked as if he were going to ask the girl a question.

"Oh don't bother, she can't hear a thing. It's why I had mercy on her when she made that error with the pills. I have no idea if she's grateful that I didn't kill her. The beating I gave her was a little rough.

But she never complained."

The Collector tipped the cup to his lips and swallowed the capsules quickly. He dropped the cup onto the tray and snatched up the second cup, washing out his mouth with a strong smelling black juice. The girl smiled at him as he nodded in approval.

"The devil only knows what she's really thinking behind that smile." He licked his lips. "It's called licorice. It comes from Earth. My time is limited. Let's continue."

The girl backed out of the room never ceasing to smile.

"He is here to find Ethan Layne." The Collector had again displayed the Private Investigator's image on the screen in front of the Agent. "I was beginning to believe our message to the mother had gone unheeded. It almost made me doubt the sacred love of a mother for her son. I never expected her to send a surrogate. But it doesn't matter. I want you to keep an eye on him. He may need some help.

"And tell me, have you covered your tracks? It would be problematic if he discovered your involvement."

"There is one more thing for me to do. It won't be a problem." The Agent smiled at the image on the screen. "And the second task?"

"Dr. Fisher has requested our assistance. I have given it some thought, and despite his rather—" the Collector had begun to think of the doctor as an irritating child, "—exaggerated anxieties, it would be wise to provide that assistance. Indirect assistance. Very indirect."

The Agent listened as the Collector outlined their next move. The Collector had to be absolutely certain that his Agent understood what was needed. They were beginning to get far more involved than he wanted. It was important that his plan be followed explicitly.

He had held his composure as long as the Agent was still in the room. Once the Agent had gone, the Collector gave up hiding his pain. The capsules were already partially digested and the chemicals raced into his intestines with genetically engineered speed. Acute pain built up in the soft vale below his sternum and the Collector knew it was only the beginning. Fire shot up through his throat burning out all it touched in its consuming hunger.

The pain meant nothing. The only thing that mattered was the cleansing: the burning, tearing cleansing through over eight meters of his digestive tract. And even as the Collector shuddered from the chemically induced attack, he knew it was good. The cleansing brought purity. Purity was life.

47

Gregor Lepov wished he had never taken Eudia Layne's money. Since he'd accepted the job he'd traveled halfway across the Euxine, been attacked by a German Berserker, been imprisoned on a quarantine planet—as if the quarantine planet weren't prison enough without jail—and met a woman who had both enchanted and betrayed him. What was next? Maybe he'd catch some wickedly deformative disease. He wasn't even sure there was such a thing, but with his luck, it was possible he'd be the first person on this moon to contract it.

What bothered him more was how little he had been able to search for Ethan Layne. There had been his discovery of the karate wunderkind who'd stolen all of his evidence. He'd been shocked the police hadn't asked him about all that stolen property, then he realized that they might not have been aware of it yet. More than likely, they were on their way to Layne's apartment right now. If so, they'd be looking for him again as soon as they discovered Layne's room had been pillaged.

Damn, Lepov muttered to himself, I never got around to telling them about that crazy Becker woman.

It was getting colder and Lepov was glad to get inside his building and out of the increasingly strong wind. A heady odor of mildew hung in the air. The rain had quit hours ago but everything still felt wet to Lepov. He wiped his shoes on a worn mat even though they weren't wet. It only felt like he should. It was that kind of day.

Halfway up the second flight of stairs, Lepov heard someone above him. A man heading down the stairs passed him on the third floor landing. Lepov paid no attention to him until the man was halfway to the next landing. He recognized him. How did he know this guy?

"Hey," Lepov called down to the man, "didn't we meet last night?"

The man stopped and peered up at Lepov.

"You're Parks, right?" Lepov wasn't sure he had the right name.

"Right," the man answered reluctantly. He stood uncertainly on the stairs, putting his weight first on one foot and then the other. "You're Lilly's friend."

Lepov descended the stairs between them slowly. Parks was acting like a kid who'd been caught sneaking out of the girl's shower room. Lepov might have been paranoid but he'd be damned if he would ignore anything that even rhymed with suspicious for the rest of the day.

"I seem a little too refined for this type of neighborhood. You weren't looking for me, were you?" Lepov was in the mood for a fight. He was beginning to get the feeling Parks was up to no good. Damn. Wasn't anyone in this rat-hole honorable?

"Looking for you? No." Parks edged backwards, one foot feeling for then finding the landing below him.

"What exactly were you doing here?" Lepov cocked his head and glanced towards the upper floors without taking his eyes off Parks.

"I was uh…" Parks stammered as he ran out of words.

"Always have a lie ready to use," Lepov stepped closer to the Lazar, "that way you don't sound like you're making it up as you stand there clearing your throat."

Lepov reached down and jammed Parks against the wall with one hand. With his free hand he reached under Parks' coat and felt around for a weapon. Parks was unarmed.

"What were you doing up there?" Lepov's growled.

"Now wait, I don't even know what's going on." Parks' eyes weren't filled with fear, but there was enough there to shine through. "I —"

Parks seemed to be reconsidering his choice of words. Lepov wasn't going to let that happen. He shoved Parks back into the corner of the landing. Parks tried to stop himself from hitting the wall with an outstretched hand but misjudged how fast he'd been pushed. His hand buckled under the impact and he slid to his knees on the landing. Lepov stood over him.

"I thought you were Lilly's friend," Parks whined.

"I don't give a damn what you thought. I want to know what you were doing." Lepov was not much bigger than Parks, but his aggressive attack had overwhelmed the man.

"I wasn't doing anything. I was supposed to meet someone."

"In my room?" Lepov nearly stood on top of Parks.

"Your room? How would I know you have a room here? I was told to go and wait in one of the dormitory rooms on the fourth floor."

Lepov didn't have to ask which room.

"And Lilly never showed? Or is she still up there?" Lepov knew she wasn't there. He had left her at the precinct.

"Lilly?" Parks looked more than afraid now; he looked confused. "What does she have to do with this?"

Lepov backed off, allowing Parks to roll to one side and sit up.

"Lilly wasn't going to meet you here?" For the first time since the cops had arrested him, he wasn't sure who had planted the PDTs.

"No."

"Who was it?"

Parks said nothing. He watched Lepov with wide eyes, obviously worried at how violent his attacker might become. It was also obvious to Lepov that Parks wasn't worried enough.

"I hope you're loyalty is worth the damage I'm gonna do." Lepov never threatened a man unless he was willing to follow through with his threat. He raised a fist.

"What loyalty?" Parks stalled, shaking. "I just agreed to meet a guy—Montillo! Carlos Montillo!"

"What were you supposed to do for him?" Lepov tried to work out the new information in his head. Montillo? Did this mean he'd been wrong about Lilly?

"Nothing! I just asked him where I could find him and he said he'd be over here. I came late. I guess he'd already been and gone."

A noise below them reminded Lepov that they were on a public stair. He grabbed Parks by the collar and pushed him up the stairs. Neither man spoke until they shut themselves in Lepov's dormitory.

"What does Montillo deal in?" Lepov asked. He needed to add a few numbers together, but he was a little short on integers.

"What? Souvenirs, junk for the travelers." Parks jerked away as Lepov threatened to backhand him with his beefy rough hand.

"What does he really deal in? What is he really selling?"

"I wouldn't know. Wait!" Another flinch. "It won't do any good to hit me. I don't know. Yeah, alright, Carlos does some illegal stuff on the side. He knows I won't do that kind of thing. He won't tell me any of it. All I know is he's got some code name. Something he calls himself."

"Well?" Lepov was ready to give up on Parks. This guy was more scared than he ought to be. He was either a total coward or he was a ham actor. Either way, he wasn't much use.

"Romeo. That's like his trademark. But I don't know what he sells."

Montillo. Lepov had not liked the man from the moment he had met him in the café. It was obvious Lilly was fond of him. But what did that mean? And what, after all, was Lilly's role in this?

He hated to base any of his deductions on the word of Shaw Parks. The only guy he trusted any less than Parks was Montillo. And if Montillo had shown up here fingering Parks, Lepov would have been inclined to disbelieve him. The fact of the matter was, neither one of these guys had any credibility.

Lilly could tell him. She could make sense of this. She was the one person he had trusted. And now he had no idea if he still could. And would it even matter if he changed his mind about her? It was unlikely she was sitting around pining for him to ask for her advice.

Lepov couldn't help but wonder: what else could happen today?

48

It hadn't been long before Helen was laughing at herself. She had been so intent on getting home and relaxing that she hadn't noticed how hungry she had become. It was only after she was soaking in searing hot water that she realized she had never eaten dinner.

One night can make a difference. Just the night before she had come home with no appetite. Yet now, after another day with Dr. Haupt—she was no longer thinking of him as *the German*—she was hungry.

Already in the cleansing waters of her bath, she had no desire to tramp into the kitchen and sweat out a fully cooked meal. That was out of the question.

It was time for her to spend some of that hard-earned money she'd been saving. Why not? There was no special occasion, save her survival through her second day with Dr. Haupt. And there was the addition of Julia as her co-survivalist. That was something worth celebrating.

In fact, if she were going to spend some money and order out for a nice dinner, she didn't see why she shouldn't invite Julia. And maybe that new boyfriend of hers. Helen frowned at that. She wasn't too excited about the boyfriend joining them. But it probably couldn't be avoided.

There was only one way to find out. Helen reluctantly climbed out of her bath, too soon really, but she was excited at the prospect of eating dinner with Julia. The presence of someone else in her apartment would be a welcome change; the exact thing she had shunned the night before. Why she should want company she could not really say. But she supposed that was simply an advantage of her freedom. She could change her mind for no apparent reason.

Wrapped in a robe, Helen padded quietly into her living room. Her bare feet sank noiselessly into the thick mauve carpeting that ran throughout the apartment. Like the full bath, this had been something else Helen had held out for in choosing her living quarters; carpeting was one of her guilty pleasures in life. She had once remarked to a friend that if she were ever to become filthy rich, she would make sure every room she ever walked into had thick soft carpet. Walking bare foot through such luxuriousness was as pleasurable as a deep body massage.

"Julia?" Helen spoke into her phone expectantly. "Tell me you haven't eaten yet."

"No, I haven't." Julia's normally upbeat voice sounded dull and disinterested.

"I was about to order something from *The Royal Aquila*. Please tell me you'll come and eat with me. If your friend is with you, he's welcome to come as well." Helen felt foolish; she'd almost said *boyfriend*. That would have made it sound as if they were all still in school.

"Thanks, Helen, but I don't think I should."

"What's wrong?" Julia never sounded like this unless something had happened. Helen tried to think of the name of Julia's friend. "Has something happened between you and Billy?"

"I don't really know. He's been gone all day. I think I had better wait here, in case he comes back in the next couple of hours."

"Have you talked with him today?"

No, Julia said in a detached voice, she hadn't heard from him or seen him since the day before. Helen asked a few more questions. She had the distinct feeling that Julia wasn't telling her the truth. Just how long had it been since she'd seen him?

"Two days." Julia had difficulty speaking. From Helen's end of the line, she could hear both fear and embarrassment in her friend's words.

"But you two went out last night to that club."

"I lied about that." Julia paused, waiting for recriminations from Helen. When Helen said nothing, Julia tried to explain. "I kept expecting him to show up. I had this crazy feeling that if you would have agreed to meet us both at the club, somehow he'd have been forced to reappear. I only wanted him to come back. I want to know he's okay."

"Did something happen to upset him?" Helen usually avoided being drawn in to this kind of thing but her life lacked anything remotely interesting.

"Maybe."

Helen's NewsVision screen lit up. An emergency report was being broadcast. Helen rarely watched the NewsVision reports but she had set her system to display emergencies.

A reporter, dressed in the sky-blue coveralls worn by all reporters, stood in front of a government building. The word *murders* scrolled up from the bottom in bold red letters on the right side of the screen.

Julia was still talking. "So if he does call, I'll be here. Of course, I'm gonna chew his butt out for disappearing like that. But thanks for inviting me. Us, I mean. I hope you understand, Helen."

"That's okay. I hope he shows up. Call me if you need anything."

Julia promised she would, though there was little sincerity in her voice. Helen disconnected the call and set down the phone. She was still staring at the NewsVision screen. From a bank of controls set into a small end table, she turned the volume up on the sky-blue reporter.

"The police aren't telling us much right now. But we'll keep looking into this. As of right now, we have no identities on the two bodies found yesterday. And while we have no evidence to connect those two bodies with the body found this afternoon, we also have no reason to suspect they are not connected. From what little we have been able to learn, all three victims were brutally beaten. Where they were found is only another bit of information the police are reluctant to release."

Helen had missed the first part of the report, but she was following the gist of it. Three people had been murdered. Violently so. Where had this happened? In Center City? Out in the residential zones? She even imagined it could have happened in one of the four quarantine quadrants. What a mess that would be, she thought.

But in their typical sloppy fashion, the NewsVision service was reporting on something on which it had little information. Helen hated that. All they could hope to do was send fear into the hearts of single women like Helen with stories like this. Someone at the controls had felt they needed to add some kind of visual clip to the report and had decided to run footage of street scenes: street scenes of commuters crowding street walks and SubTransit entrances. Helen even caught a few scenes of residential neighborhoods and, despite the incongruity of the clip, a visual shot of a deserted hallway much like the one outside her door.

Helen shut down the screen with an aggravated punch at the table console. In nearly the same motion, she snatched up her phone and began to dial *The Royal Aquila*. She wanted to eat, to take her mind off Julia and her stories as well as that stupid sky-blue reporter.

It wasn't until she'd ordered the food and given the restaurant her address that she began to worry. Once she hung up, she would have to disengage the security lock on the elevator to allow the delivery person access. Her fingers hesitated over the security panel.

It was that reporter's fault. How was Helen to know if the murderer was operating in her neighborhood or not? What was the visual shot of that hallway all about? Were the victims found in an apartment building like her own? She wanted to strangle that half-wit reporter.

Helen debated if she should disengage the security lock. It was ludicrous, or course. She did that three or four times a month. And that was only the times she ordered food. There were plenty of other times she did the same thing for service personnel. Helen was acutely aware of the magnitude of her overreaction to the incomplete report.

So much for relaxing. Helen was sure she could actually feel her heart rate pumping at an increased speed. Why did she feel so spooked? Why would that incompetent reporter have set her on edge? Helen knew it was more than the story of the three murders. It was more than her lack of knowledge about it.

Julia had unnerved her as well. Their phone conversation had felt odd; as if everything Julia had said carried with it the stain of something gone wrong. Helen tried to shake her fears. The combination of being tired, stressed out, and hungry was wearing down her ability to combat her baseless fears.

Helen jerked in fright at the buzzing that erupted from her front door speaker. *The Royal Aquila's* deliveryman had arrived at the elevator. She had lost track of time. She must have been more tired that she realized.

She could see the deliveryman on the security panel's small screen beside her door. He looked harmless enough. She even thought she recognized him from a delivery made the week before. There was nothing sinister about his face. Bordered as it was with yellow hair, he looked downright angelic.

With a shake of her head, she entered the security code and watched the young deliveryman step into the elevator once the doors slid open. Her fears forgotten, all she could think of was how hungry she'd become.

49

Despite the fact that the third bludgeoned body was fractionally less distorted than the first two, Fenelli still had trouble getting his supper to stay where he'd put it.

As expected, IHS sent over a team who hardly glanced at the corpse before coating him. MacNally simply waved them on their way, though not before he made sure a full set of visuals were taken. He also had the police coroner take physical samples.

Neither of the detectives were shocked to discover that the dead man was Ivan Rodyakov; Mikhail Rodyakov's father. It made sense to them. It made more sense to find the dishwasher dead; he'd been with the blond man in *The Blue Forty's* kitchen. What the connection was between Blondie and the child was yet to be seen.

Some good had come out of the senior Rodyakov's death, Fenelli realized. It had confirmed some of what Pete Landon had put together. There was a connection with Blondie; what that connection might be was anyone's guess.

And that left them back where they'd been that afternoon; watching Carlos Montillo.

"The trail team says he's moving down Third Street." Fenelli said to MacNally as his partner approached his desk with two cups of coffee. Fenelli took one from him. "It doesn't sound like he's going anywhere, not in a hurry anyway."

"He will." MacNally didn't look as confident as he sounded.

"I still don't think this makes sense."

"He's only got two choices. He knows we've got enough to arrest him on the PDT's. And he sure doesn't want to get tangled up in multiple homicides. So he either has to try to get out if he has the money to do it, or he hits up Blondie for cash to get out. Blondie's the one that got him in this mess. I'm betting he tries to get more money out of him."

"That's stupid." Fenelli shook his head. "He's gotta have money stashed for a run. Wouldn't you? So why risk a meeting with a homicidal maniac – to extort money from him? I didn't get the feeling this Romeo was that stupid."

"Maybe." MacNally drank his coffee and wiped his mouth with his fingers. "What do you want? You want me to say we're wasting time?"

"I merely think he's gonna jump into Delta when it closes down tomorrow. And if he does, and we miss him, we're gonna look pretty stupid. We could have him arrested in there, but we'd have to wait forty days before we could really talk to him."

"I'll tell you what, if that little Spaniard dives into Delta, I'll personally guarantee that I'll either pull him out before the doors lock down, or I'll stay there with him – for all forty days." MacNally wasn't joking.

"Did you read this?" Fenelli handed MacNally the hard copy of a report. "Wojawski pointed it out to me. That's from the Carbon Dating. Check out the timing on the injuries."

"I don't get it. All these numbers are nearly the same. What's it telling me?" MacNally had never made much effort to learn how to read the technical data from the visuals. He was happy to let others do it.

"Well, if I understand it right, the sequential pattern of injury would indicate that most of the bruising – the beating – came nearly all at once. As if both Ford and Mikhail were hit by thirty or forty hammers, but all at the same time."

"Great," MacNally glared at the report, "he told us his calibrations were up-to-date. Probably bad readings."

Fenelli wanted to agree with him. But who could really say? At least it was logical to suggest the calibration was off.

"Look," MacNally studied the report, "I'm no good at this stuff, but tell me if I'm wrong. These numbers look like the ones we got off that jumper several months ago. See? Remember, the body hit the pavement in one moment, and all the damage was at the same time. Of course, we identified it as a murder when we realized the first damage was sustained at the base of the neck forty-five seconds before all the others."

"Yeah, someone had hit the guy and thrown him off the roof. But this is different. They're nearly from the same moment in time, but not quite. And on both bodies, the damage is on all sides of them, not restricted on one side like the jumper."

"So I'm right." MacNally tossed the paper report onto the desk. "These numbers are bad."

"I guess," Fenelli hedged his answer. "Maybe when we get the numbers back from the third body…"

"Yeah, maybe." MacNally's expression told Fenelli he had zero faith in *maybe*. "Has anyone at that club been able to remember our Blondie coming into the kitchen?"

"Not so far as I've heard. They're still interviewing people, but all the most likely witnesses can't seem to remember much. From what Horsham told me, most of them don't have the proper training and certification to work in food service and are scared to death they're gonna end up with jail time or a helluva fine. They end up too scared to talk."

"So it all depends on Romeo, huh?" MacNally set his desk display to a visual feed of Carlos Montillo. Romeo was standing on a street corner checking his watch. Both detectives sat quietly for a few minutes and watched their quarry make his way up Third Street.

"Well, if he's gonna do something, I hope it's soon." Fenelli pushed one of the paper reports out of the way of the deskscreen and leaned over the image of Romeo. "This guy better do something fast."

50

"Connect me to Detective Khalid."

Gregor Lepov sat on the edge of his bed and watched one of his roommates in the dormitory. While Lepov sat with the phone to his ear, the roommate peeled off his clothes without any thought to Lepov being in the room. He was an older man and Lepov guessed he was the kind of man who didn't give a wit who watched him dress or undress. But Lepov cared who was dressing and undressing. He turned away from the old-timer and waited for the voice of David Khalid.

"What can I do for you, Mr. Lepov?" Khalid's tone was cordial, though far from friendly.

"I thought I would take the Chief Administrator up on his offer."

"You decided you want the room?"

Lepov couldn't help but glance back at the old man. Lepov was beginning to wonder if the old guy would ever put any of his clothes back on.

"I admit the offer is temping, but I was thinking of Reno's other offer."

"And that was what?" Lepov didn't mind Khalid's feigned ignorance.

"I need your assistance." Lepov took pleasure in saying that. Rather than feeling unwilling to admit he needed the help, Lepov enjoyed asking. He was well aware that Khalid would begrudge him every bit of assistance that Reno forced out of him.

It wasn't that Lepov disliked Khalid. The detective had merely done the job that had been given to him. He had actually been a pretty decent cop through the whole affair. And Lepov was aware that Khalid had been used by someone else. But Lepov had a solid lock on Khalid's kind of cop. Yes, he was fair, hard working, and an all around *good* guy. But like most cops who'd been on the job as long as Khalid, he was also arrogant, quick-to-judge, and a xenophobe when it came to private detectives.

It would do Khalid some good to have to cooperate with Lepov.

"What would that be, Lepov?" Khalid made an attempt to be civil.

"Two things. First, I'd like to be able to talk with Layne's managers; with the understanding that I have the necessary authorization to look at his work records."

"Tonight? This can't wait until tomorrow?"

"I'm behind schedule on account of your hospitality today. If you don't mind, I'd like to catch up."

"Fine. I'll arrange it if I can." Khalid's patronizing tone couldn't be masked. "And the second thing?"

"I want to know about a guy who goes by the name of Romeo."

There was silence from Khalid's end of the transmission.

"Khalid? Do you hear me?"

"Yeah, why are you asking about Romeo?" Khalid could not disguise the genuine curiosity in his voice. Lepov had struck a nerve.

"Tell me what you know about him and I'll explain it if it turns out to be relevant." Lepov wasn't about to give up one of the few advantages he had over Khalid.

"I don't really know much. In fact, there's someone else here who could explain it better. He was talking about Romeo this afternoon."

"Just tell me what you know. I'll connect the dots."

"Okay, I can do that." Khalid's interest in Lepov's angle overrode his reticence to lend a hand. "Let me look at something."

Lepov had to wait far longer than he expected.

"You still there?" Khalid came back onto the line. "Okay, now I know why you're asking about Romeo. It looks like those PDT's we found in your locker were from Romeo's magical computer laboratory. A guy by the name of Carlos Montillo."

Lepov never let on he knew who Montillo was. There was no reason to. Let Khalid hand out information like he owned the proprietary rights.

"What put you on to Montillo?" Khalid's curiosity was growing.

"So Montillo actually made these tags?" Lepov asked him. What he didn't ask aloud were the many other questions going through his head. Did this clear Lilly? Was Montillo the one who planted the tags in his locker? Or were he and Lilly working together?

"I'm not sure if he did the technical work. I know we've always sort of had him down as a broker for false IDs. We never made a move on him though. It was to our benefit to know who he was and keep an eye on him." Khalid still wanted an answer from Lepov. "What led you to Montillo? And how does that help you find Layne?"

More than likely, Lepov realized, it wouldn't help him find Layne at all. For all he knew Montillo had tried to get him arrested because he might have seen Lepov as competition for Lilly's affection. Although that possibility was less dramatic than a conspiracy to keep him from finding Layne, Lepov had learned that life normally turned out far less dramatic than people imagined it to be.

"I'll let you know." Lepov's answer apparently left Khalid unsatisfied. The detective uttered a particularly foul curse before breaking off the transmission.

It was difficult for Lepov to keep his priorities straight. He wanted to find Montillo — maybe wring his little Spanish neck until he confessed to everything that was going on — but he really needed to talk to Layne's co-workers. For all he knew Layne could have been a victim of that murderer who was beginning to get airtime on the NewsVision updates.

Nothing was going the way it should have. Lepov had only taken the job because it seemed like a simple enough scenario: Mama's boy gets too much of the wild life far from home and won't answer when mama calls. That had been a pretty good working hypothesis. It wasn't like Lepov hadn't seen it before. But so far, Ethan Layne was nowhere; like a magician's canary that's disappeared into thin air.

Forget Montillo for now. Lepov almost had to say those words aloud before he would obey them. Find Eudia Layne's son. That's what he was being paid for. He was going to be stuck in this place for a long time, no doubt, and he would have plenty of time to deal with Montillo later.

Find Ethan Layne.

Lepov remained committed to that task for nearly ten minutes. But it had taken all of one or two seconds for him to abandon his commitment.

He had hired a Center City TransitCar and given the driver directions to Layne's place of work. When he later thought about it, Lepov blamed fate for what happened next. How else could he explain seeing Montillo on the street?

Ethan Layne would have to wait.

Lepov ordered the driver to continue past the dark figure of Montillo until they were two blocks ahead of him. Slipping quickly from the TransitCar, Lepov found a hiding place in the crowded street. He allowed Montillo to pass. For now, he would only watch him.

51

Georges did not always accompany Maria to the clinic in the evenings. Maria was usually eager to arrive before Kjarsta went to sleep, and Georges saw no reason to arrive until the night shift arrived at ten p.m. But once he had been told about the mysterious young man on the SubTransit, he insisted on accompanying her.

Maria insisted he had no reason to do so. She hadn't the slightest prospect of winning that argument. Georges walked with her.

As they left their tower for the SubTransit station, the sound of clattering footsteps pounded towards them — two sets of footsteps.

"Hello, Maria," Beth Edgars crooned. Her voice changed to a more respectful tone as she addressed Georges. "Hello, Mr. Duvalls."

"Children," Georges nodded at the two little imps that appeared at his beltline. Georges was always stiff and unsure of himself around the kids. Maria enjoyed his discomfort.

"Button your coats," Maria chided them. "It's getting colder now. And what are you doing out so late?"

"We were in the park. It feels like it's going to snow!" Beth hopped up and down at her own exciting prediction.

"It don't snow here, Beth." Jack made sure the adults knew how smart he was.

"But I only said it *felt* like it was going to snow," Beth said in defense.

"And that's exactly why you should button those coats." Maria pulled at the front of Beth's coat, straitening it out before she began to button the heavy garment. She gave Jack a scolding look that he had no trouble interpreting. Rather unenthusiastically, he began to close up his as well.

"It's too dark for you to be in the park, don't you think?" This was from Georges, who was still in a cautious mode.

"Oh, no! Not at all!" Beth fidgeted while Maria finished with her coat. "We like to play like pirates in the trees. No one can find us!"

"And there's lights on the walkways. And lots of lights at the fountain." Jack continued to impress the adults with his solemn explanations.

"Does Dr. Edgars know you've been in the park this late?" Georges had apparently decided he did not like the children running around at night. "I think you had better go home. Perhaps we should escort you."

"Aw, we'll be okay." Jack stepped away from Georges as if he were afraid the doctor might grab him. Beth, bundled up by Maria, gave her a hug, thanking her for her help.

"You go on with Jack now, and listen to Georges. He's right, you shouldn't be out so late. Go straight home."

"We will," Beth promised. With a gleam in her eye, she struck a sprinter's pose—as well as she could with the heavy coat firmly wrapped around her. "And we'll go *fast* too!"

Both kids shot off down the walkway towards the other towers. Maria giggled at the sight. Georges watched them for only a moment before turning back towards their original destination.

"It is irresponsible of Dr. Edgars to allow them to run around unattended so much. Perhaps I will speak with him."

"They are so well-behaved and don't get into any trouble. I don't think it hurts anything." Maria liked to see them running free and hated to think of their father reining in their exuberance.

"I wasn't suggesting that they might misbehave. I was concerned for their safety. They are not living on Dnepr anymore. I have heard of the pastoral atmosphere of that world. But there are dangers here that must be heeded. Yes, I will speak with him."

Maria felt a tug at her good humor. There was that sense of threat again; a shadow looming just beyond the mind's eye. It saddened Maria to feel its presence intrude into what had been an enjoyable afternoon and evening. Why did it have to become thus? Why was that uneasy feeling allowed to stain this moment?

Maria was not being idealistic. She understood that certain cautions needed to be taken; a level of vigilance that had to be retained. And she was not foolish enough to blame Georges for it, no more than she expected Beth to blame her for the threat of pneumonia. But she shared the young girl's disappointment at the necessity of having to guard against such dangers. To all little children like Beth, pneumonia, like other difficult to spell diseases, was a vague, scary thing that mysteriously intruded into the happy times of our life. These scary things were more like legends out of folk tales rather than serious threats to their bodies. Maria understood. For her, the threats that lurked in the parks and alleys and SubTransit stations of life were just as scary and mysterious. For Maria, such dangers were not as vague as childhood bogeymen, but their existence was every bit as difficult to fathom.

52

Lilly Stewart sat in the darkness of her hotel room. When the light of day faded to night, she had not bothered to turn on a light. She didn't need it. There was nothing she wanted to see.

She'd been sitting for hours, shaken by her encounter with Gregor Lepov. His accusations had caught her off guard. That was undeniable. But even Gregor had no idea how hard he had hit her.

Gregor's assumptions had been wrong. Lilly knew that. She could prove that to him. She even had an idea who was responsible. But that was not the point.

Even as she acknowledged that Gregor's accusations had cut her deeply, it hadn't been the kind of cut from which she couldn't recover. Yes, she was angry that he could believe her guilty of setting him up. Despite the short time they'd known each other it should have been obvious she hadn't been the one who'd done it. Wasn't he a private detective? Couldn't he have trusted her?

But that wasn't the point either.

Something else had come out of his accusations that disturbed her more than any of those other considerations. Gregor could never have known that she'd had accusations like that thrown in her face before; accusations of betrayal from someone she had loved deeply. Accusations that had been unquestionably true.

No, she hadn't set up Gregor Lepov. But yes, she had set up her husband Shay Stewart. The magnitude of that betrayal had never ceased to grow within her. She had been tempted to deny Lepov's accusation with great indignation. But even as she had begun to plan her defense in her mind, her soul cried foul. How could she insist she would never betray a new acquaintance like Gregor when she had justified betraying her own husband?

And she had justified that betrayal. Lilly had never tried to deny it. She had pulled the strings and maneuvered her heart and mind until she could look herself in the mirror and feel proud about her decision. She had declared it to be taking action for what was right; she had known it merely to be taking action to save her own skin.

When the Sinopese Investigators caught up with her, she had been more than willing to give them everything they needed to stick Shay in jail. If she hadn't, they would have closed her down; she, too, might have done time in the orbiting prison holds. However, she had never noticed how easily she'd given him up until that first time Shay saw her after he learned of her betrayal.

His eyes—those same eyes she'd loved and adored—held no anger, no mad call for revenge. Those eyes had been so full of pain they had harbored no room for any darker emotions.

Lilly no longer cared that her husband had been working against her, spreading lies about the authenticity of her pieces, selling forgeries, undercutting bids to steal away established and once loyal collectors. Her complicated justifications broke to pieces in the weeks after Shay's imprisonment. Not because he had been blameless. No, she may have had no choice but to make the deal she had made, but it went beyond whether or not she had been right.

Lilly knew the true shame of that time. Lilly knew that she had made her decision without building complicated justifications. Those had come later, to fortify the decision she had already made. But Lilly had decided to betray her husband without the slightest hesitation. Her own survival had been her pragmatic and expedient choice.

And now she sat in the darkness, afraid of the light. Afraid to see her own reflection and see what Gregor had seen in her. She couldn't help but ask the question: had he believed her capable of betrayal because he had applied deductive reasoning to what had happened, or had he seen base and effortless betrayal harbored within her soul?

Lilly had no illusions about Gregor. She did not love him—had not known him long enough to love him. Yet she ached to think he might see such ugly betrayal in her. Hadn't she betrayed enough? Hadn't she destroyed her marriage and the man she loved and paid for it through her years of shame and guilt? Must she be labeled for her errors and lose a chance to find someone else?

Lilly switched on a lamp. A small pool of pale light danced around her feet. She couldn't indulge her self-pity any longer. She had been assailed with such pitiable thoughts because she had allowed her defenses down. She'd been hurt by Gregor's words and her hastily erected walls had not held. That would not happen again.

Her pragmatic drive to survive would take control. It had to. Without it, she would remain right where she was; sitting in the dark unable to turn to the right or the left. But nature had provided her with an alternative. She would tap that ravenous desire to stay alive and throw off her paralyzing shame.

To begin, she would find Gregor Lepov and make him see the truth.

53

They had watched Montillo from the surveillance visuals for several hours. It had been a depressing commentary on the state of their investigation. The trail team, consisting of six men and an array of visual tracking equipment, spent the whole of that evening watching and waiting with nothing to report. The two lead investigators on the case, MacNally and Fenelli, were doing the same thing from the office. No one else was involved in anything that could be considered progress.

Fenelli had never believed MacNally's plan would succeed. Putting himself in Montillo's shoes, he knew Montillo was most likely to make a run for it. There was no way he was going to contact the blond-haired suspect. MacNally was being bullheaded as usual. Once he came up with something like this, he would never admit to being wrong. Fenelli wouldn't be surprised if MacNally sat and watched Montillo for a week.

"Let's go down there." MacNally dropped his feet to the floor and jumped up, as if he'd received a sudden shot of adrenaline.

"Go where?"

"Down there." MacNally pointed at the visual feed of Montillo walking across a street.

"What is that going to accomplish?"

"I imagine by the time we get down there, he'll be meeting with our guy." MacNally was already walking out the door of Homicide without looking to see if Fenelli was behind him.

"Hold on, MacNally!" Fenelli grabbed his coat and had to dash out the door to catch his partner in the hall. "What makes you say that? Nothing's changed. We've been watching him for hours."

"The watch." MacNally sighed when he realized Fenelli did not understand. "*His* watch. Romeo's been checking it all night, at intervals of twenty to thirty minutes. Now, he's looking at it every five minutes. Wherever he's going, he's close and he's right on time."

They stepped into the elevator as Fenelli asked "How can you tell?"

"You must be tired, Fenelli. Think it through. He's taking his time. At one point he stopped altogether. Now, he's moving at a steady pace. If he were late, he'd be moving fast. If he were still a good ways off he'd be late. If he were already there, he'd have stopped. You want me to draw you a diagram?"

"You're making a lot of assumptions."

"We get paid to make assumptions."

They rode in silence towards the section of Center City where Montillo was being trailed. The cold night was heavy with threatening clouds. The cloudbank above them brooded close to the city; close enough to absorb all light like a black-iron lid.

"You don't have to."

"To what?" Fenelli asked.

"You don't have to come. You have a wife waiting for you. Drop me off down there and I'll hook up with the trail team."

"I suppose I could do that." Fenelli liked the idea. In fact, he thought it was a great idea. "Are you looking for something to complain about tomorrow? I bet I'll never hear the end of it."

"No," MacNally's answered, "I really think you should go home. Don't you still have kids at home? Of course you do, what am I saying? Now I'm the one acting tired."

"What's the matter with you?" Fenelli wasn't use to MacNally speaking so seriously. "Who's the tired one now? None of my kids are young enough to be at home anymore."

"You know," MacNally ignored Fenelli, "I can remember how you used to work all those stakeouts with me—I mean like years and years ago, when you're kids were little. You always wanted to go home. But you never did. You remember what you told me about saying no to workin' late?"

Fenelli looked over at MacNally and shook his head.

"You told me 'Mac, if I'd been able to say no to my wife those four times when we were first married, I'd be able to say no to making overtime now'. Remember that?"

"Yeah, I remember that," Fenelli rolled his eyes. "As I recall, I had to explain to you what I meant."

"The hell you did," MacNally grunted at the insult. "I may not be married, but I know how kids are made. But that ain't my point."

"Then what is your point?"

"All that time you spent late at night with me, you should've been home. Go home to your wife. Right up here, you can drop me off."

Fenelli stopped the car and turned his head to look at MacNally. Most of the time, his partner was an old grouch that went out of his way to get under people's skin. Only Fenelli was allowed to see the good MacNally. And that was only on rare occasions. This was one of them.

"Fine, I'll go home. You're starting to look uglier than usual, so I look forward to getting out of here." Fenelli was glad it was dark in the car. He could feel his face flushing red as he spoke. It was typical of them to insult one another when they were caught in an honest, genuine moment. Fenelli wished he hadn't said it, but the habit was too ingrained in the both of them.

"Oh, go home to Lynne and get back to whatever it was I interrupted yesterday. That should take all of two minutes." MacNally slammed the door.

Fenelli drove home without paying attention to the city. Most of the time he was thinking about what MacNally had said. He really had put in too many hours when the kids were young. And most of that had been necessity. He and Lynne needed the money. And even when they hadn't needed the money, Fenelli had been driven by the knowledge that they *would* need it. The most ordinary of days could blindside you. He'd learned that the hard way.

Broken legs, leaking pipes, lost shot records; there was always something happening with the family that required money. And so, Fenelli had pushed himself on the job. He had taken on extra work; he had aimed for more than working a patrolman's beat. He'd known men whose ambition had been driven by the desire for prestige and power but Fenelli had never wanted any of that. All he'd wanted to do was get higher up the ladder where the money was better and he had a better chance of keeping his job.

It was only later that the job had begun to mean something to him. It was only after he had begun to see the evil that dwelt in the city that Fenelli had found his job meant more than merely paying the rent. It was then he had realized he was doing more than providing food and clothes for his children; he was providing a safe environment for them to grow and learn and live. That had become the higher goal.

But when something like this killer surfaced on the streets, Fenelli began to doubt that he had ever done any good for his family. If this kind of threat awaited them, what had all the years of excessive hard work brought them? Security? Tranquility? Not when the NewsVision services carried stories about murder and rape, beatings and break-ins.

Riding the elevator to his floor, Fenelli knew he was being fatalistic. Things had gotten better. The streets of the Lazaretto were safer than they had been in a long time. He was only reacting to the recent shocking violence that the city had begun to believe was a thing of the past.

The important thing to remember was that his family could take comfort in the fact that he was there for them, and he was always going to be there working to make the Lazaretto increasingly secure.

It was enough for him; enough to push back the hopelessness and allow him the chance to smile as Lynne met him at the door.

"I didn't expect to see you this early," she said, wrapping her arms around him.

"Where else would I be?"

"I already ate," Lynne said apologetically while standing on her toes to kiss his cheek. "I figured with what the news was saying you'd be out most of the night."

"I nearly was." Fenelli changed the subject, asking about her day. She allowed him to; she knew he never liked to talk about work. "So what did you eat?"

"Who cares what I had for dinner," Lynne ran her hand up inside Fenelli's jacket. "Let's see what I can have for dessert."

"I care." Fenelli made an attempt to head toward the kitchen. "I'm hungry."

"Oh, really?" Lynne reached out and grabbed his arm, turning him around. "Don't you think that can wait?" She reached up and pushed his jacket off his shoulders. Once it was off she loosened his necktie.

"Well, I suppose it can."

"Are you feeling okay?" She stopped pulling at his tie and looked him in the eye. He leaned down and kissed her. "That's a little better."

Fenelli thought about MacNally out on the street with the trail team. The old man had been right. This was what Fenelli needed; for a short time, he hoped to God he'd be able to forget about those battered and bloody bodies.

54

He had never been good at tailing suspects — at least Lepov never felt he was. He always thought he was too easy to spot; as if everyone in the crowd were painted green and he was painted orange. Lepov's image of himself was that of a large and ungainly man. A clumsy man. He always felt most people were watching him and laughing at him. With that image in his head, it made following anyone an arduous task.

Montillo was now ahead of him by a good thirty seconds or more. The people on the walkways were moving slowly so the time difference did not translate into any great distance. Unfortunately, that pace allowed Montillo to turn now and again to watch for someone tailing him. For a while, Lepov had befriended an older man and walked beside him, talking to him as if they were old friends out for a stroll. But too soon, Montillo had crossed the street and Lepov had been forced to leave the old man and make his way across the street without drawing attention.

Never once, as he walked in Montillo's wake, did Lepov regret or reconsider his decision to put off his search for Ethan Layne. Layne could wait. He watched Montillo stop at a vendor selling hot drinks, which seemed like a good idea. It was getting colder as the night came on. At least Lepov's knee was feeling better, though it made little sense that it would be; he was walking way too much on the wretched thing. But as long as his luck held, he'd be able to keep up with Montillo.

Nearing a side street, Montillo stopped and turned back to watch for signs of a tail. Lepov took a bold approach. Without hesitating, he walked right past Montillo. Although they had met the day before, there were enough shadows from both his hat and the multitude of shop awnings to prevent recognition.

Right as Lepov passed him, Montillo turned and headed down the side street. Lepov had been waiting for something like this. He took a few more steps and jogged up a stoop to an unmarked door. If Montillo came back out of the side street, Lepov was prepared to knock on the door and ask anyone who came to the door anything that came to mind. If Montillo did not reappear, it would mean he had guessed wrong and he might lose his quarry.

Lepov could hear the sound of children crying behind the door. An angry woman's voice shot sharp rebukes at someone who replied with muffled apologies. Other sounds of laughter, the whine of TransitCars, dissonant music, all added to make it impossible for Lepov to hear Montillo's footfalls down the side street. He had to decide quickly if he was going to follow or not.

If he guessed right and waited, Montillo would reappear and Lepov's cover would be safe. If he decided to head down the side street and Montillo came back, Lepov would most likely be recognized. Lepov waited a few minutes more. Already, it was getting to be too long if he intended to try to follow the Spaniard. And this was why Lepov was never any good at trailing someone; he could never make a quick decision in such situations.

Stay or go?

Damn it, but he had taken too long. He might as well stay now. It was too late to try to follow. If Montillo had kept walking, Lepov would never catch up with him.

He was beginning to doubt the logic of everything he had been weighing. What if Montillo had a room down that street? What if he had been meeting Lilly down there? There were a thousand reasons Montillo wasn't going to come back out of that street. Lepov shook his head at his own ignorant assumptions.

Lepov decided to head back to the drink vendor and get himself a cup of coffee. If he was gonna stand there and freeze to death, he'd like a last cup of hot coffee.

Montillo stepped back out of the side street right in front of Lepov but turned and walked ahead of him. Lepov almost cursed loud enough for Montillo to hear him. His impatience had nearly ruined everything. Slowing his pace, Lepov allowed distance to grow between them. As he came abreast of the drink vendor, he decided he had time to get that cup of coffee. The crowds were thinning and he would be able to see Montillo from a distance.

And that's when he knew his luck was holding. Forget the fact his knee was still okay. When Lepov stopped to buy the cup of coffee, Montillo stopped and reversed his course again. Lepov was able to step to the side of the coffee vendor and hide himself as Montillo came straight at him.

This explained the wariness on Montillo's part. Whatever had made him this cautious was about to be revealed. Lepov had won the lottery. Montillo had made three distinct moves to confirm he wasn't being followed—and Lepov had been able to hold his cover. Who cares about being good when you've got this kind of luck?

Lepov took his time and sipped at his coffee, his back to Montillo. He waited a full ten-count before turning around. Montillo was heading back down that same side street. This time Lepov followed him.

Lepov eased around the corner and into a shadow on the left side of the street. The alley was empty except for Montillo who stood twenty meters from where Lepov was watching him. For several minutes, both men stood perfectly still; Lepov too afraid to reveal his position, and Montillo watching and intently listening for something or someone.

Lepov was nervous; worried that Montillo would turn around and spot him. There was nothing to hide behind. And even though Lepov was standing in the shadows, there was sufficient light from the intersection behind him to create a silhouette.

A door to Montillo's left opened a crack. Lepov almost missed the movement, so dark were the shadows. Someone was behind the door. Montillo made slow and deliberate motions with his hands. The person behind the door was obviously arguing with him. Montillo's pantomime grew agitated. Lepov heard voices but could not make out the words.

He would have to get closer. If they conducted their conversation like that, he'd never know who was behind that door. Was it Lilly? Lepov had to know. No matter the consequences, he had to know if she had set him up.

Getting closer required little imagination. Lepov had to walk straight towards them without attracting attention. He had to get close enough to be able to know who was behind that door.

Montillo was fully engaged in an argument now. Both parties were raising their voices from a whisper to a low growl. It was still impossible to tell if the voice behind the door belonged to Lilly. But at least the noise from the argument covered what little noise Lepov made.

Before Lepov could get as close as he wanted, the door swung open as Montillo uttered a particularly loud invective. A figure stepped out from behind the door and Lepov was relieved to see it wasn't Lilly.

Then, as the figure stepped into a small pool of light, Lepov cursed aloud and for the first time that night, his luck ran out. Lepov was too shocked to bridle his tongue.

"Ethan Layne!"

In direct consequence to Lepov's luck running out, all hell broke loose.

Montillo spun around, recognized Lepov and shouted "he *is* a cop!"

Layne dove back in through the door as a half dozen men streamed into the alley waving badges, RiotTamer shotguns and hand lights. Two of them shoved Lepov up against a wall and he felt his knee buckle. Montillo ran into the darkness of the street, but two cops ambushed him at its opposite end. Two more men dashed through the door after Layne.

Lepov had no idea what was going on. When he tried to ask, one of the men shoved the barrel of his RiotTamer into Lepov's ribs and it felt like Greta Becker had reappeared and kicked out one of his lungs. Unable to breathe, Lepov watched a large man in a grey raincoat walk towards him with a murderous look in his eye.

The man was big and heavy, though he carried most of his weight above his belt. Lepov had never met the man before in his life but he knew he was exceptionally pissed off.

"Who the hell are you?" the man shouted before he reached Lepov. "And what the hell are you doing breaking up that meeting?"

Lepov was wondering the same thing: why had he shouted Layne's name and run him off? He had no answer for the furious cop or himself.

"My name's Gregor Lepov, I'm a Private Investigator." Lepov couldn't understand why this cop was so apoplectic. "If you're one of Khalid's boys looking for Layne, I'm sure we can still catch him. But if we can't, at least we know he's alive. He's just been missing, that's all. Don't act like I screwed up catching some master criminal."

The big cop stared at him, obviously trying to control his rage. Lepov had the feeling he'd said something terribly wrong.

"I am not one of David Khalid's boy scouts. I don't give a damn about the fraud squad. I'm Lieutenant Ed MacNally from Center City Homicide, and that kid you ran off is our prime suspect."

Lepov could already guess what the big Lieutenant was going to say next. And why not? He'd already been arrested once today. He couldn't think of any reason he shouldn't be stuck in jail again.

But the big Lieutenant didn't say anything. He stood trembling with anger. But before he could start yelling, it looked as if the man had suddenly understood something important.

"Did you call that kid Layne? You know who he is?"

"I know a lot about him. I've been looking for him. But I don't know anything about him being a suspect." Had he been right back at the precinct? Did this explain Reno's interest in finding Layne? "What is Ethan Layne suspected of doing?"

"Ethan Layne, or whoever he is, is suspected of three murders."

Lepov thought immediately of Eudia Layne. What in God's name was he going to tell her? But he knew he wasn't going to tell her anything. Not yet. As he watched MacNally order restraints put on both Montillo and himself, Lepov knew he would have to wait before calling his client. Before he did that, he was going to have to have a long talk with Lieutenant Ed MacNally of Center City Homicide.

As the temperature continued to drop and the wind began to rush between the tall buildings of the Lazaretto's Center City, Gregor Lepov never even noticed. His heart had already turned cold as he realized he had wrongfully accused Lilly of betraying him. He had attacked the only friend he had found on this dark and corrupt world. And he'd scared off the man he'd been hired to find. He didn't mind when MacNally shoved him into the back of a PoliceTransit. Lepov knew he deserved more rough treatment than that.

Book Two

Murderer

The dead of night had arrived. Maria could feel it. Alone beside the sleeping form of Kjarsta Zoltis, she often wondered about that unnatural time of night. No matter that there were no windows in Kjarsta's room; Maria had learned she could feel it, like the arrival of an evil presence.

Without a clock, she knew when the late hours of the night watched her with menace and loathing. She was not offended. She understood she was an intruder—alive and attentive at a time when all other living souls retreated into the cocoon of visions and dreams. She did not arrogantly imagine her vigilance could hold back the passing shade of Death when it finally came to claim what was left of Kjarsta. She only wanted to attend him in comfort and peace. And when Death did make an appearance, she wanted Kjarsta to know he was not alone.

But Death had not arrived. Kjarsta rested peacefully. The lines of his worn and weary face had relaxed and softened as he slept. His round, bald head could have been that of a sleeping baby save for its great size.

Maria was thankful to God for Kjarsta's easy night. He did not have as many of them as he once had. The bad nights were beginning to be the rule, not the exception. She did not like to see him on the far side of a pain-filled night. By the time she left him on such mornings, he always looked so much older—looked as if Death really had come and Kjarsta had only lived after a great struggle with that black-hearted beast.

And at such times, she wondered why he struggled so. What drove him to survive? Maria would have given up long ago, she was sure of that. But Kjarsta would never give up. He would die one day. She was not denying Death his due. But she knew that on that day, Kjarsta would only be defeated by the narrowest of margins. Indeed, he might find a way to drag Death down to the grave with him.

As if in response to her blasphemous speculation, Kjarsta shook with a vicious cough. Had Death rattled Kjarsta's body to remind him that he is only mortal, no matter what foolish thoughts entered Maria's head?

The coughing and rattling had awakened his body, though not Kjarsta himself. His legs began to twist and stretch as if they were searching for something under the sheets. His right hand grasped nothing and squeezed it tightly. His jaw gnashed and twitched while his eyes swung back and forth under their lids in frenetic REM patterns.

Maria stood up, alarmed at his agitation. Was he indeed

struggling with that oily, black vulture Death? Was she witnessing his final battle with that cruel carrion-hunter? His spasms and tremors increased yet he made no noise save one low growl that never seemed to end.

So sudden and violent was this attack that Maria could do little but watch in distress. By the time she thought to call for assistance, Kjarsta ceased to struggle. A fleeting thought that he was dead overcame her.

"There's an angel standing over me." Kjarsta's eyes snapped open and he stared at Maria. "Did you wake me or did I wake you?"

Maria shook her head. "Neither. You were — restless."

Kjarsta closed his eyes and drew in a long, scratchy breath. Fluids in his throat popped and gurgled as he exhaled.

"I was dreaming," he said.

Maria nodded. She took a wet washcloth and dabbed at his forehead. He winced at her touch as she continued to stroke his fevered skin.

"You are an angel. It's no silly nickname. A lady like you wouldn't care for me if you weren't one." He swallowed hard and made a choking noise. He tried to sip the water Maria offered him. "But maybe I'm wrong. Maybe an angel wouldn't do this for me. Angels know stuff about us, like God does. Don't you think so, Maria?"

"I imagine they do."

"Well then, you must not be one. You'd never do this for me if you knew stuff about me. All that stuff…back when…"

Kjarsta stared silently at an empty point in space. Maria shook her head, mildly rebuking him for believing his past could nullify her willingness to care for him. She silently wondered what he had done. Could his past wipe away her compassion for him? Perhaps she would never learn of Kjarsta's past. Maybe that was best for both of them.

Keep your secrets, Kjarsta.

"Can you eat?" Maria gently broke his silent meditation on the past.

"No, I can't eat. That's how I got my start, you know? Shipping food. I had a little truck. The little colony I grew up in raised cabbages. And of course the colony's largest families had the shipping rights. What rights are those, huh? Rights paid for with lots of money. So I had this little truck. I would fill it with cabbages — " Kjarsta's weary face managed to look childishly ashamed, " — stolen cabbages, I admit it. But that's not the point. You see, I would drive two colonies over to a friend who ran a little grocery. I could sell him the cabbages for half the price."

Maria watched him tell his story. Each word took great effort as he began to tell her of the truck and the cabbages. But as he warmed to his story so did his body; the words became easier to speak, his breathing became less difficult. It pleased her to see him enjoying himself.

"I made a little money." The light in his eyes told her he had made more than a little money. "But those men with the shipping rights were angry. When they ran me out of the colony, I was lucky they did not run me off Phasis. My little truck could not fly."

Maria could not help but laugh at his little truck. Kjarsta knew he was amusing her and for a moment he looked happy. Moments like that did not last long for Kjarsta. Maria made sure she laughed some more.

"Don't encourage him." Della, the night nurse, appeared in the doorway. She was a large woman, and Maria had the idea she must have been a beautiful woman when she was younger. "He'll never shut up if you let him think you enjoy his foolish stories."

"What do you know, old woman?" Kjarsta's insulting name for Della was unwarranted. She was little older than Maria.

"I know I'm too old to waste time on a wicked man like you." She gave Maria a displeased look. She could not tell if the nurse's scolding was playful or sincere. "Maria, you're too good to that man."

"No, I don't think so," Maria said softly.

"Trust me. Kjarsta Zoltis don't deserve a sweet woman like you."

"You might be right about that, old woman." Kjarsta coughed violently then spoke again. "You might be right."

Maria wiped spittle from his chin as Della slipped out of the room.

56

Gregor Lepov was angry. He wasn't angry because his knee had been hurt during the arrest. He wasn't angry that MacNally, that big Lieutenant from Homicide, had actually booked him on charges of aiding a fugitive from the law. He wasn't even angry that he had acted like a clown in that alley and blown his case as well as the cops' case. What really made him angry was the fact that Eudia Layne's kid was a murderer.

If MacNally was right, then everything Lepov had done for Eudia Layne was a monumental waste of time. He'd flown across the whole of space and subjected himself to quarantine on a hellhole of a moon. He'd been wrongly detained twice now by a police force that seemed intent on sticking him in prison. And all of that had been done in search of a maniac who was beating the living hell out of people.

About the only consolation Lepov could see was that he had never found Layne alone. He could have easily ended up like one of those corpses in the pictures that MacNally had so eagerly shown him. Lepov just wanted to get back to Bukovina.

He would do his best to forget about Lilly. Although he would never know the truth, Lepov felt sure Lilly had not been involved in any of the shenanigans with those PDTs. And if that was the case, he had spit in the eye of the only person who'd shown him any kind of decency. Too ashamed even to apologize, he was ready to get out of the Lazaretto.

But first, he had to get out of jail—again. And that MacNally character looked a lot harder to satisfy than David Khalid. And he could forget about Reno setting him free again. He doubted the Chief Administrator could interfere with charges that involved a triple murder.

Once again, Lepov thought, wincing as he shifted his leg, this bum knee's the least of my problems.

Lepov needed to convince MacNally that he had been searching for Ethan Layne, not aiding him. But MacNally wasn't around to convince. Since they had secured Lepov to a chair in the Homicide office, he'd been left alone.

MacNally was in an office only a few feet from Lepov. Captain Samuel Jenkins' name was etched into a glass wall that obscured Lepov's view of the men inside. He could hear MacNally and his captain engaged in a pretty stiff fight. There was no way to tell who had the upper hand, but if this Jenkins was anything like Lepov's old captain back on Bukovina, MacNally could yell all he wanted; he'd never win an argument with his superior.

Lepov didn't like to think about his former captain. Captain Shojen Weig had not won his arguments because he was a stubborn, belligerent jackass. That would have been the type of boss Lepov would have preferred being in trouble with. Being fired by a real jerk allowed you to nurse your wounds with bitter spite. But Weig hadn't been like that at all. Weig had been a quiet, balanced, and humble civil servant who had won his arguments strictly with the quiet authority of his office.

He had been the kind of man Lepov wanted to work for; Lepov went so far as to acknowledge a love for the old man. And that's what had gotten him into trouble. He still did not regret saving his captain. Lepov had never even hesitated when it happened. His only regret was that Shojen Weig was living the rest of his life back on Bukovina believing that Lepov had destroyed evidence to save himself.

He had wanted to tell Weig the truth. But Weig would have insisted the truth be made public. And the whole point had been to cover up the truth. Lepov had no problem destroying evidence that would have put a good friend in prison. Even at the cost of his own career, Lepov hadn't hesitated to do it. The cover-up hadn't been designed to save a politician's career, nor the career of any high-placed official on the police force. All Lepov had been trying to do was save the life of a friend; the life of Captain Weig.

And that's why Lepov had harbored no ill will towards his captain the day he'd been fired. Weig had never been aware of the evidence that had been fabricated against him by one of the Commissioners. He had never been aware that he had been chosen to be the scapegoat for an Internal Affairs investigation. And he had never been aware that Lepov had discovered and destroyed that fabricated evidence to save his captain.

Lepov had not been surprised when Weig fired him. He had expected that; the pressure from the Commission would have been too intense. But Lepov had not expected Weig to sever their relationship. Lepov had always expected to tell Weig the truth one day. But now, more than ten years had passed, and Weig still refused to speak with him.

The real surprise had been Lepov's discovery of how much Weig's disapproval hurt. It had taken the wind out of Lepov's sails. He'd pursued his Investigator's career with little or no ambition. He'd taken to working simple cases of infidelity and missing persons; anything he could do with the least effort. Lepov had found the world to be corrupt and capricious and had no desire to succeed in it. In fact, he had made an effort to stay at the bottom of his profession. And now, twelve years after the fact, Lepov was sitting in a police station chained to a chair in the middle of the Lazaretto. He had reached his goal.

The captain's door jerked open and MacNally stormed out. If Lepov hadn't been so annoyed at the way everything had gone down that night he might have laughed at MacNally's expression.

"I hope we can start over," Lepov said as a way of forestalling MacNally's imminent outburst. "I'm on your side. We both want Layne."

"And you screwed that up." MacNally kicked at a chair beside Lepov and dropped into it. He pulled out a pack of cigarettes from a desk drawer and lit one.

"I don't deny that. Don't think you're the only one mad at me right now. Is this necessary?" Lepov extended his hand as far as the chains on the restraint would allow. Lepov gave the Lieutenant an irritated look; he might have screwed up that night, but he wasn't about to act like a humiliated supplicant.

"I guess it's not. But that don't mean I gotta unlock these. I could leave them on for spite. I just want to know one thing."

"What?"

"Why is my captain acting like you're the son of the Police Commissioner? I got my ass chewed out for arresting you."

"I guess its Reno." Lepov watched MacNally punch a four-digit number into a small plate on top of the restraints.

"The Chief Administrator? Is he your daddy?"

"Hardly. David Khalid might know what's going on. Does this mean I'm no longer under arrest?" Lepov rubbed his wrist.

"For now. Tell me about Reno."

"I don't know much about him. I know I was arrested earlier today."

"Hold on." MacNally sat up, gave Lepov a queer look, and tapped at his desk. "If you'd been arrested this morning, I would see it here."

"No record? I'm not surprised."

"David Khalid arrested you?"

"Yeah, I was set up over some fake PDT's. Don't ask me why." Lepov held up his hands when he saw MacNally about to interrupt. "My best guess is someone wanted to stop me from finding Layne. But I wasn't even aware anyone knew I was here looking for Layne. So that may not have been the reason. I really don't know."

"So what happened? What does Reno have to do with this?"

"All I can say is when I told Khalid I was hired by Eudia Layne to find Ethan Layne, within the hour, Claude Reno was personally apologizing and pushing me out the door of the precinct. He offered me a place to stay and all the assistance the police could provide.

"Reno was here today? And he dealt directly with you?" MacNally narrowed his eyes as Lepov nodded in response.

"What is this about?" Lepov had a feeling that if anyone was going to be honest with him, this MacNally was a likely candidate.

"That would make more sense. Jenkins doesn't normally give in like that. Unless you count yesterday and that mess with the IHS." MacNally's eyebrows lifted as he thought silently about his own words. He twisted in his chair to look back at Captain Jenkins' office, muttering under his breath before turning back to question Lepov. "How did you know Layne was going to be there tonight?"

"I didn't. I was following Montillo. I wasn't aware he had anything to do with Layne. Montillo's the one who set me up with Khalid's boys. Layne's appearance, if you haven't figured it out, was a surprise to me. Now are you gonna tell me why you think Ethan Layne is a murderer?"

"No, I'm not," MacNally said without apology. "You said you hadn't got too far in your search for Layne. Wasn't that your story?"

"Yes." Lepov had been forced to dodge accusations of holding back vital information. MacNally had found it difficult to believe Lepov had found out so little about Layne.

"Tell me about the girl again," MacNally insisted. "Becker, right?"

"Yeah, Greta Becker. But I already told you what I know about her. It's getting late, Lieutenant. Can't we do this tomorrow?"

"What I don't get," MacNally ignored Lepov's question and changed the subject, "is what Reno has to do with this. It's a good bet Reno is behind my orders to let you go, and that whole issue with IHS and Jack Ford's results. That's why Jenkins was so final about everything. Reno's the only one who can get that kind of response from Jenkins. Not even the Police Commission can do that. I've seen him stand up to them too many times to believe it." MacNally looked up at Lepov as if he'd forgotten he was there. "What did you say about tomorrow?"

"Can't we go home and work this all out tomorrow?" Lepov wasn't that tired but his knee was throbbing and had become impossible to ignore. On top of that, MacNally's cigarette smoke was beginning to give Lepov a headache. On days like this he was glad he'd quit smoking.

"What do you want to work out? You're not still planning to look for Layne are you? I don't want you in our way again."

"I want to talk to Montillo. I want to know why he targeted me."

"Don't get your hopes up. I was told to let you go. Don't think that means I like you now. It doesn't even mean I have to tolerate you. If you do anything to upset me—and I have an extremely sensitive spirit—I'm gonna toss you into the first open quadrant and get you out of the Laz. And I can make sure you're not allowed back in. So don't upset me."

Lepov didn't have a response to that. He understood MacNally's anger, but he wished the guy would back off all the same.

Why had MacNally assumed he wasn't going to keep looking for Layne? He was being paid to find Layne regardless of his legal status. So he was a murder suspect; that didn't mean Eudia Layne had lost her right to find out what had happened to her son. Besides, Lepov wasn't about to cut off his funding from the good Mrs. Layne. Not yet, anyway.

Lepov had changed his mind. He wanted to find Ethan Layne.

57

A shrill scream wailed in Helen's ears. It wouldn't stop. Helen awoke. Someone was repeatedly jamming her door chime. Helen reached for her robe. It was four-thirty in the morning.

Who was so desperate to get in? She pulled the robe tightly around her waist and went into her foyer where she could view the lobby.

Julia appeared on the screen. She was a mess.

Helen punched in her door code and watched Julia nearly fall in the elevator as its doors opened. There was an anxious moment between the time she disappeared into the elevator and the moment she made it to Helen's front door. Helen had it open and stood waiting for her friend.

"What happened to you? Are you all right?" Helen saw that Julia wasn't wearing a coat and she grabbed a throw blanket from off her couch, wrapping Julia in it as she pulled her into the apartment.

"I don't know." Julia had been crying.

"Well come on, you're okay for now. Sit over here and calm down. I'll get you something to drink. In fact, I might as well make coffee. I doubt either one of us will get any sleep now before work."

Julia had allowed herself to be led to an overstuffed couch and sat on the edge of its cushions, holding herself as if she were afraid to relax.

Helen left her alone on purpose. As she fiddled around in the kitchen fixing a pot of coffee, she knew Julia was too overwrought to make any sense. She wanted to stay out of the room for a minute and let Julia settle down; allow the comfort and serenity of Helen's place to ease her distraught spirit. Whatever had happened, Helen knew she'd hear more than she'd want to hear about it. It was simply a matter of getting Julia to relax enough so that she could explain everything in a logical manner.

Easier said than done. Julia had no intention of being left alone.

"Could I come in there and help you?" Julia called from the other room. "I could make the coffee. I didn't mean to make you work."

"It's nothing, Julia. You stay there. It's all automatic anyway. All I have to do is hit a button. It's one of the few machines I've got that never breaks down."

As the aroma of coffee filled the kitchen, Helen realized this episode of Julia's would be about the new boyfriend. It wasn't the first time Julia had come running to her 'big sister'.

With her hands full of steaming cups of coffee, Helen walked gingerly into her front room. Julia was still sitting on the edge of the couch.

"Watch it, that's hot." Helen gracefully passed one of the thick mugs into Julia's shaky hands. She had left enough room in the cup so that it wouldn't spill too easily. It had been a wise precaution.

The women sipped at their hot coffee in silence. Helen did not question Julia; there would be plenty of time for explanations.

Once the coffee had disappeared, and the mugs had been refilled and drained again, the time for explanations had finally come.

"Is this about Billy? Did you find him?"

Julia nodded.

"Did you fight?"

"No," Julia said without hesitation or equivocation. This time Helen waited for Julia to speak on her own.

"He came back about two hours ago," Julia said. Helen glanced at a clock on the wall. Julia continued: "I was excited that he had come back, I really was. I was glad he was safe, you know? I'd been watching those awful stories about that murderer—did you see those?—well, I got the silly idea in my head that Billy might have been killed. I know that's silly of me. But you can see how happy I was he made it home safe.

"So, I don't know why I started to get snippy with him. I guess I couldn't help it. It's just that he'd been gone for so long. I wanted him to know how worried I'd been. But he made a joke about it. That made me mad, I guess. He should have called, you know?"

"So you ended up fighting with him about it?"

"No, I told you we did not fight. I left before that could happen." That point seemed important to Julia.

"Why'd you leave?"

"He was acting funny. I couldn't understand what was bothering him." Julia held her empty mug and kept running the tip of one finger around its inside lip. "I had been asleep when he got there. I heard him in the living room, he was standing at one of the windows watching the street below. He was nervous. Really nervous."

"Did he say why?"

"I tried to ask him," Julia answered; hurt and confusion in her eyes. "I don't know what was going on, but he got angry with me. He yelled at me not to ask questions. It scared me."

Helen could see it still scared Julia. It's why she was still sitting on the edge of that couch. Her eyes would occasionally dart in the direction of the front door, watching and waiting for something beyond it. She looked ready to spring off the couch and flee.

"He can't get in here, Julia." Helen tried to beat back that fear. It was obviously wearing heavily on Julia's spirit.

"Okay," Julia nodded. Another glance at the door.

"Why are you so afraid of him?"

"I'm being silly." Julia looked down at her mug and tried to smile. "Don't worry about silly me."

"That's the fourth or fifth time you've called yourself silly since you came in here. You didn't wake me at four-thirty in the morning to tell me you're silly."

"I don't want to say it." She shrank back when Helen sighed in exasperation. "You're gonna think…"

"Don't tell me what you think I'll think. What are you afraid of?"

"I got the silly notion in my head—" Julia wasn't going to finish that sentence until she saw the annoyance on Helen's face " —maybe Billy was the one killing those people. Maybe he was the murderer!"

Helen said nothing for a brief moment. Julia shook her head in embarrassment. "Like I said, I was just being silly."

Julia had misinterpreted Helen's silence. She hadn't thought Julia was overreacting. She had only been surprised that Julia had been as disturbed by the NewsVision story of the murders as Helen had been. There was nothing more ridiculous about thinking that Billy was the murderer than Helen thinking that the *Royal Aquila's* deliveryman had been the killer.

"Did you say anything about this to him?" asked Helen.

"No," Julia shook her head emphatically. "Not yet."

"Then no harm done, huh? It's okay to be cautious. And it's not the end of the world if your imagination gets the better of you. Believe me, I know. You don't have to say anything to him, either. Simply go home after work and find a way to make it up to him. Maybe call him up this morning and let him know you're coming back tonight."

"You think?" Julia frowned and wrinkled up her forehead. To Helen, Julia looked all of fifteen years old at that moment.

"I think. Come here." Helen sat beside her and put an arm around her. Julia melted into her arms.

"That's why I come to you, Helen. You're better at this kind of thing than my mother is."

"Big sister, darling." Helen stroked Julia's hair and smiled. "I'm only old enough to be your big sister. Let's not forget that."

"I can't go to work looking like this," Julia wiped at tears that rolled down her cheeks. "I'm a mess."

"Forget about that. What are big sisters for, huh? I'm sure I have something in my closet you can wear. Should we go and take a look?"

58

Fenelli was awake by five a.m. For the first time in several days he had slept. He felt great. For one thing, he'd been able to get to bed at a decent hour. And more importantly, he'd had no nightmares about swollen, bloodied bodies.

He hoped MacNally had been able to rest, as well.

A quick shower and a hastily downed breakfast were evidence of

Fenelli's eagerness to get back on the job. He wanted to get into the office, read the reports on Montillo from last night, and hopefully do something useful before MacNally dragged in later in the morning.

Fenelli almost missed it. He had been in such a hurry to get to the office that he almost missed the note stuck to the windshield of his car. It was a small note. Handwritten. Fenelli snatched it up and read it.

6 AM. Delta Entry Lounge.

He was tempted to ignore it. If someone wanted to meet with him they could come to the precinct. What was it about? A quick look at his watch told Fenelli he had little time left to think about it. If he wanted to get to the Delta Lounge by six he was going to have to hurry.

The Delta Entry Lounge was located at the Delta Annex that allowed travelers to move between the Delta Quadrant and Center City during Delta's ten-day loading window. Once Delta was locked into its quarantine period, the Delta Annex closed down as well.

It did not occur to Fenelli that Delta Quadrant was closing its doors that day until he drove into the lower parking level of the Delta Annex. The traffic was already congested at that early hour. Thousands of people would be trying to end up on the right side of the locked doors before twelve noon. And not everyone was trying to get into Delta.

Many of the vendors who serviced the travelers in Delta were now leaving that quadrant in expectation of the opening of Alpha quadrant. Barbers, tailors, and numerous salesmen were heading into Center City to avoid being locked down where they were no longer needed. Fenelli knew that as the morning sun, shrouded by clouds, rose towards its noontime apex, tempers would flare among the last few travelers entering Delta and the vendors trying to escape.

Fenelli now understood why the note had specified the Delta Entry Lounge. The lounge would be a madhouse.

Travelers still awaiting paperwork camped out along the sides of the open lounge. They were easy to spot with their worried looks and nervous tittering; men snapping at their wives, wives smacking at the kids. There were smaller groups of Lazars sitting around small tables eating breakfast, completely at ease; they'd been through a quadrant closing too many times to worry over it. Fenelli had no trouble spotting them; they were the only ones cracking jokes or placidly reading news-screens.

The rest of the growing crowd consisted of individuals who seemed to have everything and nothing in common with everyone around them; a mishmash of people who looked as if they were all going in opposite directions. One of these would be the man who had written the note. Fenelli knew it would be impossible to pick him out of that crowd.

He would have to sit down at one of the tables and wait to be contacted. Whoever this guy was, he wanted to be in control and Fenelli had little choice in the matter.

An overworked young woman rushed up to Fenelli and asked if he was planning to order anything.

"Coffee, I guess." He could see the relief in her eyes.

"I can get you that. Nearly everything else is a real problem this morning. Sit tight, I'll be back." She pushed her way back through the crowd towards two swinging service doors that hung on a far wall.

Fenelli wondered if she was new. Things weren't that busy yet, not as bad as they were going to get. What would she do then?

Fenelli turned when he heard a woman shout at a security guard. She had attracted the attention of nearly everyone within twenty feet of where she stood. When Fenelli turned back towards his table he wanted to shout as well. A single data tag lay in the center of his empty table.

Had the waitress dropped it? Fenelli doubted it. It had to be from the man who wrote the note. A quick scan of his immediate surroundings told Fenelli he'd never figure out who had slipped it onto the table.

Fenelli palmed the data tag. There was no reason to wait around. Whoever dropped it was gone. The closest tag reader was in his car. Fenelli left the boisterous lounge for the honeycombed silence of the car.

There was nothing special about the coin shaped data tag. It could have been a Personal Data Tag, a Communications Data Tag; there were any number of uses it might have served.

Fenelli pulled a DT reader from a compartment in the driver's side door. For once, the department had spent good money and purchased newer model readers for the detectives in the field. As soon as the reader screen lit up he could see it had already picked up the data tag's signal. A secondary signal was listed on a column to the right side of the screen: Fenelli's PDT, complete with a file image of himself that he had always disliked. Also listed were the signals from his car—registration and diagnostic readings—and a last signal that was labeled unknown/non-threatening. The reader could not identify its weak signal.

Fenelli accessed the data tag he'd found on the table.

The top left corner of the screen displayed a blinking message that the tag was empty. That's how it was supposed to look. Fenelli typed in a command to open the blank screen. Again, the display labeled the data tag as empty. Fenelli had to give the same command two more times before he found a file. The dummy blank screens had been an old method kids had used for generations to hide information from nosey adults. Fenelli had expected something more complex.

The first screen to contain information showed six visual shots of a young man that Fenelli guessed to be around twenty years old. The shots were not taken from the best angles, but Fenelli could see enough of the man from the different shots to get an idea what he looked like. If he needed to, Fenelli would be able to have the precinct's compositor generate one clean image from the six images.

After studying the face for a minute, Fenelli felt confident that whoever this guy was, he had never seen him before.

Opening yet another level of screens, Fenelli found a written statement from an unnamed source who claimed to have witnessed the first murder: Jack Ford's. The witness did not want to give an official statement as it would put him in a compromising position. But the witness had wanted the police to have the visual images of the murderer.

It was the worst kind of tip. Fenelli wanted to throw the data tag in the nearest trash can. What was he supposed to do with it? The visuals were worthless. Even if he could get a name and identity from them what could he do with it? A witness who refused to come forward and refused to identify himself was useless.

The tag reader's display cleared and updated. The list of signals to the right changed slightly as the unknown signal had finally been identified. A small image of a woman was displayed beside her PDT profile.

She looked familiar. Fenelli wondered where he had seen her before and it took a few seconds to recognize her.

Fenelli looked up and tried to spot her. According to the reader, she was somewhere on the parking level with him. The reader would not have picked up her signal unless she was close. Not only was she close, she wasn't moving; the signal strength remained constant. Fenelli set the reader down and put his hand on the door.

As soon as the door swung open, he slid out of his seat and pushed off in her direction. He saw her standing beside a concrete column two cars away. She stared at him, startled that he was coming her way, then turned to run a few heartbeats before Fenelli could reach her.

"Wait!" he barked. She kept running. A foot race was the last thing Fenelli wanted. He couldn't remember the last time he'd had to run at a full sprint.

He sucked in a deep breath and started after her. She was well ahead of him, but to his surprise, she slowed down. She had run for the elevator doors instead of the stairwell, probably by sheer habit. And the closer she came to the elevators, the more obvious it became that she could not wait for the doors to open. She would have to backtrack towards the stairwell.

But she never had the chance. Fenelli hadn't run in a long time, but that didn't mean he was slow when he did. With an outstretched hand he grabbed her by an arm and held on tight.

She didn't squirm and fight like he had expected. She was no spitfire. The same fear that had set her to running now paralyzed her.

"I thought you were bringing me coffee," Fenelli said as he caught his breath. She was the waitress from the Lounge. His little joke did nothing to dispel her fear. She stared as if she expected him to hit her. "You put that data tag on the table. Didn't you?"

She continued to stare, her mouth clamped shut.

"You want to tell me about it?" What was this woman's problem? Fenelli wanted to smack her; to get any kind of response out of her except that silly look on her face. "Did you make the tag?"

A slight shake of her head was all she could muster. Fenelli wasn't surprised the tag wasn't hers. Most likely someone else had employed her to give Fenelli the tag. Maybe she could tell him who that someone was.

"First thing we'll do is go get that cup of coffee. Then you'll find out I'm not a bad guy. And then you can tell me what's going on, okay?"

She nodded twice.

"Well, that's a start anyway." Fenelli encouraged her with a smile.

59

Maria's restlessness was stronger than a cup of chamomile tea. The tea had put her to sleep but she hadn't slept long enough.

Georges had come home and now lay beside her in a deep sleep. She watched him for a few moments. Despite the Van Dyke beard and age lines etched into his cheeks he still had a childlike quality when he was at rest. That firm pragmatic façade of his that she dearly loved was modified ever so slightly to give him a soft, innocent expression, as if he were unaware of his own sharp intellect and wisdom.

She slid gently off the bed, wondering how she could believe Georges to be so wise when she knew she intended to ignore his warnings.

That question lay at the heart of her restlessness. She wanted to listen to Georges. He was right to tell her to be careful. Yet, even as her head agreed with him, she pulled on warm clothes with every intention of going out to the park. More to the point, she was hoping the young man would be there. She wanted to see him again. She wanted to prove Georges and Arturo wrong. Or was it that she wanted to prove she was right?

She pushed her head through Georges' heavy sweater and caught the scent of his pipe tobacco. No, she thought, she should not wear his sweater; not when she planned to defy his warning. She removed his sweater and chose a more delicate pink one made of thin synthetic fibers. It was as warm as her husband's heavy sweater, but it would lack that bundled-up feeling.

Guilt weighed upon her as she rode in the elevator; enough that she imagined the elevator was traveling faster with all that extra weight. But what had she to feel guilty about? Maria reasoned that Georges had been worried over something he didn't understand; therefore his warning was uninformed and unnecessary. No, the guilt came from her earlier misjudgment of the young man.

Even as the cold morning air blew chills through her hair and down her neck, Maria flushed at the memory of the fear she had allowed to control her when she last saw the young man. She hated such foolishness. She had never wished to be a man, did not wish to be one now, yet wondered why she had to be a woman. Why did she have to allow her fears and weaknesses to overrule her desire for courage? Why couldn't she live with the kind of steadfast resolve that Arturo had revealed when facing down their father? What was it like to be strong like a man?

She laughed aloud at her foolish questions. Yes, Georges and Arturo were strong men with firm wills, but their strength was in their character, not in their manhood. Maria had seen other men who lacked mettle, even as she had known women who were strong and never given to timidity. The real question was: why couldn't she reach out and take hold of courage like everyone else? What held her back?

Maria had no answer. If something held her back, it was as invisible as the wind pushing against her, slowing her progress as she pressed deeper into the park. That same invisible wind blew bits and pieces of grass and leaves at her and she tucked her chin to her chest, closing her eyes whenever possible.

If only she could find the young man again. If only she could face him again and cast out her fear—replace it with peace. She wanted that. She needed to rid her mind of its silly fears as much as Kjarsta needed to be freed from his pain.

She knew that was unfair; Kjarsta's pain was so much greater than her petty fears and the shame they brought with them. Kjarsta's pain was real and he could do nothing to stop it. Her fears were only imagined; she had only to deny them and they would vanish. She laughed at herself; she was allowing her fear to make her problems out to be bigger than they were.

"That's a nice laugh. I've not heard you laugh before."

Maria's head snapped up despite the wind blowing at her and she looked directly into it. The young man stood before her on the path. Could it really be him? Was she imagining him?

"I'm glad you like it." The first step to conquering fear was to address it, to face it and never allow it control. Maria took that first step.

"You like this park." The wind tossed his words all around.

"Yes, it's a wonderful place, don't you think?" Maria looked up at the surrounding trees. The grey light of morning dripped down through the wet branches and it made her shiver. She liked that.

"There's a lot to like about it. It's beautiful. I like beautiful things. Were you going to the fountains?" Maria was tempted to find his words odd and disturbing but she forced herself not to.

"The fauns? I guess I'm a little predictable."

"Yeah," he laughed easily, "you are a little predictable. Do you always take the path around to the fountains? Well, I wasn't sure if you knew there was a quicker way through the trees.

"No." Maria shook her head as he pointed out a natural archway through the trees off to the right of the path. "I prefer to walk along the path. It is easier on my feet."

The young man shrugged at her and didn't seem to care one way or the other. He fell in behind her as she kept to the path.

"My name is Maria." She felt it was safe enough to tell him this.

"That's a sweet name and fits you well. I'm William." He smiled then, and she liked the way his smile wrinkled the skin of his forehead all the way up to the edge of his blond hair.

Perhaps she would find a way to trade in her fears for courage.

At the fountain, the smiling faun looked down upon her as if he were laughing at her sudden confidence. She didn't mind his light ridicule; she really was getting ahead of herself. She had relied on her brother's and her husband's courage for too long to quickly develop any of her own.

"I know you like that one. You were sitting in front of him before." William walked up and stood close beside her. He blocked the chilling wind for her. "He's a happy fellow, isn't he?"

"Yes," Maria nodded.

"You don't like the sad one next. No, I'll bet you like this one here; the bored faun."

Maria laughed at that and William was startled by so much noise.

"What's so funny?" he demanded.

"The faun is not bored. He is content; at peace."

"Are you sure? He looks bored to me. Of course, bored and content are one and the same, aren't they? I mean, the most content man in the world must certainly have nothing to do. He has nothing to complain about and nothing to brag about. A content man is like a married man—he has what he wants but isn't really sure he wants it anymore."

Maria smiled weakly at his philosophy but said nothing about his analysis of marriage.

"I hope that didn't offend you," William watched her and shook his head. "I don't suppose that was the nicest thing to say. I have a tendency to make bold statements I've never really examined before. You'll have to ignore me when I wax philosophically."

"It's okay," Maria lied; she never liked to hear marriage spoken of with disrespect.

"Well, let's forget what I said, okay?" William stepped back to look at the whole of the fountain. "Then I suppose you'd still choose the sad faun before the angry faun."

"I would never choose the angry faun!" Maria insisted.

"Is that right?" He bit his lip while thinking over what she had said. "You don't like it? It's only a depiction of a mythological creature, you know. It won't bite."

"I'm aware of that." Maria did not like the turn of the conversation. She did not want to discuss the angry faun.

But why not? Was she doing it again? Allowing an ungrounded fear to take hold? No, she reminded herself, she wasn't afraid of it. She did not like it; did not like its rage and disturbed spirit. There was nothing wrong in wanting to avoid something like that.

"I think all of the fauns are important. Even that ugly one. They all tell a side of the story, you know?" William had drifted towards the contented Faun and stood staring at it. Maria followed him hesitantly. "I like to see things like this. It helps me get a better picture of what's inside—all of us."

Maria saw him move to his right, circling closer to the angry faun. She wanted to go back or let him go on alone. But she did not want to let fear control her. What was there to fear? She took a few steps to the right. The serene faun watched her placidly as if it did not care that she was about to look upon its foul and immoral brother.

Maria had not stood beneath the wicked visage of that faun in a long time. She was not even sure if she had ever looked upon it since that first time. Taking a breath, she lifted her eyes and met its burning eyes.

The faun's sharp teeth protruded from an open mouth, the lines of its neck and jaw straining as it howled in pain. The brow was constricted in pain and the eyes bulged out as if something were strangling it. The faun's horns and pointed beard were more prevalent than its brothers'; an uninhibited allusion to its satanic nature.

The body stood contorted at sharp angles. Maria imagined it was being poked by red-hot prongs. There was something hideous about the faun's continuous effort to pour out the contents of its jar. She did not like to think of what was in that jar; what infected waters were being dumped into the pool, mixing with the waters from its brother fauns.

"Well?" William stood directly in front of the odious faun. Maria stood beside him. He turned his gaze from it, shifting it towards her. "Is it as bad as you remembered?"

"It is worse. Why would a man make such a creature?" She stared at William, if only to keep from gaping at the faun.

"I couldn't say. But I'm glad someone did. I think we need things like this; in remind us what kind of creatures afflict us, what kind of creature man can be."

That thought scared Maria. But at the same time she understood what he meant. For a moment she could see the pain in the faun and it made her think of Kjarsta. Surely this was the kind of devil that feasted upon him from the inside. How alone and despairing Kjarsta must feel as he tried to fight it off. It was why she had to be there for him, to make sure he knew he had not been left alone to that vicious devil.

"Am I doing it again? Did I say something wrong?" He watched her closely. As he had before, he pressed uncomfortably close to her.

"I don't know." She could feel her uneasiness returning. She wanted to leave. She should never have come to this side of the fountain.

"Let's look at the last one. The sad one."

"No, I think I'll sit down." Maria barely managed to get the words out before she stepped quickly to her bench on the opposite side of the fountain. William followed her but did not sit down beside her.

"I didn't mean to upset you." She could hear uncertainty in his voice. He shifted his weight from one foot to the other.

"It's not your fault," Maria said. "Like you said, it's something we need to see."

"Then again," William turned back to the fountain, "we could always look at the happy fella and never go back to that other side."

"I think I'd like that." Maria wished the children would appear.

Fenelli sat with the woman—her name was Jeri—in the Delta Entry Lounge with coffee cups in front of them. The coffee had been served by another waitress who had angrily scolded Jeri for walking off the job until Fenelli had shown her his badge. The waitress had then changed her attitude from that of a shrew to that of a nosey gossip. Fenelli had been forced to order her to leave them alone.

And they were alone now, surrounded by the crowd around them; their table a pocket of isolation amidst the hustle and bustle. Jeri was still reluctant to talk, though the fear had left her eyes.

"We could go someplace more private. Are you in danger?"

She shook her head.

"Then I want to know about the tag? Who gave it to you?"

"Was it something illegal?" she asked.

"On the data tag? No."

Jeri was visibly relieved. She nervously sipped some of her coffee.

"Who gave it to you?" Fenelli repeated his question.

She was unable to look him in the eye.

Fenelli knew he should take her down to Homicide. With this girl's frame of mind they should have no trouble scaring her into talking. But Fenelli hated that idea. There was enough kindness in her eyes that Fenelli did not want to work on her like that. He believed he could get what he needed with his own kindness. He never got the chance to do things like this with MacNally by his side.

"Do you know his name?"

"Not really," she admitted.

"Okay," Fenelli thought he knew what was holding her back. "I'm not too interested in the details of your relationship with the man who gave you that tag. And I'm not here to pass judgment on it either. But you will have to tell me about him."

"We only hooked up a few times before. He's just a Lazar, you know. Comes in here every two or three weeks." She spoke softly and Fenelli had trouble hearing her over the noise of the people around them. "I could tell he'd been watching me when I waited on him. And I could tell by the suits he wore that he had money, you know? God, I sound like a real slut don't I? I don't normally do this kind of thing."

"I said I don't care about the details. When did he give you the tag?"

"Last night. He came by my place and said he needed to pass something along to someone he couldn't be seen with in public. Don't you think I knew how stupid that sounded? I'm not straight off the farm. I knew there was something funny going on. But I—it's hard to say no to a guy like him. Maybe that's why I let him up to my place that first night.

"But like I said, I knew something wasn't right. I didn't want to get mixed up in anything—"

"—illegal?" Fenelli leaned towards her. "That's why you were down on the parking level? You were curious, right?"

"I knew you were a cop the moment I saw you." She bit her lip and shrugged when Fenelli gave her a quizzical look. "I could just tell. All you cops act the same way."

It never ceased to amaze Fenelli when people told him that. He liked to think he could blend into a crowd when he had to but he was forever discovering that he wasn't fooling anyone. Even his kids made comments about his behavior when they were around other people. Most of their comments centered on his wariness—always watching everyone. It was something he apparently never switched off.

"You said he'd been up to your apartment last night?" Fenelli asked. "Do you have a door recorder that's working?"

"No." She seemed disappointed at her own answer until she thought of something she could add. "But the apartment manager keeps the elevator recorder working. He's always trying to catch kids who play around and spray paint all over the elevator's walls. If they haven't painted over the recorder you might get a look at him."

Fenelli could see that Jeri was no longer afraid to talk about her occasional lover. She even seemed eager to help him find out who he really was. Perhaps she was beginning to regret getting involved with a man she knew so little about.

Once the lines of worry had been erased from around her eyes, Fenelli realized she was an attractive young woman. He didn't find her tempting in a sexual way, she was young and vulnerable looking; a combination that left Fenelli worried for her in the same way he'd always worried over his sister Maria. Fenelli had known guys who liked to pick up girls like that. He always figured they liked to find someone they could control. But that had never appealed to Fenelli. His first instincts had always been to protect. It's why he'd become a cop.

"Would you come with me to your place?" He wanted to see those elevator visuals right away.

"Sure, why not? I don't seem to mind taking men to my place, do I?"

Fenelli could feel himself blush when she said that. She'd known what he meant but her self-esteem was low enough that she couldn't pass up the chance to aim a cutting remark at herself.

As they pulled out of the lower parking level and onto the street, Fenelli thought about that data tag and the guy who'd given it to her. Something wasn't right.

The information on that tag wasn't only missing a few vital pieces of the puzzle. It seemed designed to tell Fenelli nothing. It was designed to *not* give information.

And why give him this tag now? Why give it at all? What was the overriding purpose to this charade? It was a charade, after all. There were too many holes in its premise to be anything else. It angered Fenelli that someone out there didn't think he'd be smart enough to see it. Fenelli would have to ignore that insulting implication.

While Fenelli had been caught up in his own thoughts, Jeri had ridden beside him in silence. She'd only spoken a few times to guide him towards her apartment. The cold, gray day lent a somber mood to their silent trip across the Lazaretto.

It wasn't until they entered her building that Fenelli had put aside his speculations and began to look forward to identifying their mystery man. Jeri led him to a third story apartment that belonged to the building's maintenance manager.

The manager was a dark, wiry man wearing a white t-shirt and black suspenders that held up a grubby pair of workpants. He stood inside the door of his apartment and looked up at Fenelli with a bored expression. Yes, the elevator recorders were working. How else was he going to catch those damn kids screwing around in the elevators? No, he didn't care if Fenelli looked at the recordings.

The manager showed them a screen in one of his back rooms. He had direct access to the visual recordings. He waved them towards a controller without making any effort to show them how to operate it. He assumed they could figure it out or didn't care if they could or not. He hung around for a few minutes watching from the far side of the room.

"What time last night?" Fenelli pulled up an archive list and scrolled through the available images from the night before. He hadn't needed instructions on how to access the images. It was an older recording model that he'd seen many times over the years.

"Early, before dark. Maybe close to six."

"Was this set on continuous feed or was it set for motion?"

"I had it on all the time. Those little bastards found a way around the motion detectors." The manager had pulled out a long brown cigarette and lit it. Fenelli could smell the strong aroma of its Dneprish tobacco. Fenelli occasionally liked to smoke a cigarette or two, but he'd never been able to stomach the potent sour tobacco from Dnepr. Fenelli was beginning to dislike this little man.

"If you call down to the precinct we might be able to take care of those kids for you. We could talk to them. Set them straight for you."

"I'll take care of those little *chajaks* myself." Fenelli had recognized the man's accent as coming from somewhere on the backside of Dnepr but he didn't know the meaning of the idiomatic slang. It didn't matter; he understood its general meaning. It wasn't the kind of thing that should have been said in front of a lady.

"Tell you what," Fenelli decided he was going to ruin the manager's day, "I'll call down there for you. We'll find out what's going on with those kids. We'd love to help."

"That's him, right there." Jeri had been watching the screen as Fenelli skipped through the images.

The manager muttered a few more Dneprish phrases and left the room. Fenelli watched him go with a smile before examining the image.

"Damn it," Fenelli muttered. "He was expecting the camera. Hasn't anybody ever thought of taking a visual from any angle other than from up high? We get more shots of people's hair than any faces."

"Well that's him, I'm sure of it." Jeri bit her lip and narrowed her eyes, concentrating on the moving image.

"I believe you, lady. But there's no way he's gonna be dumb enough to lift his head. I can't do much with this. Hell, this angle's so bad your grimy little manager will never even catch kids with this thing."

"I don't understand why he'd set it like that. He's obsessed with those kids." Jeri bit her lip again, shaking her head at his incompetence.

Fenelli thought about her last words. If he was right, that manager wasn't as incompetent as he pretended to be. But he was certainly crafty.

"Hey," Fenelli called the manager back into the room. The little man walked back in with a careful step. A long piece of ash hung precariously off the end of his cigarette. "Unlock the feed from the other recorder."

The manager sucked on the cigarette and let the smoke out slowly. The ash held on for a moment longer before it fell to the carpet below. He never paid the slightest attention to it. Fenelli could see he was weighing his options. If the man were smart he wouldn't try to deny the existence of the other recorder. If he were smart at all he'd unlock the feed and keep his mouth shut.

Fenelli had reasoned that if the kids had been able to get around the motion detector, then the manager would have had to assume they would find a way to kill the recorder in some other way. So logically, he had to have hidden a second recorder, set at a lower position to catch the kids. Not knowing their height, he would have had to set it low and aim it towards the ceiling of the elevator.

The little man sucked in one last lungful of smoke and made up his mind. He pulled the cigarette from his mouth and gave Fenelli a sour look. Leaning over the controller, he typed in a short command followed by a six-digit number.

"There's your second angle." The screen split to display two separate angles; one from above and one from below. "Now, I'm helping you. And you can help me by not getting involved in my damned business. I will take care of those kids."

Fenelli ran the images forward to the point where Jeri's unnamed friend stepped onto the elevator. For a few moments it looked as if he were going to keep his back turned to the second recorder. Had he known about it as well? It looked as though the doors were going to open before he ever turned around.

But then he turned. And Fenelli knew they had him. To avoid the angle from above, he had kept his head down. And as he turned into the recorder's view, it recorded the perfect visual of his face. Whoever this creep was, Fenelli had him. It was only a matter of matching the face to a name.

"Jeri, I'm going to need you to come with me to the precinct for a little while, okay?" Fenelli turned and looked down at the manager. "And thank you for your cooperation. And don't worry about those kids. I will personally be sure to come back here and get involved in your damn business."

61

Lilly Stewart entered Lepov's dormitory late in the morning and a few of the men were still lying on their beds or moving from the showers to the beds. She passed one man who was pulling off his towel and uttered a protest when he realized she was a woman.

Gregor was asleep with an arm draped over his eyes to shield him from the overhead lights. There was precious little light coming in through the windows. The Lazaretto seemed to shun sunlight as much as the residents shunned human contact.

"I should have expected to find you still asleep, Gregor Lepov."

Gregor's arm shifted enough for one squinty eye to peek out at her.

"You remember me? The woman you slapped in the face yesterday?"

One of the men chuckled at that until she cast a deadly glare at him.

"You'd better go ahead a slap me back. I deserve it." Gregor pulled his arm away and looked up at her. He looked like hell. She almost asked him if he was alright but stopped before she did. She wasn't finished scolding him.

"You do deserve it. And don't try to be nice. Do you know how long I've been looking for you? Where have you been all night?"

"I should be able to answer those questions if you ask them again one at a time. I'm in bad need of some bad coffee. What time is it?" Gregor picked up his watch and tried to read the display. "I don't think I got three hours of sleep. And who's being nice?"

"I won't talk to you like this. Get up and put some clothes on. And meet me down at Comic Joe's. Have you been out drinking all night?" Lilly turned to leave but added one comment before she did. "I can't believe I was looking for you in the hospitals."

"You should have checked at the jail," Gregor called after her. "I'm beginning to like it there. Next time I get my own room and I can pick out my own pictures for the walls."

Lilly went down to the street, glad to have a chance to compose herself after finding him. She had been out most of the night looking for him and had begun to worry that something bad had happened. It didn't matter that he had insulted her. She wanted to find him and make him understand that. And now, seeing him so worn down and such a mess—she'd been surprised at the intensity of her relief.

But she couldn't let him see that. Likewise, she couldn't really tell him the things he'd said didn't matter to her. She would have to play her role as the injured party. Even if he insisted on being humble and admitting his guilt—it looked like he was already doing that. But she'd never keep him honest if she didn't make him pay a price for his poor judgment.

Lilly wasn't proud of such a decision, but it was a necessary factor in keeping her defenses up. And she wasn't going to let them down again.

She had two cups of Comic Joe's coffee sitting in front of her when Gregor came through the door. That same dull clank of the bell announced his entrance as it had the first time she'd seen him a few days before. But he didn't look like the same man. Gone was his little boy lost expression. She now saw shrewdness behind those eyes that she hadn't seen before; something closer to the wariness of an animal that was both predator and prey. Maybe he had decided to build his defenses up as well.

"I was surprised to see you this morning." He joined her in the booth and made a hesitant attempt to sip the steaming coffee. "I expected you'd come only if you could chop me into little pieces. I wouldn't have blamed you."

Lilly watched him talk, keeping his lips pulled back against his teeth in a perpetual half grimace. It made her think he was always about to say something both funny and impertinent. She could see mockery coming from that tightened jaw, but never cruelty; at least she had thought so until she'd met him outside the police station.

She tried not to think about that.

He continued to sip his coffee and ramble on while she silently listened. Either he didn't notice she wasn't saying anything as he rattled on or he did notice and was only jabbering to fill in the silence. She liked watching him talk, fumbling for a way to apologize for what he had said to her. He was doing a pretty bad job of it and she liked that just fine.

Her reverie was broken by something he'd said. She put out a hand as if to physically prevent him from saying more.

"What did you say?"

"I know I should have trusted you. I shouldn't have had to wait until I discovered Montillo set me up."

"Carlos?" Lilly eyes mirrored the disbelief in her voice. "You can't be serious. Why would you think Carlos did this to you?"

"I didn't, remember? But the police are the ones that convinced me of that. I was arrested for having a bunch of fake PDT's in my possession. You're little friend turns out to be a broker in these things."

"Don't talk down to me, Gregor. I'm well aware of what Carlos does." Lilly frowned as she tried to think.

"So you know this about him? Then maybe you'd know why he planted them on me. And why he wanted me arrested."

Obviously, Gregor wasn't doing much thinking. "That makes no sense. You think Carlos put them there so the police would find them? Don't you run your own business? Would you do something that puts it all at risk? Not only would he be losing the value of the confiscated PDT's, but he'd give them a route that could lead right back to him."

"Maybe they were old—useless—I don't know. Maybe he and the cops already have a deal under the table. But I didn't really believe it was him until I talked to your other shady friend."

"What shady friend?" Lilly asked, her irritation at Gregor's poor skills of deduction abated by curiosity.

"That guy from the party. Park? Something like that."

"Shaw Parks? When did you talk to him—and whatever for?"

"He was coming out of my room, where he'd been told he could find Montillo. He said Montillo had told him he was going to be at my place that morning—a few hours before the police showed up."

Lilly was beginning to get the picture.

"Gregor," she spoke in a measured tone. She wanted to calm things down between them so he would listen to her. "You need to understand something. Shaw Parks is a rotten apple. If anyone's done something to harm you, Shaw's the one. You spoke about trusting me. Then do that now. Carlos wouldn't do this. But this is right up Shaw's alley."

"I suspected Parks was no good the night I met him. But Montillo fits the bill. Not only does he make his living on contraband, he's sitting in jail right now for being mixed up in those three murders."

Lilly stared at him, convinced he had lost his mind. What was he talking about? Carlos in jail? Murders?

"Yeah," Gregor nodded, answering her stunned silence. "That's where I was all night. I was arrested for interfering with the police as they followed Saint Carlos. They were following him as he led them to the man who murdered three people. Don't you keep up with the NewsVision? I had the bad luck to be hired to search for some missing kid who turns out to be this same killer."

"I don't believe any of that." Lilly looked down at her mug and picked it up but never took a sip. She set it back down.

"What do you need, a signed confession? Why?"

"Yes, I would have to hear him confess to this before I believed it! Why? Because he's a friend. I don't classify many people like that. But Carlos is a friend and I choose to believe him. Does he admit to any of this?"

She could tell Gregor was startled by her passionate response; he had pulled out his pack of cigarettes, nervously stood it on end, and then knocked it down. That was good to know; he wasn't completely unflappable. Maybe she could get through to him yet.

"Not that I know of." He softened up his tough-guy routine. "Look, if Montillo didn't do this, then what are you saying? Parks did it? I could believe that, only what is his motive?"

"I don't know. What did you think Carlos' motive was?"

"Hell, I didn't know. For all I knew, he was jealous that I was moving in on you." Gregor had apparently said this without thinking and he flushed when he realized what he'd said.

"Oh my," Lilly laughed and arched her black eyebrows. "To think I'd be worth fighting over; and getting sent to jail for me as well. How romantic."

"I didn't—look, I said I had no idea." He was truly embarrassed. Lilly could see it in the way his hands were fiddling with his cup and his eyes refused to meet hers. It was the cutest look he'd had yet. She liked this man. He could be stupid at times, but what man couldn't be? All men were stupid from time to time. That was one of their saving graces.

"Then trust me. Carlos didn't do this to you. But we'll have to be careful with Shaw. He's more dangerous than you know. What happened when you talked with him?"

Gregor told her what had happened on the stairwell. She knew right away Shaw was up to something. She hadn't been lying when she said Shaw was a dangerous man. He was more than manipulative and scheming; he could be physically dangerous as well. When Gregor describe their meeting, it was obvious Shaw had allowed Gregor to push him around. The Shaw she knew would never have let that happen unless he wanted Gregor to think he was forcing Shaw to reveal Carlos' name.

"So he wanted me to go after Montillo?" Gregor was beginning to understand.

"Well, at least he wanted you to go after someone other than him." Tired, Lilly shook her head to clear her thoughts. "So now we ask why he wanted to get rid of you."

"Is he the type to do things on his own? Does he work for anyone?"

Lilly didn't answer right away. Her thoughts had strayed back to Carlos. She was still upset to think that he was being held by the police. Would she be able to see him? She asked Gregor.

"I doubt they're gonna let you talk to him. He's being charged with aiding a murderer. Uh-oh," he held up his watch. "But I might be able to help you. I got a detective there who promised to let me talk to Montillo this morning. Maybe I can get you in with me."

Lilly hoped so. Carlos wasn't a close friend, but he was a friend. And like she'd said: she had few friends.

62

Even though Helen and Julia had been up since the early hours of the morning they were enjoying themselves as they worked in the small conference room adjoining Dr. Haupt's office. They only had another hour of work before they could take a break for lunch.

The morning had been spent collecting files from the archives located in the lower basement levels. Helen had known the paper archives were extensive, but she had never had to spend hours walking through the disorganized aisles looking for reports and evaluations. She wondered how previous generations had relied solely on paper records. It must have been a constant headache of misplaced, lost, and outdated record keeping.

Now, with the stacks of files they'd collected in the morning, Helen and Julia were trying to make sense of them. It was necessary for them to separate the files and match them up to the list as requested by Dr. Haupt. Those files that could be copied were, and the new copy was set aside as a backup to be stored in case a question arose regarding the file's original condition. If a file was already a copy, it was set aside in order that a more thorough search could be made for the original document.

Despite the tedious strain of the work, a lighthearted mood filled the room. Dr. Haupt had not come into the office yet. He had called and said he would come in after lunch. Julia had immediately declared a holiday of sorts and unbuttoned the top button of her blouse. She'd been giddy most of the morning.

"You know," Helen told her, "you seem to be feeling pretty good. I take it your call to Billy was successful?"

"Nope," Julia shook her head with exaggeration. "He wasn't even there when I called. He got in as late as he did, and he still took off early. But I don't care about him right now."

"Okay," Helen wasn't going to argue with her. If Julia wanted to deny her worry or her anger, Helen would let her.

"I'm serious, Helen. I won't spend any more time crying over him."

"I said okay."

"What do you suppose Dr. Haupt is doing this morning? You think he found a cute little accountant last night and now they're crunching numbers?"

"I don't think so," Helen tried to hold back a smile at Julia's silliness.

"I suppose he'd take her someplace nice, like a bank. And they'd count coins or something." Julia sat in a chair and spun around in it. "Or maybe he'd sneak her into the building here and they'd fool around downstairs in the archives. Of course we'd have seen paper and folders flying everywhere. You think he'd call her 'my little statistic'?"

"You are a wicked girl, Julia. Make sure everything in this folder is an original." Helen dropped a folder onto the table in front of Julia.

"Helen," Julia dropped her chin and tried to mimic the doctor's solemn tone and accent. "Here is my new friend *Firginia*. Ve have known each other for twelve hours und zix minutes. Ve are in *luff!*"

"No copies." Helen stabbed her finger into the top of the folder. This time she hadn't been tempted to smile. "You're acting a little too strange. Perhaps you should quit mocking Dr. Haupt."

"Oh? Are you starting to like him? I don't mean to upset you."

"I don't want us to upset him by not having enough done when he gets here." Helen pushed a strand of hair back out of her eyes. "There's going to be enough people mad at us. I'd rather not get on his bad side."

"Good grief, Helen. We've done more than we ever should have. He'll start expecting this much out of us every day." Julia flipped the folder open and began to examine each page.

Helen really didn't mind Julia's foolishness. It was a nice break from Helen's own good sense. That kind of freedom had never been something Helen had felt. She'd always been too aware of herself and unable to let go and enjoy anything absurd. That had always been for the free spirits like Julia. Let them make fools of themselves, Helen had always said. She had more productive things to do.

Although she never partook of Julia's brand of living, she enjoyed observing it now and then. Julia had often served as a sweet tonic that washed away the insipid taste of too much practical living. She could add energy and excitement to any kind of day.

"What do you suppose all this means?" Julia asked. She was reading the papers in the folder that lay open in front of her.

"Don't worry about that. Please check and make sure we have—"

"—the original. I know. But look at all of this. What's it all for? Most of these are reports about other paperwork. And we're collecting these reports to make a report, isn't that right?"

Helen rolled her eyes at Julia's childish questions. "This isn't about what is in the report, dear. This is about *who* is writing the report. All these reports were compiled by IHS here in the Lazaretto. Dr. Haupt, an Earth representative, will be writing up his own reports. It's a polite way of telling us they expect our reports to be full of lies."

"Well that's pretty awful."

"No," Helen said, "it's how things work. When someone at the top of an organization wants to know what's going on, he has to rely on information that has worked its way up through a system that is run by people who are trying to protect their territory. Most of the time, the top people like the watered-down truth they receive. They know they're being lied to, but those lies are padding their own pockets, so they accept them.

"It's only when someone at the top decides they want to know the truth that they run into a problem. The system that they endorse is no longer an asset. They have to find a way around it. And that's what Dr. Haupt is here to do. To find out what is really going on."

"And he told you all of this?" Julia asked.

"No, but I can figure it out. That's why we're collecting both the raw data he needs to make his report, and the reports that have already been filed so he can recognize what lies have been told. Then he can go back to Earth and not only report accurate data but he can explain why the data previously submitted does not match what he has found."

"Now you lost me." Julia waved her hands in surrender. "I admit I really didn't have to hear all that. I'll stop asking questions and do what I'm told. I really don't care about this. I only want to make a little money so I can enjoy the weekends. I don't need to get involved."

Helen wasn't surprised. She envied Julia. She wished she could toss her hands in the air and say *I don't care*. How much simpler life would be. She hoped Julia would get her wish.

She should have been scolding Julia for her selfish ideas but Helen could not find it within herself to do so. Some people were made to worry and fret over the details of this world. Helen knew this firsthand. But not Julia. She'd been made for something else; something less serious though no less important. Julia had been made to enjoy life. Helen did not begrudge her friend this gift; to the contrary, she fed off it. It was a way for Helen to enjoy life as well; through Julia's insatiable life.

"Let's go get some lunch," Julia pushed the folder away from her and nearly leapt from her chair.

"It's early. Maybe in ten minutes or so."

"Who cares if we go early? The boss is gone, remember? Let's get out of this stuffy room."

Helen put down a report and ran a hand through her hair. Why not? Here was a chance for Helen to partake of Julia's freedom.

"Okay, dear. Let's go to lunch."

Julia led the way. Helen could hardly keep up with her eager friend.

63

Fenelli had been back at Homicide for over an hour before MacNally showed up. During that time, he and Jeri had waited while a VTech worked with the recorded image from the elevator. They were still waiting for an ID match when MacNally walked into the office.

"Where've you been?" Fenelli asked.

"Getting some sleep." MacNally stared at Jeri for an extended time before asking: "Who's this?"

"Jeri Drounett. Jeri, this is my partner, Ed MacNally."

"Come see." MacNally nodded towards his desk and walked away.

"I'll be back in a few minutes, Jeri." Fenelli stood up and put his hand on her shoulder. "Are you okay?"

"Yeah, don't worry about me."

She was a good liar. Ever since they had seen the image of the man in the elevator, she'd obviously been castigating herself over her involvement with him. If Fenelli had known her better he would have tried to console her. But he not only didn't know her, he didn't know what he could have said to make her feel any better. She was going to have to work this out on her own.

"What's her story?" MacNally asked.

"It's something I'm working on. I'd rather not say right now." Fenelli had been thinking about what he would tell MacNally. He had decided that he would follow up on the reluctant witness on his own. Until he knew what was going on he didn't want to involve MacNally.

"That's fine. I've got plenty to deal with here." MacNally allowed a rare smile. "Did anyone tell you yet? About last night?"

"I hadn't read the reports from the trail team yet. Did you guys get something?"

"Oh, we got something. I was right. Romeo went right to our guy. He met him not long after I joined the trail team."

"Our guy? We got him?" Fenelli asked.

"It's not that easy. Things went screwy. Someone else was watching Romeo and he scared off the suspect. But we know who he is now."

Fenelli tried to keep up with MacNally's narrative of the previous night. Most of it made sense until MacNally told him that the interloper Lepov had been released.

"You let this Private Investigator go free?"

"Yeah," MacNally answered, as if he thought it was a bad idea too. "That's a funny thing. I was ordered to let him go. And from what we could tell, Jenkins got the order from Claude Reno."

"What?"

"This Investigator, Gregor Lepov, said Reno was falling all over him when he found out Lepov was here to find Ethan Layne."

"That's the blond guy, right? The suspect?"

"Uh-huh." MacNally started typing on his deskscreen while still talking to Fenelli. "I guess Reno wants to make sure this Lepov finds Layne. Maybe Layne is his bastard son or something."

"So what are you going to do now?" Fenelli asked.

"I've had Romeo in a cell all night. I came in late because I wanted him to stew. I want him mad when I go in there. And when he tells me he's mad, I'm gonna jump down his throat. And then he's gonna be scared. But other than that, I didn't really have any plans."

Fenelli turned at the sound of someone calling his name. An officer held up a phone and waved it at him.

"I gotta take a call. Good luck with Romeo."

"You have fun with whats-her-name." MacNally pointed at Fenelli. "And you're gonna tell me what's going on with her at some point, right?"

"Eventually."

Fenelli hoped he would tell MacNally about it. If not, that would mean he'd been wasting his time since he found that note on his car.

He took the phone from the officer.

"Detective Fenelli." He was caught off guard when he recognized the voice. "Maria? Are you okay?"

"I'm perfectly fine, Arturo. In fact, I feel great. Have you eaten yet?"

"No. I hadn't even thought about it." He looked at a clock and saw lunch was way overdue.

"Are you too busy to eat with your sister today?" Maria always believed she was being an inconvenience.

"Well I do have a few things going on," he looked up and saw Jeri still sitting at his desk. Should he send her home? If he did, he'd have time to grab a bite with Maria. But not much. "If you don't mind a short lunch I'd love to join you."

"No, I don't want to be a problem. If you're busy —"

"How about tomorrow? Maybe an early dinner before you go to the clinic. Would that be okay?"

"Sure, I can wait." Maria sounded disappointed. Had she needed to talk about something important? "I will look forward to it."

"I'll call you tomorrow afternoon. Is that alright?"

"Yes, Arturo."

He'd pressed the switch to end the call when he remembered Maria's call the day before. Was she still in trouble? Was that why she wanted to see him? Fenelli couldn't decide if he should call her back. She had sounded upset, but that was natural for her. He had also learned long ago that he was always seeing trouble for his little sister where there was none. She'd often scolded him for fussing needlessly.

He decided he'd take her call at face value. If she'd been in trouble she would have said something.

"That was my kid sister," he told Jeri. Maria hadn't been a kid for many years but Fenelli still thought of her as one. "You'd like her. Everybody likes her."

"There is still no word from the man about the image?" asked Jeri.

"Let's find out." Fenelli pushed some paperwork out of the way and keyed in a request on his deskscreen. The screen flashed a set of numbers before displaying a report. "Well thanks a lot, guy. Looks like he had a match on that ID a while ago. He could have let us know."

Jeri stood up and leaned in to see what was on the screen.

"I don't know this guy. Never heard of him. But if this is right, I can find him. Does this look like your boyfriend?" Fenelli regretted using that label after it was too late. He could see she didn't like it.

"That's him. But I never heard him use that name."

"There's not much information on him. Most people's files are much more complete than this. But if that's him, I'll find out what I can from him. You're absolutely sure?"

"Yes." Jeri answered without the slightest hesitation.

"Well, that's all I need from you for now. I'll take you home and you can get some rest. Or would you rather go back to work?"

"No, I'll be fine. You don't need to drive me home. I'll walk. There's always the SubTransit if I need to take it."

Her tone was flat, as if she were half-asleep. Should he insist on taking her home? Should he find a female officer to escort her?

In the end, he let her make her own decisions. He followed her out of the precinct and onto the street. She was still worrying over her mistakes, that much was easy to see. But she seemed to have found a level of resignation that was either wonderfully therapeutic or dangerously self-destructive. Fenelli wished he could help.

Watching her walk away, he understood that he couldn't always help despite his best intentions. The best thing he could do for this woman was find the man who'd used her. Maybe then she could move on and never have to look back and remember any of this.

Fenelli went back inside to find MacNally. He found him in the hallway outside the elevator talking with a man and a woman. The man was big, with broad shoulders and short, salt and pepper hair. The woman was slender; with dark skin and white hair held together in a ponytail from high upon the crown of her head.

"I'm heading down to interrogate Romeo." MacNally stopped to talk with Fenelli as people pushed past them in the crowded hall. "This is Gregor Lepov, the Private Investigator I told you about."

Fenelli nodded at Lepov and turned to nod to the woman.

"This is Lilly Stewart." Lepov introduced her.

"Can you give us a minute?" Fenelli asked them. He stepped away and MacNally followed him.

"What do they want?" Fenelli asked.

"I'm gonna let Lepov talk to Montillo after I do. The woman's just going to observe from the other room. I think she's a friend of Montillo's. Anyway, I told Lepov last night I'd let him ask Montillo a few questions. I don't see the harm in it. Where's that little thing you had with you?"

"Jeri." Fenelli supplied her name for MacNally so he wouldn't have to call her *that little thing*. "She left. I have something I need to follow up. There's someone I need to question. It might be something, it might not. Until I talk to him, I won't know."

"You don't want to join me while I interrogate Montillo?"

"No, let me take care of this." Fenelli looked down the hall at Lepov and the woman. "I can't help but wonder..."

"About Lepov?"

"Yeah. What's Reno's interest in him? You know as well as I do that Claude Reno doesn't get his hands dirty for anything. What could get him out of his top floor office? Have you learned anything about the kid Lepov is looking for?"

"Horsham and Amony have been researching him since this morning. Maybe when you get back we can see what they've found." MacNally scratched at his chin.

Even though it was only a few minutes after noon, Fenelli could hear the scratch of MacNally's stubble on his hands. The man must have to shave three times a day, he thought.

"I'll come back as soon as I can," Fenelli promised.

64

Gregor Lepov opened the door to the interrogation room annex and held it open for Lilly. They both sat in chairs on the same side of a table. The room was small, with wall screens on two of the four walls. Seated at the table they could see two images of the same interrogation room displayed on the wall in front of them. The same two images were also on deskscreens on the surface of the table.

The interrogation room was empty.

MacNally came in a few moments later and stood across the table from them, crossing his arms like an angry parent.

"Let me remind you," he addressed Lepov, "that you wouldn't be in here without Reno's directive to assist you. I take that to mean within reason. So don't push your luck. I'll allow you to watch me question him. You don't come in until I say. When you do, you ask him what you need to know and if he cooperates, fine, if not you leave. Is that clear?"

"You don't have to bully me, Lieutenant. I'll be a good boy."

"Okay." MacNally turned his attention to Lilly. "I don't know what you're doing here. But you stay in this room. No arguments. I don't have any orders concerning you and I could kick you out of here if I wanted. You're here at my discretion."

Lilly nodded without comment. Lepov was glad to see she did

not rise to meet MacNally's challenge. Lepov had expected nothing less. As he was learning, Lilly was no stranger to tight situations.

Lepov and Lilly were willing to allow MacNally to say anything he liked. He was the man in charge and they needed his permission to get to Montillo. They weren't going to make him angry by responding to his belligerence with anything but grace.

On the screen behind MacNally, Montillo entered the interrogation room. MacNally saw it on the deskscreen and turned around to watch the larger visual. None of them said anything as they watched Montillo take a seat at the table. The image to the left showed him from behind. The image on the right gave them a good look at his face.

Montillo looked like he hadn't slept all night. He was clean-shaven, but there were bags under his eyes. He was wearing a grey shirt buttoned all the way to his neck. The collar was too tight and a bit of skin hung over the stiff collar despite the fact Montillo was thin.

A uniformed officer unlocked Montillo's restraints and mumbled a strong warning that he stay in his chair. As soon as the officer walked out of the room and closed the door Montillo reached up and undid his top button. At the same time he stood up and walked around the perimeter of the room. His hands were fidgety, first in his pockets, then rubbing together, and then scratching at his face and scalp.

Lepov knew what MacNally was trying to do. He had done it himself as a cop. Make the man sweat before you talked to him. Make him wonder what is going on. Make him mad.

"Well, I suppose I'll go see what Romeo knows. You're a friend of his?" He directed his question to Lilly.

"We know each other as well as business partners might. We don't do business together but we end up in the same circles." Lilly looked up at MacNally with a guarded smile.

"So is he nervous? Agitated?" They all looked back at Montillo.

"No."

Even Lepov stared at her with an odd expression when she spoke. Lepov could see MacNally didn't believe her any more than he did.

"He's playing a role for you. He wants you to get on with it. Don't think you're the first cop to do this to him."

"Well, fine." MacNally yanked open the door. "I'll get on with it."

They watched MacNally enter the interrogation room. Montillo stopped moving when he saw the detective.

"Sit down." MacNally jerked a chair back from the table. The metal legs cracked hard against the bare floor.

"He doesn't get a lawyer?" Lepov asked Lilly. He watched Montillo sit in the chair.

"This isn't Bukovina, Gregor." She spoke in a near whisper as if she were afraid she'd be overheard by the two men in the other room. "Colony Law might have been abolished on your planet, but it's alive and well here in the Laz. And no one's been able to change it."

MacNally half-sat, half-leaned on the edge of the table and looked down at Montillo, simmering a few degrees below angry.

"I want to get this over with as soon as possible," the big detective said, "so don't play stupid. You were seen with a prime murder suspect last night. I want to know how you contact him. Anything less than that gets you accessory to three murders."

"Carlos is smarter than that," Lilly whispered.

"But does he have to be?" asked Lepov. "I mean, when it comes down to it, why fuss over giving up the whereabouts of a murderer? I don't know the man, but I can't imagine he wants to spar with the police over three murders."

Montillo hadn't responded yet to MacNally's demand and MacNally grew impatient.

"Where is Ethan Layne?" MacNally's eyes locked with Montillo's.

"Who is Ethan Layne?" Montillo didn't look away.

"So much for civility." Lepov shifted in his chair and rubbed at his knee. Thank God it wasn't hurting since he'd awakened.

Lilly nodded. Montillo wasn't going to give in without a fight. But it also looked like he wasn't going to give MacNally a reason to come down hard on him. He was sly enough to appear dumb, but not uncooperative.

"Why's he doing this?" Lepov asked.

"Would you give MacNally what he wanted?" Lilly asked.

"If you're asking if I'd roll over on a friend that I thought was innocent to save my own skin I'd say no. But if you're asking whether or not I'd give up the name of a client who was a killer three times over I'd say yes. If my skin were part of the bargain I'd say yes twice as fast."

She didn't reply to that. He had expected her to disapprove of him for that kind of talk. It was apparent she was less on the side of the law on a day-to-day basis than he was. But she was hard to read. Her eyes stared at him but it seemed as if she did not see him. Whatever was going through her mind had taken her light-years away.

As the interrogation dragged on, Lepov was beginning to wonder if she'd ever come back. She hadn't said another word. She merely watched Montillo fend off MacNally's questions with feigned ignorance and stubborn resolve. He was good. He still hadn't given MacNally the opening he needed to raise his threat level.

And that was driving MacNally mad. Lepov could see it. MacNally stopped asking questions and stood over Montillo. His size was intimidating but Montillo wasn't fazed by it. MacNally wasn't looking at Montillo anymore. He was looking into the recorder. After a few moments, MacNally turned his back on Montillo and left the room.

"He's coming to get you." Lilly finally spoke. "He needs you to unbalance Carlos."

"Does that bother you?" Lepov asked.

"No," Lilly shook her head. "I've seen enough to know Carlos isn't completely clean in this. I still don't think he set you up. But he does know something about this kid you're looking for."

When MacNally opened the door, he didn't say anything. He jerked his head at Lepov in a gesture that plainly said *it's your turn.*

It occurred to Lepov as they walked to the interrogation room that he was the wrong person to question Montillo. Lilly should have been asking the questions. Not only would Montillo be more open with her, but she knew the right questions to ask. There was no way, of course, that MacNally would go for it. He had a hunch that MacNally was only allowing him to question Montillo because the interrogation had stalled. If he had gotten what he wanted, MacNally might not have allowed Lepov in the room.

So be it. He would take what he could get.

Montillo seemed genuinely confused when he saw Lepov enter.

"What is he here for?" Montillo asked MacNally.

MacNally didn't speak. He stepped over to a corner of the room and stood as still as the statue of Justice. Only his eyes weren't blindfolded; they were locked on Montillo.

"I'm only here to talk, Montillo. You don't mind, do you?"

"I told Lilly you were a cop."

"Is that why you tried to get rid of me? You thought I was a cop looking for trouble?"

Montillo didn't answer but he was clearly intrigued by the question.

"You look curious, Carlos." Lepov spoke the man's name with disdain. "So I'm gonna fill you in on what we know. That way, when we come to the blank spots, you can fill 'em in for us. Oh, and don't hesitate to stop me if you start to get lost.

"The first thing you need to know is that I'm not under arrest for the fake PDT's. I don't know how much value there was in that stash, but you wasted it all. Not only that, but there's a cop here who was able to trace the PDT's to you. By the way, that's kind of vain leaving your signature all over them like that."

Montillo shifted his gaze from Lepov to MacNally and looked as if he might speak. Lepov paused to let him talk but Montillo said nothing.

"These guys also know you supplied Ethan Layne with a false PDT." Lepov held up his hand to silence MacNally. "Hold on, Lieutenant. It's not gonna hurt anything for Mr. Montillo here to know more than you've been telling him."

MacNally thought about what Lepov was trying to do. He reluctantly stepped back into his corner and resumed his silent watch.

"What I don't know is how you learned I was searching for Ethan Layne. I hadn't told anyone that yet."

"I don't know what this guy is talking about." Montillo said to MacNally. "I'll ask you again, why is he here? Is he a cop? Do I have to answer his questions?"

Lepov approached MacNally and leaned in close, lowering his voice.

"Show him what you've got. The PDT's, the ID Layne was using. I really don't think Montillo is going to go down for murder if he sees how strongly you've linked him to this thing."

"It's too early to do that. I want to give him time."

"Take all the time you want, but he's not gonna give us anything. Lilly's right. Montillo's too smart to give up anything. I won't even bother asking more questions unless you can get some leverage on him."

"Okay." Once MacNally agreed with Lepov he almost looked as if he liked the idea. Lepov wasn't going to wait to see if he'd change his mind.

65

"Helen, please close the door." Dr. Haupt sat behind his desk. He was dressed in the same black suit and grey tie he had worn since he had arrived. His short-cropped hair remained perfectly combed. His white skin remained tight against his cheekbones. His cold, blue eyes were surrounded by porcelain whites without a hint of red.

So much for Julia's theory. Helen's thoughts strayed for a moment. She had been right. The doctor had not experienced a wild night.

"The revised lab protocols; you still cannot access them without elevated authorization, correct?"

"That is correct."

"What I am about to give you will remain between us. You are not to speak of this to Miss Maiden."

Helen nodded. Somewhere in the back of her mind she realized she had never told him Julia's last name. But, of course, he would have seen it in her personnel file. And there was no question that Dr. Haupt would have read over her file. She was beginning to expect that. Dr. Haupt pulled a data tag from his coat pocket and held it out to her.

"This is a key tag. You are to use it to access whatever you need to verify the revised lab protocols and any further data that you will need in the course of our investigation. No one here at IHS will know of this authorization or this level of access."

Helen took the key tag and held it in her palm. It was slightly smaller than a normal data tag but it was much heavier; as if it were weighed down by the authority it concealed.

"I want to see everything you do on this. And no one else sees it."

"Yes, Dr. Haupt." Helen knew a simple nod would not have satisfied him. He had watched her answer with great care. There was an intensity to his manner that went beyond his usual gravity.

"Do you know how to use it?"

She did. She had never used a key tag before but she understood how it worked. When she powered up her desk screen, she would have to hold the key tag in her right hand, pressing her thumb and index finger against it. If her fingerprints matched those on the key tag's file, the proximity readers would pick up a signal verifying the authorized access.

"I believe it will only work if my fingerprints are on the file."

"That has been taken care of."

"I'll get right on those protocols." He had already encrypted the key tag with her fingerprint data? How had he done that? She couldn't even remember if she'd been fingerprinted when she hired on at IHS. Again, Dr. Haupt had been thorough; had in fact been busy that morning. How he had managed to get the necessary authorizations for the key tag made her wonder. He had impressive resources.

When Julia returned, Helen put her back to work in the conference room. She'd been bursting with curiosity about Helen's meeting with Dr. Haupt but Helen would not tell her anything. Julia wore a hurt look and complained about being left out. Helen didn't worry. Julia loved a mystery. Spending the rest of the day wondering what was going on was the best kind of therapy for Julia.

Helen tried the key tag as soon as Julia left the room. The deskscreen quickly noted the presence of the tag, listing it on the queue directory, and waited for the fingerprint match to initiate the authorization.

Once she pressed the key tag between her fingers, Helen had expected some kind of official seal to fill her screen along with whistles and bells. But to her surprise, the screen cleared, with only a small icon blinking in the bottom right hand corner. She couldn't make out what the symbol was and she wondered if something had gone wrong. Had the match been negative? Was she about to get a visit from IHS Security?

She watched the blinking symbol long enough to guess that no one was going to come running into the room to arrest her. So what did the symbol mean? Helen decided to give the strange little figure a try. She leaned forward and lightly touched it with the tip of her index finger.

Again, the screen cleared. The words *master access* flashed twice then disappeared.

"Maybe I should have asked him to explain this." Helen spoke aloud as a tonic for her nerves. There was no reason to stare at it any longer. Either the key tag had worked or it hadn't. There was only one way to find out. It was designed to provide her access to the lab protocols. So that's what she would do.

She keyed in the request. Without hesitation her screen displayed the file directory for Laboratory Protocols/SOP/EOP. Helen was tempted to stare in awe at the success of the key tag. But she was aware that Dr. Haupt was waiting for her. There was no reason to be impressed. He had told her it would give her the necessary access. She should never have doubted that it would.

A subdirectory labeled *Revision/Update* led her to the file of which the lab tech had spoken. It was all there. She tabbed the digital document for retrieval then ordered a printout of it. A shadowbox appeared on her screen asking if she wanted to lock down the document.

Helen had never seen such a request. She stared at the shadowbox for a few moments trying to understand what it signified. It must be the access level, she thought. That had to be it. She was seeing master administrator options that she had never been privy to in the past.

Lock down the document. Helen understood the procedure but did not know if she should do it. If she locked it down, no one would be able to alter it or delete it without her approval. Obviously she did not have that kind of authority. But the key tag had given her the option. And it would preserve the document in case Dr. Haupt decided to use it.

She decided she would lock it down. If Dr. Haupt disagreed with her decision she could always come back later and unlock it.

The revised protocol had been authored by Dr. Phillip Stride two weeks before Jack Ford's body came into the lab. Stride was a department head from Research. Helen could see that Stride had not only named the exact symptoms that Ford exhibited, but he had also detailed that these bodies be treated as a *non-contagion/pathogen*. The procedure called for informing Dr. Stride personally if any body was found with symptoms that were remarkably identical to Jack Ford's. One last detail was added: anybody that met the criteria was to be treated with Shipper's Formula.

As a follow up on the protocol, Helen secured all available data on both Dr. Stride and the Shipper's Formula. These she edited, trying to determine what data was significant enough to add to Dr. Haupt's report. By the time she had finished with it, she had archived it on a personal storage data tag as well as on a limited access module on her desk system. As an added precaution, she pulled the system monitor data of all activity and folded it into the index of the report. She wanted to make sure no one could accuse her of abusing her Master Access key tag.

Finished, she printed the report before scrubbing her system. Now, aside from the hard copy, the only trace of it was on her storage data tag and on the limited access module. Her data tag stayed with her at all times, and the module was accessible only with a twelve digit alphanumeric code with a rotating daily cipher. It was an old school password routine that was surprisingly effective against the majority of the modern workforce.

As she handed Dr. Haupt the report, she explained her security measures to him. She hoped he would tell her they had been unnecessary. His silence worried her.

"Is there anything else, Doctor?"

"Please, sit down. I want to go over this with you." Dr. Haupt pointed at a chair and Helen sat immediately. "We will start from the top and work through it. I believe we will discover something important."

Helen thought she saw a hint of eagerness in the doctor's eyes. Up until that point, he had shown a basic devotion to duty, as if he had no interest in the task set before him. But now, he almost looked excited.

66

Fenelli drove through the west end of the city, past deserted walkways and storefronts. By now, Delta Quadrant was closed. Everyone who wanted to be in had better be in. The cost-prohibitive grace period was only an option for the extremely wealthy and stupidly desperate. For the money, the two days that could be saved were never worth it.

Despite the wind and cold, the sky was white; the sun wasn't visible, but there was more light than usual. The bright streets looked that much emptier. Fenelli was not surprised at the amount of trash that blew along the wet edges of the street. On its best days the West End was never clean. Adding a quadrant closing day to the mix compounded the mess. And Fenelli knew no one would demand that the mess be cleaned up. No one cared what happened in the West End.

The West End had once been the only residential district in the Lazaretto. Its twelve square blocks of apartment buildings had been the main housing for IHS at the opening of the Lazaretto. Many of its first occupants had been the builders of the Shipping Port. Once this automated phase had been finished, the workers had cleared out of the Lazaretto for construction work on the fast growing planets of Dnepr and Phasis. As the size of Center City grew, many West End residents moved out to the residential zones south of Terran Park.

By now, most of the West End was empty, save for a few hundred holdouts still in their homes. At street level the businesses that had once been grocers, clothing stores, newsstands, small restaurants, and coffee shops had been replaced by liquor stores, strip clubs, pleasure brokers, and fortunetellers. Most of them thrived on the business of traveling Lazars who had not yet been locked down in quarantine. With the closing of Delta, the sullied world of the West End had been virtually shut down.

But Fenelli wasn't slipping through these grimy streets for sensuous pursuits. For one thing, he'd seen too much of the seedy side of it to ever want to partake of it. For the moment, he was there because the man that he had seen in the elevator image was somewhere in the West End. At least the man's personal data tag had last given off a signal in that vicinity.

The signal had not been strong enough for an exact location. Fenelli was now driving down each street, hoping his tag reader would pick up the signal. It should be able to get a better fix than the reader back at the station. He was following the grid pattern of the streets, making a full coverage sweep.

Fenelli was determined to find his man. He had not taken the bait that was in the data tag; if he had he would have been locked down in Delta Quadrant now. Had that been the goal? Was this guy trying to hamper their investigation? If so, Fenelli knew he'd have to be careful when he approached him. As that thought entered his mind, he reached inside his coat with his left hand and felt the butt of his police issue revolver in its shoulder holster. Maybe he should have told MacNally where he was going.

It made little difference, he decided. No one was on the street. He had a funny feeling he was never going to find this man. Not in the West End. He had run down all but two of the streets without finding any hint of a signal. This guy was long gone. That last faint reading had been two hours ago. That was more than plenty of time for him to engage in whatever squalor he'd been after.

As a mere exercise in thoroughness, he drove the full length of the last two streets to confirm what he already knew. The PDT signal, and the man who it belonged to, was long gone.

Fenelli parked the car beside a strip club with a malfunctioning sign lit in the shape of a licentious vampire. Fenelli thought he could see someone inside the heavy looking door watching him through a dark window in the center of it. It was hard to tell.

He would call MacNally and see how Romeo's interrogation had gone. Then he would tell MacNally what was going on. He was going to need help. He had wasted too much time on this deep space chase.

Before he could complete his call to MacNally, the tag reader chirped at him. A small icon blinked in the left column with an ID tag number. Fenelli looked up in shock. The signal was strong. Too strong. The man he'd been looking for had to be right on top of him. But where was he?

Grabbing the reader, Fenelli shoved open his door and stepped out into the street. No matter how much light forced its way through the cloud cover, the air was still cold. Fenelli pulled his coat tight and cinched it with a belt, pulling the collar up to keep the wind off him as he watched the reader's display.

The signal was moving and growing weak. Fenelli spun and looked back down the street. He turned in every direction. Was he tracking a ghost? The only movement on the street was a white transport truck that stopped in front of a liquor store. The driver jumped down from the cab and slid open a cargo door revealing cases of cheap alcohol.

Fenelli suspected the reader had malfunctioned then he spotted a handrail a few feet from where the driver was unloading his order. Of course! A SubTransit station was directly below him. Sprinting across the empty street, Fenelli ran down the station steps three at a time.

The station was empty now. He could hear a SubTransit car receding down a tunnel. The signal was stronger below ground. If he took the next car, he might be able to keep the signal within range. It depended on how soon the next car arrived. It was either wait for it, or head back to the street and try to track the SubTransit from above.

Judging by the stronger reading below ground, he had a better chance of keeping up if he remained below.

Another car shushed into the station earlier than he had expected. The data tag signal was still strong as his car gave chase.

67

Georges watched Maria prepare a late lunch for him in their small kitchen. It was not used for serious cooking. Maria had little experience in that area. But she enjoyed making sandwiches for Georges. He was easy to please: there was little he would not eat.

"Do you wish I were a better cook?" she asked.

"You couldn't make a better sandwich, Maria."

Maria smiled at him. "You're sweet," she said, placing a plate in front of him. His sandwich was bursting with lettuce and tomatoes and onions.

She did not mind that Georges dodged her question. She had not expected him to actually answer.

"You went out this morning," he said.

"Yes. A walk in the park." She waited, hoping he would not ask about William.

"I think I know what is going on." Georges had not picked up his sandwich. He was paying too much attention to Maria. "Maybe we should talk about it."

Maria nodded, sure that Georges knew about William.

"I understand why you're so restless. You have taken on a heavy burden. And it is not getting any lighter. For some time I have wanted to interfere. To step in and protect you from getting too involved. But I have tried to allow you to handle this on your own."

Maria was relieved when she understood where Georges was headed. He wasn't thinking of the park or William at all. She raised her head, not so afraid of what he might say.

"But as I knew you would, you have allowed your compassion for Kjarsta to overwhelm you. You are getting no sleep. You worry over him, not only at the clinic, but here as well. Trust me, I can see it. You are distracted; many times you don't even hear me when I speak to you."

"Don't ask me to stop." She raised her head even more, daring to look him in the eye. The request was not an attempt to be dramatic. She would obey him if he demanded she stop watching over Kjarsta, but it would wound her. He had to know that. Could she dare tell him that?

Georges was silent. There was still kindness in his eyes. He wasn't angry with her. She was glad to see that.

"I'm sorry I've been inattentive with you," she began to say. The last thing she wanted was to cause a problem between them. "I will try to—"

"Maria," he interrupted, "listen to me. I said I understand. When I said I wanted to interfere I did not mean I would ask you to stop. I know how that would upset you. You would be even more distracted, is that not true?" Maria nodded. "Of course you would. But I cannot allow you to carry this burden alone. Not anymore. And that is why I feel compelled to see what I can do for your friend. I will look at his files and see if there is anything that can be done. I won't promise anything. You understand?"

"Yes, I do. But Georges, you have so little time. Your responsibilities are already so great."

"I will make the time. If I am not mistaken, Kjarsta is afflicted with an unknown pathogen, correct?"

Maria nodded. Kjarsta had never known what it was that was eating away at him. The IHS had merely identified the pathogen as terminal, possibly contagious, and incurable. It was not only a fatal diagnosis, but a sad and lonely one as well. Patients like Kjarsta were given little information on why they were being left to die and the IHS would make no effort to find a cure. Singular Event Pathogens like Kjarsta's—and even ones that occurred two or three times—were simply ignored. A threat must manifest itself many times over before time and money would be spent to combat it. It was so much easier to simply quarantine rare threats like his and hope it died out with the patient.

"Give me time and I will see what can be done." Georges reached out and put his hand on Maria's.

"Thank you, Georges," she walked behind his chair and put her arms around him. Leaning her head against his, she could feel the scratch of his Van Dyke as he turned to look back at her.

"I make no promises. There may be no reason to thank me."

"I have every reason to thank you. You are a good man. An uncommonly good man." She kissed his cheek.

"Well, we will see. We will have to wait and see."

68

Lepov was disappointed, but not terribly surprised. He stared at Montillo and knew that the Spaniard was doing the only smart thing he could do. But all things being equal, he still didn't like it.

Montillo had listened to the thread of evidence that linked him to Ethan Layne and the three murder victims. It didn't matter that there was a certain amount of speculation involved. As Lilly had pointed out, this wasn't Bukovina, and Lepov was learning how much it wasn't Bukovina. Colony law, once a temporary form of law for the outer planets, was light years away from Earth law. And Montillo knew it; was well aware of how damaging the tenuous thread of evidence against him could be.

But he was also keenly aware of the value of his information. It required little logic to conclude that MacNally had no way of finding Layne without Montillo. And so Montillo wanted to deal.

He wanted the PDT evidence against him expunged, as well as a guarantee that there would be no charges brought against him regardless of what happened with Ethan Layne. Lepov half expected him to ask that his bag of fake PDT's be returned.

But Montillo had been smart enough not to push his luck. Judging by MacNally's agitated state as he left the interrogation room, Montillo had pushed hard enough.

"Well?" Lepov followed MacNally back into the annex where Lilly was waiting for them. "I guess you'll get what you want."

"You think so? I'm not so sure." MacNally chewed on his lower lip. Lepov was willing to bet there was a lot more activity than normal going on in MacNally's head. MacNally turned towards Lilly. "I suppose you'll tell me I should trust him."

"I would. Can you give him what he wants?"

"I think he can get what he's asking for, but it wouldn't come from me. I'd have to talk to my captain. I won't do that strictly on what he's told me so far. I want to know what he's gonna give me."

"He said he'd tell you how to contact Layne." Lepov sat down and rubbed his knee from habit. Even on the days it didn't hurt it felt good to give it some attention.

"But you scared Layne off," MacNally reminded him. "What are the chances that Layne will show up again? Pretty damn low by my count."

"So you have to trust that Montillo can draw him back out." Lepov was beginning to wish he hadn't come in to see Montillo. It was clear he wasn't going to learn anything about why Montillo had set him up.   And now he was being sucked into MacNally's investigation.

His best bet was to get back to Bukovina. That's what he wanted to do until he caught sight of or thought about Lilly. Then he wasn't so eager to jump a flight back to the old home planet. He couldn't remember the last time a woman made him change his plans.

"Montillo's position is not as strong as he thinks." MacNally was still looking for a reason to not make a deal with Montillo. "I do want to get this guy before he kills again, though. And there's no indication he's done beating the life out of people."

"So tell your captain to take the deal." Lepov had no love for

Montillo, but if Layne really was a murderer, he couldn't see what the fuss was all about. Montillo's little illegal enterprise was hardly worth worrying over.

"Soon, but not yet. I want to talk to him again. You wanna come?"

"I'm not sure." Lepov eyed Lilly as if she'd know what he wanted.

"I need to go. I have an appointment," Lilly said.

"Would you like me to tag along?"

"No, that's okay. This is business."

"One of those art collectors you were telling me about?"

"Yes," Lilly had walked to the door and stood waiting for MacNally to move out of her way. "I don't mean to run out on you like this."

"It won't bother me," MacNally said, stepping out into the hall. Neither Lilly nor Lepov laughed at the big detective's joke. "Stay or go, Lepov. I don't care either way."

Lepov wished MacNally would shut up. Lilly was about to leave and he couldn't think of the right thing to say. He wanted to make sure he would find her again but didn't want to ask her where she was staying. It would remind her too much of how little they knew each other. He followed her into the hall.

"I'll be at—"

"I'll find you." She cut him off. "I'm good at that, remember?"

"Lepov!" MacNally shouted from the other end of the hall.

"Don't let him mistreat Carlos." There was sadness in her eyes. "Please, for my sake."

"Okay," he promised. It was a meaningless promise—Lepov had no control over MacNally—and she had to know that. But at least she would know he wanted to do something for her. If it made an impression on her he couldn't tell. She had already gone.

By the time Lepov made it down the hall to the interrogation room MacNally was already inside. Lepov had to knock twice before he was allowed to enter.

"...so I want to know." MacNally didn't allow Lepov's entrance to break his rhythm. "And don't think I'm stupid. I want to know why you think you can still contact Layne. He's gotta be spooked by what happened last night. There's no reason to believe he'd let you contact him. For all he knows, you might have been the one to set him up."

"I already told you I could contact him. How or why is none of your business. Not until you agree, in writing, to my conditions."

Lepov could see MacNally's frustration but he couldn't understand it. If anyone had a reason to hold a grudge against

Montillo it was Lepov, not MacNally. Why didn't the cop want to give Montillo a deal?

"You seem to think we won't find Layne without your help. But you're overestimating your value," MacNally said.

"I know what you're thinking and you're wrong." Montillo nearly made the poor decision to laugh. That would have guaranteed MacNally's non-cooperation.

"No I'm not. We know what PDT you gave this guy. We'll track him down."

"Like I said, you're wrong. And here's where I'll give you some free information—no strings attached. You guys were lucky when you caught that PDT signal twice. That PDT is designed to change ID information randomly. The ID numbers that came up never should have appeared on the same night. The odds that would happen are ridiculous. It'll never happen again. I'll bet that number hasn't popped up anywhere on the system since that night, am I right?"

Lepov waited for MacNally's answer. He was convinced that Montillo was telling the truth. MacNally's silence confirmed Montillo was right; Layne's new PDT hadn't hit the system again.

"So what do we look for?" MacNally couldn't help asking. Montillo smiled.

"You are stupid. Like I said, make the deal and I'll tell you—"

Despite MacNally's size, he took the three steps needed to reach Montillo before Lepov could interfere. The big detective jerked Montillo out of his chair and threw him on the table. The lightweight Spaniard bounced once and tumbled backwards to the floor. The back of his head striking the edge of a metal chair.

Lepov grabbed MacNally from behind and yanked him off balance. Lepov was smaller than MacNally, though not by much. When MacNally regained his balance, Lepov was glad he was big enough to absorb the impact of MacNally's swinging arm. Only he wasn't big enough to absorb it and stay on his feet. Lepov dropped to one knee. It was only after the knee crashed into the tiled floor that he realized he was dropping to the wrong knee.

"Dammit!" Lepov grunted as his knee surged with high voltage pain.

"Don't ever do that again!" MacNally tried to catch his breath. He'd moved fast for a big man but the brief exertion had winded him. "Get out of this room right now."

"I wish I could, but I made a promise to a lady." Lepov was painfully aware of three things. The first was the flash of red smeared on the floor and chair seat that told him Montillo was bleeding heavily. The second was the pain in his knee when he tried to straighten his leg. And the third thing he was aware of was how deep in trouble he'd just become. His old man use to say *in for a penny in for a pound*. And no matter that he never really knew what the origin of the phrase was, he could remember it popping up at times like this.

"You dumb Mick! Go tell your captain to make the deal. What the hell is your problem?"

"If you'd seen that kid in the stairwell you'd know. I'm not playing games. I want to find this killer."

"Then tell your boss not to screw around." Lepov winced and groaned as he stood. The knee was killing him. He limped over towards Montillo and put himself between the cop and Lilly's friend. "And leave him alone."

MacNally stood at his full height and watched Lepov try to staunch the flow of blood from Montillo's wound with a handkerchief. Lepov wanted to shout at him — tell him to leave — but he didn't want to push his luck. He simply ignored him until MacNally finally left the room.

"Carlos, if he makes the deal, you better be able to give him Layne."

Montillo nodded, despite the pain in his head.

69

The day was wearing out. Fenelli's attempt to find his quarry was taking much longer than he had hoped. Following him in the SubTransit tunnels had only been the start of a long afternoon. Now, as the shrouded sun began to set, Fenelli began to second-guess his decision to go after this man alone.

Fenelli had followed the PDT signal through the tunnels until it had returned to street level. When Fenelli left the SubTransit station he was surprised at how much colder the day had grown. He had come up at the northern edge of the Lazaretto in a warehouse district. The warehouses were erected against the forty-foot wall separating the main Lazaretto from the lifeless expanse of the shipping port.

The signal was now in a large brick warehouse that looked abandoned. The warehouses in that section were storage houses for Lazaretto supplies that were first treated in the shipping port before being allowed into the main Lazaretto. Fear, superstition, or good sound science had dictated many years ago that supplies be isolated in warehouses like this one for an additional five days upon arrival.

Just inside an open truck-sized door, he watched the display on his tag reader. The signal was strong but moving away. Unless he was wrong, Fenelli judged the man was heading for the barrier on the north end of the building.

Skin hairs rose and fell along the nape of his neck. It wasn't possible that his quarry was headed *into* the shipping port, was it? He would have to realize how dangerous that was. If he wandered into a docking bay that was being sprayed or had recently been sprayed he would be as good as dead. Nobody would be that stupid.

Fenelli crossed the great open floor of the warehouse. If the signal led him across the barrier, would he follow it? How important was it to find this man? So far, he hadn't even seen the man; he had only been following the man's PDT signal. Fenelli didn't even know if crossing the barrier was possible.

The empty warehouse smelled of raw plastic — probably used to wrap bundles of supplies — as well as heavy oil. A black slick of it was smeared along an arrow painted isle. It was evident that something had spilled in transit and the leak had not been noticed as the bundle was dragged through the bay.

The back wall had large docking bay doors spaced every four meters along its entirety. The closed doors were made of heavy black iron and were sealed with a soft polyplastic seal as well as an eight point mechanical seal. Large red buttons labeled with warning icons decorated the doors.

The signal was strongest in front of one of the doors. Fenelli might have been fooled into thinking the man had passed beyond the door into the shipping port if he had not seen the small junction box on the wall. Fenelli recognized what had happened. The PDT signal was a ghost. Whoever had been on the SubTransit had somehow managed to implant the PDT's signal into a local circuit. Fenelli had been led by the nose and now the one doing the leading wanted him to know it.

A klaxon siren blared a head-splitting signal. Fenelli backed off and watched as every single bay door clanged to life. As one, their mechanical seals broke free and a great hiss exhaled from the soft seals as each door pulled back from the wall and swung up on its top mounted hinges. The grinding of gears and smack of iron on iron echoed endlessly through the warehouse. Fenelli backed away.

A tearing, screeching whine erupted high above him like metal being torn in two. A framework of automated articulated arms dropped down near the now open bay doors like the menacing legs of gigantic mechanical spiders. At the same time, an elongated truss extended out of each bay wrapped in a black conveyor belt. Each belt turned at the speed of a casual walk. Before each one of them was extended beyond its bay door to its full ten-foot extension, bundles roughly the size of small cars began rolling out on the belts.

The spider legs reached down and grasped each of the bundles as they cleared the bay doors. Fenelli would have found the completely choreographed dance fascinating had he not been angry about the ghost signal. The man had known he was being followed.

Someone had succeeded in running him around for a full day.

Fenelli left the spider legs to their intricate dance.

It was tempting to give up and head back to the office. He could tell MacNally all about his wild goose chase and that would be the end of it. But Fenelli was insulted. He'd been played all day long, and he wanted to turn the tables. First, he had better stop following standard procedures.

The Personal Data Tags had radically revamped the traditional methods of police work. Once society had completed its transformation over to the PDT identification system, official protocols became fixated on the PDT signature. Many aspects of government activity allowed the PDT signature to overshadow an individual's traditional identity. It was why Fenelli had set out looking for this man with a tag reader and a PDT signature as his target. He had little interest in the man's name or his home address. The assumption had been that regardless of where the man lived, Fenelli could find him wherever he happened to be.

Riding the SubTransit back to the West End, Fenelli pulled up the man's file on the tag reader. He should have done that back at the office. It was a sad commentary on how much he'd come to rely on technology.

His personal phone whistled and Fenelli stabbed a thumb into it.

"Fenelli," MacNally was pissed off, "where the hell have you been?"

"I'm out on the West End," he answered. He didn't want to explain his misadventure in the warehouse district.

"Why aren't you here? Get your ass back here and get on the job."

Fenelli knew that tone. MacNally was angry, but not at Fenelli. Whenever MacNally was this mad he liked to spread it around to everyone.

"You said you didn't need me, remember? And I can't come back yet, I'm tracking someone."

"Who?" MacNally demanded.

"Funny you should ask, I'm reading over this guy's file now. His name is Shaw Parks. A lazar who just annoyed the wrong cop."

"You?"

"Yeah, you'll hear it all when I catch up with you. Now what's got you so grouchy?"

"I could've used you a few minutes ago. Romeo got under my skin."

"Uh-oh," Fenelli knew what that meant. "Is he hurt badly?"

"Oh, he'll live. But you would have kept me out of trouble. That

Lepov is a poor excuse as a substitute for you. Tell me about this Parks."

"I will, I will. But later. You sound like you need to relax, maybe knock off early. I'll call you as soon as I know something, okay?" Fenelli didn't leave the transmission open long enough for MacNally to object.

"Now," he told himself as the SubTransit car came to a stop, "it's time to do some old-fashioned police work."

70

Helen and Dr. Haupt had gone over every factor in her report. She had been amazed at the doctor's attention to detail. He had been careful not to overlook any fact, no matter how small. And by the time he was done he had found what he was looking for.

"Helen, treat this data with the same precautions you took on the initial report. Scrub not only my system, but yours as well. I also want you to backtrack our system searches and archive activity."

"Yes, Dr. Haupt." Helen tried not to think about what his instructions might mean. Instead, she thought over the necessary steps in her mind and tried to anticipate any difficulties that might arise. "I should be able to eliminate any footprints that might be seen by first and mid-level access. Only the highest tiered access will be able to see what we've done. But that is only Dr. Fisher here at IHS."

"There are others outside of IHS?" Dr. Haupt frowned.

"As I recall, the Senior Lazaretto Commission members would have that kind of access. But there are only three of them, including the Chief Administrator."

"No," Dr. Haupt shook his head, "I don't want anyone to see what we've been investigating. Surely you can take care of that with the key tag I provided you?"

"Maybe," Helen said tentatively, unsure of how true her answer was. "I think I should tell you, Doctor, that I can't be one hundred per cent certain. That would require oversight directly from Baltimore. It's a question of visibility. I can clean up what I can see. But if there is a backup sentinel program that I am unaware of, then I can't unlock it with the key tag to clean it. I'm sorry."

"No need to apologize. Your knowledge and skills are commendable. You are telling me something I should have anticipated. I will have to leave for a short time. Please do what you can and I will try to be back as soon as possible. But this must be taken care of today."

As she began to clean up both desk systems, she realized that her own precautionary measures—which had seemed unnecessary when she first took them—were nothing compared to Dr. Haupt's. Why all this need for secrecy? It was true that what they had found seemed to incriminate Dr. Fisher as well as other highly placed IHS officials. But so far, they had not been able to find out what had actually happened.

The majority of the information they had gathered was centered on Dr. Stride in Research. There were a great deal of memos flowing to and from Dr. Stride and Dr. Fisher. Some of the memos were missing; several memos referred to memos that could no longer be found. But whatever had been in those notes had something to do with the revised protocol that was sent to the lab.

For all of that, Dr. Haupt still had few facts. So why was she covering their tracks?

The door to the conference room opened and Julia stepped slowly into the office. She said nothing as she moved across the open floor and dropped into a chair.

"What are you still doing here?" Helen asked. She had expected Julia to leave almost an hour before. "Aren't you heading home to make up with Billy?"

"He's not there," Julia answered listlessly.

"Doesn't he have a personal phone?"

"Never carries one that I've seen. Helen, what's wrong with me? I mean, doesn't there have to be something wrong with me?"

Helen finished the second system scrub on her desksystem before she looked up at her young friend. She had done all she could for Dr. Haupt and would have to wait for him to return. Until then, she could give Julia her full attention.

"Okay, girl, what's the matter?"

"Isn't it obvious? I can't find a decent guy no matter how hard I try. I've never thought I was the most beautiful girl in the heavens, but there's nothing distasteful about me, is there?"

"You think this has to do with your appearance?" Helen tried not to smile.

"I'm serious, Helen. Why would Billy leave me like he did? And when he did come back he was so cold. I don't deserve that. I've done everything for him. But it's not only him. It seems like every guy I find ends up leaving me. I've got to have more value than that. Don't I?"

Julia stood up and tried to see herself in the reflection of the glass office door, pouting as she pulled at her blouse and fixed her hair.

"I always wished I could be beautiful. Really stunning, you know?"

Helen allowed a rather noisy sigh to escape her. Julia was getting maudlin and Helen was not in the mood to play along.

'Julia, listen to yourself. You told me this morning you'd been worried sick about Billy. But now you've turned this into something that is all about you. Maybe you should stop worrying about how attractive you are and start wondering what is wrong with Billy."

"I'm supposed to sit at home and worry about him as he traipses all over Center City? I'm not his wife for god's sake."

"You could sit around and worry about him. It depends on how much you care about him. That's true whether you're his wife or you aren't his wife. Believe it or not, not all wives care enough to worry over their husbands. My mother never did. But that's not my point, dear. You might want to consider that there is something wrong with him, not with you. His behavior would support that theory, don't you think?"

"Wrong like what?" Julia asked.

"It may be something as simple as bad manners. I don't know. Maybe he's in trouble. He may have serious mental problems. I doubt you know him well enough to decide he's perfect and you're the cause of all your problems. Why don't you give yourself a break?"

"I was worried about him." Julia looked up at Helen with the eyes of a child seeking approval. "Maybe he is in trouble. Do you think?"

Helen wasn't surprised that Julia avoided acknowledging that the problem might lie with Billy. She was too eager for his companionship and too quick to blame herself to entertain such a thought.

"I think you need to get some sleep. You didn't do much of that last night and now you're overtired. Go home and forget about him." It was the best advice Helen could give.

"Maybe. Are you coming now, too?"

"I wish I could. But I'm waiting for Dr. Haupt." Helen didn't mind staying late but she hated to think of Julia making that trip home alone.

"It's okay. I'm okay." Julia tried to smile as she held onto the door. "You really don't think there's anything wrong with me?"

Helen shook her head.

"I like that thought. I might have to think about that."

Thirty minutes passed before Dr. Haupt finally returned to the office. His manner was brusque. Passing through the outer office, he barely said a word. Helen followed him into his office and waited as he seated himself behind his desk and sat staring at his blank deskscreen. Cocking his head at Helen, he examined her with hard eyes. She realized she had never seen him angry before.

"We will have to accept your precautions as sufficient," he finally pronounced. The look on his face told her he wasn't about to accept them as sufficient. "Have you done what I asked?"

"Yes, Dr. Haupt."

"I was unable to provide you with the oversight codes from Baltimore. So we must assume that it will be possible for someone to see what we have been investigating. However, as long as we have only observed the data, it should eliminate the activation of any sentinel program that might flag our intrusion. Baltimore has assured me that only changes made to a file's archive status would be noticed."

Helen did not like the sound of that but she could not understand why. Dr. Haupt was right. They hadn't changed anything; they had only accessed and read the data. She still did not understand fully the reasons Dr. Haupt was so insistent on covering their tracks. Yes, Dr. Fisher seemed to have some explaining to do, but she had an idea that Dr. Fisher would be able to do so. In fact, Helen wondered why Dr. Haupt hadn't already gone down to speak with Dr. Fisher.

"That's all for today, Helen." Dr. Haupt did not look up at her. He brushed his hand on his deskscreen and it lit up with a pale blue glow.

"Goodnight, Doctor." Helen watched him for only a moment; long enough to confirm that he did not say goodnight in return.

71

Fenelli contacted Pete Landon and had him run down the SubTransit visuals to determine if someone had ridden back from the Warehouse District. That was simple enough. It did not take Pete long to find an image of Parks reentering a SubTransit car about five minutes after Fenelli had stepped out of his.

The SubTransit tag readers had him listed as Thoma Li Chen. An unlikely name that suggested Parks was using a random generating Personal Data Tag. Pete quickly confirmed that Parks was using one of Romeo's PDT's. It was the kind of information that Fenelli liked to receive. Although it did not explain why Parks had deceived him, it did suggest that this was no unrelated contact.

"I think I can track the PDT," Pete called back to explain.

"That's all well and good but I don't want to put too much stock in that." Fenelli wasn't about to track another signal. "If you can track him, make sure you confirm each tag signal with any available visuals. What I really need is to get ahead of him. Figure out where he's going. Let me go through his file and see what I can come up with."

By the time he'd left the SubTransit station and ascended the stairs to the street where he'd left his car, Fenelli had decided Parks' detour out to the Warehouse District had been a standard maneuver to mislead any possible tail. Parks had been headed in that direction long before he could have detected Fenelli tailing him. And if he was making this big of a move to clear a trail, then Parks was about to do something he didn't want seen.

He didn't know enough about this guy to anticipate his moves. The sad fact was he had little options but to rely on Pete. It irritated him but he couldn't allow his pride to get in the way of finding Parks. Not if something were about to happen.

"Pete," Fenelli said before making the call, "don't let me down."

After answering the call and listening to Fenelli's idea, Pete assured Fenelli he'd do his best.

"So can that work?" Fenelli asked.

"I think so. I'm trying it now. When your man ghosted that signal, there was a brief overlay when the signal doubled. He couldn't turn his off first, since the system might have picked that up as a termination. The chances of setting off a red flag for any kind of surveillance are greater for a signal termination than a redundant signal. And he must know that because he did turn his off only after the ghost signal activated.

"And what that means is I can set up a scenario capture of what happened to his signal before and after that ghost double appeared. If he's done this before, I might be able to find it in the system. Of course, getting a clear signal in the city depends on all sorts of things like weather, signal congestion, tag relay reliability…"

"Pete, call me back if you find anything." Fenelli may have had to rely on the technology, but he sure as hell wasn't going to learn every step in the process.

"I won't need to," Pete said. By his tone it was evident he was quite pleased with himself.

"Why not?"

"I've already got something. Hold it…yeah, wow. It worked. I'm looking at it. Give me a second. Your man did this three times in the last couple of days; once way down at the south end of the residential area, once at the Beta Entry Lounge, and then at Delta Passenger Registration."

"And how long does the ghost last?"

"Never more than two hours."

"And where does the original signal reappear? Does he go back to the ghost location?"

"Nope." Pete was silent for a moment and Fenelli gave him time to elaborate. "Looks like the signal doubles before the ghost signal terminates—that's as expected. But each time he's done that, the signal is somewhere near Seventh Ave."

"Okay, that's where he stays. He has a room there. But each time he's done this he's misdirected his signal away from Center City. And with only two hours time, he must be going back into the city for only a short time. He's careful, but he's too lazy to go return to the ghost site."

"Or he doesn't have time."

Fenelli wanted to bang his head against the window of his car. An opportunity was slipping away and he could feel it. There was no way to make a proper search for Parks.

"Pete, try this. Take a square out of Center City — say Masthead and First are your x and y axis. Run that out about four blocks and make that our grid. Do you still think you can run a search on that Romeo PDT?"

"I can look for a couple of things that make it stand out. Not that exact PDT he's using, but ones that act in the same manner. But that's not going to get a lot of hits."

"Yeah. But we can match them with any visuals that might resemble Parks. He'll keep his face screened from recorders, but his basic size and hair coloring doesn't change. Can the system handle a search like that?"

"Hey, Fenelli," Pete was offended, "don't pretend you can think of something complex enough to confuse the system. Just because you have junk equipment doesn't mean the main system's junk. Besides, the real value lies in the system's exceptional system techs."

"Well, tell those guys I appreciate the help."

"*Those guys*?" Pete barked in mock protest. "*Me!* Thank me, you dumb cop!"

Fenelli continued towards Center City. It was wishful thinking. Unless Pete called back with a location, he really had no place to go.

The place he wanted to go was home. It was getting late, the sun had set long ago, and the cold night had taken over the city. It still felt early, there was too much activity on the street to suggest it was late at night, but it felt much too late for Fenelli. Lynne was home alone; he had called to tell her he'd be late. By now she would have eaten and cleaned up. She never liked to eat late. Through all the years on the job, he'd also known she never like to eat alone. But that was something she had never voiced. And she hadn't had to say it. There had been the kids, and they had provided companionship for a time, but they were gone now, and he knew Lynne felt it deeply. Hell, Fenelli thought, I can feel it too. And what made it worse for him was the knowledge he hadn't been with his kids as much as he had wanted.

Old regrets were easier to manage if you made the changes necessary to eliminate new regrets. But as it became increasingly evident that he'd be away from home for another evening, Fenelli could feel a tightening in his chest—a sudden panic—as he realized nothing would ever change. He was forty-seven-years old, and for all the years he'd told himself he would quit working late, he was still doing it this very night. He wanted to declare this would be the last night—never again—but he knew it would be a lie.

Knowing that Lynne was home alone, waiting for him, worrying about him, and willing to forgive him each and every night only made it worse. She deserved better than that. A lonely life like that might have been bearable on Phasis; she would have had her family to ease her solitude. But here, in the Lazaretto, she had nothing to shore up her empty nights. Even the kids had fled this prison moon. Fenelli couldn't blame them. Who in their right mind would raise a family in such a place?

He had. Maybe when all was said and done he hadn't been in his right mind all along. Maybe it was the source of his agitation since he'd seen that Rodyakov child lying in a bloody heap. For a reason unknown to him, the Rodyakov's had attempted to raise their son in a dark and hopeless world. To what purpose? To what end? Their child had died and would never get out. And though Fenelli's kids had been able to break free, what scars had they taken with them? Could anyone live on this island of fear and death without staining their soul? Fenelli hated to think what punishments awaited him if his children's souls had been tainted by the choices he'd made. But what punishment could await that would be worse than the Lazaretto? He wasn't sure if he was more afraid of discovering Hell was more horrifying than this life or finding that this life had been Hell all along.

Pete Landon called back as Fenelli drove down Masthead Ave. The computer-brain/puzzle-wizard sounded like he had finally solved a puzzle that had been vexing him for years. Plainly said, he was ecstatic.

"You owe me dinner, Fenelli. And I don't mean with you, I mean with a beautiful woman. I've got your man."

"If you can give him to me, I'll put on a dress and be the woman. Where is he?"

"I said a *beautiful* woman, man. Do you want to hear the details on how I found him? Because you told me to go out four blocks from Masthead and First but I set my outside perimeter at six blocks. After that I—"

"To hell with your details, Pete. Come on, give me a location."

"Long story short: he ends up on Masthead, down around the High Rent section. Close to Dardanelle."

"Down by the Administration complex?" Fenelli asked. It was

the central hub of the Lazaretto Administration.

"Yeah, I guess so. But I think it has more to do with the Overlords. I think that's where he ends up. That's where the big shots live, you know. I did a Beat there for a year once. Rich bastards did not want us uniforms to get in their way. Guys like Kai Fritsch, Roma Phen, and Cam Raley might own half of the Lazaretto but they don't have to act like it."

Fenelli knew what Pete was saying. The Overlords were a pair of one-hundred-plus meter towers that housed the homes and offices of the leading companies doing business in the Lazaretto. Most of them were only satellite offices; their corporate headquarters were back on one of the colony planets. And only Cam Raley actually lived in the Overlords.

"You aren't gonna be too welcome there," Pete chuckled.

"How soon does he usually show up there after he ghosts the signal?" Fenelli was worried they had wasted too much time.

"Never less than an hour. I think you have time to get there ahead of him. But I can't tell you which Overlord he enters. I'm doing this from street recorders and as you might have guessed those recorders in front of the Overlords haven't worked for a long time."

"They don't worry about security?"

"They've got their own security, man. And I can't get into it. I've tried." Pete sounded angry and embarrassed at such an admission.

"Okay, I'm almost there now. I don't know how to thank you."

"Dinner, man. Beautiful woman. You're no math wiz, but I'm sure you can add the two together."

Yeah, Fenelli had to agree with that concept. Dinner with a beautiful woman was exactly what he'd been missing. Dinner with Lynne.

Fenelli left his car parked in an alley under a wall with the message *no parking* painted on it in four or five places. He stepped out onto Masthead and walked a block south to where Dardanelle crossed Masthead. He had to cross both streets to approach the street side entrance to the northernmost Overlord.

The Overlords were actually named Pha Nohm Sae Towers One and Two. But no one ever called them that. Few people knew who Pha Nohm Sae had been and even fewer cared. The Overlords nickname had come from a series of articles written by a cynical reporter who found the massive blunt structures a fitting but malignant display that captured the oppressive spirit of the wealthy businessmen who lived in them. The nickname stuck.

Overlord One and Overlord Two were identical and stood in that order from north to south. Fenelli passed the entrance to Overlord One and kept moving until he was midway between the two entrances. Stepping into the cone shaped shadow created by wall lamps that failed to overlap, Fenelli leaned against a wall of glass and hoped Overlord Security wouldn't show up to discourage loitering. His guess was they wouldn't notice him for a few minutes, but the longer he had to wait the better his chances of being spotted. He would have to leave his shadow from time to time if Parks didn't show up within the next five minutes.

Conventional wisdom would have dictated that he watch the back entrance, but Fenelli never even considered it. Buildings like the Overlords had great security on the front entrance and even better security on the back entrance. The back entrance was the gateway that allowed cleaning crews, servicemen, and suppliers access to the building; a class of people who were suspect merely by their status. Rigorous protocol was followed for rear entrance access. The front entrance could expect a fair number of unexpected yet high class visitors who would not always be on a list or would take offense at access protocols.

If Parks was going to enter the Overlords, he'd come suitably dressed and walk right through the front door. Skulking was the surest way to attract attention at the Overlords.

Fenelli would have bet money that he'd have to wait thirty minutes or more until Parks showed up. That was the kind of luck he had. But he had guessed wrong. Parks walked right past him only four or five minutes after Fenelli had leaned against the wall.

As expected, Parks' head was tucked down into the collar of his coat. Avoiding the recorders, Fenelli noted, though it was possible Parks was only avoiding the cold night air. Fenelli didn't care what his reasons were; it kept Parks from noticing the middle-aged cop standing in the shadows.

Parks never hesitated as he reached the entrance to Overlord One. A doorman pulled open a door and Parks slipped inside.

As the door swung shut on Parks, a TransitCar pulled up to Overlord One's entrance. Fenelli thought he recognized the woman who stepped out of the back. As she leaned back into the Transit to pay the driver, Fenelli remembered who she was. The white ponytail sprouting from the top of her head was too memorable to forget. She was the woman that had been with that Private Investigator—Lepov.

Fenelli couldn't remember her name. What she was doing at Overlord was more important at the moment. Did she have something to do with Parks? He wanted into that building. And he wanted access to their recorders. But the men living in those towers had been labeled *Overlords* for a good reason: a homicide detective like Fenelli had little authority with men like that.

72

The Collector was irritated that circumstances had unraveled to the point where direct intervention was required to maintain control. That was a tricky business. Direct intervention allowed those in the game a chance to see who was really in control. Much like a man in a storm is given a flash of light to see the extent of the storm; if he is looking in the right direction when the lightning strikes, he will see what is hidden in the dark.

"On time as always," the Collector said as the Agent stepped off the elevator. "I have much to say and little time to say it. A new development has arisen that must be dealt with immediately. Your efforts to delay the police have failed."

"I will get this done. It will take time—"

"There is no time. They have what they need. They will find him. You must stop them. There is an opportunity. But time is short."

"I'll be discreet."

"I don't give a damn about discreet!" the Collector shouted. He took two slow breaths in order to control his temper. Too many things were getting out of hand. He had to regain control. "You get down there and do what I tell you. That's an image of him. But then again, you don't need that, do you? I believe you know him. He is assisting the police. I want you to kill him."

If the Agent felt any compunction about killing an acquaintance the Agent didn't allow those feelings to surface.

"Now about the other matter. The doctor has already found something. It is a small thing, but it is the first of many steps on a dangerous path. I am beginning to think there is little reason for discretion here as well. The woman who works with him has locked out files that should have disappeared. We will have to get them unlocked and then wipe them."

"I still cannot touch the doctor?"

"You won't have to. Not if you're smart. But you will have to be persuasive. He's a cold-hearted bastard. Threats to the woman will be of no use. You will have to make sure he knows your level of commitment."

"And if I can't get the files unlocked?"

"You will not come back here and tell me you were unable to unlock the files." The Collector stared at the Agent with suppressed anger. "Now do as I said. And leave now, you have little time."

There was anger in the Agent's eyes betraying a sense of indignity. The Collector was being highhanded but it could not be any other way. The Agent would have to accept it.

"Is there anything else?" asked the Agent sarcastically.

"You had better use the back exit. I believe you are being followed."

That stung. The Collector could see his remark had scored painfully. The Agent opened his lips as if to deny the accusation but said nothing.

The elevator closed on the Agent and the Collector tried to calm down. Despite the tension he was beginning to feel with the Agent, he knew the Agent would accomplish all that he had asked. The Agent was resourceful and proud. He had only to stay focused on his task.

And with the belief that everything would eventually work out as he desired, the Collector was able to relax even further and turn his attention to something more pleasing. He sat behind his desk and spoke.

"Tell her to come in."

The elevator doors opened. The Agent was no longer in the elevator. Instead, a graceful woman with long white hair stepped into the room and smiled at the Collector. She carried a large leather case in one hand.

"Lilly, my flower. I'm sorry I couldn't see you sooner." The Collector neither rose to greet her nor reached out a hand. He gestured towards a chair and offered her a drink.

"Thank you." She set the case at her feet and accepted the drink from an automated butler, sitting carefully on the edge of a high-backed chair. Crossing one leg over the other, she sipped at the drink then set it down. Her left hand never strayed from the case.

"You have it? You have my piece?" He eyed the case with excitement.

"Have I ever failed to procure a piece for you?" Her eyes locked with his as her hand slid over the leather.

"You really did it." He stood and moved around the desk, unable to mask the excited tremor in his hands and not caring if she could detect it.

This time, she picked up the glass and lifted it to her mouth, slowly taking in the strong liquid. She knew he was impatient for her to put down the glass and open the case; her delay reminding him that she was still in control of the piece. He liked that. It was exciting in its own way.

She was exciting in every way. But he never once desired her physically. Yes, he could feel lust for her, but the Collector would never allow himself to have physical contact with another person. The image of two bodies in contact exchanging germs and bacteria revolted him. There were no treatments or cleansing procedures that could eradicate the traces of such activity. He was content to look at her, and be excited.

"Would you like me to open the case?" she teasingly asked as she set the glass back down. Her smile told him she was enjoying every second that she delayed. He didn't mind her childlike mischief.

"Over here," he led her to a table near the wall of windows overlooking the city.

She laid the case on its side, and entered a numbered sequence into a small keypad beside the handle. A pressure seal released with a hush as a latch released. She lifted one side of the case, opening it. Clear gel foam surrounded a small black urn. It was a simple glazed, clay urn with no ornamentation. Scratches along its squat rounded sides gave evidence to its age and poor treatment.

"You have provenance?" It was more of a statement than a question. He knew Lilly would never bring him something like this without the proper documentation.

"Chain of custody is undeniable. The documents that were with it have been verified by a complete modern set of tests. As promised, there are three new supporting opinions written on it by professors from Oxford, Stanford, and Berlin." Lilly had accessed a panel that slid out of the back of the case. She pulled a sheaf of papers from it and laid them out on the table. The Collector waited for her to withdraw a few feet before he stepped forward and looked over them. His hands remained clasped behind his back.

"So it is undeniable."

"This urn contains the remains of Simon of Auxbury."

"A prominent landowner who died during the Black Death in 1359. Think of it, a man of wealth, position—a man of power. A man reduced to ashes by disease carried by fleas. Ignominious, pitiless, foul death. Unbelievable really." The Collector passed his hand a few inches above the gel foam that encased the urn. As his hand did so, he jerked it back as if he'd been bitten.

"The urn was scanned for pathogens. It is perfectly safe," Lilly said. "The gel will remain constant and hold its seal for fifty years and will be nearly impossible to see in its display case."

"You're a miracle worker, Lilly. No words can express my thanks." He was moved by her success, though practical enough to remember she was being well compensated for her efforts.

"I'm always available when you need me."

The room became silent as the Collector stared at the urn.

"You're leaving soon?" he suddenly asked.

"Delta closed down today, as you know. I will be leaving with the next quadrant."

"A great waste of your time. I hate to see you stuck here. I can get you into Delta and pay your fee. Consider it a bonus for a job well done."

Lilly pondered his offer with no hint of what she was thinking. The Collector hoped she would take the offer. He wanted her out of the Lazaretto. Each time she came he wondered if this was the time. Had she learned the truth? Did she know who he was? Did she know who *she* was?

"I will consider it," she said.

The Collector nodded and returned his attention to the urn.

73

When Lepov returned to Homicide, he found MacNally sitting at his desk. The big detective had one hand wrapped around a cup of coffee and his other hand tapped nervously on his deskscreen.

"Where've you been?" MacNally asked him.

"I was making sure the man who knows how to contact Ethan Layne would live. Have you calmed down or should I sit across the room where I won't be within your reach?"

"Hitting you ain't the worst idea I could think of. You made a mess of that back there." MacNally's expression told Lepov he was serious.

"I made a mess of things? If I didn't know any better I'd say you weren't grateful that I stopped you from making matters worse. If I'd let you keep hammering on him, he'd be worthless to us. My guess is, his jaw wouldn't open 'cause you'd have broken it and even if it would open he wouldn't tell you the weather report, let alone where Layne is. But people tend to get like that after you mistreat them."

"You finished?" MacNally looked up at Lepov, amused. "My partner usually keeps me in line but even he wouldn't go on like that."

"I'll shut up now, if that's what you're getting at." Lepov pulled a chair over and eased himself down onto the seat.

"What's with the knee?" MacNally noticed Lepov favoring it.

"To tell you the truth I don't know what the deal is with it. One day, when I tried to extend it, it suddenly felt like someone stuck a rock under my kneecap. Now, the pain comes and goes. It didn't help when that crazy girl kicked it, or when you knocked me down on it."

"I don't know about the girl kicking you, and I deny knocking you down, but I'd wager the real problem is the same problem I've got—you're getting old."

"That's a comforting thought." Lepov was all too aware that his body was getting older. "So what did your captain say about the deal?"

"Nothing. That's why I'm sitting here. I told him why we needed the deal and he sounded like he was going to agree with me. But he had to check with his boss. We're still waiting for an answer."

Lepov didn't understand. This police department had funny ways of handling urgent matters. He wondered if it was the Lazaretto—a prison-like world that looked and felt as if it were doomed—that fostered such odd behavior or if it reflected the character of the men in charge. Either way, precious time was being lost. And although MacNally looked frustrated, he also looked as if he were used to such delays.

"So will he live?" MacNally asked Lepov.

"Who, Montillo? He'll live. You tore a pretty nice gash in the back of his head. I took a lot of guff for you. The MedTechs seemed to think I had something to do with it. Funny thing, though. When I mentioned you they quit looking at me funny. I guess they know your procedures."

"I'm surprised you stopped me. I thought you were the one who was angry with him."

"Well," Lepov confessed, "I don't like people who try to put me in jail. And that includes you. But I hadn't planned on splitting his skull over it. I just want to find out why. Isn't that reasonable? But Lilly seems certain that Montillo didn't set me up. I'm not so sure. She thinks some guy by the name of Shaw Parks is involved."

"Then why did you want to talk to Montillo?" MacNally asked.

"Call it a lack of faith in Lilly. That's no reflection on her, mind you. It only points out a shortcoming I have. I tend to be a suspicious cuss."

"So you were with Montillo while they patched him up downstairs?" Lepov nodded. MacNally actually seemed worried. "Is he still interested in a deal?"

"He'll do it. He hates you now, but he still understands this is his way out of trouble." And that was what Lepov had advised Montillo. After being thrown to the floor, Montillo had sworn not to help the police. Lepov had been forced to point out that Montillo had little choice in the matter if he wanted to stay out of jail. Montillo's anger hadn't been assuaged, but he had been practical enough to agree that the deal should go through as planned.

"Hold on a minute," MacNally sat up straight. "What was the guy's name? Parks?"

"Yeah, Shaw Parks. Why?"

"The name rings a bell, but I can't figure why."

"Have you heard from your partner?" Lepov asked him.

"Not for a while."

Lepov needed to get out and look for Layne. He wasn't doing any good sitting around with MacNally. But he had few leads to follow up on. The pain in his knee reminded him of Greta Becker. Now that the police were involved, maybe it was time to talk with her again.

"Are you going somewhere?" MacNally watched Lepov push himself to his feet. The knee was an obvious problem.

"Can you get me the address on a woman?"

"Let me guess: Greta Becker?"

"Good guess."

"Yeah, well that one's been on my mind, and we don't have a lot of people available to check her out. You want to talk to her again?"

"I want to find out what she really knows. She left in the middle of our conversation last time. She didn't like the questions I was asking." Lepov pulled on his coat and picked up his hat.

"Here's her address. We pulled it up after you told us about her. There's little chance she'll be there, but you might as well give it a shot." MacNally grabbed a pen and notepad, scribbling the address for Lepov and added a few simple directions so Lepov could find it.

"I'll check in on Montillo as I go. You better go talk to your boss again. You need to know what Montillo knows."

Lepov walked out of Homicide and down the hall towards the elevators. It was after dinnertime and most of the station was empty. A few cops could still be seen behind their desks in small rooms off the hallway, but there weren't many. Lepov's shoes echoed off the hard wood floors as he approached the first elevator. He pushed the call button and waited for the doors to open. When he did not hear the cable wench motor or the rumble of the approaching elevator car he pushed the button again. Each of the three elevators failed to respond.

"Murphy's Law must be standard operating procedure in this place," Lepov complained aloud. He walked a few meters to the stairwell door and pushed it open. Somehow, it seemed to make sense that there was only one bulb working in that vertical tunnel. I'll fall and break my neck, he thought, and all because of a bum knee and poor lighting.

Every step down aggravated his knee. It was the kind of pain you never got used to. In fact, it was the kind of pain that only got worse. No matter how he tried to ease up on that knee, it hurt. He tried to put his weight on the old iron banister but he could feel it shake under his weight. No wonder his knee hurt. If an iron banister couldn't hold him, why should his knee be able to?

And if getting down stairs was this difficult, how did he expect to be able to hunt down Greta Becker? She could easily kick him again. One more like that and he might end up in a wheelchair.

He was near the third floor when he heard breaking glass and the stairwell became pitch black. Below, someone pounded down the stairs then crashed open a door. It slammed shut with the sound of cannon fire.

Lepov made it to the second floor and sought out the guard stationed at the holding cell gate.

"What was that all about?" Lepov asked him.

The young guard did not know what he was talking about.

"Someone from this floor ran like hell down the stairs. They smashed the only working light in the stairwell, too."

"I didn't see anything. But I wasn't watching the door to the stairwell. That's not my job." The guard stared into Lepov's eyes, daring Lepov to challenge him.

"Well, it's no concern of mine." Lepov wasn't going to get into an argument over what might have happened. He didn't work there and he sure as hell didn't want to, either. "I want to check in on Carlos Montillo. Detective MacNally should have cleared me."

"Yeah, he did." The guard gestured towards a deskscreen and shrugged. "Put your hand on that, then go on in. Cell 18. If you need anything else, go back upstairs and ask MacNally."

The guard turned his back to Lepov.

"You aren't going to escort me in?"

"Do you need me to hold your hand?" the guard asked. Lepov couldn't see his face but he was sure the man was laughing at him.

When Lepov thought about it later, he understood there was nothing that could have given him the idea that something was wrong. There was no way he could have suspected what he would find when he opened the door to cell 18. But as soon as he did, something deep inside him told him he should have seen it coming.

He pulled open the cell door. The pair of shoes on Montillo's swinging feet were expensive, and their black leather matched the belt wrapped around both the single light fixture and Montillo's neck. The light fixture didn't look strong enough to hold Montillo's weight, but what did that matter? These were trivial observations.

This was not what it looked like. This was no suicide. Carlos Montillo had been murdered.

Lepov sat on the edge of the cell's bunk. He wanted to vomit. What was he going to tell Lilly?

74

By the time Fenelli had seen the white-haired woman leave the

Overlord Towers he knew Parks had slipped out unseen. It was a stupid mistake on Fenelli's part. He had assumed that if Parks was bold enough to use the front entrance he would come back out the same way. But he had waited over an hour, and according to Pete, Parks had never spent that much time at one of these meetings.

It was readily apparent that Fenelli was unable to track Parks without help from MacNally or someone else from Homicide. Trying to catch Parks at his rooms would be as problematic. It would save time in the long run to head back to the office and tell MacNally what was going on. Then, with help, they could bring this guy in.

And so Fenelli had driven straight to the station. As he slowed down to turn into the station's garage, he nearly drove into a PoliceTransit in front of him. To his shock, Shaw Parks was hurrying out the entrance to the garage on foot. He was *leaving* the police station. Fenelli took extra care to make sure that the man was indeed Parks. The streetlights provided enough light for him to be certain.

What was Parks doing at the station? Fenelli watched as Parks crossed the wet street and hailed a TransitCar. There was little time to do anything but follow. For once, Fenelli might actually have an advantage over Parks. He was already in his car and behind the TransitCar. He accelerated, keeping close to the lead car. It was dark, and Fenelli hoped enough rain was falling to prevent Parks from spotting a tail.

The TransitCar headed south, and Fenelli easily stayed with it. Traffic was light but there were cars on the streets to hide amongst. He made sure his tag reader was turned off. He wasn't about to announce his presence with an electronic signature.

As the two cars passed through traffic, Fenelli tried to think. He wanted to stop Parks and question him but he had to know what kind of questions he was going to ask. He also wondered what he could arrest him for if Parks refused to answer any questions.

Although he had little proof, he knew that Parks had tried to misdirect Fenelli into the Delta Quadrant as it was closing down. That was clearly an attempt to keep him from pursuing the murder investigation. But that was only clear to Fenelli. Would anyone else see it that way? He doubted it. MacNally would back him up, but MacNally would have done that regardless of whether or not Fenelli was right.

And although Parks had ghosted his tag, that was a minor violation that could only lead to a small fine. He wasn't even sure he could detain him for that. Parks could produce all kinds of excuses for such behavior. Parks could say he was trying to lose a woman who had become too attached after a one-night stand. Anything would sound plausible next to Fenelli's accusations.

And Parks' stop at the Overlord Towers was even more innocuous. It left Fenelli with no leverage. But that didn't dissuade him from his belief that Parks was dirty. And he was still offended that Parks had thought he could confuse Fenelli with that ridiculous message.

The TransitCar turned right and began skirting the perimeter of Terran Park. The dark mass of trees loomed ominously over Bosporus Avenue. The lights from the street could not penetrate their thick tangle of branches and wet leaves; light was swallowed up as if by a black hole. Fenelli remembered spending a day in that park with his children, many years before. It had been unusually warm and dry. The sky had been cloudy, of course, but a pale sun had shone through enough to make them feel as if they were enjoying the brightest summer day on Phasis. How many years ago? He couldn't remember anymore.

As the two cars worked around to the south side of the park, Fenelli looked up at the six steel and glass skeletal fingers of Terran Towers. Maria was probably leaving for the clinic, if she hadn't already. Her dedication to those suffering in the clinic was hard to understand, though he greatly respected her for practicing such diligence and mercy on people she did not know. His admiration of her was immeasurable. He had often wondered if he could do the same for someone he did not know and was ashamed to believe that he couldn't.

How could Maria give of herself so freely? How could she put herself in harm's way, knowing she was vulnerable to the same diseases that imprisoned her patients? Surely he came from the same blood, the same set of genes, yet clearly he had none of the courage and self-sacrifice so prevalent in his sister. What made her do it? It couldn't be the fact that she was a woman. Maria's husband was cut from the same audacious cloth. So why them?

He had wanted to raise his kids to be as selfless. He had wanted them to succeed in whatever they attempted only so they might give back when they were able. And yet, what had he ever shown them but a father who was too busy at work? A man who couldn't be home for dinner most of their lives? What kind of message did that send them? What kind of image did they have of their father?

Fenelli knew he was getting tired. He always allowed such mawkish thoughts to crowd his mind when he began to wear down. It was best if he steered clear of such worries. The life he'd led could never be changed. Those decisions had all been made. It was better to simply concentrate on the day at hand and forget what had passed before.

If only it were that easy, he thought. He concentrated on the

TransitCar in front of him. That was one thing he could do.

75

Maria arrived at the clinic early. Della had asked her to come in early. If Georges had gotten the message correctly, Kjarsta wanted to see her right after dinner. It was an unusual request and one that both intrigued and worried Maria. Was he feeling worse and expecting to die soon? She was troubled at the possibilities as she entered his room.

"You came," Kjarsta said. He spoke with a throat-clearing growl.

"Yes, I came." Maria was already reaching for a cup of water to give him but Kjarsta waved it away.

"Sit down, sit." More gravel sounds followed after a hard cough. "You're lovely, Maria. I couldn't wait until later. I couldn't wait for you."

"Yes, they told me." Maria lowered her head, as if she were ashamed to be so needed.

"What is wrong, eh? You look upset."

"I was worried that you were…I didn't know why you wanted me."

"Hey, I didn't call you because I was about to die." He raised his hand towards her, though it only moved a few inches off the bed. "You don't have to worry about that. I won't call you when that time comes. I do not need to pass through the gate while you hold my hand. It would be unfair to you. And I am ready for it. Don't worry about that."

Maria nodded, unable to reply. He talked as if he knew when he would die and she wanted to believe him. Somehow that made it better. He couldn't know, of course, but it provided some dignity to pretend he had some small token of control over his life.

"As a matter a fact," Kjarsta coughed sharply before continuing, "I feel pretty damn good. Pretty damn good. That's why I asked you to come. I want to talk with you. I want to tell you a story."

"About your little truck?" Maria smiled, wiping away a tear.

"No, I left the little truck behind, remember? When I left Phasis. The little truck is still there for all I know. Maybe it is gone. No, but I will tell you about something even more interesting than my first attempts as a cabbage salesman. I want to tell you how I came to the Lazaretto. But first, the water, please."

Maria took the cup and lifted it to his lips. She spoke gently to him, easing the cup over until the water rolled into his open mouth. She pulled back after only a little had dribbled in. Kjarsta's rough scabbed lips scraped together as he swallowed. Maria tilted the cup three more times, each time as patiently and carefully as the last. Each time Kjarsta's head jerked back with the effort to swallow. His tongue broke free from the thick saliva that held it to the roof of his mouth with a viscous sucking sound. The water seemed to cause him more discomfort than anything.

"Thank you, that's nice." He exhaled with a low growl. As he continued to speak, his words were often interrupted by deep breaths, a soft grunt, or a strained attempt at swallowing. But despite all of this, he was determined to tell Maria his story.

"I came to the Lazaretto for the first time forty-five years ago. It was different then. Everything was new. It was an important place. Memories of the violent plagues still haunted us, and the Lazaretto was a promise to eradicate the plagues forever. A time of much sorrow, but yet such hope. I had lost much of my family back on Phasis: a brother, two sisters, my parents, and many others. But I survived. I was strong, and able to fight off so many of the diseases that harassed and harried us. It was like I was chosen by the gods to carry on the Zoltis name. I know that's silly. But you feel like that. In the middle of something so scary and difficult to understand. You grab at straws to make sense of the insanity. It is what I did, anyway.

"So I looked for a way to take advantage of my good fortune. I wanted to do something that would make my survival something important. And the Lazaretto was such an important and new world. I was certain that I would find a way to make my mark on life. Do something meaningful."

Maria glanced at him when he paused. His breathing was erratic.

"Remember that, Maria. Remember I wanted to do something meaningful. Because when I came to the Lazaretto, I forgot all that."

Maria nodded, though she dared not say anything. Kjarsta's words sounded as if they had come out of a confessional; there was no bravado in his tone, nor was there any shame. Maria could only hear the self-assured voice of a man who knows his audience will understand and forgive. It was intimidating to be in that position; to be so trusted.

"There were so many ways to make money then. A man could cross the street and before he was halfway there he could make a deal worth a week's wages. For someone like me—unscrupulous like me—the possibilities were dazzling. Before I knew it, I was bidding on construction jobs. And all the time without a crew. I would low-ball a bid, and when I had been awarded the job, I'd sell it to a legitimate builder. There wasn't a lot of oversight then. Hell, I must have done that more than a dozen times before the real building contractors threatened legal action against me. But by then I had enough money for other things.

"Now don't get me wrong, I never went in for drugs, or whores — sorry, Maria — I never trafficked in prostitutes. Not that I never indulged in that stuff, but I wasn't going to make it my business. That seemed like something the other guys should do. I wasn't no religious man but I kept a kind of standard, you know? Who needed that kind of low-class trade when there were so many other ways to make a fortune.

"I put in a bid on the maintenance contract for all the automated machinery in the shipping port. Biggest bluff I ever made. Stole a copy of the bid put in by the first company that installed and maintained all the robotics, and rewrote it with a lower bottom line. When I won the bid, I had a crazy notion I'd actually keep it instead of selling it to another contractor. Best crazy notion I ever had.

"I hired guys from the first contractor — guys who were suddenly out of work — and before I knew it I was the custodian of the shipping port. Have you any idea what that meant, Maria? It was like giving a bank robber the keys to the safe. All that cargo moving in and out without any supervision. I was in paradise."

Maria tried to pay attention to Kjarsta's story. She understood few of the details he related, but she understood he was trying to unload a lifetime of corruption.

"I wasn't the only one who realized the position I was in. That's when I met my partner. To be more precise, he made sure I met him. My partner invited himself along for the ride and there was nothing I could do about it. You see, while I was an unscrupulous businessman, my partner was an unscrupulous politician. And that made him dangerous.

"But don't have any sympathy for me. I was out to get what I could and my partner was out to get what he could. We deserved each other. He kept me out of legal trouble and I kept his accounts well fed.

"It was fun, you know?" Here again, Maria could hear a lack of shame in his voice. He had a way of telling her these things as if he were explaining the technical workings of a machine. Did such a disdain for self-consciousness come from his close proximity to death? Or had he always been so free with his conscience? She did not know which explanation made him a better man; maybe neither one.

"It was fun because neither one of us needed to do what we were doing. I had made enough money to withdraw to a life of leisure or whatever I wanted. And my partner was successful enough in his political world to never need to be so corrupt. But we were both driven by the basic character that saw an opportunity and couldn't pass up the chance to take advantage of it. It was like a game, I suppose."

It had taken Kjarsta a long time to tell his tale. The effort was beginning to show on his face. His cheeks were flush and his breathing was shallow. Maria gave him more water and placed a wet towel on his forehead. He allowed her to leave it there for a few moments before asking her to remove it.

"I think you had better rest now." She never gave him orders. It would have shamed him to be reminded he no longer controlled his life. She made sure to suggest things to him rather than dictate.

"Later. Rest later. Let me talk. Am I boring you?"

"No," Maria assured him, seeing the childlike desire for her approbation. It wasn't about being bored or interested to Maria. She was only concerned that Kjarsta not overextend himself. But at the same time she could see that this was something he needed. There was a veiled sense of urgency behind his rheumy eyes. Perhaps he knew he was dying and had to speak of things long held in secret.

"I don't want to bore you." His head fell back, sinking into his pillow. With eyes staring at the ceiling, he opened his mouth and drew in several deep breaths. It wasn't until his eyes closed that he was able to speak again; his mind picturing those years that lay so far in the past.

"I never spent much time worrying about ethics. I'm not even sure I knew what they were when I was young. I told you I stayed away from the uglier side of corruption. I don't think it really matters, but it feels good to point that out. Does it matter to you? I suppose it might. But not to me. At the end, it all looks ugly.

"You shouldn't be here, you know?" He regarded Maria as if seeing her for the first time that night. "What are you doing with an old jake like me? You shouldn't be here. I'm endangering you. You're my angel, and I'm a danger to you. There are things within me that will hurt you."

Maria did not know if he was speaking of the disease that ate at his body or something less tangible; the stain of age-old sins. Perhaps she would never know of what he was speaking. He had ceased talking as he drifted out of consciousness. It was quite possible he would remember none of this when he awoke. She would never speak of it to him.

He was asleep. That was good. There was no need to dredge up old sins; no need to unbury the dead. She prayed that he might forget it all when he awoke. It would be better for him. Better for them all.

76

Helen welcomed another night at home; another night to relax and allow the stress from her day to melt away. She had eaten the leftovers from the previous night's dinner and pampered herself with another long hot bath. She needed it. This business with the lab protocols and Dr. Stride had left her unsettled.

And the bath had done its job—almost. Wrapped in her robe, she sat on her couch with her legs stretched out across the cushions. She did feel better, though she couldn't ignore a vague sense of distress. It was far too faint to be able to define; far too faint to be able to understand what caused it.

Helen reached over and pressed a button on her table console. The soft introduction of Antonin Dvorak's *Stabat Mater Dolorosa* seeped into the room. If she wasn't careful, the warm tranquil music would put her to sleep. That wasn't a bad idea.

Julia would do well to sit alone with Dvorak as well. Helen was surprised that Julia had not called her. Did that mean Julia and Billy had come to some kind of resolution? Or was Julia alone at home, crying again? Helen was glad to be free of such relationship conflicts.

There were so many advantages to being alone. And as the music washed over her, completing the cleansing that the bath had begun, she felt at peace over her solitude. Not even the NewsVision's threat of murder could dissuade her from that peace.

No fear tonight. The building was locked down, as it was every night. What could she possibly fear?

Sifting through her thoughts as they melted into the music, Helen wondered: what had she just said? Something there had been important. The singers' plaintive cries added their voice to her own. They would not allow her to disregard her thoughts. She could hear them asking repeatedly: what had she just said? The soprano's voice ceased singing and Helen heard her articulate one word. *Lockdown.*

Helen's eyes flashed her. Had she been dreaming? Dvorak was still playing. Both the man and the woman continued to sing to each other. She knew now what had been bothering her since she had last spoke to Dr. Haupt. *Lockdown.*

She had locked down the revised protocol. Helen could see the shadowbox as it had appeared on her screen. How could she have forgotten that she had locked down that document? Now she understood why Dr. Haupt's words had bothered her. He had said *only changes made to an archive's status would be noticed.* Locking the document had certainly sent up a red flag.

Helen was not sure how important that might be. But judging by Dr. Haupt's concern over the possibility of a sentinel program, she had to assume he would see this as important but unwelcome news. Would he see it as important enough that he should be told immediately?

The answer to that was obvious. If she informed him about the document later, he might think it was too late. There were fewer disadvantages to doing something too early. She knew she would have to tell him right away.

She wondered if she would be able to contact him. Sending an open call was futile if he had not listed her on his receive list. And surely he would have his connection removed from the universal call lines. But as Helen picked up her phone to attempt the call she felt certain that Dr. Haupt would have thought of that and taken the necessary steps so that she might contact him as needed.

She spoke the doctor's full name into the phone carefully. The system's voice recognition program was an old one and apt to misinterpret names. As she had expected, the call was immediately put through to Dr. Haupt. He had indeed made arrangements for her. He was, as always, efficient and thorough.

"Yes, Helen?" Dr. Haupt answered immediately.

She was nervous as she explained why she had called. She was actually more worried she would be scolded for bothering him rather than forgetting to tell him about locking down the revised lab protocol. He waited until she had finished before speaking.

"Thank you, Helen. I am glad you told me. Would it be difficult to unlock this document?"

"I couldn't do it here at home, Dr. Haupt." Helen was relieved that she had not angered him.

"No, of course not. We will have to go to the office."

"Tonight?"

"No, no." Dr. Haupt said softly. "We may not even need to unlock it. If anyone was watching those files, they will already know we have it. And if that is the case, unlocking it only gives them a chance to delete it."

"I'm sorry about this, Doctor. Perhaps I should not have locked it down. And I should have remembered it and told you right away."

"Your apology is unnecessary. Do not trouble over it. Locking down the protocol was appropriate. It gives us a measure of control."

"Yes, sir." Control? Helen wanted to ask what was really going on. But she hardly felt that she was in any position to ask questions.

After Dr. Haupt had ended the call, Helen tried to do as he had suggested. She would attempt not to trouble herself over her mistake. And the only way to do that was to go to sleep. If she could get to sleep she could distance herself from everything that had happened that day. The next day might turn out better.

Her central control panel for the houselights, music, and communications was a wall unit in the small hallway leading from the front room to the kitchen. Activating it, Helen put her apartment to bed, as Julia liked to say. With one push of a button, she could program the lights to cut off in fifteen minutes, set the kitchen to clean itself, and set the security system on its highest setting.

The panel gave Helen a view of the hallway outside her door, the elevator at both the street level and her floor, and the front doors of the building. These visuals were reliable, and Helen had never seen them not work. It was disturbing to see the front entrance views blank. Her building's superintendent took great pains to make sure the security systems were in good working order. He was lazy about dripping water supplies and clogged waste lines, but he took his duties on security quite seriously. He knew that many of his tenants were women working for IHS and other government employers.

What did it matter? She scolded herself for allowing the blank screen to worry her. But even as she tried to ignore it, the screen that provided the view of the elevator from the first floor flashed bright blue then went as blank as the front entrance screen.

That should have panicked her. But instead of panicking, she watched the remaining screens, paralyzed with curiosity. She could see the doors of the elevator, only ten meters from her front door. They were closed, and Helen waited to see if they would open.

And then, with the slow, deliberate surety as if from out of a dream, the doors slid apart. A tall blond man stepped into the hall. His head was down and she was unable to see his face. With calm measured steps he moved down the corridor. Helen held her breath. There was no reason to believe he was coming for her.

But belief requires no reason. And Helen not only believed the man was coming to her door; she knew it. She even thought she might know who he was. She had never seen him before, but she had a feeling it was Julia's friend Billy. But why Billy would be coming to her apartment was a mystery to her.

She was surprised when he knocked on her door. She had expected him to walk right in and ignore the lock system. It took her a moment to realize he was waiting for her to open the door.

For a moment, all of her irrational fears of the NewsVision's murderer had slipped away. And in that moment, they had been replaced by an irrational belief that Billy had come to speak with her. She unlocked the door.

"Are you Billy?" she asked as she pulled the door open.

"Who the hell is Billy?" the man asked as he raised his right hand and smacked her across the right side of her face.

Helen fell to the floor, pain overriding thoughts of Billy, Julia, or anyone else. The man grabbed her by her hair and pulled her back to her feet. Before she could regain her balance, he threw her against the wall of the foyer. Her head rammed into a metal wall sconce which crumpled under the impact, its sharp edges slicing into her scalp.

The attack was so fast and aggressive that she had no time to feel fear. Shock and pain overwhelmed her. As she slid to the ground, with her vision losing focus, she wondered why the man was not Billy. It was a pointless question, but it gave her something on which to concentrate.

"Can you hear me?" the man asked in a calm voice.

Helen stared at him as if he were insane. Maybe he was. Why was he asking her if she could hear him?

"Helen—" he knew her name "—can you hear me?"

Helen winced as she tried to nod.

"Good. I'm going to make this easy. I want you to call the doctor and tell him I want the code to unlock the protocol. Are you going to give me trouble?"

Helen's scalp burned. Blood tracked down through her hair. She could remember his assault, though it seemed such a long time ago, but she could not understand the part about the doctor.

"Won't talk, huh?" The man stood over her. Helen sensed rage beneath his words. "You will. I'm awfully persuasive."

Talk? Helen wanted to tell him he was wrong. Doctor Haupt did not know the code. Didn't this man know she had the code? His threats were ludicrous. Why didn't he ask her for the code?

She would like to be brave. She would like to hide what she knew. But she could see it in his eyes. He had a strength she could never fight. If only she could speak loud enough to tell him.

But as she tried to speak, another voice spoke. Another voice from someone she couldn't see.

"Put your hands where I can see them."

"Who the hell are you?" the man asked, even as his hands rose slowly to shoulder level.

"My name's Fenelli and I've been looking for you."

To Helen, it seemed as if the whole room exploded with violence. She heard a gun fire, both men slammed into each other in a blur of motion, and she saw blood burst in the air above her.

77

Lepov didn't know how he did it, but MacNally had managed to make it down to the second floor only a few minutes after Lepov sounded the alarm. Lepov was glad he had. He needed a friendly face. And despite MacNally's usually gruff exterior, his was much friendlier than the skinny little guard's.

"What happened?" MacNally asked Lepov and the guard.

"That's what I want to know," the guard said. He was doing his best to throw blame in Lepov's direction. "This guy goes into cell 18 and the next thing I know your guy's dead. Hanging from the light."

"Careful, now. That's the way rumors get started." Lepov had to consciously refrain from smacking the scrawny little guard. "Someone was in here right before me, and he left through the stairwell. I heard someone running to beat hell down those stairs and he had to pass right by you to get to those stairs."

"Officer Simmons," MacNally read the guard's badge, "don't try to put this on Mr. Lepov. You'd better start explaining what happened. You left your station, didn't you?"

Simmons stared at the floor. The dull tile looked as if it hadn't been waxed in months. It seemed to fascinate the guard.

"Sit down," MacNally grabbed Simmons by the arm and shoved him into a seat. "Wait here until your supervisor gets here. You can give your excuses to him."

MacNally and Lepov crowded down the hall and stopped outside number 18.

Montillo's body was no longer swinging.

"Lieutenant," Lepov pulled a folding knife from his pants pocket and snapped the blade out, "I'd like to cut him down from there if you don't object."

"You don't think he's still alive, do ya?" MacNally asked.

"No. I'd say he wasn't alive when the cord went around his neck. I'd lay odds your MedTechs will find he was killed before he was hung."

"Okay, but we can't cut him down. Not yet. We'll have to get Visuals on him. I don't want any of this to go wrong. I want to catch the sonofabitch who did this. Who did this right here on our own ground."

That seemed to be the prevailing attitude as the Visuals team arrived and began recording everything they could find in cell 18. Both techs were taking extra precautions to ensure their data was complete and uncontaminated. At the same time, they were as efficient as they could be — they weren't wasting any time.

Lepov and MacNally stayed out of their way and let them work. MacNally was angry, Lepov could feel it, though it was obvious the big man was insulted more than angry. Losing Montillo was bad luck for the investigation, but MacNally wasn't devastated by the Spaniard's death.

But Lilly would be. Lepov wondered how he would break the news. It's true that Lilly and Montillo weren't the closest of friends, but from what he could tell she cared about him. And when someone has so few friends, losing any of them is damned hard.

Would she blame him? Could he have done anything to stop this? He wasn't sure how he could have seen it coming. The best way he could help Lilly now was to help MacNally find out what had happened.

"We've got to find Ethan Layne," Lepov said to MacNally.

"What do you mean?"

"Montillo was going to tell us how to find him. And someone knew that and killed him. Someone out there doesn't want you to find Ethan Layne. I don't know about you, but when someone tells me not to do something I'm inspired to do that exact thing."

"Okay," MacNally nodded, "and we've just been told not to find Ethan Layne, right?"

"That's the message. But don't listen too well. Do you?"

"Lt. MacNally?" The tech in charge of the Visuals team walked over to them and peeled off a pair of gloves. "I'm Joe Barnes, I'm overseeing the Visuals. We're finished, and you can go back in the cell. But I wonder if you'd mind an observation?"

"Well?"

"Your strangling victim was more than likely tortured. I'll get the report to you as soon as possible, but there's evidence that tells us he was tortured before he was killed. I can't imagine why they would have done that, but what I can imagine doesn't really matter."

"I can imagine why." Lepov took a few steps toward the cell. "Can't you MacNally?"

MacNally slowly nodded in answer to Lepov's question. "Yeah, I can imagine. They want to know where Layne is too."

"So now the question is *what did he tell them?*" Lepov walked back to the cell, knowing the answer to his own question. There was no way to tell what information Montillo had given them. Only a fly on the wall would have known what happened in that cell. By the time Lepov realized he should ask MacNally about recordings taken in the cellblock he knew what MacNally would tell him. If the detective hadn't mentioned them already, they obviously weren't an option.

"I bet I don't like the answer to my next question." Lepov's self-assurance had run out. "Are there any recorders down here?"

"You're right. You're not gonna like the answer. No, we don't have visual recordings of the cell blocks or the halls leading to them."

"God Almighty, MacNally!" Lepov felt a chill pass over him. "This place is some kind of rat-hole."

"Like I don't know that?" MacNally shrugged off the insult. "I told you before this ain't a high priority department. The health services get all the money in the Lazaretto. We had visual recordings when this place was built, but that was ages ago. No one's gonna spend money on that kind of maintenance."

"That's convenient." Lepov had already seen how MacNally

treated people he questioned. "I'm sure you guys pulled all the stops trying to get the recorders repaired."

"Something like that." MacNally didn't have to acknowledge that Lepov had guessed the real reason there were no recordings in the cellblock.

When they reentered the cell, Lepov couldn't keep from looking at Montillo's face. It was cocked at a hard angle; the belt came up around his right ear. No matter how much he had disliked this man, Lepov felt the weight of the tragedy before him. The man's death was a colossal waste; a gross sin in the middle of this transitory, unhealthy, crummy little world. A man's life had been traded for a piss-poor scrap of information that was more than likely useless.

Lepov stared at the body, still hanging and twisting on that light.

"Help me get him down," Lepov had his knife out again.

"The MedTechs will get him. They'll be here in a few minutes."

"Forget the damned MedTechs, will ya? Hold on to him. He ain't got no disease. Not any more than you or I have. This hellhole has already killed him, there's no point in letting it disgrace him more. How can you people live like this, afraid to touch anyone? Half of you must die from despair every year. Now support his weight while I cut the belt."

Lepov's anger had surprised the both of them. And yet, on a certain level, Lepov knew that MacNally understood where that anger had originated. He may have been an outsider, but he surely had no proprietary right to the righteous indignation the Lazaretto inspired. A man didn't need an outside perspective to feel it. He only had to have a heart; a basic fragment of humanity.

With a joint effort, the two men worked quickly to lower the dead man's body, laying it with a sudden gentleness on the wall-mounted bed. Lepov hoped it would somehow make a difference; that when he broke the news to Lilly she would be able to handle it better if she knew they had shown Montillo some respect. Maybe it wouldn't. Maybe it would only make a difference to Lepov.

Once they were finished, both men stood looking at the body.

"I want to find Greta Becker." Lepov had an idea she was their only link left to Ethan Layne. And this time she'd damned well better cooperate.

"I'll help you find her." MacNally looked as angry as Lepov felt. "But let me call Fenelli first."

78

When Parks swung around and attacked, Fenelli had not been ready for it. He fired without hesitation, but his shot missed the narrowing profile of Parks. The second shot hit Parks in the shoulder, but it did not slow him down as he launched himself at the detective. Fenelli weighed more than his attacker, but his feet weren't set to take the impact and he was thrown back against a wall. His gun hand was pinned down by his hip and he struggled to raise the weapon.

Parks wasn't going to let him. He grabbed the gun and twisted it out of Fenelli's hand. For a moment, Parks had it, but Fenelli hit the barrel with his fist and sent it banging across the hallway floor.

The fight had come upon him too quickly. Fenelli could not keep track of each blow. He had wanted to keep an eye on the woman but Parks was too much to handle.

Fenelli hadn't expected any of this.

After Parks had entered an apartment building, Fenelli thought he had caught a break. Maybe Parks was leading him right to someone who could answer all of the questions that were piling up. Maybe Parks was even leading him to Ethan Layne. Fenelli knew that was a long shot, but he felt confident something was about to roll his way.

Without waiting, Fenelli followed Parks into the building. He wasn't going to lose track of him this time. Parks' elevator had stopped on the twenty-third floor. That had been precious time lost but Fenelli jumped into another elevator and coaxed it to lift him faster.

When the doors had finally opened, Fenelli had wanted to rush out into the hall. The elevator doors opened at the end of a long hallway. He had stood silently outside the doors, listening for any sound that might tell him where Parks had gone. It hadn't taken long before he'd heard a crash; something metal had been smashed and thrown to the ground.

By the time he'd heard the woman whimpering and moaning, he drew his service weapon and came around the corner of the open apartment door. In an instant, he could see a woman in a bathrobe on the floor and Parks standing over her.

And that's when he'd made the mistake of talking to Parks instead of pistol-whipping him in the head. That's what he should have done. Fenelli knew that now. But only after he'd lost his gun and Parks had hit him hard enough to send him to his knees.

Parks was on top of him now, lifting his left arm with his right hand to determine the extent of his wound.

"You shot me—stupid cop." Parks dropped his arm and turned his full attention on Fenelli.

Fenelli was only vaguely aware that the woman had begun to crawl out of the apartment. He wanted to keep Parks from paying her any attention.

"I'm gonna shoot you again, you sonofabitch." Fenelli was trying to think of something MacNally would have said. "And then I'm gonna shoot you again strictly because I can."

It was wishful thinking on Fenelli's part, and Parks knew it. But it had been sufficient enough to draw his wrath. Parks shouted something that Fenelli couldn't understand and kicked him in his ribs. Fenelli turned away from the attack and rolled onto his left side in the fetal position. His back was exposed and Parks took advantage of it, kicking him repeatedly in the lower back.

"Run, lady!"

Fenelli had intended to keep Parks' attention for as long as the woman needed to get out of there. But he hadn't thought that Parks would attack him so swiftly and so brutally. At some point, he no longer had the ability to keep or hold Parks' attention. He was merely trying to keep from passing out.

And Parks knew his assault had been effective. Worse, he hadn't forgotten about the woman. Fenelli heard Parks walk back into the hall. The woman was obviously crying and doing her best to make it to the elevators. Fenelli straightened himself, pain tearing at him as he did so, and made an effort to pull himself towards the still open doorway.

He couldn't let Parks catch up to her. Fenelli knew he was in no shape to overpower Parks. It was no longer a question of subduing him and then helping the woman. Whoever she was, she was going to have to get out of there on her own. And Fenelli's only hope was to slow Parks down long enough to allow her to get out.

Dragging himself to the doorway, Fenelli could see the woman had reached the elevator. She'd made it to her feet and was now standing inside the elevator, jamming frantically at its panel switches. Parks strode towards her; he had maybe four or five meters to go before he reached her, though he made no effort to hurry. The woman's terrified eyes shifted from Parks to the panel then back to Parks. She was scared, her breathing ragged. Trickles of blood ran down the side of her neck and soaked into the collar of her robe.

Fenelli could see all of this but had no idea how to interfere. Pulling himself to his knees, he felt his phone in the pocket of his long coat. He yanked it out and saw right away it had been broken in the fight. It couldn't even be powered on.

Fenelli raised the useless phone to his mouth.

"Officer requesting backup! I repeat, officer requesting backup!"

Parks hesitated. He turned and looked back at Fenelli. With a barely audible shush, the doors of the elevator closed. Parks twisted back around and lunged at the buttons on the wall. He was too late; the elevator remained closed.

Fenelli felt a sense of relief. Whoever the woman was, Parks had seemed determined to get to her. For the moment, she was safe. He had to keep Parks' attention only a little longer.

"Standby for location." Fenelli spoke into the broken phone. He stared at Parks, who was walking back towards him.

"You dumb bastard." Parks closed the gap between them and kicked Fenelli in the ribs again. Fenelli tried rolling away from the kick but misjudged Parks' speed. The burst of pain was alarming. Something important was damaged inside. He had no idea what it was, but the pain was far greater than any he'd ever experienced in his life.

He knew the phone was no longer in his hands but couldn't remember how he'd dropped it. He had to get it back. He had to call MacNally. MacNally would be wondering what had happened to him.

"Why were you following me?" someone asked. Fenelli couldn't remember who it was. Before he could come up with a name he was hit in the side of the head. Fenelli thought someone—the man who'd asked the question?—had hit him with a rocket engine. His ears were ringing and he had trouble keeping the horizon at a flat angle.

Something important had definitely been broken inside him. He could hear his own breathing and it was wheezy; he could hear liquid as he exhaled. Damn, but that couldn't be right. He needed to get away from the man asking questions. He could come back later to answer them, but for now he needed to get to a doctor.

Again, he felt the overpowering blow; this time in his back. *My God*, Fenelli tried to yell, *stop it for God's sake! That's enough!*

It wasn't enough. There was more. A lot more. He felt a full sized vehicle run over his chest. Who was driving in the hallway? And why was that voice still asking questions?

"Did Haupt send you?"

Whoever was asking the questions obviously didn't care about answers. Fenelli knew one of the last blows he'd received was directed at his mouth. His jaw hadn't been broken, but it was sore, and his lips were already swollen. It didn't matter. He had no idea who Haupt was.

He wished MacNally would come. MacNally wouldn't let this happen. Sure, Ed could be a real jackass at times. But Fenelli knew he wouldn't let someone beat the living daylights out of him. Lynne always insisted Ed was goodhearted. She always saw the good in people.

But she wouldn't be able to see any good in the man asking questions, would she? After all, he was still hitting and kicking him. But at least he had slacked off. Fenelli couldn't feel each blow anymore. He found that if he thought about Lynne more, the pain pulled away. That was Lynne; she always made things better.

If she hadn't helped him out like that, Fenelli decided, this beating would have been murder. It would have been too much.

All bravado aside, it was too much. He hated to have to say so. Ed would be disappointed in him. But it really was too much. He was too much. Fenelli finally understood that each pounding blow was an attempt to smash him into a hole in the ground that was much smaller than his body. Each blow jammed more of him into that hole.

God, but it hurt. No matter how much pain Lynne was able to take away. This beating would be the death of him. That's something even his father hadn't been able to do. And his dad was still trying to do it. But Fenelli refused to allow his old man to see him hurting. If he kept the old man looking at him, Maria would get away. All she had to do was get in the elevator. All Maria had to do was get far, far away.

It had always worked. Fenelli would have laughed if everything didn't hurt so much. His old man always fell for that bit. And Fenelli could always make sure Maria got away.

It worked this time. Maria was safe from this murderous bastard. And wasn't that who it was? Fenelli shook at the thought. Images of a bloody body in a doorway mixed with images of a child in a stairwell.

This was him! I got him! Where was Ed? He needs to know I found the murderer. He was trying to kill Maria, but I stopped him. I've got him right here!

And he's killing me. I can still feel it. I can't hear his questions anymore. But he's still at it. I'm in the hands of a psychopath and he's beating the life out of me. My God, what about Lynne? She'll eat alone for the rest of her life. If only Maria would sit with her. Maria will have to do it. If only Maria survives.

And Maria will survive. I saved her. I stopped the man from hurting her. No, it wasn't Maria. It was another woman. I don't even know her name. I don't even know who she is.

I wish it would stop. How can it still hurt so much? Can't anyone make it stop? Lynne? Ed? Maria? God?

79

Maria placed each step with exaggerated caution. The rubber soles of her shoes threatened to squeak on the freshly waxed floor. She slowly took three more steps, each one a display of her practiced ability to circumvent any noise that might awaken the man in the bed. As her last step landed in the corridor, she allowed herself to relax. She stopped only long enough to listen for signs that she had awakened Kjarsta. His shrouded form, hidden in the shadows of the room, had not moved. He continued to sleep.

Maria continued down the hall, careful not to awaken the other patients in that wing. A nurse's station sat at the end of the hall. A second hallway ran crossways to it at that end. The nurse's station jutted out into the intersection enough that any nurse sitting at the desk could look down all three hallways. Maria could see Della watching her as she walked towards the station.

"Hello, Darlin'." Della had a way of making Maria feel like a little girl though she was barely older than Maria. Della had the heart of a loving mother and she didn't care how old you were; she was going to mother you no matter what. "How's the old grouch?" Della asked, tossing an accusatory glance towards Kjarsta's door.

"He's asleep." Maria smiled at Della's playful insult. "Is there any coffee?"

"Come around that counter and sit down, honey." Della gave her a look of disbelief as she headed towards the back of the nurse's station. "When are you gonna realize I'm here to take care of you? I had that coffee made ten minutes ago. I knew you'd come slipping out here, sneaking around like a little cat burglar. Now go on and sit down."

"No," Maria shook her head gently. "I'd rather stand. I've been sitting for quite awhile. Della, can I ask you a question?"

"Now, sweetheart, don't spend time asking questions you know the answer to. You can ask me anything. I can't guarantee the right answer all the time, but don't let that stop you from asking." Della handed Maria the coffee then pulled up a chair and settled into it.

"Tell me what you know about Kjarsta. Tell me about him."

"Maria, you feeling alright?" Della leaned forward and scrutinized Maria's face. "I don't believe anyone in this clinic knows Kjarsta Zoltis like you do. What would possess you to ask me?"

"I've seen the way you talk to him. You joke with him, poke fun at him. No one does that here. Not with these patients. Everyone is so solemn. But not you and Kjarsta. You poke fun at him, no matter how tragic his situation. You must know him. Am I right?"

Maria flushed at her own boldness. It was none of her business if Della and Kjarsta knew each other. Especially considering Della had not broached the subject herself.

"Despite your quiet ways, Maria, you do surprise me." Della was silent for a few moments after this vague response.

"I'm sorry," Maria hid her embarrassment behind her cup of coffee. "My mistake."

Della allowed a big laugh to roll out of her.

"Don't be sorry, dear. You made no mistake. In fact, you're

correct. I do know Kjarsta. I've known him for a long time."

Maria raised her chin in surprise. She had not been prepared for an answer like that. She had only wondered if Della had been the first nurse to look after Kjarsta when he had arrived in the clinic. She had been hoping to learn about Kjarsta's frame of mind before the sickness had worn him down. Della's answer was something else entirely.

"I've known him for over twenty-five years. When I first came to the Lazaretto—fresh out of nursing school—I was unhappy with my duties at IHS. That's where I first worked. I was assigned to help with the screening process. We tested travelers who showed signs of sickness.

"Every day we worked through the never-ending line of patients. My God, I thought, what am I doing here? The work wasn't as bad as you might think. But it was never ending. Most of the young girls who hired on there didn't last long. It was simply overwhelming. We saw so many sick travelers; kids, mothers, grandparents. And it never stopped. I was one of those girls who didn't last long."

"And you came here?" Maria prompted.

"No, I wasn't about to do that. That would have been equally depressing. No, I needed an easier way out. And then I met Kjarsta."

Maria could see a cloud pass over Della's eyes. She had stopped talking abruptly. Something was on her mind but she looked as if she were unable to speak of it. She looked uncomfortable.

"It's okay," Maria said softly. "I need to go back to the room. You don't need to say anymore."

"Stay in your seat, Maria. I'm okay. I'm somewhat amused to discover I still feel embarrassment over what happened so long ago. But it won't kill me to talk about it. It might even do me good."

Maria stayed in her seat. She sipped at her rapidly cooling coffee and watched the nurse search for the right words.

"I met Kjarsta in his early forties. But heavens, he was something to look at even then. A big man, as you can guess. But his size was only a part of it. He was important. At least, in certain circles. That was appealing to me. I suppose I wanted him to get me out of IHS. We signed contracts that were difficult to get out of in those days. But I knew that if anyone could get me out of there, this man could.

"You can imagine what I was prepared to do to make that happen." Della laughed in response to Maria's barely perceptible nod. "It's wasn't as bad as you imagine. The truth is, I discovered I wasn't as prepared as I thought I was. I don't know if some latent form of morality grabbed hold of me or I simply got scared silly, but I ended up—well to be quite honest—I ended up running out on him. It's okay to laugh a little at me. I was young and didn't know what I was doing. I'm glad of that, now."

"And do you think he remembers you?"

"But, wait, my dear little Maria. That's not the end of the story. You might think that Kjarsta was hopelessly angry with me. But he wasn't. He sought me out, and made sure I understood that he wasn't angry. In fact, if I might say so, he seemed to respect me more than he once had. In the end, he gave me a job."

"A job?" Maria asked.

'That's right, darling. He hired me away from the IHS and settled my paperwork involved with them. I soon discovered that Kjarsta had a daughter. She was only a few years old at the time. I took care of her. I was her nurse..." Della's focus shifted to those long ago days.

"She became sick?" Maria asked.

"That's another story, dear. One I won't tell."

"I'm sorry." Maria dropped her chin.

"Don't be." Della rubbed away tears.

"I didn't mean to bring back unpleasant memories."

"There was nothing unpleasant about his daughter."

"Did she...?"

"After I finished caring for her, Kjarsta arranged for me to work here. I was grateful to him."

The sound of coughing echoed weakly down the hallway. Maria turned to look in that direction. That was Kjarsta. She recognized the cough. She should be there in case he awoke.

"I need to go back." Maria pushed the coffee cup towards Della and stood to leave.

"I'll walk with you," Della said. "I need to stretch these old legs."

The two women began to walk down the hallway. The overhead lights were dimmed at that hour, and the edges of the wide hallway were covered in shadow. Della walked as quietly as Maria, though the sounds of their steps still echoed softly down the silent corridor. They paused outside Kjarsta's door, speaking in whispers.

"I think you should know something, Della." Maria watched Kjarsta's still form. "The disease is not all that eats away at him. There is much that he regrets."

"There are things that eat at all of us, dear. We all have regrets."

"Regrets stick around like old friends," a deep, scratchy voice came out of the shadows.

"And why are you awake, old man?" Della stepped into the room. "And shame on you for eavesdropping to two honorable women like ourselves."

"Two beautiful women, you mean." Kjarsta tried to chuckle at his comment but only ended up coughing.

"You're no charmer, anymore, Kjarsta Zoltis. I might have fallen for it when I was a young girl but I'm much too old to listen to your flatteries. Now go on back to sleep."

Maria listened to Della scold him. She wasn't easily convinced that Della was only joking with him.

"I don't like to sleep," Kjarsta countered. "I'm getting too old to sleep through the time I have left. I can sleep later, when it's all over."

A violent cough racked Kjarsta's body. Maria could hear phlegm choking his air passage but before she could move in to help Della had already leapt forward and grabbed him by the shoulders. She turned him on his side as quickly and gently as she could. Maria pressed a cotton towel into the nurse's hand and Della held the towel up as she helped Kjarsta expel the partially congealed grey matter from his throat.

Even after the foul substance was cleared away—some of it cleared by Della's own fingers—Kjarsta continued to cough fiercely. Maria watched helplessly as Della held him in place. She was trying to keep him on his side in case any more thick fluid sprayed up into his throat.

After what seemed like hours, Kjarsta's body finally stopped trying to exorcise the now phantom blockage. Mercifully, his breathing rediscovered its normal cadence. It was still raspy, but at least it was a rhythm that did not exhaust him.

80

Run.

It was a word that had little meaning for Helen. It made little sense. But it was a word she couldn't get out of her mind.

Run.

Why had that word been branded into her thoughts? She was frightened. She was terribly upset. But she had enough presence of mind to know that she should not be thinking of that word.

Run.

There is was again. No matter how absurd it was, it wouldn't go away.

Run!

I can't run, Helen wanted to say. Was she the only one who understood that? Why was someone yelling at her to run? She wished he would be quiet. She knew he meant well. But despite that, the fact remained that she was unable to run. She was too shaken up to run. Even walking was too much. She was shaking so hard it hurt.

If only he would tell her to crawl. She could do that. She thought she could anyway. And maybe it would make him happy. At the least it might get him to stop shouting.

Run, Lady!

Helen was tired of it. She decided that no matter what he said, she was going to crawl. She had to crawl. She was too terrified to do anything else. But when she tried to bend her knees they wouldn't respond. If she couldn't crawl she'd never get away. That was bad. That was very, very bad.

Lady!

Helen tried to ignore him. That voice wouldn't stop yelling.

"Lady?"

Helen looked into the man's eyes. His head was twisted back so that he could look at her.

"This is it. Your friend's place. You said it was this building, right?"

Helen looked in the direction he was pointing. As she stared at the tall, cold tower, she began to remember.

No one was yelling at her to run. That had been back at her apartment. The policeman; he had yelled at her to run. But she'd had to crawl. I remember now, Helen thought. The images were coming at her fast, as if she were accessing image files with a high-grade computer; the man at her door, blood hitting the carpet all around her, the man coming at her, her fingers mashing the buttons on the elevator.

"Didn't you tell me 614 Dardanelles?"

"Yes," Helen could remember getting into the TransitCar, now. It had taken an effort to convince the driver to let her in. With no way of paying for the ride, and standing at the street in her robe with blood running down her scalp, it was a miracle he had even stopped. "Yes, this is it. I'll go up and get the money to pay you."

That's what she had told him. That she could get the money from Julia once she talked with her. He had wanted to take her to the police. Helen knew that's where they should have gone. But she was too shaken up to think straight. All she could really remember was demanding that the driver take her to Julia's place.

"Lady, I may look new at this, but I'm not all that new. I'll come with you. Okay?"

Helen turned from looking out the window and examined her driver. He did indeed look young. That was unusual for a Transit driver. Most of them were older men or women who had few prospects left for decent employment. He would have looked even younger if he'd of had a head full of blond hair.

And Helen would never have gotten into the TransitCar if he had.

Helen flinched as the image of the blond-haired man passed over her eyes. It felt like he was swinging the back of his hand at her all over again.

"You okay?" asked the driver.

"Yes, I'm fine." Helen took several deep breaths and pulled the robe tighter around her. Was she still shaking? "I'm sorry about this. I appreciate your help."

"I haven't done anything. Only trying to make a fare. With Delta closed now, I can't be choosy about who I let in my car. Wait there."

He jumped out of the car and hurried around it to open Helen's door. Helen's eyes flickered, trying not to flinch as he yanked the door open and offered her his hand. If she wasn't careful, he might decide she needed to go to the police or the hospital no matter what she told him.

"Come on, we need to get you inside. It's freezing out here and you ain't really dressed for this." He grabbed her gently and hurried her into the front entrance of Julia's apartment building.

The wind pushing down Dardanelles was quick and bit hard at Helen's cheeks. Most of it went right through the cotton robe. It was warm enough if she was curled up on her sofa with a book, but running around the city in it was pretty foolish.

"Thank you," she said as he guided her away from the cold entrance. "You've done more than you know."

"Well, I couldn't leave you standing there in the street. Besides, my mother had the same problem."

"I'm sorry?" Helen asked.

"Your accident." The driver's pity could be clearly read in his eyes. "My mother's third husband. After she married him, she had a lot of accidents like yours."

It had been a way to explain the blood. Again, Helen didn't know why she had lied to the man. She simply didn't want to be forced to talk to anyone about it. When she had told him she'd had an accident, it was obvious he had believed her to be talking about something else. The misunderstanding had been beneficial and she did not correct him.

He kept one hand at the small of her back. Without pushing her, he eased her towards a bank of three elevators. The lobby was nicer than the one in her building. Julia had not hesitated to spend money on a nice apartment. The elevators all had faux wood décor surrounding them.

As the right set of doors slid open, panic seized Helen. The doors weren't locked down. Something was wrong! But no, Julia's building had a different kind of security. Helen remembered Julia telling her about it the first time she came to visit. It was far more advanced than the old system at Helen's. Still, she wanted to stay away from that elevator car. She took a step back and felt the driver's hand hold her in place.

"What's the matter? You do know what floor she's on, don't you?"

"Wait, please." Helen tried to get her breathing under control. She saw her attacker rushing towards the elevator again. No one could stop him. The policeman was lying on the ground like a coat that had been dropped to the floor.

"You aren't afraid of elevators, are ya?" The driver eyed her with disappointment. "If you are, I sure hope your friend is only on the second floor. I don't want to climb no stairs. Elevators don't break down and fall down the shaft, you know? That only happened in the old Earth stories. You gotta know that."

It wasn't the thought of falling that scared her. Once she saw the inside of that elevator car, she thought about the ride down as she fled from the blond man. It had been the longest ride of her life. She kept thinking that the man would be waiting for her in the lobby. It made no sense, and she should have ignored the imaginings of her mind. But no matter how logical she tried to be, she felt the terror in her grow as the elevator continued to drop to the lobby.

"Lady, I'm not climbing stairs, come on." He put his hand against her back and pushed her forward. Helen stiffened in resistance. She was being silly. That's what she would have told Julia. And Julia was at the other end of that elevator. The thought of seeing her friend gave her courage. She wanted to see Julia. She needed her. Julia would stop the shaking.

"You can't stand out here in that robe, you know. Someone's gonna come along and wonder what's going on. And that blood's kinda easy to spot. You need to get to your friend's place and I need to get paid."

Helen made up her mind. No matter how much the elevator terrified her, she had to get in it. She was trembling too much to make it up the stairs. She focused on the image of Julia meeting her at the door. That helped. Seeing Julia was all she needed. Then she could talk to the police. Then she could face whatever came next.

Taking a step forward, she could no longer feel the driver's hand on her back and that helped too. Inside the car, she pushed the button for the seventh floor. Helen remembered the security system would read her fingerprint. It had registered her print the first time she had come and Julia had added her to the access list.

"This is a nice little hut, ya know?" The Transit driver looked around at the interior of the elevator. "Your friend must be rich, huh?"

"Not really," Helen answered automatically, uninterested in small talk.

"Right. Is she married?" he asked with hope in his eyes.

"No," Helen said. It seemed an absurd question. Everything was beginning to feel that way. Some monster had attacked her in her own home, and she'd barely escaped. For all she knew, the man was still fighting with that policeman. And yet, here she was, riding in an elevator with a young kid who was interested in Julia because she might be rich.

"Which way?" the driver asked, stepping out onto the seventh floor.

"This way," she pointed right. "Number 736B."

The hallway was carpeted, with textured walls that absorbed sound. Helen felt as if they were walking through a funeral parlor; ordered and beautiful with the hint of death beneath. Helen hadn't noticed that when she had visited Julia before. It had seemed pleasant then.

Helen knew she was coming apart. She had arrived at Julia's in time. She would not have lasted much longer.

"Hello?" The driver rapped at Julia's door with the back of his hand.

Helen wondered what time it was. Julia was no doubt still awake. But there was no response and Helen began to worry. What if Julia was out? She might not be back for hours. The thought had never occurred to her until that moment. God, she shook, don't let her be gone.

The driver knocked two more times and they both stood uncomfortably in that silent hallway.

"Lady, you should be able to get in. This system should accept your print if it accepted it in the elevator. So you go on inside. Forget the money, okay? If anyone ever needed a free ride it was you. But I hope you'll take my advice about something, huh?"

"Advice?" Helen didn't understand.

"That accident you had." He nodded at the blood on the collar of her robe. "I don't care how much you love the guy—don't let him do that. Call the police and put a stop to it."

Helen nodded absently. Yes, she ought to call the police. Though, undoubtedly they already knew.

"Thank you, for everything." Helen tried to smile at him. The driver watched her to make sure the door would open. Once she wrapped her hand around the brass door handle, a green light above it flashed twice and the door began to swing inward.

"There ya go, I told ya." He backed away a few paces then turned and walked down the carpeted hallway.

Helen took a deep breath and made herself stop shaking. She would be safe in Julia's apartment. Julia would be home soon.

Everything would be alright.

As Helen entered the foyer, she could see a light on in the kitchen. That was a surprise. Even at Helen's place, the older systems knew to shut down lights once the occupant exited the apartment. Maybe the higher scale suites gave the residents more options. A light had already turned on once she was fully in the foyer. When she closed the door, two more lights came on; one in the living room adjacent to the foyer, and the other in the short hallway that led to the kitchen.

The bedrooms were on the other side of the living room, and Helen needed to go find some clothes and take a shower. She was pretty sure she could do that, even if the shaking hadn't stopped completely.

But first she needed to drink some water. She could taste iron and realized her mouth had been bleeding. She needed to wash out the taste of it. She was sure she tasted bile, though she couldn't remember if she had actually vomited. God knew she'd wanted to.

She could smell it before she reached the kitchen. Something had gone bad in the there. Maybe the self-cleaning system had broken down. But even if it had, Helen couldn't imagine what would smell that awful. It was almost strong enough to keep her from entering the kitchen. She stopped at the doorway and put a hand to her mouth. The taste of bile and blood combined with the odor made her gag.

"What in God's name?" she whispered. There was something on the bright tiled floor. Spots of something smeared on the cream-colored squares. Dark, viscous smears. She only had to take a few steps into the kitchen to see it more clearly. To see her.

To see Julia.

Helen knew it was Julia. It didn't matter that the body was horrifyingly battered and bloody. It didn't matter that the swollen face was unrecognizable. It didn't matter that the long silky hair was streaked dark with blood. Helen knew she was looking at Julia.

She had lost her mind. She knew because she could no longer smell the overpowering odor of death, could no longer taste the bile and the blood, her eyes failed to see her friend on the kitchen floor, just as her ears failed to hear her own screams. The only thing Helen was aware of was the incessant shaking of her body. And there was nothing that would stop her from shaking that hard for all eternity.

81

Gregor Lepov knew he should never have taken MacNally up on his offer. He was an outsider and he didn't belong there. He could not explain why that mattered. And maybe it didn't. But at that moment, it was the only logical thing on which he could concentrate.

If Lepov was going to be honest about it, he really didn't want to belong. He didn't want to be there.

When MacNally had heard that Fenelli had been found in the hallway of an apartment building, he had unhesitatingly told Lepov to come with him. Lepov hadn't even thought about where they were going. He had followed along as if he were now a member of Lazaretto Homicide.

They had received spotty reports about Fenelli's condition, most of them too confusing to get any kind of accurate picture of what had happened. But Lepov had been able to judge MacNally's despair and anger enough to know that the big detective held out little hope for his partner. Yet, despite that, Lepov had never considered what they would find. If he had, he would have held back and stayed out of the way.

Now, in that hallway, he wanted to get back in the elevator. He had no business being there. This was something MacNally and his fellow officers had to deal with. With something like shame, Lepov was glad it was their friend and not his. Why had he come along?

He had done something stupid like that as a rookie cop; something just as foolish. He had only been a patrolman for six months when he had been called to the scene of a house fire. The location of the fire caught his attention and even though it was outside his coverage area he rushed to the address without hesitation.

The house fire was at his father's parents' house. And by the time he made it there, his grandmother was dead. She had been laid out on the sidewalk a short distance from the still smoldering home. Lepov had never been close to her, but he knew that his father worshiped her.

And then, without a thought as to what he would do when he arrived, Lepov sped towards his father's home. The only thing he had felt was an overwhelming urge to tell his father that his mother was dead. He never once thought of what that shock would do to the old man. He only felt he had to act; to get to his father as fast as he could.

It had been something akin to divine intervention when his mother answered the door. He could still remember the smile on her face as she reached out to hug him and asked what had prompted his visit.

And then he'd blurted out his news. Grandma was dead. That was all he'd said. His mother's smile faded, and Lepov watched her draw herself up as if she were preparing to enter the King's presence, then walk softly into the house to give her husband the news.

Lepov had watched his father break down that day as his mother gingerly held him in her arms. Lepov wondered what would have happened if he had rushed into his father's house and delivered such a bombshell.

It seemed to Lepov that he had learned nothing from that experience. For now, standing a few steps away from the dozen or so policemen in that hallway, Lepov wanted to get off that floor. He wanted to get back down to the lobby and walk away. This was not the reason he had come to the Lazaretto. He had only come to earn a small commission on a simple job.

MacNally stood a few feet in front of him, lighting a cigarette. He was wearing his long coat, his hat left behind in the mad dash to get out of the police station. Thin wispy hair covered a white scalp that was prematurely spotted with age. He looked old.

Lepov could see it in MacNally's stance; his shoulders rounded down, as if his arms were affected by the gravity of a large planet; his back arched in a way that suggested MacNally was suffering from arthritis and standing upright was painful.

Lepov knew that Time was not to blame for this. He was watching a man who'd been ruined by horrific news concerning his dearest friend: Arturo Fenelli had been brutally murdered.

Lepov could see an exaggerated pulse of blood pumping beneath the skin of MacNally's temple. This wasn't despair. This was about to become something else entirely. Lieutenant Edward MacNally was filling with rage. Lepov knew the man would never be able to contain it.

With annoying predictability his mind returned to his earlier thought. He wanted to get away; to get away from MacNally, to get away from Fenelli's brutally savaged body, to get away from that hallway.

He began to edge towards the elevators.

"Lepov, where are you going?" MacNally hadn't even looked in Lepov's direction. But he had known what Lepov was doing. More than likely, Lepov conjectured, he had even known why.

"I should wait downstairs." Lepov cleared his throat, he was afraid his voice sounded like a scared child's. "I don't belong here. I'll only be in the way of you and your friends."

"My what?" MacNally turned around and stared at Lepov with hard eyes. It seemed to Lepov that they were the only part of MacNally that didn't look vulnerable at that moment.

"The other officer's — your friends. I understand, losing one of your friends. This is no place for outsiders."

A young MedTech approached MacNally and stood waiting to speak. He reached out a hand to get MacNally's attention.

"Hang on," MacNally brushed him away and took several steps towards Lepov. "Losing one of my friends? Is that what you think happened here? That's not one of my friends lying there in his blood. That's my only friend. What the hell makes you think any of these people here are my friends, huh?"

The MedTech, along with the other officers within earshot of MacNally, dropped their heads and backed away from MacNally.

"You know what you and I have in common, Lepov? I'll tell you what we have in common. I'm as alone in this hellhole as you are now. We're both standing alone in the middle of a disease-soaked world looking for some madman named Ethan Layne. And that's a hell of a thing to have in common.

"So do me a favor. Don't go anywhere." MacNally used the stub of his cigarette to light another one.

"Sir?" The MedTech approached MacNally again.

"What, dammit?" He dropped the stub on the carpeted floor and stepped on it.

"Well, Sergeant Barnes wanted me to give you a message—he's busy taking the visuals right now. But he said he's already seen something that you should know."

"Well?" MacNally asked, clearly still shaken.

"He says the pattern's not right. Whoever killed Detective Fenelli wasn't the same guy who beat those other victims. He'll give you the details later, but he thought you'd like to know this as soon as possible."

Lepov wanted to ask the MedTech about the details but waited to allow MacNally to respond. The big detective didn't say a word. But it looked for a moment as if life was returning to MacNally.

"Look out," MacNally put out a hand and pushed the MedTech off to one side.

Lepov gave the kid a sympathetic smile and hurried after MacNally, who was headed down the hall to where his partner's body lay.

"What'd'ya got, Barnes?" MacNally nearly ran into the Sergeant, who was standing a few feet away from Fenelli's body with a small box-shaped machine in his hand.

"Watch it, don't bump me. I want to get this right. I'll be done in a few minutes and then I'll explain it to you." Barnes spoke softly, his attention focused on Fenelli's body as if he were taking pictures of beautiful scenery, not a bloodied and broken man.

"How can you tell this wasn't the same guy?" MacNally lowered his voice. He kept his eyes to one side, never looking at Fenelli's body.

"Well, I'm no Doctor, but I can see the bruising is all wrong." Barnes seemed to forget he had told MacNally to wait. He spoke in that same soft voice. "There are places on the body where the skin is split, as if it were punctured."

"He was stabbed?"

"No, I mean punctured after the swelling had begun, as if many of the blows came later than the first ones. The victims from earlier in the week all had bruising consistent with nearly simultaneous bruising. Remember? Well, anyway, I'm sure these visuals will confirm it. Also, there is bruising below the beltline. That is inconsistent with the others."

Lepov made himself look at what use to be Fenelli. From what he could see, Barnes was right. But if he were, then who would have done this? The smell of MacNally's cigarette gracefully interfered with the smell of Fenelli's body. He had to admit a cigarette didn't sound like a bad idea at that moment. He tried not to think of the pack inside his coat.

MacNally's breathing was becoming audible. It sounded as if he were trying to force more air out of his lungs than he was taking in; an ancient steam engine—complete with smoke—beginning to pick up speed. Lepov put out a hand to steady the detective.

"Come on, maybe we both need to go down to the lobby, for a few minutes."

"Why?" MacNally jerked away from Lepov, his voice loud and full of anger. "So I don't stand here and see the obvious? Leave so I don't realize what's happened? It's too late for that. And I wouldn't avoid it if I could. I may not be the brightest cop on the force, but it doesn't take much to figure this one out!"

"What are you talking about?" Lepov asked.

"I'm talking about why my partner and best friend just died. That's what I'm talking about. Someone out there thinks I'm an idiot. Oh, God!" MacNally looked as if he might double over in pain. "Fenelli! They killed you and tried to make it look like you were just another victim. Goddamn 'em! Why'd they do that? Would somebody tell me what the hell is going on? Why the hell did my friend just have the life beaten out of him? Who's playing games with me? Why?"

Lepov watched MacNally ball his fists and smash them into the crown of his head, stumbling around Fenelli's body in a drunken gait. Twice, Lepov reached out to grab him—to calm him—twice, MacNally swung a fist at Lepov to make him let go.

Then finally, MacNally turned and took a moment to study the body of his partner. He dropped to his knees beside Fenelli's swollen figure. When Lepov tried to move the detective from where Barnes was still taking visuals, Barnes waved him off. He had finished and was shutting down the recorders.

"Arturo," MacNally kept moving his hands in stuttered

movements, unsure of what he should do with them. "What were you doing out here? Why did you let me leave you alone? Lynne'll never forgive me. I was supposed to watch out for you."

MacNally choked and then sobbed. Despite his large size and hardened façade, Lepov was not surprised to see tears falling from MacNally's eyes. He had known next to nothing about Fenelli. And he knew precious little about MacNally. But he could see how close these two old detectives had been.

"I'm sorry, Arturo. I'm sorry. I'm gonna find him. I'm gonna find the monster that did this. I'm gonna..."

Barnes quietly walked away, leaving Lepov to watch over the kneeling figure of MacNally. He was staring at his partner and muttering something so softly that even Lepov could not make out what it was.

Book Three

Pathogen

Ed MacNally sat at his desk with an empty coffee cup in his hand. He had too much to do. He was investigating the murders of Jack Ford, the two Rodyakovs, Carlos Montillo, Julia Maiden, and Arturo Fenelli. Good God, what was going on?

MacNally did not know where to begin. He felt sluggish but he knew another cup of coffee wasn't going to do him any good. He needed Fenelli to help him sort things out. That's what he really needed.

But some bastard had killed Fenelli. MacNally really didn't need to be reminded of that fact. The truth was it had been all he'd been able to think about for the past two days. That was the reason he couldn't set priorities on what he needed to do. There was only one thing that had priority over all of his other responsibilities: he had to find the man who had killed Fenelli and beat him to death. That was what he had to do. He didn't care about any of the other victims. He wanted to exact some old-fashioned vengeance. That was his priority.

Fenelli would have argued about that. He would have told MacNally to not let his anger get the better of him. He was always saying things like that. Fenelli was forever acting like a mother. *That's not the right way to do this. That's not following procedure.* Well, to hell with procedure, MacNally wanted to yell.

And if he had, Fenelli would not have yelled back. He would have waited patiently until MacNally had calmed down, then he would have convinced him to do it the right way. That's what Fenelli did; he kept MacNally balanced.

MacNally needed that balance now. He had to move forward.

One step at a time. The most important step was to investigate the girl's murder. She had obviously died the same way as the first three victims; the way Fenelli's death was supposed to look. But that was only a ruse. A crude attempt to link Fenelli to the other murders. But this girl's death had been no ruse. Her body was identical to the other bodies.

So he would start with the girl. And that should be easy. He already had someone at the station to interview. The woman who had discovered the body had been waiting in a side room for fifteen minutes. MacNally had known all along he would have to talk with her. But he had been too preoccupied with Fenelli's death to be able to show any interest in questioning her.

He stood up from his desk and decided he had better get his head straight. If he couldn't get anywhere on these four murders, he was never going to get the chance to look into Fenelli's death.

With two cups of coffee cradled in the palm of one of his large hands, MacNally opened the door and spoke as he entered.

"Miss Segal? I hope you like your coffee with milk and sugar. I used a little of each." He set the cup down in front of the woman and watched her reaction. She kept her chin up; not arrogance, but a good deal of self-assurance. He liked that.

"Thank you." Her voice was even, no sign of nervousness. MacNally was glad of that; he didn't need to talk to some skirt who was too nervous to remember her own name.

"I told you yesterday that if you wanted me to bring in a female officer during this conversation I could do it. But you never gave me an answer about that."

"It really isn't necessary is it? I mean, there's little point."

"That's for you to decide. But if you were really looking for my opinion then I would tell you I don't see the point either. I'm not that hard to get along with. Although others might disagree. To be blunt, I'm not one for small talk, so could I just ask my questions?"

"Yes," the woman nodded.

"Good, I hope this won't take long. For the record, we are discussing the events from two nights ago. I should tell you that I have had little time to look over the initial report from the officer in the field. So tell me your story as if you are telling it for the first time, okay?" MacNally sat facing the woman and crossed his arms over his chest.

"Should I start with finding Julia, or start with the attack?"

"Start at the beginning," MacNally suggested. She was middle-aged with a plain but pleasant face. Her hair was simply done. She wore little make-up. She was thin—too thin—and it was most noticeable in her face. The report said she wasn't married, and that was no surprise. But he doubted she sat around whining about the fact. She seemed sensible enough.

MacNally decided that for a woman, she would be a fairly trustworthy witness.

"I was at my home and had finished taking a bath when the man came to my door. On my security panel, I watched him come out of the elevator but I didn't see him in the lobby. Something was wrong with the cameras on that level. But I opened the door when he knocked. I know that was stupid of me. And then he just attacked me."

"And you said in the report you don't know why he attacked you?" MacNally scanned the report on the table's deskscreen.

"No, I don't." The woman looked him in the eye when she said that. Had she hesitated? Or was he only imagining it? It was the one thing he had noticed when he glanced at the report. She had been unable to give a reason why the man had chosen to attack her.

"Okay, go on." MacNally wasn't going to fight with her over it. If she were lying, he wouldn't have been surprised. If there was one thing he had learned over the years it was that women never hesitated to lie. If she were hiding anything, he would eventually find out what it was.

"After he threw me against the wall, I heard a voice—that was the detective, though I didn't know who he was then—tell the man he was under arrest, or something like that. I was pretty dazed and can't remember exactly. Is it important what he said?"

"It could be. Did the detective call the man by name?" It seemed absurd to MacNally to be speaking about Fenelli as if he were a nameless participant in a crime scene.

"I don't remember." The woman thought about it for a moment, then shook her head. "No, I don't think he did. I think he might have said his own name. I'm sorry."

"Go ahead. Keep going."

"That's all I can say. I knew I had to get away. And I tried to crawl away as fast as I could. They were fighting and the detective yelled at me to run. I think he knew he was in trouble. The other man was so fast—so brutal. All I could do was force myself to get to the elevator."

"You did good. If that's what he told you to do, then you did great."

"I understand he was your partner?" There was kindness in her voice. "I can't express how grateful I am..."

"He was the best—a good man. Can you describe your attacker? I have what you told the officers on the scene. But you've had time to think about it. Was there anything else you remembered?"

"No. I wish there were. I told you he was blond. Maybe taller than I am. But I'm not sure of that. I know that I saw his face but his attack was so fast that I didn't have time to think about what he looked like. Do you understand that?"

MacNally nodded, but he wasn't really listening anymore. He was thinking about Fenelli again. What was Fenelli doing there? Simple coincidence that he was on her floor when she was attacked? That was impossible. So why was he there?

"There is too much I don't know," MacNally said. "Why did he attack you? Why was my partner there?"

The woman looked irritated, as if she wanted to get away.

"I'm sorry if this is bothering you, but you may know something that can help us find this guy." MacNally's tone was heavy-handed.

"Oh no, Lt. MacNally. You've misunderstood me. Something is bothering me, but it's something that your partner said. I can't quite remember it, but it may help you in some way if I can remember it.

Please, give me a moment."

MacNally nodded silently, allowing her to think.

"He told the man to leave me alone. And the man asked him who he was." Miss Segal shook her head as she tried to replay the scene in her head. "He said —" she shook her head.

"That's okay; I understand you were shaken up." MacNally decided he was finished with her. It had been wishful thinking to believe that questioning her again would bring any kind of new results. He tapped a symbol on the desk screen and it went black. MacNally was back to square one.

"He said —"she spoke again, as if she hadn't heard him, " — I've been looking for you. That was it. He said 'I've been looking for you'."

"Fenelli was looking for this guy?"

"Yes, I'm certain of it."

MacNally was both excited and disappointed. He was glad she had remembered what Fenelli had said, but he was disappointed with himself for letting Fenelli leave without telling him what he was doing. He would have to go through Fenelli's desk screen and see if there was anything there that might tell him who had murdered his friend.

83

Maria lay in her bed, wishing desperately to slip back into sleep. But no matter how dark she made her room, no matter how much daylight she kept out of it, she knew that sleep was impossible. She kept replaying the last two days over in her mind. Despite resisting them, the images came of their own volition.

After a long night with Kjarsta, Georges had told her the news of Arturo's death. There had been no sleep that day, only long, black moments of dull pain and even longer periods of tears. A headache had dominated most of the remaining day, and she had been forced to stay home that night. That had only made her feel worse knowing that Kjarsta was alone. She would have gone, despite her pain and grief, but Georges had intervened. He would not allow her to go.

But that had not meant she had slept that night. She had wandered about the apartment in despair, her mind conjuring up all kinds of nonsense. If she had insisted on eating lunch with Arturo, would he be alive now? Had he died in great pain? Had it been quick without any time to realize what was happening? No one would tell her what had really happened. She couldn't stop the speculation.

Now, she was supposed to be sleeping. If she couldn't, Georges would never let her go back to the clinic. And she had to get back there. Watching over Kjarsta was the only thing she could do. She had wanted to go to her sister-in-law but she knew that she was in no shape to be of any help. Lynne was a strong woman and she would only end up comforting Maria.

Sleep had come in small doses; enough to allow dreams of Arturo and Kjarsta and her father, enough to give her hope that all three men were alive and healthy, enough to leave her with fresh pain each time she awoke to the realization that hope had abandoned them all.

The death of her brother was nothing like that of her father's. With Arturo there had been no fissures left between them. They had never been close, but theirs had been a relationship based on familial love that was stronger than most. They had even shared the pain of their childhood and it had been the tie that bound them together whenever the business of life allowed them to drift apart. Losing Arturo would be like losing a part of her soul.

The same would happen when Kjarsta died. She had come to terms with the fact that he would die. Grief would not harass her. Shame was the bigger threat. Shame at being a part of a society that would allow a man to die alone, shoved aside as if he were nothing more than an unfortunate animal that did not even deserve the mercy of a quick death.

Maria would find a way to sleep. She would do what was necessary to convince Georges she was ready to get back to the clinic. Kjarsta needed her. She would be there for him. He would not die alone. Maria would make sure of it.

84

The Collector stared at the image of his agent for a long time. His agent was sitting on a bench in the outer chamber of the Collector's office. This was not the front lobby where most visitors waited. This was an anteroom that had a discreet entrance near the back of his office. But no matter how discreet it was, he did not consider his agent's visit safe or welcome. He was becoming more and more disappointed with this man.

The Agent sat at attention, shoulders back. Undoubtedly, he was only too aware of the size of his mistake and he was making a brave show of it. The Collector shrugged. He could be as brave and bold as he wanted. The fact of the matter was that mistakes like that could never be tolerated.

But the Collector would deal with that later. First, he needed his agent one last time. It was irritating to be forced to rely on him, but time was short and he had no choice. He had to make his agent believe that he still held some trust in him. He had to make his agent believe that he had not made a fatal error. He had to give his agent hope.

"Do not disturb me until you hear from me." He spoke to his secretary, knowing she would recognize his tone and be sure to obey him.

With the push of a button the door to the anteroom opened a few inches. The Collector watched his agent turn and stare at the partially opened door for a few seconds before he stood and walked towards it.

"Don't touch the handle." The Collector said sharply. The Agent stopped his hand a few centimeters from the polychrome handle. "Push it open with your foot."

The Agent pushed the door open and stepped into the office.

"Your fear of germs is getting out of hand, don't you think?" The Agent smiled though the Collector knew no joke was intended.

"How is the injury?" The Collector saw no sign of a bandage.

"Like new." The Agent put a hand to his shoulder. "Your man has talent. But I'm sure you know that. Why do you ask?"

"You made a mess of things. I need to know that you're healthy enough to fix them. You understand? Yes, my man told me he repaired your wound. But I need to hear it from you. That you are able to take the next step."

"And what would that be?" The Agent's curiosity was evident. More than likely he had expected to be disciplined, not given more work.

"It's time to kill the doctor. He's too close, and with this mess you made of his assistant and this lockdown code, we can't afford to be careful and discreet. Kill him, the woman too, that should end this."

"What about Layne? Aren't you forgetting him? I don't like loose ends."

"Leave Layne to me. I don't leave loose ends." The Collector hoped his smile covered the fact that he *had* forgotten about Layne. He was getting sloppy. It was why he didn't like doing things in a hurry. And he was doing too many things in a hurry lately.

In fact nothing was going the way he had planned. But that would change. Soon, he would tie up those loose ends his agent was worried about. And after that, he could wash his hands of everything.

"You were stupid to kill the cop." The Collector saw the Agent's eyes and knew he had caught him off guard. He had not wanted to bring that subject up but it was evident he had to put his agent back in his place.

"He came after me. I had no choice."

"I understand that. I was referring to your methods. I only hope you cleansed yourself sufficiently after all of that contact with his blood. Especially since you were brazen enough to show up at my office." The Collector was sincere about that last part. The thought of the cop's blood contaminating his office was unthinkable. He would have to schedule a third level purification of the office as soon as the Agent left.

"I'll kill the doctor. But you must do something." The Agent still had some fight in him. "I want into Delta. The grace period is over in about an hour. I won't be done by then. But I want you to get me in, I don't care how. This is the last thing I'm going to do. I want out of the Lazaretto. And I don't intend to come back for a long time."

"That can be done on the condition that you kill both the doctor and the woman. I had every intention of this being your last task."

The Collector shut the door to the anteroom on the heels of the Agent with the push of a button. He had already decided a third level purification was not enough. It would be sufficient for the office, but he would need a sonic bath, as well as a light treatment. He sent a message for preparations to be made. "Damn him," the Collector cursed his agent. "What a waste of my time."

85

"Helen, why are you here?" Dr. Haupt was not pleased to see her.

"I'm fine, Dr. Haupt. I need to return to work. I can't sit at home. I was released from the hospital last night, and slept surprisingly well. After a short interview with the police this morning, I felt I had to come in."

She had not expected her answer to sway him from demanding she go back home and she prepared to launch into an even more detailed defense of her reasons for coming to work. He surprised her by simply nodding.

"Then I will update you on what has happened since you were last here. Please come into my office. And Helen, I am sorry about Miss Maiden's death. It was tragic and wasteful."

Helen could only nod; a weak form of acknowledging his words of consolation. From anyone else, his words might have seemed cold and abrupt. But for the doctor, they seemed to be backed with real emotion. Helen realized that Julia would have liked hearing him speak like that. She might have allowed that he had a little humanity in him after all.

"I will be brief. We have much to do, and time is short," he said as Helen took her seat. "I have been studying many documents since yesterday. Your call the other night, and the subsequent attack upon you, made me go back and look at that revised lab protocol. And I had to ask myself how Dr. Stride could have anticipated such details about murder victims that had not yet been murdered."

"Had they already been murdered?" Helen asked.

"No. That would have been easy to detect. No, I did not spend much time on this because there is only one simple solution. And I was not going to overlook an answer because of its simplicity. The easiest solution was that Dr. Stride knew what to look for because he had seen these symptoms before. And when you consider that Dr. Stride works in the IHS labs, we can guess that he has seen them here at the IHS labs."

"Are you saying someone was murdered here at IHS?"

"No," Dr. Haupt shook his head with disdain. "You are not thinking clearly. Dr. Stride is one of the head physicians at IHS. His primary function is to work with pathogens, viruses, diseases of all kinds. There is no reason to look beyond this fact."

"Are you suggesting that Julia, and the others, died of some kind of virus? That's impossible. IHS would have—"

"Ignored it. As they had been told to do with the revised protocol. There have been no murders. But something is killing people, and Dr. Stride knows what it is."

Helen was silent, trying to catch up to Dr. Haupt's line of reasoning. She would have said he was out of his mind until she stopped to consider his theory. And when she did, she was astounded to discover it not only made sense, it was incredibly obvious.

"How could we, or anyone, not have seen this?" she asked.

"The IHS has dominated the Lazaretto since its inception. No one does anything here without their approval, is that not correct?" Helen nodded. Dr. Haupt continued. "So when IHS told the police that this was a non-pathogen, they would have automatically believed them."

"But they didn't. Remember the two detectives?" Helen asked.

"Precisely. And that is why I went to Dr. Fisher before you returned. I decided that he knew something. It was possible Stride was working under Fisher's orders. I had hoped that if I applied pressure, Dr. Fisher would reveal what he knew."

"And did he?"

"No. But his reaction to my questions told me enough. I feel quite certain that Dr. Fisher knows what is going on. He denied the existence of the lab protocol even after I assured him I have the original file locked down. I could not show it to him, since I did not have you here to unlock it. And that seemed to give him some sort of confidence; enough to deny it existed, anyway."

"Do you think he sent the man who attacked me?" Helen could never believe that Dr. Fisher would do something like that to her, but it was the most likely explanation.

"I do not know. If I thought he had done this, I would have been tempted to beat a confession out of him. However, I hesitate. Tell me, do you think Dr. Fisher capable of such decisive action?"

Helen had worked many years for Dr. Fisher, and she wanted to assure Dr. Haupt that such a thing was impossible. But she realized she really didn't know. Could anyone really know what another person was capable of?

"I think the time for discretion has passed, Helen. I am going to call a meeting with Dr. Stride and Dr. Fisher. I will link the meeting with Baltimore. That might force some accountability on them."

"Would you like me to prepare something for the meeting? I can print out the lab protocol, as well as the reports on each of the bodies." It troubled her to think she had just labeled Julia a *body*.

"Yes, in fact, I will send you a list of what I want. But Helen?"

"Yes?"

"I want you to know that I think you should be home, resting. However, I'm glad you are here. I will need your help."

"Will you be contacting those detectives?" Helen remembered that one of them was dead only after she had asked the question.

"I think we had better do so. But I want to speak with Stride and Fisher before I speak to the police. Right now, we have only speculation. I want more facts before we go to them. We will call the detectives and ask them to be here some time after the meeting,"

And then the doctor dismissed her. She sat at her own desk and needed a few minutes to collect her thoughts. Was that all there was to it? Julia had died from some form of virus or pathogen? Had all of this originated here at IHS? She had believed the NewsVision's reports of a murderer. Was she supposed to ignore it now?

The most difficult part of believing Dr. Haupt was what she had seen at Julia's apartment. Such a violent and bloody scene made the reports of a murderer quite real. How could that not have been the results of a deranged maniac?

Helen felt a tremor in her hand and she knew she would have to stop thinking about it. She had spent half the day in the hospital trying to quell the shaking. Hour by hour it had slowly faded. She did not want to let it start again. She remembered her helpless feeling when it seemed as if she would never again stop shaking. She'd been able to peer deep into the future with the foreknowledge that the shaking would never stop. She had no desire to feel that way again. She pushed thoughts of Julia and those bloody bodies out of her head and focused on her hand.

The shaking stopped.

It had taken Lepov most of the previous day to realize he needed to quit tagging along with MacNally. His partner's death was certainly a tragic blow but it ultimately seemed to have little to do with finding Ethan Layne. And Lepov had come to the conclusion that regardless of Layne's involvement in the murders, he was going to find him. That's what he had been hired to do. He also wasn't going to be paid in full if he high-tailed it back to the home planet empty-handed.

No, Lepov told himself, he was going to find that kid, and Greta Becker was going to make that happen.

He had never completely bought her story. Too much of it made no sense. But Lepov had been trying to keep a low profile when he first tangled with her. Well, he chuckled, my low profile's been shot to hell, so I won't let her rattle me the next time we talk.

But first he had to find her.

Her apartment was in the West End, a part of the Lazaretto that looked strikingly familiar to Lepov. Back in his hometown where he'd cut his teeth as a rookie patrolman, there were two sections of town that supplied these kinds of services to the populace. It appeared that no matter how worried travelers were about the possibility of transmitted diseases, some things never changed.

Lepov sat in a rented parked car in front of a small gambling house. A dim light was barely visible through the grungy windows. So far, no one had come out complaining that he had been parked in front of their door for most of the night and all of that morning.

The Becker woman's apartment was three doors down from the gambling house, on the other side of the street, and three floors up. The outside of her building looked as if it had once been on fire. The first floor of her building was a bar; a windowless affair that Lepov had entered the night before. It had been dark enough inside that he couldn't see what the bartender had poured into his glass. Dark enough that it would have been impossible to see Greta Becker if she had been next to him.

He had made no attempt to enter her apartment yet. He was going to wait her out. He hoped to God she wasn't shacked up with someone else. If she didn't show by the end of the day, he would start asking around. But that was something he was only going to do as a last resort. This part of town was trouble enough without stumbling around asking for someone who didn't want to be found.

Lepov's mind wandered to the subject of Lilly. He'd been shocked by her reaction to the news of Montillo's death. She had blamed him for it. Her anger had sounded much like MacNally's anger over his partner's death. He understood that and tried to give her space. He was, in fact, using this search for Greta Becker as a way to hide from Lilly. But there were also legitimate reasons for tracking down Greta Becker. Besides, he muttered to himself, Lilly was free to join him if she wanted. He wasn't hiding from her at all.

As a TransitCar pulled up to the front of Greta's building, Lepov sat up to clear his head. He was getting tired and the coffee had run out hours before. He would watch to see who was in the TransitCar, then he would have to get out and stretch his legs; maybe even find more coffee.

He almost didn't recognize her. She was smaller than he remembered her. Her little boy's haircut was hidden by a tight-fitting, black hat. But as she argued with the Transit driver over the fare, he recognized her defiant gestures. He had most certainly found Greta Becker.

As if to verify he had found the right woman, his knee began to ache as he climbed out of the car. He made a promise to himself that he would never let her get close to kicking his knee again. He had no qualms about hurting her if he had to. Who gave a damn if she was a woman? She had proven she wanted to be treated the same as any man.

Despite the brief pain he'd felt getting out of the car, his knee was actually feeling pretty good. And that was important as he hurried to close in on her. He did not want to catch her on the stairs. He wanted to be able to catch her right as she was entering her apartment. Pushing through the old, badly painted door, he could hear her shoes on the wooden stairs. She was a full floor above him. He would have to hurry to get there before she closed her door.

It would be impossible to mask the sound of his approach, and he had to trust to luck there. If she guessed something was wrong and made a run for it he would never make it. She could barricade herself inside and he'd catch hell trying to get to her. More than likely there were back doors that he couldn't find before she'd get away. The thought made him push up the stairs all the faster.

He could no longer hear her steps; his own steps echoing harshly up the dim stairwell. He felt his knee start to protest; nothing serious, a standard complaint. It was a good thing she didn't live on the top floor. Hell, he admitted to himself, if she lived on the fourth floor he would never make it.

And then he was there. Her room was right by the stairs and she was standing half in the doorway, staring at the stairs with the eyes of a hunted animal. As soon as she saw him she realized her mistake. She should have slammed the door shut as soon as she heard the heavy rumble on the stairs. Her effort to duck inside was quick, but

Lepov, spurred by the memory of their first meeting, was quicker.

"Hello, Greta!" His large hands reached out and grabbed her by her shoulder. The heavy canvas of her jacket bunched in his fingers, he pushed her further into the room and kicked the door shut behind him.

"Damn you!" She tried to regain her balance while at the same time she swung around, her foot seeking contact with any part of him she could reach.

He dropped a hand down low and caught her foot in midair. He smiled and he held her there as she tottered on one leg. His grip tightened as she struggled to break free.

"Let go of me, asshole!"

And he did, after shoving her back over a low table. The table acted as a blocker, knocking her legs out from under her. Momentum carried her across the table and she landed on a tattered throw rug. She grunted as the air was knocked out of her and for a moment she didn't move.

Lepov would have felt sorry for her if he hadn't been so irritated that she had tried to kick him again. He stepped over the little table and knelt down beside her. His knee was definitely starting to hurt again, a consequence of running up the three flights of stairs. He tried to ignore it. He held Greta by the collar of her jacket.

"You can't do this. I'm calling the police this time." She reached up and tried to pry his hand off her. Lepov smacked both of her hands away with his free hand.

"I not only can do this but I'm doing it as we speak. Now, are you gonna stop squirming around or am I gonna have to tie you up? Don't think I won't."

"What do you want, huh?" She laid still, her eyes straining to see something to her left.

"I want to sit and chat with you. You were so charming last time."

"I can't stay here. I have to go. You can't make me stay."

"In a hurry?" Lepov turned and spied a clock hanging on the wall. "It's eleven-fifteen, if that's what you're looking at. What's your rush?"

Her face hardened and stared straight ahead. Lepov felt a flush of blood to his face and he tried to catch his breath. Getting up those stairs and grabbing her had taken more out of him than he had thought it would. MacNally was right; he was getting old.

"Talk then." Her body had gone rigid under his grip.

"You're going to help me find Ethan."

"I don't know where he is."

"Of course not."

Lepov took his eyes off her long enough to look around her apartment. The rooms were nearly bare. Besides a few pieces of mismatched furniture, it looked as if no one lived there.

"Anything else?" she demanded.

"You might start by telling me where all of Ethan's junk went. I can see you didn't bring it here."

She glared at him then. Her defiant eyes widened enough that he recognized she wasn't acting. "You think I know where he is? You think I took all of his shit out of his apartment and brought it to him? You're out of your mind. I told you I was finished with him."

"I know that." Lepov slowly released his grip on her jacket collar and stood back up. "I don't think you took it to him. I think you sold it all. I only want to know who the girl is."

He was ready for it. She rolled away from him like a cat dodging the neighborhood dog. Lepov already had his foot in the air. He jammed his heel into her back and sent her sprawling across the floor. He crossed the floor in three big steps, and this time he grabbed the back of her collar and yanked her to her feet.

"Don't make me sit on you," Lepov chuckled, tossing her into a stuffed chair. He backed up enough to stay out of kicking range.

"You're an animal!" she hissed.

"I'm a bully, I won't deny that. Now tell me about the woman."

"What woman?" Again, the mention of the woman seemed to upset her, though she didn't run this time.

"The other woman. Ethan's latest woman."

"I don't know anything about her. Get out of here." She sat back in the chair, unable to get away from him. She fumbled in her jacket pocket and pulled out a pack of cigarettes. She was beginning to shake.

"Now see," Lepov watched her light the cigarette, "I believed you when you told me that the first time. But not this time. Hell, I never should have fallen for it the first time. You don't seem the type to fade away when someone else takes your man. You wouldn't allow another woman to take Ethan. You found out who she was, didn't you? Of course you did. Who was she?"

And then she did something that even Lepov had never expected. She started to cry. Tears rolled down her hard, proud face. With the same hand that held the cigarette she tried to brush the tears aside.

"I've got to get out of here, do you hear me? I have to get out!"

"Why?" Lepov asked. He looked back at the clock. "What's so special about now? You need to get out of here before noon, is that it?"

"If I tell you about the woman will you let me go?" She was rocking now, clearly agitated.

"Maybe." Lepov watched her; there was more fear in her eyes now than defiance.

"I didn't do it," she whispered.

"Do what?" Lepov leaned in, trying to hear her.

"I didn't do anything." She took a deep drag on the cigarette and blew the smoke out hard. "But that doesn't matter, you know? If I didn't do it, then whoever did will probably come after me. Let me out of here!"

"Who is she, Greta?" Lepov wasn't going to let tears distract him. "I'm not letting you go anywhere. At least not until twelve. Not unless you give me a name."

Her eyes shifted to the clock again. He was right about noon. Something was happening then and she didn't want to miss it. What was significant about twelve o'clock?

"You did sell all of Ethan's things, didn't you? What did you do with the money, huh?" The talk of the money seemed to rattle her almost as much as mentioning Ethan's new woman.

"I didn't..." she whispered again. This time, she couldn't even finish the sentence.

"Didn't what?" Lepov prompted her.

"Kill her! I didn't kill that woman! Don't you see? If someone killed her, they'll be coming after me!" She didn't jump up and run though Lepov was ready for it.

"The woman on the news?" he asked. Greta nodded.

That shouldn't have surprised Lepov. If Layne really was the killer MacNally insisted he was, then it almost made sense that he would eventually kill the woman who was hiding him.

"You think Ethan will come after you?"

"Ethan? He didn't do this. Is that what you think?" Her eyes narrowed as she spoke. "Ethan couldn't do this thing. I'm getting out of here. I told you who she was. I don't have any more time."

She stood up, clearly expecting him to stop her. Lepov watched her, but did not make a move to interfere.

"So that's where the money is, huh? You're buying your way out. I'm surprised you can afford the grace period fee. Will they refund you if you don't make it there in time?"

"What the hell do you care?" She backed away from him into the kitchen. Tossing her cigarette into a pot that was sitting on top of an old stove, she ducked into a small room off the kitchen.

"What did you forget?" Whatever it was, Lepov figured it had to be important, or she would never have returned to the apartment.

"It would be meaningless to you." She returned to the main room and reached for the door. He caught a glimpse of gold clutched in her other hand.

"Come to the police station, Greta. They can protect you." Lepov hoped he was right. A brief image of Montillo swinging from a light passed before his eyes.

"The cops will think I killed her. I've been to her place; I was going to confront them. But I never did. I'm sure the cops know I was there. They'll never believe I didn't do it."

Part of him suspected she was right. Even MacNally would have to treat her as a suspect.

"You know," she opened the door stood still for a moment. After taking a deep breath, she confessed: "I'm not sorry she's dead."

Lepov couldn't say why, but he let her close the door. He even hoped she would make it into Delta on time.

87

The Segal woman had pointed MacNally in the right direction. The fact that Fenelli had been looking for her assailant meant Shaw Parks was Fenelli's killer.

Searching through Fenelli's desksystem, MacNally found the VTech's report with Shaw Parks' image. He was blond, just like the woman had said. That was the good news. The bad news came when he tried to locate Shaw Parks' PDT signal: it had vanished.

He returned to Fenelli's desksystem. There had to be something else. He saw the report on Jeri Drounett. If he couldn't find anything else he'd call her. She might be able to tell him something. But from what he could see in the report, she wouldn't be able to help much. She knew nothing about Parks.

MacNally's next step was to check Fenelli's call sheet. Every call to or from an officer's personal phone was logged. MacNally saw the call from Maria; the call Fenelli had gotten the last time he'd seen him.

He didn't want to think about that. But that really had been the last time he'd seen Fenelli. MacNally was never one to spend time blaming himself for things he couldn't control, but he couldn't help it this time. Why had he been so inattentive to Fenelli that day? He should have asked more questions. Should have demanded that Fenelli wait until he could join him. Maybe if he had insisted that Fenelli stay for that interrogation, he would still be alive today. Hell, there was no maybe about it. Of course he'd still be alive.

There were several calls to and from Pete Landon. The puzzle guy? MacNally felt a brief surge of hope. Pete must know something.

If he had wanted to, MacNally could have easily pulled up a transcript of the calls. But he wanted to hear from Pete. He couldn't say why. Maybe he wanted to talk to the man who had been helping his partner. Maybe he did not want to read Fenelli's last spoken words.

The last thing MacNally noticed about the call list was the absence of his own number. Fenelli had never called him. There was only the one call that MacNally made to Fenelli. Why? After all those years together, was it possible Fenelli hadn't even thought to call him when he needed help? Did their partnership mean nothing? What was so special about Pete Landon?

MacNally called Pete from Fenelli's deskscreen.

"Ed, I'm sorry about Arturo. Are you alright?"

"I will be when I catch the man who did this. What were all those calls about between you and Fenelli?"

"We were trying to find Parks."

"You do know this Parks killed Fenelli, don't you?"

"Yes. Do you guys have him in custody yet?"

"We would if we could find him."

"That's what I thought. I've been working on that. I was about to call you." Pete launched into a quick summary of the trouble he and Fenelli had run into while trying to track Parks. MacNally could not follow most of it, but he let Pete finish. This was exactly why Fenelli had called Pete instead of MacNally.

"So what's the bottom line?"

"His signal keeps changing. I can't get a read on it. The damn thing's changing way too fast. But what I can do is anticipate the change. I've been able to isolate the number pool he's drawing from—"

"I'm not following you, but I don't need to. Can you trace him?"

"I can get his signal briefly, but maybe only once every third or fourth time it changes. So I can trace him intermittently. The last hit I had on him was back at the Overlords. But that was over an hour ago."

"So you can only trace him in the past?" MacNally wasn't joking when he said he didn't understand. "The information is an hour old?"

"No. When I get a hit, it's real-time. But I can never keep it for long, and I might not get another one for an hour."

MacNally wanted to choke Pete for not calling sooner. But at least now he had something to do. It didn't matter that he had told himself to forget about Fenelli. And there was always the chance this Parks could lead him to Layne.

"Can you call me every time you get a signal?" MacNally was anxious to move.

"I can do better than that. Do you have a PDT reader?" Pete asked.

"Yes."

"I'll link my program to your reader. The data will be real-time."

"Okay, do you need the number off my reader or something?"

"No," Pete sounded amused. "I've already found it in the system. I'll have you linked before you get to the garage."

"Thanks." MacNally reached out to kill the connection when he hesitated. "And Pete? Thanks for helping Arturo the other day. I'm sure he was glad you were there for him."

"I don't know about that." Pete's light tone could not mask the guilt he felt. "I think it'd have been better if I hadn't helped. He'd be alive."

"And that woman would be dead. Don't forget that."

MacNally grabbed his coat and hat and ran out of the room. It was the first time he had something useful to do in the last twenty-four hours.

88

Lilly Stewart sat at a table in the now empty Delta Entry Lounge. A waitress sat at a table near the kitchen's swinging doors as a busboy was pushed a cart through them. Delta had been closed for two days and the grace period would be over in fifteen minutes. One other man was sitting at a table near from Lilly. He had not looked up from the table's news-screens since she had arrived.

The waitress was smoking a cigarette. It made her think of that silly pack in Gregor's coat. The waitress had already checked with Lilly and she had not ordered anything. The busboy came back through the doors without the cart. He had a wet rag in one hand and made a few lazy swipes at the table next to the waitress before he gave up pretending to work and sat across from the waitress.

She laughed at his poor work habits. He faked an embarrassed smile, but even Lilly could see he was actually rather proud of himself. It was his way of impressing a woman. If the waitress was anything like Lilly, she was probably falling for it. More of that little-boy-charm.

That made her think of Gregor again. She was being unfair, blaming him for Carlos' death. And though she knew it, that didn't stop her. It only made her feel guilty. It only made her want to get out of the Lazaretto.

That was the reason she was taking her client's offer. When he had offered to pay her grace period fee, she had not even considered taking him up on it. But when she'd heard the news of Carlos' death, she had known that she had to get away. Of course, she knew that Gregor had not killed him. And she knew that the police had let it happen, not Gregor. But after seeing Gregor, actually being in his presence, she had known that she would always see him as culpable. Even worse, he had readily recognized that she unfairly blamed him.

She refused to do that to him. She refused to pursue any kind of life with him. It had been a crazy idea, anyway. They hardly knew each other. And there was no reason to believe that they would make any kind of connection that went beyond a passing acquaintance.

She looked at her table screen: Delta would close in twelve minutes. She would have to get moving soon. She was cutting it close. A bag full of clothes and a few accessories had already been sent into the zone. She had a room reserved in her usual hotel. There would be little to do there for thirty-eight days. But once she got off the quarantine planet, she'd have a chance to get on with work. Three clients were already trying to hire her. There would be plenty to do. One of them wanted her to find a piece that was last seen on Earth. She hadn't been on Earth for quite some time.

The busboy laughed. The waitress only smiled at him. Maybe she was not taken in by charmers like that, Lilly thought. Maybe she was smarter than that.

Ten minutes and she would be locked inside Delta. That would make her client happy. Why? Lilly had been insulted when he first made his offer. She never liked being told what to do. What did he care if she stuck around or not? If she had not been so eager to get away from Gregor, she never would have given her client the satisfaction of accepting his offer.

It was vanity, she knew, but it really bothered her when she thought about it. Why would he care? What difference would it be to him if she did not make it into Delta in time? What gave him the right to force her to do one thing over another?

Gregor had been the same way. Only he had tried to convince her to stick around. He'd bungled it, which did not surprise her. He tried to ask her to stay, sort of ordered her to stay, and ended up telling her she was making a bad decision to leave so soon. If his attempt to control her had not been so irritating, she would have laughed at him. Why did everything he do seem so charming to her?

A small woman came rushing through the Lounge. She had short hair, nearly identical to that of the busboy's, and a cigarette hung from one of the corners of her mouth. She looked worried, almost scared, glancing behind her every now and then. Lilly would have sworn someone was chasing the woman.

Lilly knew she ought to stand up and get over to the entry gate. Time had run out. In five minutes she would have to be inside the gate.

A man came rushing past Lilly. For a moment, she imagined it was the someone who was chasing the small woman. But really, he didn't look the type. He was slightly overweight, and soft, rosy cheeks. His tight curly hair, combined with his round face, made his head look like a child's doll. The deep anxiety etched into it added to the childish effect. He was moving as fast as his legs could carry him, intent on making it through the gate on time.

It was time. She should get out of her chair and through the gate.

Lilly had not noticed the waitress approach until she was standing beside Lilly.

"Aren't you going in?" the waitress asked.

"I'm supposed to. Whether I want to or not."

"Well, which do you want?" the waitress asked.

"That's a good question." Lilly had only two minutes left. She would practically have to run to make it.

"Well?" the waitress tapped the table, pointing to the time.

"Some guy wants me to get through those gates, and another guy wants me to stay." Lilly gave the waitress a funny smile. "Life's little choices."

"Well, the choice is probably easier than you think. Which guy do you want to keep happy?"

Lilly wondered if it were really that simple.

"Would you do something for me?" Lilly relaxed into the chair.

"What can I do?"

"Pour me a cup of coffee." Lilly knew she could never make it. Had she ever actually intended to leave?

"I've got some old coffee, but I doubt it's any good."

"That's perfect," Lilly smiled. "I love bad coffee."

89

Helen set a stack of papers down on the conference table. Dr. Haupt had been adamant that they require both Dr. Fisher and Dr. Stride to come to their conference room. Dr. Haupt refused to go to Fisher's office. This was a meeting that he had called, and he would not play the role of supplicant.

The doctors were expected to arrive in a few minutes. Dr. Haupt stood at the head of the table, looking over the documents Helen had prepared. He nodded several times in satisfaction. As he was reading one of the reports—Helen estimated that he must have read all of them four or five times—he abruptly dropped the report onto the stack of papers in front of him and pointed at Helen.

"May I ask a personal question?" Dr. Haupt eyed her carefully.

Helen answered with a nod, giving his sudden request little attention.

"Are you married?"

"No." Helen carefully checked to make sure she had placed the right pages in the stack. These would be given to Dr. Fisher.

"Widowed?"

"No."

"Very irregular," Dr. Haupt announced.

"I'm sorry?" Helen turned and focused on his comment.

"It is irregular that a woman as well-mannered, well-educated, and with such pleasing features would be single. Do you have something against marriage?"

"Inasmuch as it requires a man to volunteer to join me, I have everything against it." Helen found his direct questions easy to answer. They left no room for emotion—no room for embarrassment.

"That's nonsense," the German pronounced. "Now, it appears you have everything here that I requested. Thank you."

Helen tried to refocus on the pages in her hand. Had Dr. Haupt actually said such things? Had she imagined it? *Nonsense*? She didn't know if she was more surprised at his use of that word or at what he was implying. She tried to catch a glimpse of him; to read his thoughts. His face betrayed nothing beyond his usual stone-hardened attention to his work. Helen filed Dr. Haupt's odd words for later analysis.

She prepared to leave the room when Dr. Haupt's voice stopped her.

"Helen, you are to stay in the room. I want you in the meeting."

She nodded and chose a chair that was not at the table but set back in one corner of the room.

Only a few minutes passed when they heard the outer door to the office swing open. A tall, rail thin man stepped into the conference room. Standing a few feet from the end of the conference table, he looked as if his back were slumped against an invisible wall.

"I'm Doctor Isaac Stride. Someone wanted to see me?" He was not only tall, but he had a long face, with sour lines dragging down the corners of his mouth. His unhappy disposition nearly turned his pale skin lime green. Helen wondered if the man was sick or if he were perpetually ill at ease.

"I did. I am Doctor Gerhard Haupt. Thank you for cooperating." Helen knew that Dr. Haupt was under no illusions; Dr. Stride had only agreed to come after he had been assured that the request for a meeting was backed up by authority granted from Baltimore. "Please take a seat, over here. As soon as Doctor Fisher arrives we shall begin."

The room grew uncomfortably quiet. Neither of the men would make eye contact as they waited. Helen, sitting in the corner, tried her best not to be restless; she had already decided that her best course of action was to make as little noise and gain as little attention as possible.

The uncomfortable silence grew into an unbearable awkwardness. Fifteen minutes had passed, and Dr. Fisher had not been seen, nor had he been heard from. Both of the men at the table continued to avoid eye contact. Helen was beginning to wonder how Dr. Haupt would break the void left by the silence. He would have to do something. They could not wait all day for Dr. Fisher.

"Helen," Dr. Haupt spoke, as if they had not been sitting in complete silence for over a quarter of an hour, "please call Dr. Fisher's secretary and confirm his appointment."

It took only a few minutes to confirm that Dr. Fisher's secretary — the new woman who had taken Helen's job — thought that Dr. Fisher was already at the meeting. A thorough inquiry revealed the truth: Dr. Fisher was no longer in the building. Dr. Haupt was the first to suggest that the IHS Chief had simply run away.

"You sound as if you expected this," Helen said to him. They were standing in her office; Dr. Stride was still waiting in the conference room.

"No, I must admit I did not. If I had, I would have had him watched. No, I did not expect this, but I am not surprised by it either. It would appear we are closer to the truth than we suspected."

Dr. Haupt stepped through the doors of the conference room and approached Dr. Stride. He waited for Helen to follow him and did not speak until she had shut the doors.

"It is time for us talk, Dr. Stride. You should be aware that Dr. Fisher will not be joining us."

"What's that?" Stride asked, looking even more physically ill.

"Dr. Fisher has left the office. It would appear he is not willing to answer my questions. Do you have any idea why that would be?"

Stride was uncooperative. He seemed determined to parry any direct questions from Dr. Haupt. It was only after Haupt was informed that Dr. Fisher had taken refuge in the Delta Quadrant that Stride began to understand that he had been left holding the bag.

"Dr. Fisher might have done you a favor," Dr. Haupt told Stride. "You have no choice but to cooperate with me. Now, at least, you can tell the truth. You can tell your side of the story. Dr. Fisher will not be here to keep you silent. Do you understand what I am saying?"

Stride nodded, his long face betrayed his demoralized state.

"So," Dr. Haupt sat at the head of the table and held up a sheaf of papers, "let's begin with the lab protocol revision."

Dr. Stride nodded. He evidently did not need to ask which protocol revision Dr. Haupt was referring to. He was not surprised to see the document on the table.

Helen had trouble keeping up with the two doctors as they talked. She was having a hard time reconciling Dr. Fisher's actions. There was no other way to interpret what he had done. Her boss — presumably now her former boss — had actually attempted to flee from the investigation. It made no sense. Surely he understood that Dr. Haupt would arrange to detain him in Delta. He had to know he would never be allowed to leave the Lazaretto.

Helen did not want to think about how this might connect with Julia's death. It was still painful to remember her friend was dead. It was unbearable to think that Dr. Fisher was somehow involved. How could he have been? Why?

Helen knew that these were the kind of questions that were about to be answered. She cleared her mind and focused on Dr. Stride's answers. They would come. She had only to be patient.

90

Burdened with the reality of Arturo's death, Maria walked through Terran Park. The cold and heavy rains of the last few days had been replaced that midday by a nearly clear sky. The Lazaretto had no warm southern winds that might make an occasional appearance, but the absence of wind could feel warm in comparison to the near constant frigid winds that blew in off the waters that surrounded the miniature continent. And as the sun reached its pale zenith that day, Maria could feel no wind at all.

She paused in the glade and closed her eyes, allowing the ivory light to warm her cheeks. It was good to do so; to pretend as though she were on a warm planet, where men's lives were worth more than the whims of a maniac or the protocols of a government institution.

Someone called her name. She looked back and saw George walking towards her. She waved at him as he crossed the glade. He seemed out of place; nature was not his natural habitat.

"I was looking for you. And I found you." Georges took her hand. "When I woke up, you were gone."

"I'm sorry, I needed some air." She did not have to say more. She knew he understood her restlessness.

"Well, I'm not here to take you back. But I did come to speak with you. I have something important that I must tell you. And this might be the best place to talk of these things." Georges looked up at the trees.

Was something wrong? Maria had been alarmed when she first saw Georges. He did not like to come into the park. There had to be a strong reason for it; it would not be good news. Georges began to walk ahead of her into the trees, pausing after a few steps long enough to ensure Maria followed him.

"There is something that I have found that I did not tell you about right away. I wanted to know the outcome before I spoke of it. I did not want to make you anxious. Unfortunately, I will not be able to avoid that now. What I am about to tell you is not encouraging. Do you understand?"

Maria did not understand. Georges was never a man to beat around the bush. Yet, he was doing that now. She only nodded so that he would continue and arrive at his point. Sadly, she had been right. He was not bringing good news.

"When I told you I had decided to look into your friend's records—your friend Mr. Zoltis—I decided to see what had been done for him, and I wanted to know if there was anything else I could do. So often, the patients that are left to die are ignored. There are usually too many of them for us doctors to research their condition. It is shameful, but we accept that we cannot help most of them. You know this, Maria.

"So I examined his records. I hoped I might find something that had been overlooked. Something that might bring you hope. I am sorry to say that I have not been able to do that."

Maria nodded, lifting her head to let Georges know his news did not upset her; she had lost any hope for Kjarsta a long time ago.

They walked through the last of the trees and came out at the fountain of the four fauns. Georges watch the water pouring forth from their pitchers as he continued. Maria did not gaze upon them; she did not want to associate them with Georges' news.

"I have discovered something that puzzles me, Maria. And I think you need to know of it. You may be the only person who knows this man, and maybe you can help me understand what I have found. But you should know that what I have found is not good. I hesitate to upset you, yet I am compelled to do so."

"It is okay," Maria said. She sat on one of the benches and put a hand on Georges' arm. "I would do anything to help Kjarsta. Stop worrying about me. I will be fine," she bravely added.

"I know you care about him deeply. So I will tell you what I have found." He no longer hesitated; having once made the final decision to speak, he no longer worried over the consequences. "I did not have to do much investigating. I was startled that no one else noticed this. Your friend did not become infected with a random, unknown virus. That is what his report says, but it is not accurate. You see, he has been infected by a genetically engineered virus; it is a virus made by man. But not only made by man. It was designed by one.

"I was careful not to jump to conclusions about this. I asked Dr. Edgars, the new virologist, to look at it as well. That is why it took me two days to be certain. Otherwise, I would have been done after only a few hours of research."

"I don't understand," Maria said.

"There is a simple battery of tests that the IHS lab runs on anyone who exhibits symptoms of sickness in the quadrants during the quarantine period. These tests determine who is pulled out of quarantine and forced to remain in the Lazaretto. But they also tell us a few fundamental things about whatever is making them sick; bacteria, virus, and so on. When Mr. Zoltis was classified as *nullus exitus*, there was no qualification of his sickness. It was labeled unknown. This happens on rare occasions, when someone has been traveling widely and they pick up a rare, unknown pathogen from one of the wilder planets. More often than not, these things are picked up on Arcobia. There are still many parts of that swamp-filled planet that we know little about.

"But even when a pathogen is labeled as unknown, there are basic things we can know about them that we learn from that first set of tests. This information was missing. I could see right away that the tests had not been run. Maria, I can say this with absolute certainty; someone at IHS deliberately made sure those tests were not run."

"You might be mistaken," Maria suggested.

"Impossible. You see, if those tests had been run—only a few of them, mind you—the computer system would have tagged the anomalies that were so obvious to me. And it would have been impossible for any health professional reading his report to miss the fact that he had been infected with a man-made virus. It would only have been a matter of time before a more serious fact would have been discovered."

"Which was?" Maria could see this other fact disturbed Georges.

"Dr. Edgars saw it first. I am not sure I would have seen it. But he is an excellent virologist with a great deal of the most recent training available. He could see that the virus was not only engineered by someone; someone had deliberately infected your friend with this virus. This was a cold, cruel act of murder."

"How can this be? Dr. Edgars must be wrong." The idea was too malicious for her to believe. She had watched what that virus had done to Kjarsta over time and the thought that someone had designed such a brutal death was too much for her.

"I understand enough of what Dr. Edgars explained to know he is not wrong. I could not explain it well enough to you to make you believe it. But to put it in simple terms, the virus was developed to attack a specific DNA; Mr. Zoltis' DNA."

"It is..." Maria could not even put into words what she felt. Kjarsta. He had suffered so much. To say it was unfair, it was horrific; such words did not begin to suffice. "You have told the police?"

"No." Georges shook his head. When Maria's questioning gaze flared at him, he held up a hand to check her anger. "This is not a simple murder. Did you understand the first thing I told you? Someone at IHS has taken steps to bury this. That cannot be done by an ordinary employee. That kind of action is practically impossible. The Interplanetary Health Service is rigidly designed to protect billions of people. There are safeguards that cannot be tampered with. For someone to do this, they must be powerful. Your friend had an enemy of the most powerful kind. If we tell anyone, we must be cautious."

"What do you mean *if* we tell anyone?" Indignation flared within her. She would not allow Kjarsta's suffering to be ignored. It was already unbearable to know that he, like so many others, was being left to die on his own. This new indignity could not go unpunished.

"Please listen, Maria. I am not worried for my own safety. But I do not want to put you in danger. Right now, we know so little. We cannot rush off crying 'murder'! We must be wise, discreet."

Maria could not prevent the tears that filled her eyes. A sudden thought overcame her; the knowledge that there had been someone she could have trusted with this information. That now, when she needed him most, her brother was dead. Arturo would have known what they should do. He would have made sure Kjarsta was treated with justice.

"Yes, it makes Arturo's death that much more of a tragedy." Georges read her thoughts. "I miss his counsel in this. It is why I have told you; if only to get this off my chest, there is no one else I feel I can trust. I am sorry to burden you with it."

She had never seen Georges like this. It was clear he was disturbed, as anyone would be. But there was something else. His uncertainty was alien to her. Georges had always been a man who knew what to do. She wanted to be strong for him, but that was impossible. She did not have the kind of strength that Kjarsta exhibited from day to day.

"Georges," she said softly, "maybe there is someone who can help. Someone who would know what to do."

"Go on," he said, willing her to continue.

"Someone who is stronger than the both of us, and will not be intimidated by any man, no matter how powerful he is. I think I should speak to Kjarsta."

To her surprise, Georges agreed immediately.

She stood up from the bench, taking a moment to look at the fauns. She could see the face of the sad faun and she knew why the sculptor had formed such a downhearted figure; sadness was a key part of life. It was everywhere. And it was never something you could ignore.

She refused to glance in the direction of the raging faun. The seed of anger was already planted in her; anger at the heinous crime committed against Kjarsta. It would do nothing but fuel her anger to look upon that hateful and cruel visage. It would have been unthinkable to feed that same rage that had viciously attacked Kjarsta.

91

When Lepov called MacNally, he was caught off guard by the detective's excited manner. Something was going on.

"I'm right in the middle of something, Lepov. If you need something, make it quick."

"I may be able to find Layne. Is there somewhere we can talk?"

"Nope." MacNally swore under his breath, the curse barely carrying through to Lepov's end of the transmission. "Hang on. This damn reader's...there. Well, the kid was right. This thing works. Lepov, I really have to go. I will try to call you back."

MacNally had not been kidding. Lepov lost the connection, and that was it. He was on his own.

He needed to get into Julia Maiden's building security system. If he could do that, he might be able to verify that Layne had indeed been hanging around the murdered girl. And that would be another damning piece of evidence against Eudia Layne's kid. As he considered illegally breaking into the building, his phone rang. MacNally had not been kidding about calling back, either.

"I thought you were too busy to help," Lepov said when MacNally said he could meet with him.

"My lead on this suspect literally disappeared. I'm out near Delta Quadrant right now. Where are you?"

They decided on a central meeting point. Lepov met MacNally after a fifteen-minute drive. MacNally was waiting for him at the corner of Masthead and Dardanelle. MacNally opened the side door of his car and Lepov climbed into the passenger seat.

"I have to stay with my car." MacNally had a small electronic box sitting on his console. A display flashed information that Lepov did not bother to read. "Tell me what you need."

Lepov told him about Greta Becker and Julia Maiden. He was worried that MacNally would shout at him about letting the Becker woman go free. To his surprise, MacNally didn't even mention it.

"So, you think Layne was in and out of her building?"

"Well it seems like the logical assumption. And unlike most

people, I've come to put a lot of faith in logical assumptions."

"But even if you get a look at their security," MacNally scratched at a visible layer of stubble on his chin, "you're gonna need more than that. We know he was using Romeo's tag. So even if you get that, it will have changed by now. You're gonna need someone else's help."

"Like who?" Lepov asked.

"Our resident genius. Let me call him, and you can go talk to him."

"You mind if I asked what you're up to?" Lepov couldn't help but ask. "You said something about a suspect."

"That's a courtesy, calling him a suspect. Between us, I've found that bastard who killed Fenelli. I just need to get my hands on him."

MacNally had not hesitated to share his information with Lepov. The gesture was not lost on Lepov. MacNally had lost his partner and he needed to talk with someone. Lepov knew what it was like to lose a partner. When he'd been fired, it had taken a long time to get used to not having a partner who could help him think out loud.

"Who is he?"

"This guy, right here." MacNally pointed a thick finger at a printout of Parks' image. "His name is — "

"Shaw Parks." Lepov filled in the name himself. "My God, MacNally, I've met Parks. Several times. You sure this is the one who..."

"Positive." MacNally left no room for discussion. Lepov hoped the detective was right. With that kind of single-mindedness, in a place like the Lazaretto where justice was not meted out in the same manner as the home worlds, an innocent man could be ram-rodded into an unwarranted execution. "How do you know Parks?"

Lepov gave MacNally a rundown on the two times he met Parks.

"Your lady friend knows him well?" MacNally asked.

"I have no idea how well. Why haven't you picked him up yet?"

"That's complicated. I'm working on it." MacNally glanced at the box. "Look, I may need to take off any minute. So let me call the guy I mentioned before. His name is Landon. He should be able to help you. I'll also get you that building's security data. By the time you get to the precinct, I'll have all of that arranged for you."

Even as Lepov climbed back into his rental, he could hear MacNally's engine begin to fire. Lepov heard him take off like a rocket breaking free from a planet's atmosphere.

Whoever this Officer Landon was, Lepov hoped he could help. Just maybe, Lepov dared to think, he had taken another step closer to finding Ethan Layne.

"You are repeating yourself, sir," Dr. Haupt said in exasperation. "I don't want to hear how Dr. Fisher ordered you to change the procedure. We are all aware of that. Furthermore, I do not want to hear a detailed account of what those changes were. We have the revision right here on paper. I have not asked you to tell me what the revision's changes were."

Dr. Stride's face seemed to have grown longer as his mood became more sullen. His sickly pallor had only worsened. A few times Helen had even feared he would become physically sick and she worried that she would have to clean it up.

The conversation between Dr. Haupt and Dr. Stride had not been as illuminating as Helen had hoped it would be. As Stride tried to explain his actions surrounding the revising of the lab protocols, his level of cooperation began to wane. It seemed to Helen that he was becoming more and more aware of how much trouble he might be in. He was taking longer to answer questions: weighing each answer with an increasing amount of thought, unwilling to give details, and losing his ability to remember specific bits of information.

She could tell that Haupt saw this as well. The German did not show it, but she was certain he had to be feeling the pressure to discover what had really happened. For the first time since she had met him he appeared nervous. Not to the degree most normal people might exhibit anxiety, but much more than she had ever expected to see from him.

"Can I infer from your silence that you have reconsidered your decision to cooperate with us?" Dr. Haupt tossed the revised report onto the table. He was fighting to hold on to his composure.

"No, that's not it." Stride's voice was difficult to hear. He made a show of swallowing with difficulty. Helen offered to get him a glass of water. "What I would really like is something to eat."

"Helen, arrange for something to eat," Haupt said curtly.

"I don't want to eat here. I want to get out of here."

"There is no reason to leave here. You are stalling for time."

"If you want me to talk, then we will go and eat off IHS grounds." Stride set his long face, ready to repeat his demand.

"One moment, Helen." Haupt pulled at his jacket, flattening the edges of it at his waist. "I see no reason not to agree. We will eat in one of the small cafés outside. All of the quadrants are closed now. There is no place for you to run, Dr. Stride. Keep that in mind."

They locked up the office suite and cleared through security in fifteen minutes. The gray light of the early afternoon lit up the buildings in a way that Helen was not use to seeing. She so rarely got a chance to be out during the day, especially days when the clouds were so thin.

They chose a crowded café across the street. Meals were ordered. Dr. Haupt did not waste time with trivial comments on the café or the weather. He demanded that Stride explain himself.

"Will you speak, now? Were you trying to say you did not want to talk at IHS? Have our offices been wired for recordings?"

Stride shook his head. "But I feel a whole lot better getting out of there. I have spent too much time within the walls of that building. The IHS is a world unto itself; a world with its own atmosphere, its own landscape, its own vistas."

"Very poetic," Dr. Haupt said. It was not a compliment. "Put it in a book. Be more specific."

"They have their own way of thinking, their own perspectives, and even their own rules. Working within that world wears you down. Over time, you begin to believe in that world. If you want me to stop thinking like them, then I have to get out of there. I have to get someplace where I can be healthy again."

Helen could already see a difference; he had regained some of his color. At least, he had lost some of the shades of green that had haunted him.

As a fellow employee of the IHS, Helen had some empathy for what Dr. Stride was trying to tell them. She knew the feeling of impregnability that permeated that building. IHS officials never requested anything from other government and civilian organizations; the IHS demanded, ordered, announced, and implemented. Anyone who came to the IHS offices did so as a supplicant. This corrupting atmosphere was impossible to ignore.

"Begin," Dr. Haupt persisted in his demand. "Laboratory Protocol Revision. What was the root cause of this revision? And I did not ask *who*. Begin."

"It was a mistake. We were working on something that was supposed to be controllable. Something that could not get out of hand. But any time you begin this process, you make mistakes. It is part of the process. You make mistakes, you learn from them, and you move on. That is all you can do. I might go so far as to say that our project had fewer mistakes than most. We worked within tight parameters."

Helen expected Dr. Haupt to insist that Stride get to the point, but he sat erect in his chair with one arm resting on the table and waited patiently for Stride to continue.

"What was the project?" Helen could not refrain from asking.

"We were to develop a pathogen that fit a precise set of criteria." Stride paused as a waiter approached and distributed their meals.

Helen glanced listlessly at her plate. She was not hungry and had only ordered as a matter of habit. While the waiter fussed over them she moved her chair to one side to provide room for the waiter to refill their drinks. As she did so, a chill ran through her.

A man was sitting at one of the tables near the front entrance. He was sitting alone, his back turned partially away from them. She could see enough to recognize his profile and blond hair.

She must have physically reacted to seeing him. Dr. Haupt asked her what was wrong. Panic threatened to overtake her as she tried to breathe.

"That man, by the door." She could not help but draw their attention to him. He was not looking in their direction but he might turn and look at them at any time. Helen's hands trembled.

"What about him?" Dr. Haupt made no attempts to hide his scrutiny of the blond man. "You are upset. Why?"

"That's him. The man in my apartment."

"What is this all about?" Stride leaned towards Dr. Haupt and lowered his voice. "What is going on?"

"Miss Segal was attacked in her apartment several nights ago by the man at that table by the door." Dr. Haupt casually reached out to the table screen and proceeded to call up a display.

"We should get out of here." Helen started to stand.

"Stay where you are, Helen. Do not get up." The German continued to work on the table screen. "He will follow you no matter if you go out the back door or the front door. What was the name of the detective you were speaking with this morning?"

"Detective—" Helen drew a blank. She could not remember the man's name. "It was Irish or Scottish. I can't think of it."

"Was it MacNally?" Dr. Haupt looked from the table screen to Helen, who nodded. "I will contact him. Continue, Dr. Stride."

"One of our long range goals had always been to develop a virus or a bacterium that was programmable. One that we could give specific orders. What I mean is, we could make this pathogen attack and destroy other pathogens. A disease for diseases. Of course, one of the more important factors in such a pathogen would be its inability to make humans sick. Unfortunately, we are still a long way off from doing this. But someone heard about our research and wanted to take it in a slightly different direction."

Helen could not take her eyes off the man by the door. How could Dr. Haupt remain so calm? She didn't understand why he would sit there, knowing that the man who attacked her and killed that policeman was sitting only a few tables away from them. She did not expect the doctor to try to detain the killer. She could still remember with stunning clarity how fast and violent the man could be.

What, in fact, could she expect Dr. Haupt to do? She had no answer for her own question, and this made her uneasiness all the more troubling.

"Helen?" Dr. Haupt spoke her name softly. "The police are attempting to get my message to the detective. We cannot leave. We will wait. Do you understand?"

Did he know what he was asking? He could not imagine the swift terror of that attack. He could not know how much fear controlled her at that moment. She folded her hands and held them under the table so neither doctor would see how much she was shaking.

"What direction were you to take this research?" Dr. Haupt asked.

Helen could wait no longer. She had to get out of that café. Pushing her chair from the table, she stood, looking for an exit at the back of the room. There was only one door, used by the staff to access the kitchen.

She turned back to watch the blond man. He had seen her stand up and was rising from his chair. Helen could hear Dr. Haupt calling to her, but his voice sounded far away. Catching her foot on the legs of her chair, she stumbled hastily towards the back door.

93

"Oh, hell. The woman's getting up from the table. Not now, lady!" MacNally was still outside the café, waiting for a backup team. He reached the door in three steps and shoved it aside. Parks was already out of his seat and turning towards the woman and the men at her table. One of them would be Haupt; the doctor who had called with the message.

Parks had not seen MacNally rush through the door yet. His attention was still focused on the others. MacNally intended to make the most of it. He sure as hell wasn't going to give Parks a warning.

He expected Parks to follow the woman but he'd been wrong. Parks had only taken a few steps before pulling a gun from the pocket of his jacket. He was standing only a few feet from the men at the table. Lifting the gun, he said something to one of the seated men, but MacNally couldn't hear what it was.

Before Parks could pull the trigger, MacNally grabbed a wrought-iron chair and hit Parks behind one of his ears hard enough to put Parks down. Parks dropped to his knees. The gun fell from his hand.

"You're under arrest," MacNally said and swung a second time.

Parks crumpled to the floor.

"Detective MacNally?" one of the men at the table asked.

"Yeah," he nodded.

All three of the men stared at Parks' body on the floor. MacNally was still holding the small spindly-legged chair in his thick hand. Most of the cafés patrons stood well back from the spot where Parks lay. A few of them, taking advantage of the confusion, slipped out the front door without paying for their lunches.

"Is he dead?" The second man, a thin noodle of a man, was still clutching his sandwich as if it were going to jump out of his hands at any moment. He looked like he was going to be sick.

"I don't know," MacNally said honestly. He looked down at Parks for signs of life. "Ain't one of you a doctor?"

"We are both doctors, Detective. This is Dr. Stride, an IHS researcher. I am Dr. Haupt, from the home office in Baltimore." The somber-faced Haupt left his chair and knelt beside Parks. "Neither one of us have donned our physician's robes for many years. However, I do believe I am still qualified enough to tell you that this man is alive. Blunt trauma force to the back of the head can be life threatening, but for now, he is alive."

MacNally wasn't happy with the doctor's tone. It sounded as if he were criticizing the way MacNally had saved his life.

Saving this doctor's life had been a coincidence. MacNally had only been a half a block away when the Doctor had called the police.

Landon's tag tracer had worked. After Lepov had left the car, MacNally had seen a signal from Parks' PDT and rushed into Center City where the reader was picking up the signal. The signal had been strong enough to give him a fairly clear area to search. However, he had been frustrated to find that the area on the grid was packed with lunchtime crowds. By then, the signal had been lost and MacNally had been left standing on one side of Masthead with no way of finding Parks.

He'd spent ten or fifteen minutes scanning the crowd for a glimpse of his suspect. As each minute passed he had known his chances of finding Parks were rapidly diminishing. And then the call had come in.

Haupt had called from a café that was only a short distance from where MacNally had been standing. It had only taken a moment for him to spot Parks through the front window. The Segal woman and her companions had appeared safe enough for MacNally to call for backup.

And then the woman had stood up.

"I must find Miss Segal." Haupt stood up. "I will bring her back in case you need to speak with her."

"Okay." MacNally set the chair beside Parks' body and sat down on it. It looked like he was sitting on a child's chair.

"I don't think he'll wake up," the ill-looking Stride said to MacNally. "No need to restrain him."

"Maybe," MacNally said, pulling out a pair of old-fashioned chrome-plated handcuffs from a coat pocket, "but I don't care if he is unconscious. I like cuffing people. It reminds me that I'm the cop."

Two uniformed officers arrived shortly afterwards and Parks— having regained a semi-form of consciousness—was taken away. MacNally insisted that the café owner close down for the day. He begrudgingly agreed. By the time the last of the lunch crowd left, the woman was back at the table. MacNally sat down with of them.

"You didn't tell me the whole story, did you, Miss Segal?" MacNally's scolding tone matched his disapproving look.

"It is not her fault, Detective." Haupt deflected the criticism away from the woman. "I asked her not to mention certain things from the other night. We are in the middle of our own investigation and I did not want this information exposed at the time."

"You nearly got yourselves killed over it. Parks' attack on your assistant the other night was no random act. And today's attempt was not aimed at her. He was after you. You'd better tell me what's going on."

"I am still in the process of discovering what is going on, Detective." Haupt's tone wasn't touchy, but it was getting there.

"Then you'd better tell what you *have* done and I'll join your investigation." MacNally was starting to get pretty touchy himself. Fenelli had been killed because of all this. He was not going to allow this fussy little doctor to hold back information. No matter what had been going on at IHS, MacNally was determined to take control of it.

"I may not be able to explain all of it to you, Detective."

"Haupt, you don't listen too well. I'm telling you that you have no choice in the matter. You will tell me everything that is going on."

Haupt regarded MacNally. MacNally stared right back at him. There was no reason for MacNally to back down. Haupt might be from Earth, but that didn't mean much to MacNally. IHS may have jurisdiction over much of the Lazaretto system, but Fenelli's murder had changed all of that. They'd have to fire MacNally before he backed off from these bureaucrats now.

"Dr. Stride," Haupt spoke to the other doctor without taking his eyes off MacNally, "we will continue as soon as I finish with Detective MacNally. Please wait for me back at the office."

"Stay there, Stride." MacNally was not going to let him leave. Haupt's attempt to send Stride away irritated MacNally. "All four of us are going to stay right here until you tell me what is going on. Let me help you start. Explain to me why IHS would send someone all the way out here from Earth."

"I won't be bullied, Detective. You cannot keep us here."

"You're suffering from long distance travel syndrome. Are you familiar with that?" MacNally didn't stop for an answer to his question. "That's where a good little citizen of Earth flies all the way the hell out to a colony planet and discovers that the laws he grew up with don't relate to the ones that are now in effect. So try to remember one thing, Haupt: if I determine that something is putting the sanctity of the Lazaretto system in jeopardy, then I can do anything I please to remove that threat. And from what I can see, you guys at IHS might be putting the whole system in jeopardy. And that means I can do whatever I want with you."

"We have the same goal," Haupt said in a mollified tone. He seemed to get MacNally's point. "I did not want to discuss this in front of Dr. Stride. But you have left me no alternative."

"That's right, Doc, I haven't. So talk."

"I was sent from Baltimore to investigate the administrator of your IHS; Dr. Fisher. We have seen evidence that suggests private research is being done here with our facilities; research that is both a drain on our limited resources, and ethically questionable. We could not, however, discover the exact nature of the activity. It was decided that I should be sent here in the guise of an efficiency investigator."

It was easy to see that both the woman and the other doctor were not aware of Haupt's mission. The Segal woman accepted his story with mild curiosity. Dr. Stride looked both angry and afraid.

"So what have you discovered?"

"I have discovered that Dr. Stride can explain everything."

Stride began to tell his story. MacNally interrupted him.

"You're the director of the IHS lab, right? You're in charge of testing the bodies we send you, right? I've got questions for you."

"We have the same questions," Haupt said. "It was because of your visit to Dr. Fisher the other day that I was able to discover Dr. Stride's involvement. And it was for this information that the man attacked Helen. So you see, Detective, we are looking for the same answers."

"Okay. But save the technical details for your report. I only want to know about the lab reports. Those reports were wrong, weren't they? They sure weren't complete."

"They were more than just wrong or incomplete." Stride took a deep breath before he continued. "They were fabrications. Lies. No one murdered those people. They were all victims of a virus—our virus. Dr. Fisher's virus, to be exact."

"What virus?" Dr. Haupt asked.

"What people?" MacNally wanted Stride to be specific.

"The virus was a failure. It didn't do what we wanted it to do, so we destroyed it. Only, we missed something. As for the people, I meant Ford, and the father and son, and —"

"Julia?" Helen Segal stared at Stride. "Are you saying Dr. Fisher was responsible for Julia's death?"

"Are you telling us there is a virus out there that turns people to a bloody pulp? And you made it?" MacNally didn't want to think of the implications of that. A virus like that running rampant in the Lazaretto would be a disaster. There was nowhere for anyone to get away from it. Their only saving grace was the fact that it couldn't get out of the quarantine. Or could it?

"How containable is it?" MacNally was afraid of the answer.

"It's containable. Fully. It should be."

"What were its orders?" Haupt asked.

"What does that mean?" MacNally didn't like the sound of that.

"Dr. Stride was telling us that part of their research centered on trying to program the virus' DNA. Originally they tried to program it to go after specific diseases. But what was this virus programmed to do? Was a mistake made in the programming?"

"No," Stride answered reluctantly.

"Which disease was it programmed to destroy?" Haupt asked suspiciously.

"It wasn't programmed to destroy a disease." Stride was barely speaking loud enough to be heard.

"What was it programmed to do?"

"It wasn't my idea."

"We have been over that!" Haupt shouted. He leaned in closer to Stride. "What was it programmed to do?"

"It was only supposed to make people —" The more he spoke, the more Stride looked as if he would get sick. " — something that would be easy to discover and easy to beat."

"What did you say?" MacNally hoped to God he had misunderstood.

"What was it programmed to do?" Haupt's repeated question had still to be answered.

"We programmed it to make people sick. But only enough to put them on record. It was supposed to discolor the skin — enough that it could be diagnosed. And then it would simply go away over time."

"What is he telling us, Haupt?" MacNally turned to the unflappable German for a clearer answer.

"I believe they trained a virus to make people mildly sick, but the virus had other ideas. Is that right, Dr. Stride?"

"Yes," he nodded.

"What was that about putting them on record?"

"What he means, Detective, is they were trying to increase the number of people found to have a pathogen of some kind while coming through the Lazaretto. The IHS tracks the number of people infected."

"What are we talking about here?" MacNally turned from Haupt to Stride. "Quotas? Is this about funding or something?"

"We will get to that later." Haupt dismissed the question. "We need specific information on this virus. We will need to know its transmission rate, its replication rate. I will need to see all of the data available."

MacNally wanted to see it too. But for the time being, he was going to have to concentrate on not yanking the table out of his way and strangling Dr. Stride. There was no compelling reason to keep him from doing it, save that there was a woman present at the table. And she had been through enough in the last two days.

94

"So let's find your Ethan Layne." Pete Landon cleared away a space on his desk that was big enough for him to power up his deskscreen. "No one is impossible to find."

"You really think so?" Lepov looked over his shoulder but the view did him no good. The screen was full of numbers, graphs, and scrolling lists that made little sense to Lepov.

"You don't know me too well, yet, so I'll ignore your open suspicions about my skill. We'll call them ignorant reservations."

"Has MacNally arranged access for us to the building's security?"

"Now that's insulting, Mr. Lepov." Landon shook his head in despair. "Would you suggest Van Gogh needs help painting a chair?"

"Who's Van Gogh?"

"Never mind," Landon shook his head again, his great head of hair shaking with it. "I don't need MacNally to get into that building's security. Here, I'm already in. You are looking for this image, so we simply crosscheck the recorders with this image of Layne."

"That's it?"

"Well," Landon stopped typing on the screen, "which time period?"

"Ever since he's been missing, I guess. Make it four weeks."

Landon whistled a warning. "That will take a few minutes. Not that my system is slow, but the security system they have is. And four weeks is a lot of images to sift through. Okay."

The screen went dark. Lepov, watching from behind, leaned in for a closer look.

"What happened?"

"It's fine. It's doing its thing. Be patient."

"Can you do something else? I want to see Layne's work schedule. His last three days of work. Pull that up for me."

"You sound like you have confidence in my talent, Mr. Lepov. I won't even ask you where he worked. And don't tell me."

Landon's fingers flashed quickly across the screen. Like a magician, he brought up displays with a wave of his hand and made other displays disappear. Lepov suspected that most of the wild movements were for show. There was no harm in that as long as he got results.

"There, his work record of his last five days on the job."

"Now let's see what he was up to those last few days. Light schedule, only a few calls to make repairs." Lepov continued reading down the list. Nothing caught his eye on the last few days.

"Does any of this mean anything?" Landon asked.

"It doesn't look awfully helpful. But this last entry will be a place to start. He made a repair run to IHS the morning he disappeared. That was either an all day job or he left early for the day. He was listed as unavailable. Is that like calling in sick?"

"I doubt it," Landon gave him a funny look. "Not many people are willing to call in sick around here. That's the surest way to be tagged for tests. One bad result and you're left with the terminals— whether you're sick or not. And once that happens you're never getting out of the Laz."

"That great. A real five-star hotel you got here. What's the catch?"

"Catch?" Landon ran a hand through his thick hair.

"Why would anyone put themselves in this kind of place? I've been scratching my head about that since I got here. I understand why someone would pass through. But what the hell are you doing here?"

"Why does anyone work anywhere?"

"A woman?"

"No," Landon chuckled. "The other reason people do anything. Money. I can make three times as much here. And if I survive, and actually get out of here, I can retire early. That's all I want."

Lepov wanted to tell this whiz kid he was nuts, but he didn't. The fact was, Lepov was there in the same Lazaretto for the same damn reason; money. He'd like to think he had taken Eudia Layne's case because she looked so pitiful, or he felt bad for her son. But the simple truth was he had flown all the way out to this rat-trap for money.

"So Layne didn't call in sick. He must have called in something, because his employers didn't miss him for a while."

"You're being impatient. I found it. Listed right here. Says E. Layne called in and said he'd been in a vehicle accident. Needed a few days off according to his doctors."

"Can—?" Lepov tried to ask but was interrupted.

"I'm already on it. Medical logs for all Center City hospitals and clinics." Landon muttered disapproval at a display and wiped it away with one sweep of his hand. "Let me try this; traffic control report on vehicular incidents. Nope. No reports of an accident involving Layne."

"Okay," Lepov shrugged, "so he lied. Maybe he was sick."

"He was out at IHS for about three hours."

"So I talk to someone at IHS."

"Hold on," the deskscreen lit up with a blue background and a chirrup announcing that the system was finished attempting to find image matches. "I've got a half-dozen possibles. Take a look."

Lepov slid into a chair beside Landon and looked over the display. All of the images were of a young man with blond hair. Four of the shots were of the young man with a young woman. Two when he was alone. All of them were a close match to Ethan Layne but Lepov could not be positive. He did not know Layne well enough to recognize him with a different hairstyle.

"Well, that looks like him. Probably the best image you'll get of him is the third one. The probability on that match is higher than most." Landon sounded optimistic.

Lepov agreed. This was Layne. He had no reason to doubt it. He'd been hiding in plain sight for weeks. But where would he be now? The depressing truth was Layne would be nowhere near that apartment anymore. He'd killed the girl and would be long gone.

"Don't be glum. Have you forgotten why MacNally sent you to me?"

Lepov glanced over at Landon and nodded. He had to admit he could not remember why MacNally suggested he talk to Pete Landon. Well, no one had ever accused Lepov of being the sharpest detective.

"This Layne kid; he was using one of Romeo's PDTs, right? Well, I can track him, sort of. Let me simplify it. I can tell you, from time to time, where he is. It doesn't last for long, and I can never guarantee I'll find him again soon after that. But if he's not moving around much, or at least always returning to wherever he's holed up, then we can find him."

Maybe he would catch a break. Maybe Lepov wouldn't fail after all.

As if to mock his newfound confidence, his knee shot a jolt of pain through his leg as he stood up from his chair. Lepov did his best to ignore it. This was his first real chance to get Layne, and he wasn't going to let his dysfunctional knee stop him.

"Can you call me when you find him?" Lepov wanted to take a look around the dead woman's apartment. He wasn't going to sit around until Landon got his signal.

"Jot down your number on this screen and I'll call as soon as I can."

"And I thought it would be an insult to offer you my number. I'm surprised you don't already have it." Lepov grabbed a stylus and scribbled his number on the glass screen.

"I do, I didn't want you to feel like I was getting too invasive."

As he headed out the door, Lepov made a call to MacNally. He'd need the big detective's clearance to get into the apartment.

"I'm glad you called, Lepov." MacNally answered immediately.

"Well, I hope you keep up that enthusiasm. I need you to get me into Julia Maiden's apartment. Layne was definitely there. I might find something that could tell me why he's gone psychotic on us. Or maybe something that will tell me where he's gone. At any rate, I need your clearance for this. That Landon guy's trying to track Layne right now. We're hoping to get lucky."

"Lepov," MacNally sounded hesitant to continue, "I've got some news that you need to hear. But I don't know how much I want to say over this connection."

"Is it about Layne?"

"Yeah, he may not be what we thought he was."

"And what was that?"

"What we talked about." MacNally's vague references weren't making for good communication.

"What did we talk about?" Lepov wasn't playing dumb, he just didn't like word games.

"For pity's sake, Lepov. You're a lot of help. I'm only going to say this once, okay? You'd better hope to hell nobody's monitoring this. I'm sitting here with a couple of stiffs from IHS who've just told me that some kind of rogue virus is responsible for Ford's death. The same goes for the Russians and Julia Maiden. According to them, we've got a Typhoid Mary out there in Center City. None of these people were murdered. Not directly, anyway."

"What is a Typhoid Mary?" It sounded like a mixed drink.

"That's what I asked. She was some skirt who had a deadly disease centuries ago—ran around infecting people without getting sick herself. She was a carrier for this disease. And that's what we've got now. Someone in the Lazaretto is carrying this thing around."

"That's a helluva thing for a woman named Mary to do. I would believe it from a woman with a name like Greta, but you don't expect that from a girl named Mary."

Lepov suddenly had little interest in combing through Julia Maiden's apartment. He was much more interested in learning more about this virus. Most importantly, he wanted to know how infectious it was.

"Can I meet you at IHS?" Lepov asked.

"Come on. I'm still trying to find out what's going on."

And that was Lepov's aim. If MacNally had his facts straight, then Layne wasn't a murderer. So what did that mean? Was Layne dead now? Lepov was ready to find some answers and then he really ought to get out of the Lazaretto. Of course, that was not easy to do. He certainly couldn't get out of there in a hurry.

A rogue virus in the Lazaretto? At least Lilly had made it out. It was ironic, considering he had told her she was making a mistake. He should have known she would have turned out to be right.

95

It was time for Maria to go to Kjarsta. She had to be strong when she told him of Georges' discovery. And she would have to do it alone. Georges could not help her.

Georges had hired a TransitCar to take them to the Clinic. And now they stood outside Kjarsta's room. For once, he appeared to be unsure of what he should say. He reached out a hand and touched Maria lightly on her arm.

"Don't wait." She covered his hand with her own. "I will need to take this slowly. Go on to your office. I will come and find you if he is able to tell me anything."

"He is fortunate to have a friend in you, Maria Lucia." Georges turned and left her alone.

"Maria," Kjarsta's voice startled her as she entered his room. It was far weaker than she had ever heard it. His greeting sounded more like a cry for help.

"I'm sorry I haven't been here for the last few nights."

"No, no. I am sorry." He tried to shake his head but only managed to turn it to one side. "They did not want to tell me—about your brother."

His breathing was shallow, with pauses in between each short breath. His eyes closed and Maria had the feeling it was too much effort for him to keep them open. She pulled a chair beside his bed and sat down. They said nothing for a few minutes. She listened to his labored breathing; it looked as if he had fallen into a painful sleep.

"I wanted to tell you so many stories."

When she looked up at him, Maria wasn't sure he had actually spoken. His eyes remained closed and his breathing had not changed. Then his eyes slowly opened, the crow's feet at each corner looked dried and cracked. There was, however, dull color left in those eyes; evidence of life still within. It was vaporous life, at risk of evaporating into the sterile darkness of that room; yet it still existed.

Was the strength she had counted on still there? Maria was not sure. But it had to be. The kind of strength she was looking for had never been linked to his body's vitality. Kjarsta had strength that was locked into his being; something that no disease could ever take from him.

"What is wrong?" This time she knew he had spoken; his voice was firmer, closer to the Kjarsta of old. Perhaps he had seen the worry on her face and had fed off her need for him. Men often died when they no longer felt needed. Why couldn't he revive if he felt she needed him?

"I want to tell you a story," Maria whispered. Summoning courage and resolve she was sure she did not have, she began to tell Kjarsta everything Georges discovered. There was no easy way to explain it. No gentle way to break the news. She was telling a friend that he had been cruelly murdered a long time ago. There were no gentle ways to do that.

Once finished, she wondered if it had been too much for him to absorb.

"This is a bad thing," Kjarsta said, coughing weakly. "I never wanted you to know."

Maria was amazed at his response. Even as she told him such a hard truth, he worried about how it would affect her.

"Do not worry about me, Kjarsta. It is I who am worried about you. I was afraid this news might be too painful for you."

"No, my angel. This is not news to me at all. I knew this from the start. You just confirmed what I always suspected. But you were sweet to worry over me. But, if you were so worried, why did you say these things to me? What is it you want?"

"My husband, Georges, he knows that someone influential is behind this. We do not know who we can inform. We need to know to whom we can safely give this information."

"There is no need," Kjarsta actually had the energy to chuckle. It came out mostly as a strangled cough, but Maria recognized it. "No one need ever know. I am no innocent man whose blood demands justice. And I have no need to see the man responsible hunted down. He will have his rewards, as I am getting mine."

"You know?" Maria leaned in closer to him. Her words were barely more audible than Kjarsta's. "You know your murderer?"

"Too well, I am afraid. The partner I was talking about. I knew as soon as the diagnosis came out what had happened. I was at peace with my fate when I was first told about it, and I am more so now."

"Will you tell me? Tell me who he is?"

"I can't. And even if I could I wouldn't. These are things that you don't need to get involved in."

Can't? Maria wondered at that. For a man who was on the brink of death he seemed to still clutch at his world. A man with nothing to lose would never tell her he could not reveal who had infected him. There would be no reason. What, after all he had been through, did he have to lose? What was he protecting?

"Tell me about her." Maria saw the recognition in his eyes and knew she had guessed correctly.

"You're the only *her* I know anymore."

"I did not say you know her. But you did, a long time ago. Does she know about you?" Maria would not let him keep silent. She remembered his talks, his need for confession. His daughter had to be alive. He had to be protecting her.

"Della should not have said anything." Kjarsta tried to sit up as a deep cough rumbled through him. His body was trying to force something thick out of his throat. Seconds passed and he could get no air. His gut contracted two or three times as it fought the blockage. Maria grabbed a towel and held it in front of him. She tried to help him sit up with her other arm. As weak as she was, the barrel-chested Kjarsta was light and she lifted him enough to expel the pasty phlegm.

With raw effort he freed his air passage. Maria cleaned his lips and chin, and helped him sip some water. She could feel his body shaking from the sudden exertion.

"What do you think I could tell you?" Kjarsta asked after he had recovered enough to speak.

"Does she know who you are? Does she know who her father is?"

Kjarsta was barely able to shake his head.

"Does your partner know who she is?"

"I always hoped he didn't. But I'm sure he does."

Maria was having trouble pressing him for information. She felt the despair and heartache that overshadowed his imminent death and it made her ache for him. She felt foolish for trying to discover who had infected him—who had inflicted this horror on him. In the short time he had left, that could not have any meaning for him.

Kjarsta had fallen asleep. Maria watched his labored breathing and wondered how much time he had left. She busied herself cleaning up Kjarsta's room in a conscious effort to stop dwelling on it.

The Collector sat behind his desk with a tall glass in his hand. A vibrant pink liquid filled half of it. The glass was cool to the touch but the drink burned as he drank the remainder of it. Of course it burned. It was evidence of the presence of contaminants. And he could never avoid contaminants completely when he was outside his home.

He should have followed his instincts and gone home after his agent had polluted his office. He could be in his suite now, freshly cleansed from his sonic bath. But his instincts about his agent had been correct. The Agent had failed. The Collector had been forced to act.

If everything had been done as he had asked, the Agent would no longer be a problem. If not, then he would be ready for that as well.

It was a recurring difficulty that the Collector grew weary of; not everyone did what he demanded. And when he was ignored there were always consequences.

Lilly Stewart had ignored him, though she had unquestionably understood his intentions. And at first she had agreed to his request. He had even paid the damned fee to get her into Delta. But she was still in Center City, and that might lead to problems.

If she had been anyone else he would have made sure the consequences were heavy and immediate. But he would have to be careful how he dealt with her. There was more than his pride at stake.

How odd, he mused, that she should hinder his attempts to protect her. His only aim in getting her into Delta and out of the Lazaretto had been to keep her safe. Now, her behavior suggested that her safety was not the only factor. She would have to be dealt with. Perhaps that time had come.

A noise like a great breath of air broke his reverie. The Collector turned in time to see his agent open a small door—the same one he had used hours earlier—and walk boldly into the room. The Agent no longer approached him with the respect of a subordinate. His face wore an arrogant and angry expression.

"You didn't expect this, did you?" The Agent carried no weapon; he held both hands at his side with palms showing. "Right now you're wondering what happened to the man you sent to kill me."

The implication hung in the air. The Agent waited to hear if the Collector would deny it.

"And?" the Collector asked, "Are you going to tell me?"

"Having murdered a man in police custody a few days ago—by your orders, I want to add—I knew you would send someone. I knew you had little time to act and so I expected it would be someone on site. One of the patrolmen. You'll notice I survived the attack without injury. He was really below standard."

"As you said; it was short notice." The Collector nodded to the Agent, conceding the point. "But I should point out that you have performed below standard of late. It was your sloppy work that forced me to act."

"I won't argue with you. My time is short. The police will be looking for me, if they haven't started already." The Agent took a step towards the Collector.

"No doubt you want me to get you into Delta. It is a wise move. Were you aware that Dr. Fisher was smart enough to get into Delta? I get the feeling he was afraid for his life. To be honest with you, he was smart. I doubt I would have let him live."

"He wasn't smart," the Agent countered. "He ran away from you. I, on the other hand, know that the only thing that makes you something to be feared is me. You should remember that. Be afraid of me."

The Agent took a few more steps towards the Collector. The Collector pushed his chair back and stood up.

"Now who's afraid?" The Agent smiled. "I'm beginning to like being in control. I like the feeling. Now, you tell me. Who's smarter?"

"There's no question who was wiser," the Collector said with firm resolve. "Dr. Fisher was wiser than you. Some people know when things have gotten out of hand. And the smarter ones know what to do about it. Dr. Fisher knew, and he got out."

"And so will I."

"The grace period is closed."

"I didn't intend to get out of the Lazaretto by way of Delta. There are other ways off this rock." The Agent took two steps closer to the Collector, who took as many steps to stay away from the Agent.

"You could say that," the Collector laughed.

"Is something funny?" the Agent cocked his head to one side.

"There are other ways out of the Lazaretto. There is my private shuttle. But you would need my authorization codes to get it into the air. And I'll never give them up. Even if you threaten me, I'd only give you bad codes. You could cross over into the shipping zone. But you would have to don a fully encapsulated biohazard suit. And then you could hide out on one of the cargo ships as it was being released. But you aren't going to do that. You're going to take a different way off the Lazaretto; a more final path. You did touch the door handle coming in, didn't you?"

The Agent shot a look back at the door and then down at his hand.

"That's been your problem." The Collector watched his agent

with disgust. "You've done sloppy work. I told you the last time you were here not to touch the door handle. You never know what deadly germs or viruses can be picked up on this cursed little planet. I do, however, know what you picked up when you opened that door."

The Agent rubbed his hand. He looked as if he couldn't decide whether the Collector was bluffing or not.

"Your hand won't tingle. It is possible that your mind will project some kind of symptom there, however, since I told you the infection came through your hand. But the symptoms to come will be real enough. You're already feeling flush. That's the body recognizing an attack and raising your temperature to kill its attacker. But in this case, heat will only make it stronger."

On cue, the Agent put a hand to his forehead. It began to turn red.

"I came here to kill you," he said. He stepped towards the Collector. Only the desk separated them. "At least I can infect you too."

"No, if that were the case, you could accuse me of being sloppy. But the fact is this little bug is not greedy. Once it finds a host, it will not seek out another one until the host is dead. As you might imagine, I thought of that little detail myself. My engineer had a great deal of trouble getting it right, but he did get it right.

"Is your vision blurred yet? You'll see lights, too. The first place it attacks is the brain. It begins to hack the brain, as if it were a computer system. It will search for ways to shut down sensory input. And the visual feeds from the optic nerves are the least complicated to interrupt."

The Agent tried to close on the Collector but he bumped into the desk. He reached out both hands towards the man he wanted to kill.

"I'd describe to you why your hands will begin to lose coordination. It is a fascinating devolution that involves the sense of touch and its relationship with motor skills. But by the time I am done, your hearing will have been disabled, and most of what I say will go unheard."

The Agent lurched to one side, stumbling on an unseen piece of furniture. He was no longer moving in any one direction. His attempts to find the Collector were already wasted. The Collector merely moved six steps to the right. His agent no longer had the ability to locate him.

"If you can still hear me, there is one advantage to all of this. It won't hurt. When the bug goes after your heart and lungs, you won't feel a thing. That's far more merciful than you were with that detective."

The Agent collapsed to the floor; his body lay twisted as if his skeletal system had somehow been removed from within. The Collector did not bother to look at the body. He had already headed for the elevator doors.

Once he had the body removed, he would schedule that third level purification. He would have them run it twice. It was an inconvenience, but it would be necessary. There were all kinds of messes to be dealt with. And there were many different ways to deal with a mess. But the goal was always the same; one had to clean it up.

His agent had only been one part of his mess. There was more cleaning to come.

97

Helen was stunned by the magnitude of Dr. Fisher's complicity in Julia's death. She was even more unsettled to think that he had sent that man to her apartment. How could he have condoned such violence merely to cover his tracks? It was cruel. Julia had died by his incompetence, but Helen might have died by his cowardice.

She was alone in her shock. Dr. Haupt and Lieutenant MacNally were too busy trying to pry information out of Dr. Stride. Helen had remained with them as they re-entered IHS, but her heart was not in the investigation. She was certainly alarmed at the news of the virus, but she was more worried about what Dr. Fisher might still do. As long as he had people like Parks to call, he could still be dangerous.

"So let me get this straight," MacNally was sitting at the conference table reading at the deskscreen in front of him, "You guys were trying to make a mild virus that would make people sick, sick enough to be listed on the IHS logs. But your attempts to do it were hampered by an overly aggressive virus, right?"

"That's one way to put it." Stride had never lost his sickly pallor. He was slumped in the chair opposite MacNally. "To be more precise, the DNA programming was hampered by our use of an unstable virus whose DNA strands were unreliable. If the programming called for an attack on the skin, and then a retreat of that attack, it might never get the second command. If this was never corrected, the looped command might escalate the attack to a fatal level."

"And whoever is the carrier for this is capable of distributing this virus everywhere?" MacNally turned to Dr. Haupt; they needed to control this situation as soon as possible.

"I don't know for certain which virus the carrier has. There were a number of failed viruses that were supposed to be destroyed. I don't know the exact properties of the virus that is active."

"Can you give us transmission rates?" Haupt was attempting to compile data that he and Helen could use to create threat models. "We need to know the probability of carrier to carrier transmission."

"I can answer that question." Stride sat up. For the first time he looked interested in helping. "There can be only one carrier. That was part of the design that never failed. We were able to create a non-replicating carrier. That was one of the reasons we really thought we could do this. The carrier was isolated, the virus was contained. That was important to our goal. We wanted control. And that part worked."

"So if we find Layne, we stop it?" MacNally asked hopefully.

"Yes," Stride tried to sound definitive in his answer but even Helen could hear his hesitation.

"What else?" Dr. Haupt asked.

"The carrier can switch hosts. At least, that was the case for several of the virus's that we had to abandon. If it was one of them, then even if we identify who the initial carrier is, we cannot be sure it has not switched to another host."

"Are we looking at a massive outbreak within the Lazaretto?" MacNally was getting angry.

"I doubt it," Dr. Haupt answered. "Judging from the current rate—four deaths in the last few weeks—I would think it is safe to say the transmission rates are low. Would the virus have narrow parameters?"

"I think it might," Stride made no pretense to being sure of his facts. "Nearly every virus we worked with had specific factors it needed before a system could be infected."

"System? Don't you mean person?" MacNally asked petulantly.

"Yes," Stride nodded, "a person had to meet certain requirements before he or she could be infected. We used all kinds of dynamics to control it. First of all, we only wanted to infect healthy people who had healthy enough immune systems to fight it properly. But we used different combinations, and there is no telling which one is out there."

"If you could have studied the bodies...?" Haupt suggested.

"We might have been able to figure it out, with enough subjects."

"But the Shippers' Formula destroyed most of what you could use, right?" MacNally asked the same question Helen had been thinking of.

Stride only nodded in answer. He slumped back in his chair then, his face hardening under a mask of self-pity. Helen thought she heard him mumble something about it not being his fault. How could that possibly matter at this point, she wondered? What kind of man could look for justification after helping to create a virus this brutal and deadly?

At some point in the discussion, Helen had ceased to worry about the danger from Dr. Fisher and she began to understand the real danger this virus posed to the Lazaretto. As Dr. Haupt and MacNally focused on getting a clearer picture of the virus' true nature, Helen knew something had to be done quickly to find the carrier.

As the men talked, Helen determining who could have been the initial carrier. She had no idea how long ago the viruses had been destroyed. But from the little she had heard Dr. Stride speak about a time frame, she guessed that it had been eight to ten weeks. Given that period, she tried to calculate the number of people who had been in contact with Julia. If she thought about her hypothesis, it would have frightened her to think that she had been exposed to the same people. But Helen tried to ignore that thought. It was unproductive at a time when she needed to be productive.

Based on the few factors she had put into her equation, the number of possible carriers was in the hundreds. She would need more specific factors before such equations would give them anything worth looking at.

"What is this?" Dr. Haupt had seen the numbers on her screen.

Helen explained what she was trying to do.

"That's as specific as we can get," Stride responded. "It could be any one of those hundreds of people. Factor in the possibility of the virus switching carriers and the numbers get out of hand. It's why we never bothered to try to track down the carrier. It was impossible. No one could know who it was."

"Someone knew." A man whom Helen had never seen before walked into the conference room. He was broad-shouldered, with gray hair visible under his hat. He favored one of his legs as he approached the table.

"Someone knew who the carrier was? Who is this someone?" Haupt demanded of the newcomer.

"The man who hired me to find him."

"And you are?"

"He's Gregor Lepov," MacNally stood up and pointed to a chair. "Sit down before that knee gives out. You think Layne is the carrier?"

"I'd be willing to bet he is. I heard most of what you were talking about. Pardon my eavesdropping, but you have fascinating discussions in this little room. From what I can understand, someone here at IHS picked up this little bug and has been spreading it around the city for weeks. Is that right?"

"Yeah, but Layne doesn't work here," MacNally said.

"He did, one day. His last day of work. He was out here on a maintenance call. Working on the air system. And it looks like he was in a relationship with the last victim."

"The filtration system." Stride nodded as he spoke. "That could have been it. If the scrubbers had not removed the virus properly."

"But if it was Layne, why has he been in hiding? Would he know he was carrying a virus?"

They all looked at Stride.

"He would have felt a few minor symptoms. Nothing serious. Nothing that would make him want to disappear. That makes no sense."

"It does to me," Helen spoke up. All four men turned towards her.

"What do you mean, Helen?" Dr. Haupt prompted her to continue.

"If it made him feel sick at all, then he would have a good reason to disappear. Any employee of the Lazaretto Administration, whether he is employed by the IHS or the City, must be given a full range of tests at the first sign of sickness. If he had anything to hide, he would have had to disappear until his symptoms passed."

"So for all we know he might have illegal drugs in his system?" MacNally jumped to this conclusion with the single-mindedness of a cop.

"Or," Helen had a different viewpoint, "if he had symptoms that were bad enough, he might have been declared *nullus exitus* and he would have been stuck here for life. He would have lost his job. People often disappear for this reason. It's the system that makes them do it. No one wants the chance of being left to die."

"Where is Layne now?" Dr. Haupt asked.

"We have no idea," Lepov said.

"I think I can help." Again, all eyes turned on Helen. She wondered if she had spoken too soon. At this point she was only guessing. "This man Mr. Lepov is talking about is blond, correct?"

"How would you know that?" Stunned, MacNally watched her carefully as she answered.

"Because Julia wouldn't stop talking about her new blond boyfriend. She called him Billy."

Lepov and MacNally exchanged glances. Helen wasn't sure if she had irritated them with her nonsense or if they were glad she had said something. To her relief, Dr. Haupt caught her eye and nodded approvingly at her.

98

As leads went, the woman's lead was useless. The fact that Layne had been calling himself Billy—or at least Julia Maiden had been calling him that—did not make him easy to find. Was that simply an alias he used verbally, or was it on his PDT as well?

"She never mentioned a last name?" MacNally asked Helen.

Helen shook her head.

MacNally paused to consider their options. Pete Landon could probably find the full alias without much trouble. But with the Maiden girl dead, Layne would never use his PDT again. He said as much aloud.

"His tags in the bottom of a sewer." Lepov agreed. "So that leaves us right back at the beginning. I haven't done much for my client, have I? Here I am still looking for Ethan Layne."

"Wasn't your client this guy's mother?"

"Eudia," Lepov nodded.

"I thought you said something when you walked in about the man who hired you. What was that all about?"

"I'm beginning to think I wasn't hired by Eudia Layne. Oh, she called me, made the pitch. Probably meant every word of it. But there's something I never liked about that. When she first told me her son was missing, I asked her how long it had been. She told me it had been three weeks since she'd heard from him. When I asked her how often she heard from him, she said he only called her two or three times a year."

"So what made her think he was missing?" MacNally asked the next logical question.

"That's what I was wondering. But I needed the job and didn't ask. I didn't want to offend her. I figured she was relying on motherly instinct."

"That doesn't fly." MacNally had an idea where Lepov was going. "Someone told her, right?"

"An official message from Lazaretto Administration. Mrs. Layne was informed her son was missing and if she wanted to find him quickly the most efficient way to find him was hiring a private agency to locate him."

"The only way to find him," MacNally corrected him. 'No one was looking for him. There were no reports of him missing."

"Dr. Fisher knew the young man was infected. Is that what you are saying?" Dr. Haupt had been listening carefully to the two investigators.

"I was only saying someone knew," Lepov pointed out. "Was it Fisher? I don't know."

"Was it Fisher?" Haupt asked Stride.

The rail-thin doctor shook his head, more as a sign of his weariness than in answer to the question. "I suppose he did. He gave the orders to change the lab protocol. So I guess he was expecting Layne to infect people. How he knew this guy was infected though—I don't know."

"This does not help us find Billy. Why don't we simply put out an alert asking him to turn himself in? He won't want to stay out there infecting people." The Segal woman's face betrayed the doubt over her own statement.

"This kid has to know he's infecting people." Lepov didn't hesitate to disagree with her. "He knows he's sick. And like you said, ma'am, he doesn't want to get imprisoned here for the rest of his life. If he was going to turn himself in, he would have done that a long time ago."

MacNally had never been accused of passing up a chance to jump at a conclusion, but for once he had trouble making the leap. Fisher might have been a bad egg, but what kind of man would allow a virus to spread through the general population unchecked? That was unthinkable.

"Are we suggesting Fisher knew Layne was infected and he deliberately failed to raise the alarm to cover his own tracks?" MacNally's question held everyone's attention. "Haupt, when I asked you if this was about funding you said you'd answer that later. Answer me now. Were you here to cut purse strings? Was that your real mission?"

"No, I was sent to investigate Dr. Fisher."

"And no one knew this?"

"Correct. In fact, measures were taken to conceal my mission. Rumors of budget cuts were circulated. We leaked that rumor to the Lazaretto Administration before I arrived. We hoped that when Fisher heard of it, he would not suspect our true purpose. Why do you ask?"

MacNally was beginning to believe that something else was going on; something more than Dr. Fisher's lone attempt to cover up his misdeeds. But he wasn't going to tell anyone else yet. It was only a hunch.

"If I may," Lepov answered for MacNally, "it seems to me that Fisher would never have gone this far on his own. Besides, there are bigger things out there than guilt and complicity. I'd guess this was about money. And if someone thought money was in jeopardy, then this makes more sense. Fisher would have allowed Layne to spread the virus. That was the original intent, right? To make people sick?"

"Yes, but only to make the Lazaretto indispensable. Not to start brutally killing people." Stride was on the defensive. "God, you must think Fisher was psychotic. He would never have taken it this far."

"Lieutenant MacNally," Dr. Haupt cleared his throat, "there is much that I wish to discuss with Dr. Stride. Most of it will make no sense to you. I suggest you allow me to continue this investigation on my own, while you search for the carrier. I will inform you immediately if we discover anything else that is pertinent to your investigation."

"Okay." MacNally had to admit the doctor was right. He wasn't getting much done sitting there having an open discussion with a room full of people. "But you call me if you find anything you even think might help. Understood? We have one more decision to make, also."

"About informing the public?" Haupt suggested.

"The public? Hell, no. I was only thinking of my captain and maybe someone else here at IHS. But until we know if anyone was helping Fisher, we really can't tell anyone. But if we don't, we are putting people at risk, right?" MacNally directed the one question at both doctors.

"The risk is there whether we tell anyone or not." Haupt answered. "The carrier is out there. And until he is found, he risks infecting anyone he comes into contact with. The probability of that infection is in question, and we will work on discovering what it is if there is time. But telling people to beware of a blond man who may or may not go by the name of Billy could cause more problems than it solves."

MacNally didn't like what the doctor was saying but he had a hard time arguing with him. The general public of the Lazaretto was already a paranoid creature that was afraid of its neighbor's shadow. Giving that shadow a name and a vague description would ratchet up the tension in ways no one could predict.

The best way to get through this was to find Layne as fast as possible. MacNally had a bad feeling that they had little chance of success.

MacNally left IHS with Lepov. It was good to have the private detective at his side, though he would never have admitted it to Lepov. No matter how he tried, he was sure the disappointment showed on his face when Lepov informed him he wasn't going to stay with MacNally.

"So what are you going to do?" MacNally asked as he pulled out a nearly empty pack of cigarettes.

"I gotta get some sleep before I continue looking for Layne. I've been up all night. You remember telling me we're getting old? You weren't kidding."

"I can wait for you back at the station." Damn, MacNally cursed to himself, he didn't want to have to ask Lepov for help. But maybe he should. He was actually starting to like the guy. And it was getting difficult to find anyone at the station who would willingly work with him. Fenelli had been the only one who could stand him.

"Well, to be honest, I figure we shouldn't work together. I might be able to look in places you can't go."

Lepov didn't have to say any more than that. MacNally knew what he meant. But that didn't make MacNally feel any better. He had a feeling he was being brushed off. It was times like this he needed Fenelli to tell him to quit worrying over trifles.

"I'll call you if I find out anything," MacNally said. He wanted to demand that Lepov do the same but he didn't want to sound like he was relying on him. All the same, he was disappointed when Lepov only nodded and walked away.

It wasn't that MacNally was surprised that he missed his partner so much. He simply hadn't expected to need him so much. But he did. And not only as an investigator. MacNally had the distinct feeling that a great big piece of him had been ripped away and the gaping wound was visible to everyone around him. Maybe that was truer than he realized. When MacNally thought about it, he reacted in the only way he knew how; he got angry. And that made him want to get back to the station and question Parks.

And the questions were going to hurt Parks a helluva lot more than that wrought-iron chair had. MacNally would make sure of that.

99

Kjarsta awoke hungry. Maria fed him. That had always been a difficult process. Now, in the advanced stage of his disease, feeding him had become nearly impossible. He could not eat anything solid. None of the liquids he sipped at curbed his hunger. There were places in his mind that recalled the pleasures of eating and could not be fooled by the tasteless nutrients the doctors prescribed. No matter how much he forced himself to swallow, Kjarsta was starving to death.

"Stop. Don't." Kjarsta raised a hand and tried to push the spoon away. He had no more strength to push Maria's hand away than a healthy man had to push away an onrushing truck, but Maria pulled back all the same. It did no good to force the soup down his throat. He choked on and spit out most of what he wanted to swallow. There was little chance of getting him to swallow something he didn't want.

"That wasn't enough," she scolded him. If she could get him to try more it would be worth it. If not, at least he could feel like he was still in control of something. And that was worth it too.

"Don't make me hurt you," he whispered.

Maria smiled. He tried to smile back. With imagination she could see it on his face. What a rogue he must have been, she thought. Maybe, she realized, he had been too much of one. Would she have been able to love him as much then? Maybe. She hoped she would have.

And that made her wonder about his daughter. Had she ever had the chance to know him? Had Kjarsta even wanted her to?

"You look nothing like her."

The comment from Kjarsta caught Maria off guard. Maria looked him in the eye and thought for a moment. She did not want to pursue the topic anymore if it was going to upset him. But he looked as if it actually brought life into his eyes.

"You've seen her recently?"

"I kept an eye on her. I always kept an eye on her. Did she know? I don't think so." For once, his breathing remained steady and unlabored.

"What happened?" Maria dared to ask.

"I sent her out of the Lazaretto. I would have been a bad father. A monster. She was better off."

Maria was startled by the hardness of his eyes. It did not last long, but the message had been clear. This was no casual self-deprecation. There was cold truth in what he said.

"You don't know that," Maria said, thinking of her father. He too had been a bad father. But in the end, there had been that part of her that desired something more than relief at his death.

"I won't tell you." Kjarsta closed his eyes. "Leave her alone. It is the one good thing I ever did for her. And forget about my partner. I should never have told you any of it. What he did—what I did—none of it matters now. We all get our rewards. Now. Later. It doesn't matter."

Maria said nothing. It was the only answer she could give.

"I'm sorry. I should have left you alone too. Stay away from me." Kjarsta said these last words with great effort.

The day was wearing away, and the noise in the hall had ceased. No one was moving about. Maria allowed the growing silence to fill the room, holding still so as not to disturb Kjarsta as he faded into sleep. He had never spoken like that. It was the closest he had come to revealing a side of him that was more than a charming rogue. She had seen it more in his eyes than heard it in his words. And she knew why it had surfaced. He wanted her to back away. She couldn't help but wonder if that meant he was preparing to die.

Once certain that he was asleep, she went in search of Georges. She needed his solid presence. He had never been a charming rogue and she was glad of that. When she found him in his office, she made no effort to conceal her need for him. She desperately needed his embrace.

"His time is so short." Maria looked up at her husband, unable to let go of him. He had all the strength she would ever need.

"I can check on him. See if there is anything I can do."

"I'd like that." Maria knew there was little Georges could do.

"Did you learn anything?"

"He says he knew all along someone had infected him. He doesn't want us to do anything. He says it doesn't matter."

"I can understand what he means, but this is not only about him. If there is someone out there who can do this kind of thing, your friend might not be the only one affected by this. Didn't he tell you anything?"

"He only said it was his partner. But he won't say who his partner was." Maria knew that Georges would not remain silent without a good reason. "Please, Georges. Be careful. I think Kjarsta is protecting someone. We cannot tell the wrong people."

"I know, Maria. And I have been thinking about that. There may only be one person we can trust."

Georges said no more, and Maria did not press him. She recognized the expression on his face. He was trying to decide the best way to proceed and she was willing to trust him to make the right decision. She was relieved that she could allow him to make that choice. Her own emotional involvement with Kjarsta was clouding her ability to remain objective about what should be done.

100

Each flight of stairs beat hell out of Lepov's knee. At least there was a bed waiting for him at the end of his climb. He really shouldn't sleep. Lepov knew that as late as it was in the day he would only end up sleeping through the whole night. But after staking out the Becker apartment all night and spending the day looking for Layne and an afternoon at IHS, Lepov had to admit defeat. He was exhausted. If he slept all night he would worry about it in the morning.

Then maybe, just maybe, his traitorous knee would quit feeling like someone was digging around in it with a blunt knife. Getting old? The knee was making him feel downright ancient.

When he walked through the door to his dormitory, Lepov quit thinking about his knee. Seeing Lilly again, sitting on his bed as she had only a few days ago, erased all the pain over which he had just been obsessing. In that one moment he felt relief that Lilly had not been locked down in Delta. At the same time he felt sick. She should have left when she had the chance.

"Have you been waiting long?" It was all he could think to say.

She was sitting up, her hands folded in her lap, with an almost embarrassed expression on her face. She looked more like a schoolgirl in trouble than a strong-willed interplanetary businesswoman. She had never looked vulnerable to Lepov before. It made him feel slightly unbalanced. Something was wrong.

"You're limping badly," she said, ignoring his question.

"Someone told me I was getting old. I didn't think I'd see you again."

"You don't look happy about it."

"About getting old?" Lepov knew what she meant.

"I thought you wanted me to stay."

"I did," Lepov said.

"You changed your mind."

"Move over." No longer shocked to find her there, the pain in his knee could no longer be ignored. He sat stiffly beside her and tried to stretch his leg out but the pain was at its worst as much then as it was when he tried to bend it completely. He awkwardly settled for something uncomfortably in between.

"I did want you to stay, but I thought I'd been taken off your list of favorite friends." It was a flippant way of saying she'd unfairly blamed him for Montillo's death and he was sorry he'd said it.

"Never taken off," she said. "I may have been angry but that was only for a time. I was beginning to worry that you'd slipped into Delta. I thought maybe you'd found your man and made a run for it."

He laughed. She hadn't said anything funny but he laughed anyway. It took guts to laugh since sharp pains shot up from his knee at the slightest movement.

"What's the joke?" she asked.

"You said that like it was possible I could find anyone. You don't know me very well so I'll let it go. But if you ever did get to know me you'd find out what a lousy private detective I am. Do you know this is the first decent case I've had for a long time?"

"I can't decide if you're trying to be funny or if you really mean it."

"The second thing you said. The fact that I'm sitting here is proof of that. I came back up here to get some sleep. And do you know what? I'm not a bit closer to finding Layne than I was when I landed in this scabby little world." Lepov pulled his hat off and threw it down on the bed. He ran a hand through his thin hair and he wasn't laughing anymore.

"You need sleep."

"I need a cigarette." Being exposed to MacNally's cigarette smoke was wearing him down. And his resistance to them was weakest when he was exhausted. He felt around in his coat for his unopened pack.

"You don't need one of those. Two years, remember? You're just over-tired, Gregor."

"Think about it, Lilly. Have you seen me do anything remotely constructive in my search for Ethan Layne? Aside from being assaulted by a short little German nutcase, I haven't done anything. You know why Eudia Layne hired me?"

"Take this off," Lilly pulled at his raincoat. He allowed her to work one arm out of the sleeves at a time.

"She hired me because I'm cheap. She hasn't got money. She's a poor old woman who could barely afford to hire an unwanted detective to find her boy. And the hell of it is, even if I did find him, it's not gonna matter. He's already dead. Even if we find him alive, he'll still be dead."

The coat lay stretched out behind him, half of it still underneath him. Lilly got up from the bed, turned, and knelt in front of him. She pulled off each of his shoes and lined them up against the wall.

"Now you're not making any sense," she said. "When is the last time you slept?"

"I ain't that tired, Lilly. I know what I'm saying. Layne is sick with some kind of man-made virus. It seems he has this killer virus that's pretty random. From what I gather, at some point, he'll die from it too. This whole damn thing's been about a virus."

Lilly peered intently at him, trying to decide if he was talking nonsense or not. He stared at her, trying to give her his most lucid expression. That was nearly impossible to do given his level of fatigue.

"If you keep this up I might start to believe you." She put both hands on his shoulders and pressed him back onto the bed.

"What were you doing here?" Lepov looked up at her.

"I'm putting you to bed."

"No," he shook his head, "I'm serious. Why were you waiting for me? Something isn't right. You were mad at me. Now you're here doing this. What made you come looking for me?"

As tired as he was, Lepov knew he was right. She hadn't waited for him simply to play nursemaid. Lilly wasn't the nurturing type. She might have had a tender side, but he didn't believe they had reached that level of friendship where she would allow him to see it. He might have been a lousy detective, but he could recognize when something wasn't right. He just couldn't always see what was wrong.

"Sleep." She tugged at his coat until it slid out from under him. With great care she spread it over his legs, taking care to avoid his sore knee.

"Hey," he reached out and grabbed her wrist. "I said I hadn't accomplished anything, I didn't say I was stupid. Why are you here?"

"It can wait. I need your help. But you can sleep first. I won't need your help until later tonight. Okay?"

"And just like that you think I'll help you?" he asked. She nodded at him. "Okay. I'll sleep. But you forgot something."

"What?"

"You didn't take off my shirt and pants. I don't sleep that well fully dressed." As tired as he was he managed a sly smile.

"I said I needed your help. I never said I was desperate." She leaned forward, kissing the stubble on his chin. "I'll wake you in a few hours."

Lepov gave up and closed his eyes. This was why he didn't like to get involved with women. He barely knew this one and she was already pushing him around.

101

Although the conference room had no windows, Helen knew that night had descended on the Lazaretto. The air in the room felt cooler regardless of the building's consistent environmental controls. The cold white glare of the overhead lighting no longer felt like daylight. Even in the hazy atmosphere of the Lazaretto, Helen, like every other inhabitant there, needed and sought out the warmth of the sun no matter how muted it was. And so as each night approached, she was aware of the sun's retreat; even within the enclosed conference room.

When she had told Dr. Haupt that she was able to work she had never imagined that she would stay late. At some point she would have to tell Dr. Haupt that she could no longer stay. She decided to give him ten more minutes. Judging by Dr. Stride's appearance, he wouldn't be able to last much longer than that anyway. His sickly green pallor was turning chalky gray. Thin long bags had formed under his eyes and he couldn't seem to stop rubbing at them.

"I've told you everything you need to know," Dr. Stride sighed. "We are going back over things I told you already."

"And there have been a number of times that you have contradicted yourself. I must be sure I get the truth," Dr. Haupt insisted.

"I'm tired. I'm not lying to you. But I'm getting mixed up. The more we talk the more likely I am to make mistakes."

"Then clear this up for me. How can you say the virus poses no threat to the worlds outside the Lazaretto?"

"You want me to say it again? Fine. The carrier, even if he goes into a quadrant in preparation for leaving the Lazaretto, will not be a threat. The virus will die after five weeks. That's how we designed it. That's regardless of whether or not it stays with the original host."

"That is how you designed it? As I recall, you designed it not to switch hosts, yet you said certain test viruses ignored that design. That was the point, right? You found you did not have the control you expected." Dr. Haupt was walking slowly around the conference table. Dr. Stride sat on one side of it. He stiffened each time the German came near him as if he expected to be attacked.

"Don't you think we would have made an effort to find Layne if we thought he could get out of the quarantine zone?" Dr. Stride allowed anger to back his words. Helen could see his frustration growing.

"No. To be honest with you, I don't believe that. Your goal was to increase the sickness rate to prove the necessity of this system."

"What were we supposed to do? Admit we knew about the virus?"

"Now that is the closest you have come to speaking the truth." Dr. Haupt stopped circling and leaned on the table, staring down Dr. Stride's defiant glare. "You allowed this virus to spread because you were worried about your career!"

"We were only trying to keep you from shutting us down!" Dr. Stride shouted. "I didn't believe the dangers of interstellar travel were over. You were putting the public's safety at risk."

"Do you know the tragedy of this, Dr. Stride?" The German leveled a devastating look of disgust at the laboratory director. "No one in Baltimore was talking about cutting funding or shutting you down. Less than two years ago we audited this facility and recommended that the Lazaretto remain in operation. There is plenty of evidence to support this view. Did you think we would be so stupid not to realize this? Or did you think the home office was so blinded by its political ambitions that we only wanted to shut this moon down regardless of the dangers to the planets?"

"What are you saying?" Dr. Stride stared at him in horror. "This was all in vain? We did this to people for nothing? That's impossible."

"The fact is, there would never have been a good reason, regardless of Baltimore's intentions. You've murdered innocent people with this virus, and more importantly, the virus may still be out there for a long time. I'm no virologist, but I know that if this virus survived your deliberate attempt to destroy it in the lab, then it has the capability to survive in the real world." Dr. Haupt stared at Dr. Stride with cold dispassionate eyes. "Your virus is going to kill more people, Dr. Stride."

Helen could not see Dr. Stride's expression but his head was bowed and his hands lay limp on the table. What little fight he had possessed was gone.

"Go home," Dr. Haupt said. He turned away from Dr. Stride

without waiting for a response and left the conference room.

Helen sat still, watching as Stride pulled his long frame up and out of his chair. With hands sunk deep in the front pockets of his pants, he dragged himself out of the room.

Helen felt no pity for the man, though she found it impossible to hate him. She wanted to. She had every reason to. But it seemed pointless to her. Julia was dead and there was no way to change that.

She found Dr. Haupt in his office, standing behind his desk. He was shutting down his desksystem and preparing to leave.

"Dr. Haupt?" She stood in the doorway, waiting for him to acknowledge her. After a pause, he looked up. "What about Ethan Layne? How will we handle him when he is found?"

"There is nothing we can do." He came out from behind his desk and waited for Helen to move before pulling the door closed.

"What do you mean?"

"It is clear why no one here was searching for Mr. Layne. Their knowledge of this virus is so limited, there is nothing of value that can be done. For all we know, Ethan Layne is no longer the carrier. Maybe the original virus has found a way to replicate itself. Even if we get lucky and it hasn't, there is nothing we can do for him. Isolate him, yes. That will be done. But that is all. The police are looking for him. That is all they can do. There is nothing else we can do. Too much time has passed. There are too many possibilities.

"Besides, Helen, you must go home. I can see how tired you are. Stay home tomorrow. I will not need you. I will spend the majority of the next few days writing up my report. I can handle that on my own."

Dr. Haupt reached out as if he were going to take her by the hand but stopped before touching her. "I'm sorry about Julia. And do not blame Dr. Fisher too much. I am certain he could never have done this on his own. Someone far more important than Dr. Fisher is involved. When we are able to question Dr. Fisher, we will find out who it is."

102

MacNally charged into the office and headed straight for his captain's door. One of the newer detectives was standing in the way and MacNally would have shoved him backwards over a desk if he hadn't scrambled out of the way.

"Jenkins!" he shouted as he threw open the captain's door, "what the hell happened with Parks?"

Captain Jenkins sat calmly behind his desk. He was a short man, with stiff bristly hair sticking out of his head in every direction. A bristle brush mustache covered most of his mouth, concealing the expression on his face. If he was angry with MacNally's intrusion no one could tell.

"We're trying to find out right now."

"When did it happen? Why wasn't I called?"

"First of all Ed," Jenkins scratched the top of his head, a move that only seemed to insure that his hair remained unruly, "I did try to call you. For some reason, calls aren't getting through to you. But at any rate, there wasn't anything you could do. Parks is gone. One of the guards from the holding cell is dead. We found him in Parks' cell."

"Simmons?"

"As a matter of fact it was. How did you know?"

"Because whoever Parks was working for may have tried to kill him like they did Montillo. And either Simmons killed Montillo or he assisted someone else. Hell, I wouldn't doubt if it was Parks that killed Montillo. But how did Simmons get into the cell? I thought he'd been suspended over the Montillo thing."

"I don't know, Ed." Jenkins bit his lip. "The only way he could have gotten in was if he knew the daily key code. But let's move on for a minute, okay. Where have you been since you grabbed Parks at the café?"

MacNally had not yet decided how much he was going to reveal to Jenkins. But once the question was asked, he told Jenkins everything. Starting with the research at IHS, he told the story of Layne and his infection, and ended with the bad news that Layne had disappeared.

"And this Dr. Fisher—" Jenkins thought a moment, "—I've met the man for God's sake. He and I were on a committee last year. I can't remember what the heck it was about but he seemed like a decent guy. You said he's behind all of this?"

"I'm not so sure about that." MacNally was too agitated to stop moving around the office. "The kind of stuff Fisher was doing—changing IHS procedures, tampering with crime scenes, endangering the whole quarantine system—you met Fisher, do you think he's the type of man to make such bold moves? On his own? I don't believe it."

"So who? Someone at IHS? From Earth?"

"Maybe." MacNally didn't believe that, but it was possible. "I was thinking of someone closer to home. Someone here in the Lazaretto."

"Who?" Jenkins asked with wide eyes. He either couldn't believe someone like that could be involved or he was scared at the possibility.

"MacNally?" The door opened and the same young detective MacNally had nearly run over leaned inside. "You got visitors."

MacNally pushed past the detective and saw a man and a woman standing near his desk. The man wore a pointed beard with a head full of black hair. The woman stood with her head bowed. Both of them wore expensive wool overcoats; certainly more costly than MacNally could afford. It took MacNally a moment before he recognized Fenelli's sister.

"Detective MacNally," the man held out his hand—he was wearing leather gloves. "I'm Dr. Georges Duvalls. This is my wife Maria."

The man spoke with a foreign accent of some kind. MacNally was pretty sure Fenelli had told him his sister was married to a Frenchman. If the accent was French he had no way of knowing; he didn't know a damn thing about French. He shook the doctor's hand.

"Your wife is my partner's sister." There was a pause as each of them realized what MacNally had said. "I'm sorry. Real sorry about Arturo. He was more than a partner. A real friend. He spoke of you often."

"Thank you, Detective." Maria looked up at him with soft eyes. "My brother mentioned you many times. Always with kindness."

"Well, you don't have to say that. We were good enough friends that I'm sure you're exaggerating. Please sit down."

"We would like to talk with you about something important, but it should not be here." Dr. Duvalls made no effort to conceal his unease.

"Something more private? Follow me." MacNally led them around the stacks of paperwork in the center of the room and into a smaller room with a sign above its door that read *Holding*.

They took seats around a small table.

"How can I help you?" MacNally asked.

"My wife and I work for the *Terminal Clinique de Lazaretto*. I am the director there. My wife volunteers with the patients. All of our patients are in advanced stages of terminal illnesses."

"I'm familiar with the Clinic," MacNally assured him.

"We did not know who we could speak with regarding one of our patients. It is an unusual case and we do not believe we can report what has happened through ordinary channels. We had hoped that you could listen to what we have to say. There is no one else we can trust."

"I'm pressed for time, Doctor. But I don't know when I won't be pressed for time. Tell me what this is about and maybe I could tell you who it would be safe to speak with."

MacNally had heard similar conversations before. It wasn't

uncommon for people to believe—to want to believe—that they were privy to information that was explosive or dangerous. Most of the time it turned out to be nothing at all. He was willing to give them a few minutes for Fenelli's sake but he couldn't spare too many minutes.

"My wife has been caring for a man who has been suffering from an unknown virus. One of our newest virologists helped me research the virus. What we found was unbelievable. The virus had been *designed* to sicken this man. Someone had actually programmed the virus to attack a specific DNA. I have never seen this before. The deadly nature of this virus convinces me that this is an act of premeditated murder."

MacNally didn't say anything. He was thinking about Stride's virus programming. It did not match the same signature as the virus in the doctor's story but it was too close to be coincidence.

"I would have reported this to your department through the usual channels but for one thing. I have seen evidence that suggests someone at IHS knew about this; someone who was powerful enough to cover it up. I know this must sound difficult for you to believe, Detective, but I can show you. I have the information here, on this data tag."

MacNally took the data tag from Dr. Duvalls and left it lying in the palm of his large, open hand. He wanted to tell the doctor that he was wrong—it was easy to believe his story—but he did not want to explain why. Not yet, anyway.

"What's this patient's name?"

"Zoltis—" Georges began to say.

"Kjarsta Zoltis?" MacNally surprised them by asking.

"You know his name?" The woman raised her head sharply.

"Know it well. Everyone here at the precinct knows it well. Every cop knows about Kjarsta Zoltis. Would you like me to tell you why?"

"No," Maria answered, shaking her head.

"I'll admit no one here is gonna grieve over him when he dies. Are you trying to say someone infected him—murdered him? Who?"

"He says it was his partner," Georges answered. "But we do not know who that is. Lieutenant, do you understand what it is we are trying to tell you? Why we must be discreet?"

"Yes. Someone important was able to cover this up." MacNally had been saying the exact same thing to Jenkins before they arrived.

"My wife was not certain that we should have told you about this. But I am concerned what this means. Someone has access to medical laboratories that can produce a virus like this. That same someone is manipulating our system. I cannot remain silent about this."

"You'll have to for a while." MacNally saw the distress on the doctor's face. "Not long. Trust me, okay? You came to me with this, now let me handle it."

Maybe he should have told them he knew Kjarsta Zoltis' partner. But he told them nothing. And they left the office completely unaware that they had supplied MacNally with the big break he'd been seeking.

103

The Collector stood looking out over the darkness of the Lazaretto. A west wind was blowing fog in off the water, blanketing the city in a thick screen. From the top of the Overlord Towers it was difficult to make out the pinprick-lights of the city. The glass windows ran wet, obscuring his view even further.

There had been much that obscured his view in the past few weeks. He had been convinced he could fix other people's mistakes. He had been positive that taking control of events would bring an end to the mess that had been made. All that had been required was positive action on his part. Mistakes could be corrected; messes could be cleaned up.

But what he had never been able to see was how much he had been forced to rely on the commitments and talents of other men. His mistake had been to believe that other men were as talented and committed as himself. That had never been the case and would never be the case. The simple fact was he should have never relied on anyone other than himself.

So he waited. He alone would have to take the remaining steps to bring an end to the disorder that had been created by others.

One of those steps had been taken; Parks was dead. That had been easier than he had imagined it would be. It had also been more satisfying than he had anticipated. A great deal of the blame could be laid at Parks' feet. There was no question that the Collector had allowed it to happen, but that did not exonerate his agent. Parks had failed to handle his business carefully. Well, the Collector thought, Parks no longer mattered.

Fisher was another story. He should have anticipated Fisher's flight into Delta quadrant, but there was no reason for hand wringing over that. Fisher was out of reach for the time being. Opportunity would arise soon enough. The Collector did not worry what Fisher might tell the authorities; Fisher was too stupid to betray him. Fisher would go to his grave with his secrets, convinced that he was too heavily involved to be able to make a life-saving deal with the government.

At least he wouldn't have to worry about Phillip Stride. That had been the one thing Fisher had done right: Stride believed that Fisher had been acting on his own. He had no idea that the Collector existed. Fisher's competence in this matter had saved Stride's life.

The Collector knew that he had to wait out Ethan Layne. Either the ill-fated kid would be killed by the virus he carried, or he would eventually be found by the police. Layne was the only solid evidence that could prove what had really happened. And the Collector knew that he still had enough influence to be able to make that evidence disappear. He had always hoped that Layne would be found by that bungler Lepov before the police figured out what was going on. Again, he had been betrayed by someone else's incompetence. Maybe Layne would never be found; maybe he was already dead and would never be found. Maybe.

The Collector looked at an ornate clock on his wall. One hour. One of his loose ends was about to be tied up in one short hour. He felt no satisfaction in taking this step. He even recognized the smallest measure of regret.

This was the step that proved how committed a man he really was. Killing Parks had been easy; he despised the man and had only ever intended to use the man before he disposed of him. Getting rid of Fisher would be as easy; Fisher was never more than a subordinate of little value. It was easy to order the killing of rats like Carlos Montillo. But only a committed man could take the more difficult step; the committed man could kill someone he cared about. And the time had come to erase all of his connections to the past.

The past had lost its value. The Collector could see that he had little chance left to preserve the world he had built. It was a law of civilization: empires rose and empires fell. Only the emperors who stood and watched them fall were caught by the fall-out. He would never allow that. He had always been prepared to make a timely exit.

Getting out, however, was not enough. He had to get out clean. He had to erase every link to the past. He had made that commitment long ago. The first step had been taken years before; it had been a cruel, immature step, the Collector was all too aware of that now. Killing his partner Kjarsta Zoltis had been necessary, but the method hadn't been. The Collector was glad to hear that Kjarsta was finally near the end. It did not matter anymore that his partner had been plotting against him. The man had suffered enough.

The only move left for the Collector, once Kjarsta finally died, would be to eliminate the last person that might possibly know of his connection to the old crime boss. And this last tie to the past would be eliminated soon. Somewhere, down in that fog, the last person who could possibly know of his sins was about to die.

104

If anyone had ever tried to convince Lilly Stewart she would be sitting in a men's dormitory watching over a man to ensure he slept soundly she would have laughed. Yet here she was sitting on an empty bed beside Gregor's making sure he slept. Twice, men had come into the room, and twice she had warned them off. That they had obeyed her was surprising. But it was nothing compared to her surprise when she thought about what she was doing.

Even as Shay's wife she had never played the mother hen for him. She had often boasted that she'd be damned before she tucked him into bed or straightened his collar. Yes, she had agreed to be his wife. No, she had never agreed to be his domestic slave.

She'd been younger then and those things had seemed important. Was that the difference? Was she getting older? Was she becoming indifferent to the battles of her youth? Or was there a simpler reason why she would be tempted to treat Gregor in ways she never treated Shay? What was it about this man who lay sleeping under his wrinkled raincoat?

He was difficult to understand. He was strong-willed, a stiff and stubborn man; as broken inside as his knee. She had seen that when he allowed frustration to overwhelm him. He was quick to jump to conclusions—he had never hesitated to accuse her of setting him up— but he had never hesitated to apologize either.

Did that matter? Shay had his peccadilloes as well. What man didn't?

As if disturbed by the course of her thoughts, Gregor turned onto his side, facing her. He was beginning to wake. His eyes were still closed but she could see the change in the rise and fall of his shirt.

Lilly stood up and walked over to a small table at the back of the room. A small coffee dispenser sat on it. An old machine, Lilly could not make it work. An elderly man in a faded military uniform was kind enough to show her what she had been doing wrong.

Gregor would have loved to watch her fight with it. She was never going to be a housewife of the year. Maybe it wouldn't matter. Maybe Gregor wouldn't be interested in that kind of thing.

With a cup of the much-contested coffee in her hand, she walked back over to Lepov's bed. His eyes were open by then and he was trying to focus on the fog-shrouded windows.

"What time is it?" he asked, taking the coffee from her.

"Time to get up. You feel any better?"

"Not yet." He tried to sit up and immediately reached down for his knee with his free hand. "You got a cure for old age?"

"You need a cure for stubbornness. You should see a doctor." Lilly's teasing was only meant to conceal how worried she was about him. She wasn't worried about his health for his own sake; she needed him. It was time she told him that. "Take this; it'll help kill the pain."

She handed him a small tablet. He closed one eye and held the tablet out at arm's length to get an exaggerated look at it. He shrugged and tossed it in his mouth.

"I hope that wasn't anything illegal," he said.

"You're still trying to accuse me of setting you up. I ought to walk away and never come back." It felt good to joke with him.

"I agree. You ought to." Gregor's expression was deadly serious. "So why haven't you? Are you going to tell me now?"

"Yes, as a matter of fact. If you quit being so suspicious I'll explain it to you. Are you awake enough yet? I guess it doesn't matter. There isn't much time left. I let you sleep as late as I could."

"This sounds like fun."

"I'm in trouble, Gregor. I need your help. Something's not right, and maybe you can help me figure it out." She took a deep breath. "You remember my client? The man who paid to get me out of the Lazaretto?"

"How can I forget?" Gregor asked. "I've never met the man but I already despise him. What has he done now?"

"Nothing, yet. But he called me when he found out I hadn't entered Delta quadrant. How he found out I'll never know. He acted strangely, demanding to know why I hadn't left. At first I was glad I stayed. It seemed to make him mad and I liked irritating him. I don't like to have someone demanding I do what he wants."

"We're gonna be a fun couple when we're seventy."

Lilly was caught off guard by Gregor's one-liner. No man had wanted to stick around until she was seventy. "If we live that long."

"What does that mean?"

"I'm getting jumpy. After what happened to Carlos, well, maybe I'm being paranoid."

"Oh, hell," Gregor sighed, sitting up straighter.

"What's the matter?"

"You might have a reason to be jumpy. You haven't heard about your buddy Parks yet, have you?"

"Shaw Parks? What about him?"

"Parks is in jail. We think he killed that detective the other night." Gregor looked as if he might say more but didn't.

"Shaw murdered him?" Lilly had trouble accepting that.

"That's what MacNally's saying. And Parks was arrested

attempting to kill someone else. I don't know what's going on with him, but he's involved in some pretty rough stuff."

Lilly felt a shiver run through her. Gregor must have seen it because he put out a hand and asked if she were alright.

"I'll be okay. It's not the best of news discovering that you're paranoia is justified. My client has demanded that I go see him." She saw the funny look on Gregor's face and knew what he was thinking. "Oh, he didn't put it like that. I wouldn't have agreed to see him if he had. But no matter how he worded it, I could tell he was ordering me to come to his place. That's not what's bothering me."

"So what is?" Gregor asked.

"What you said — about Shaw. He killed that detective — "

"Arturo Fenelli," Gregor supplied the name.

" — right, Fenelli. Shaw killed him two nights ago, isn't that right?" Lilly thought back over that night. "That was the same night I went to my client. I delivered a piece to him. As I arrived, I'm sure I saw Shaw enter his private elevator. But when I was allowed to go up, I didn't see Shaw anywhere. That was the same night Carlos was murdered."

Gregor stared at her, working things out in his head before speaking.

"Well," he finally said, "my knee's feeling better. What time were you supposed to meet this client?"

"In a few minutes. Gregor, maybe we shouldn't go."

"I'll admit I'm not excited about this little get-together, but you might not have a choice. Besides, we're stuck in this town with no place to go." Gregor stood up from the bed, obviously masking the pain in his knee. "You're right. You're in trouble and you need my help. So let's make a social call. You should be safe if I come along."

He still looked tired, but to Lilly he also looked downright heroic. He could have told her she was on her own. He could have told her to go to the police. But he hadn't done any of those things. He had stood up on his bad knee and lied straight through his teeth. He didn't think meeting with her client was any safer than she did.

"You said he has a working elevator?" Gregor stopped at the door to the stairwell. Lilly nodded. "Well, this may not be so bad after all."

105

Maria was still not sure she and Georges had done the right thing. Kjarsta had asked her to forget the things he had told her. Maybe she should have. Maybe they never should have spoken to Arturo's partner.

She tried not to think about it as she and Georges returned to the Clinic. Georges was going home but he wanted to be sure she made it to the clinic safely. He escorted her into the front lobby where the ever-faithful Karl stood waiting to take her up to Kjarsta's room.

"Thank you, Karl." Georges had called ahead and requested Karl's assistance. "If you are here in the morning, would you see that Mrs. Duvalls gets to the SubTransit station safely?"

"Yes, I'll stick around until she leaves." Karl gave Maria a big smile as if he were a small child proud of some grade school accomplishment. It brought a smile to Maria's face to think of Karl as a small child. It was hard to believe the big man had ever been smaller than a fifteen-year-old.

"Don't say it isn't necessary, okay?" Georges immediately turned towards Maria, expecting a barrage of protests. When he saw she was not going to contest Karl's escort duties, Georges relaxed. "I'm glad you're going to be sensible about this. I don't like it when we quarrel."

Maria did not answer. She was in no mood to banter.

"Should I come up with you? See how he's doing?" Georges could see something was bothering her.

"No," she shook her head, "he's been tremendously tired lately. I don't expect he will be awake. If he sleeps most of the night, I'll come home early. I won't stay too late."

Georges kissed her lightly on her cheek. Karl walked with her towards the elevators once Georges left.

"If you don't mind my saying so," Karl looked down at her, "your husband cares a lot about you."

"He is only being a husband. It is what they do."

An elevator opened its doors and Maria stepped in. Karl stepped in behind her and poked the button for the third floor with a finger that was bigger than the button.

For the first time in a long while Maria wanted to giggle about something. Karl was such a strong young man that even his fingers looked as if they had been stuffed with muscles. It felt good to giggle. Maybe, if Kjarsta woke up during the night, she would find something to joke with him about. He needed a reason to laugh as much as she did.

She would never get that chance.

As soon as the doors opened Maria knew something was wrong. The nurses' station was empty and there was too much activity down the main hall for that time of night. She could hear nurses talking urgently and heavy carts being rolled quickly down the hall.

Karl heard it as well. Gently, he put out a hand to hold her back as they stepped out of the elevator.

"Wait here, Mrs. Duvalls. I'll see what's happened."

She ignored him. By then, she could see the activity centered on Kjarsta's room. She rushed down the hall. *Not now!* She shouted to herself. *Wait!* This wasn't how it was supposed to happen. She had been expecting this night for months, but not yet—not yet!

She was stopped at the door. A male nurse stood in her way with a short, fat cart full of little machines. He was flipping a switch on the top machine and telling someone else that he wasn't getting any power. Beyond him she could see Della standing with one of the young doctors beside Kjarsta's bed. She could not see Kjarsta. Three or four other health technicians were jammed in the room.

Breathing became difficult for Maria—speaking was out of the question. She tried to call to Della but could not get enough breath to speak. She felt as if the weight of all those people in Kjarsta's room was bearing down on her lungs. They had no right to invade his little room. They had no right to bother him at this last terrifying moment of his life.

And that's what this was. She was sure that Kjarsta was dying if he wasn't already dead. But she had no way of knowing for sure. No one would tell her anything.

If only she had stayed. If only she had not listened to Georges. She had failed Kjarsta when he needed her the most. Della had been there for him. Maria had not.

The weight become unbearable. Maria stepped backwards, shaking with the effort to stand up under the pressure. She could not make it. Vaguely aware that she was falling, Maria felt as if the weight would not only knock her down, but that it would push her through the floors below her until she was buried beneath the cold bedrock of the Lazaretto.

She did not fall as long as she had expected to. When she opened her eyes she saw Karl's face full of alarm.

She could clearly hear Kjarsta asking her what she was doing on the floor. And then he asked if she could stand up. Hearing Kjarsta's voice was a shock. She thought he had died. He asked her again. Only this time, it was not Kjarsta's voice.

"Can you stand up, Mrs. Duvalls?"

It had never been Kjarsta's voice. Karl repeated his question.

"I don't know," Maria tried to say. Her head hurt. She felt dizzy.

"Maria?" Her mind was playing tricks. Kjarsta called her name then she saw Della standing over her. "He asked for you. He needed you."

Karl lifted her as if she were a delicate bouquet of flowers. She felt so small and unimportant in his arms.

"Put her here," Della ordered him.

Karl set her down in a chair. Maria had lost track of where she was. There were several people standing around her. They were not paying her any attention. Their backs were turned to her, looking at a figure in a bed.

The tears came even before she could remember who was in the bed. She cried to God, *Why now?* After all this time, why this night? How could a man fight for so long only to die alone in his bed, unwanted by a world that had abandoned him? A world that did more than abandoned him; the world of the Lazaretto had damned him.

She had no right to pass judgment on anyone. She should have been there. He had needed her. Maria felt smothered as she thought of that. He had known she wasn't there. Had it been his last thought?

Kjarsta. She could see him now, all alone in the bed. He was coughing, trying desperately to clear his throat so he could breathe. Maria didn't help him. She stood in the doorway watching him struggle. His eyes locked with hers and she heard him call her name.

"Maria."

Ashamed, she walked away.

"Maria, look at me."

Maria felt someone lift her head. She looked up and saw Della crouched down in front of her holding a glass of water.

"Drink this."

Maria and Della were the only ones in Kjarsta's room. The overhead light was off; the soft glow of a small table lamp illuminated the empty bed in front of them.

"Feeling better?" Della smiled as she took the glass from Maria.

Maria could see the weariness and sadness behind Della's smile. That had been all she needed to know that Kjarsta was truly gone.

"We knew this would happen," Della said softly. "I would have thought you of all people were prepared for this."

"It's not that." Maria turned away, unable to look Della in the eye. "I was overwhelmed when you told me he had called for me. That he had needed me. I failed him."

Della cocked her head to one side, wrinkling her brow with exaggerated effort. "What was this I told you?"

Maria repeated what she had heard Della tell her in the hallway.

"Darling, I never said anything of the kind. Kjarsta never said a word. I was in the room with him and he was asleep. I only noticed something was wrong was I couldn't hear the rattle of his breath anymore. I don't know what you thought I said, but you can forget about it.

"You did more for that man than anyone will ever know. You didn't fail him, darling. You loved him."

"I tried to. I wanted to." Fresh tears fell down Maria's cheeks. All Maria had wanted to do was show a dying man that someone cared. That even in the middle of this cold, cruel Lazaretto, the passing of a fellow human would not go unnoticed.

106

By the time Lepov and Lilly stepped out onto the stone steps that connected his building to the street, he was fully awake. The pain in his knee guaranteed that as he gingerly lowered himself down the last seven steps to the sidewalk.

"Do you have a vehicle? Or were you hoping to walk all the way to wherever the hell we're going?"

"I had planned to take a TransitCar." Lilly's voice trailed off and Lepov looked up from his knee to see what had caught her attention. She was staring at a large silver car hovering in the street. It was impossible to see who was inside the windowless vehicle.

"Someone you know?" Lepov asked.

Lilly didn't answer. He could see the anxiety in her eyes. Lilly Stewart did not easily panic but this silent machine had her worried.

"I don't suppose you hired this to save me from walking across town on my bum knee." Lepov took the last step and turned to Lilly. He held out his hand. "Shall we?"

As Lilly took his hand, a door seal hissed on the silver car. He didn't have to turn around to know that one of its doors was sliding open. Lilly's eyes were concentrated on the vehicle behind him.

"Might that be your client waiting for us?" he asked her. She nodded. "Chief Administrator Claude Reno, if I'm not mistaken, right?"

That broke Lilly's concentration. She looked him in the eye and did not need to give voice to the question that was evident in her stare.

"How did I know your client's name?" Lepov had not yet turned to face the open door. "I'll go into details later if you like. For now, let's say I didn't have to use too many of my poor detective skills to figure it out. He was really about the only man who could be your client. But we're being rude. I suspect he's waiting to speak with us. At least he's saved us a trip to his home."

Lilly allowed him to lead her to the open door. The interior of the vehicle was lit with pale light.

"Hello, Lilly." Lepov could hear Claude Reno but he could not see him. "Will you join me?"

Lepov held Lilly's hand as she ducked her head and entered the car. As Lepov climbed in behind her, the door slid shut.

Once inside, he could see they were in a spacious bay with two white divans facing each other. The entire bay was covered in white.

Lepov had tracked black grit all over the floor from the fog-dampened sidewalk. Claude Reno sat on the opposite divan watching Lepov inspect the mess he had made.

"Don't worry about that, Mr. Lepov." Claude Reno waved dismissively at the floor. "I do not have a white floor for aesthetic reasons. It is purely practical. The white floor enables the cleaning system to identify the dirt more clearly. A white floor means a clean floor.

"We've met before. I'm Claude Reno." Reno did not offer his hand as he had back at the police station.

"Yes," Lepov nodded, "my savior from the other day. I hope you didn't bother to drive all the way over to this part of town because you thought I needed saving again. I don't mean to sound ungrateful but a man should only be obligated to another man for one thing at a time. More than one and both men will begin to get irritated with the other."

"Is that so?"

"Oh, I mean no offense, Mr. Reno. I was only making an observation; something I've learned over the years. I have a lot of experience in that area. It seems someone's always being forced to pull me out of a fire of some kind."

"I assure you that I'm not the type of man to offer assistance and then become irritated when it is accepted." Reno pointed towards a white recess above his divan. "Would either of you like something to drink?"

"No," Lilly shook her head.

"I could use whatever you've got." Lepov accepted a glass tumbler half-full of gin from Reno and took a sip. "Again I don't mean to be rude, but you might be surprised at how easily irritated you would become if someone like myself became indebted to you a second or maybe a third time. Especially when that someone—again, I'll use myself as an example—begins to show signs of ingratitude in place of gratitude. There's no excuse for it, I realize, save the fact that men are easily ashamed of accepting another man's help; regardless of that man's willingness to help the other man."

Reno looked puzzled.

"I'm sorry if that didn't make any sense." Lepov sipped the gin. "That was a clumsy way for me to say I'm both grateful for your help the other day and at the same time I'm embarrassed to be in your debt."

Reno turned his attention to Lilly.

"Lilly," Reno leaned forward, "you look uncomfortable. I hope you don't mind that I tracked you down. I realize you were coming to see me, but I decided not to wait. I was eager to see you."

"Did you think I wouldn't come?" Lilly asked.

"No, no. Nothing like that. Of course you were going to come. You told me you would come. As I said, I was impatient."

"Lilly and I don't mind at all." Lepov shifted his weight as he sought a more comfortable position for his leg. His knee had not let up. "All you've done is saved us a trip on a cold, damp night. And as I've been learning since coming to this Lazaretto, catching any kind of flu around here can have fatal consequences."

"Now you're suggesting I've saved you yet again. In the interests of keeping our relationship irritation free I ask that you do not consider yourself indebted to me again."

"I feel like I'm intruding," Lepov said after another moment of silence. "I'd offer to leave you two alone but this car is moving."

"No intrusion, Mr. Lepov. As you might have noticed, I came to your place specifically expecting Lilly to be here with you. I had an idea she might have sought you out."

"And why did you want to see me?" Lilly finally found enough voice to ask Reno a direct question.

"All you had to do was leave. Walk away."

Lilly looked too puzzled to speak.

"If you're angry about the money you spent on her grace period, I guess you could say that's my fault." Lepov knew it had nothing to do with the money.

"I wish I could believe that." Reno's tone had changed dramatically. "But I don't need much imagination to guess what she is doing. Now that your father's dead, you must be feeling the urge to take action."

"My father died many years ago," Lilly said.

"You can drop the act, Lilly. I never knew if he told you, right until the end. Not until the moment you refused to go into quarantine. What was your plan? Expose me? Had you hired Lepov to kill me? Did you think you could kill me, you little bitch?"

"Now I *am* getting irritated." Lepov sat forward and set his drink down on the floor in front of him. "Any fool could see that Lilly doesn't know what you're talking about. Even a fool as big as you. She stayed behind because of me. It's kind of a romantic thing. Something you probably don't have any experience with. But none of that matters anymore, does it?"

"Even if I believed you it wouldn't matter." Reno sat back and folded his arms.

"What do you mean, Claude?" Lilly looked from Reno to Lepov as if both men were enjoying an inside joke. "Gregor, what does he mean?"

Ever since they entered Reno's car, Lepov had felt he was missing something; that nagging feeling that no matter how hard you look at a picture you weren't seeing what you were supposed to see. Lepov had been examining the interior, cataloging everything he could see and still he knew he was missing it. The pain in his knee was distracting, but it wasn't enough to keep him from thinking clearly. No, there was no excuse. Reno had something up his sleeve and Lepov simply could not see it.

The smile on Reno's lips told Lepov that he was right and that Reno knew Lepov had failed to see what was happening. But what could that be? There was nothing to see. They were sitting in the bay of a totally enclosed vehicle as if they were sitting in a small room; a room without even windows. Lepov couldn't be expected to see anything.

And that was the point. Lilly and Lepov couldn't see anything beyond the two white seats and the man sitting across from them. It had been assumed that Reno was taking them to his place. That was, after all, where Lilly was supposed to have met him. But the fact was they couldn't see where they were being taken.

"I could make a pretty good guess, but I don't see the point in that." Lepov undid the front of his coat. "Do we get to hear an explanation or are we supposed to never know what's going on?"

"Explanation?" Reno shook his head. "Full confession? Is that it? That's slightly old-fashioned, don't you think?"

"Sure, it's old-fashioned. And unnecessary. Looks to me like you made a big mistake. You think Lilly knows something that threatens you and so you take steps to shut her up. You were wrong but you can't back down. Basically you're an idiot." Lepov didn't feel half as cavalier as he was trying to sound.

"I'd tell you to be careful but you seem to realize it hardly matters."

"What the hell are you two talking about?" Lilly asked.

"The Chief Administrator is about to—how should I put it, Reno?"

"Silence you."

"God, that's weak." Lepov pulled at his leg in another attempt to lessen the pain in his knee. "Murder is the best way to put it. He's going to murder us. I don't know why. And it doesn't matter why. It's my fault, Lilly. I thought we'd be okay, with our images being recorded as we went to meet him. But I doubt there are recorders in front of my dormitory. I should have thought of that."

"Is that right? You intend to kill us?" Lilly turned on Reno indignantly. When Reno nodded, she reached out to slap him. Reno caught her hand mid-slap. "Damn it, Claude. What are you doing?"

"No explanations," Lepov said, "remember?"

"You just tried to get me out of the Laz for my own safety, Claude. Now you want to kill me? You're acting like a lunatic!"

"You're the one who's acting. Give it up. Your impatience gave you away. If you intended to come after me you should have waited. Let some time go by. You might have caught me off guard. I always liked you, Lilly. I always hoped this wouldn't happen. It's why I let you live so long. As long as there was a chance that you did not know about me and your father I was not going to touch you."

"My father? What are you talking about?" Lilly stared at Reno. "I told you my father's been dead since I was a teenager."

"I could believe in your ignorance if you had stepped into that quadrant."

"Why aren't you doing anything?" Lilly asked Lepov. She looked as if she were about to jump at Reno.

"First of all, my knee's killing me and I doubt I could do anything that would be considered useful. And secondly, I bet Reno has a plan."

"I do." Reno withdrew a short-barreled pistol from the inside of his jacket. "I realize pulling a gun must look excessively theatrical."

"Well, at least I guessed something right. I hope you mind if I smoke." Lepov dug out his pack of cigarettes and unwrapped it. He offered one to Lilly but she only glared at him.

"Don't light that in here." Reno raised the gun to emphasize his order.

"Never threaten a man who's already expecting to die. He'll ignore you every time and you'll end up losing your control over him." Lepov lit a cigarette and blew smoke in Reno's direction. "Besides, you won't shoot me over a cigarette. Not in here. No matter how hard your cleaning system works, blood's not gonna clean up on this white fabric."

"So smoke your cigarette. You have little time left to be clever." Reno tried to pass off the cigarette as insignificant but Lepov could see the panic in Reno's eyes. "Condemned prisoner's prerogative, and all that."

"So grant one last request. We know about the virus. Tell me how Fisher knew Layne was infected. How you knew to contact his mother. I get it that you hoped she would draw him out, so you could grab him, get him off the streets. He was the kind of evidence you didn't want walking around. But how did you and Fisher know about him?"

"You have been busy, Mr. Lepov. Dr. Stride must be talking a great deal. I don't think it will hurt anything to tell you that Layne's exit scan from the laboratory wing recorded vital signs consistent with those of a carrier of the engineered virus. Fisher was the first to see the report. He destroyed it, and told no one but me. Now, no more questions. No more answers."

"Lilly, when I count to three, cover your eyes and be ready to get the hell out of here." Lepov stared at Reno and took a long drag on the cigarette.

"I'll shoot her before you get to three." Reno swiveled the gun towards Lilly.

"Then I won't count at all."

Lepov reached down and pulled at his leg again, grimacing at the tenderness of his knee. His foot dragged past the glass sitting on the floor and with a painful shudder Lepov kicked the glass and its contents towards Reno. At the same time, he flicked the cigarette at Reno. Reno burst into flames.

Lepov felt the vehicle drop hard and lurch to a stop. Fire suppression systems fogged the compartment as doors on both sides of the bay slid open. Lepov tried desperately to disregard the sharp pain tearing through his leg as he grabbed Lilly by an arm and shoved her out into the night. Rolling and scratching along a wet concrete surface, he shouted a curse. At least one wild animal must have been trying to eat his knee. It hurt bad enough that he hoped his damned leg would simply fall off. Anything would have been better than what he was feeling right then.

He was vaguely aware that Lilly was beside him, yanking him to his feet. He thought he had been rescuing her but that was no longer the case. She was trying to support some of his weight; his knee could no longer take the punishment of carrying half of his body.

Lepov cried out as his knee took his full weight for a brief second. Lilly readjusted her position and drove her shoulder up under his.

"You're gonna have to live with the pain, Gregor. I can't carry you." Lepov had an idea she was enjoying some of this.

"Where are we going?" Lepov gritted his teeth and tried to look back at Reno's vehicle. "And what the hell happened back there?"

"You set the man on fire. He's not dead, if that's what you're asking. I'm sure the fire was put out before it did any real damage. We need to find some place to hole up until we can call the police."

"I threw a cigarette at the man. That doesn't set a man on fire." Lepov looked up at the buildings surrounding them. "I know this place. Why was he taking us down here?"

"Is there a place where we can get out of the open?"

"Yeah, Greta Becker's apartment is right next door and she's not home." Lepov reached out as they passed a stone stoop and grabbed an ornate newel post. "But I got bad news."

"What?"

"We gotta climb three flights of stairs."

107

The cleaning system on the Collector's vehicle was the most advanced system available. When Lepov kicked over the gin, the system's superior programming went into action: the instant the cigarette was launched in the air, the system calculated the location where the discarded debris would land and sent a series of commands throughout the compartment. First, to minimize damage to the white fabric on the floor, a stain-resistant detergent soaked that sector of the floor. At the same time, an aerosol cleanser was dispersed from overhead nozzles, knocking down dangerous aromatics and bacteria that might have been associated with the debris.

Both the detergent and the aerosol cleanser were flammable.

The leading edge of the aerosol spray was thin enough to match the concentration necessary for the low ignition spark provided by the cigarette. The initial flames consumed Reno's clothing and body hair as well as the exposed layers of his skin. This fire burned up the available oxygen in the bay. Descending Halon fog stifled the flames, clearing the compartment of fire and heat. Fire suppression shut down. Detecting smoke, more aerosol cleanser was pumped into the contaminated atmosphere. Fire detection systems shut down the engines and slid open the doors for quick egress. Oxygen from the outside rushed in to fill the void left by the fire and fog. The fire, still smoldering on the detergent-soaked floor, roared back to life.

As the detergent-fueled flames reached up and consumed everything in the vehicle, the aerosol cleanser lit up in a burning ball of pinks and greens.

The initial rush of blistering heat and blinding flame crippled the Collector's ability to produce cohesive thoughts. His first reaction had been to pull the trigger of the pistol he was holding but his fingers never squeezed hard enough to complete the action before his hands jerked back to protect his face. The flash of his pistol scorched his already burning face. Flames attacked him from above and below.

He never had the luxury of his senses shutting down. In fact, for all he knew, he continued to feel, smell, hear, taste, and see the raging inferno that enveloped him for hours and hours and hours.

108

When MacNally got the call he was standing in the middle of the street. It took no time to find the right door and climb the worn, wooden staircase.

"Lepov!" MacNally called out for the private detective before he laid eyes on him. He found him sitting on a couch with his leg stretched out on the worn cushions. "Are you out of your mind?"

"You got here fast enough, didn't you?" Lepov's face was white and he looked badly shaken.

"I asked you if you were out of your mind—you just murdered the Chief Administrator of the Lazaretto! Are you out of your mind?"

"Are you gonna keep asking that? I don't intend to answer you."

Lilly Stewart came out of the kitchen wiping her hands on a towel. She pushed back a few strands of hair that had fallen out of her ponytail and nodded at MacNally.

"Is he out of his mind?" MacNally knew he sounded ridiculous but he couldn't help himself.

"Is he really dead?" Lilly tossed the towel on the back of the couch then circled it to examine Lepov's knee. She probed the knee to determine the extent of his pain.

"I think it's safe to say he is. Hell, Lepov, you set the whole damn car on fire. I couldn't believe you two rolled out of it in time."

Lepov winced as Lilly poked and prodded his knee. He pushed her hand away. "Are you saying you were there when it happened? You saw us come out of the car?"

"Damn right I did. I ought to arrest you two. You'd better be able to explain what happened down there." MacNally dropped into a chair facing the sofa and wished he hadn't. The damned thing was hard as a rock with an errant spring sticking up in the center of it.

"I don't mind telling you what happened down there but you're gonna have to believe us. The honorable Claude Reno was about to kill the both of us." Lepov reached into his jacket and pulled out a pack of cigarettes. "These crazy cigarettes saved our lives."

"What are you doing?" Lilly asked Lepov. He was tapping a cigarette out of the box.

"What's it look like?" he asked her, the cigarette now in his mouth.

"Stop it." Lilly reached out and snatched it from him. He grabbed her wrist and they both stared at his hand. "Gregor, let go. You're not going to start smoking."

MacNally didn't know what was going on between them and he didn't want to. He cleared his throat, interrupting their standoff.

"Reno tried to kill you?" he asked, disbelief in his voice.

"He was pointing a gun at Lilly and was taking us God-knows-where to kill us." Lepov let go of Lilly's hand and watched her as she stuck the pack of cigarettes into her coat pocket "And before you ask let me answer: I have no idea why he wanted to kill us. He said something about Lilly's real father dying. Lilly didn't understand what he was talking about but we both understood the gun pointed at us."

"So you burned him alive in his car?"

"I guess so. To tell you truth, I didn't really think it through. I only meant to distract him. All I did was kick over a glass of gin and throw my cigarette at him — give Lilly a chance to get away."

"Well," MacNally grunted, "I'd say you did that pretty good. But what am I supposed to do with you now?"

"Why were you watching us?" Lepov's mind switched gears and he wanted details. "Shouldn't you be looking for Ethan Layne?"

"A little old couple gave me some information tonight that told me Reno might be involved in all of this. It wasn't much in the way of hard facts, but it was enough for me to look into it. I thought I would go and see Reno. But he ends up going to your place. And you and Miss Stewart climb in with him. That's it."

"But what about Ethan Layne?" Lepov didn't give up. "I thought it was decided this kid has to be found."

"No one knows where to look." MacNally didn't like his own answer but it was the truth. "My guess is he'll show up one day dead in some alley. Maybe he already is. From what I could tell from those two doctors, it sounds like no one really knows what this virus can do. For all we know, it's spread all over the place. Even their idea that there is only one carrier could be completely wrong.

"May I?" MacNally reached out and pointed towards Lilly's jacket. She looked down at where he was pointing and finally understood. She pulled out the pack of cigarettes and handed it to him.

"Have a cigarette," Lepov said sarcastically.

"That's what I'm doing," MacNally said with genuine pleasure. He blew smoke out between his front teeth slowly. "You know, Lepov, I've been thinking. You may have done us all a favor."

"I didn't give you the cigarette. Lilly did."

"I was talking about Reno. I have a feeling we aren't going to find much evidence to link him to Fisher or even Parks. It may be the best outcome we could have hoped for."

"And what do you do about me?" Lepov asked suspiciously.

"What about you? You spilled a drink and dropped a smoke. I can't arrest you for being clumsy."

It was the best solution for everyone. There was no need for anyone to get a conscience and demand an investigation. Whatever Reno was guilty of, it didn't matter now. The damage was done. The best thing MacNally could hope for was that everyone involved walked away. It's what his captain would want. It was what the

Lazaretto would need. The news of the virus was going to make ugly headlines for a long time. A prolonged investigation into the upper management of both the Lazaretto and the IHS would only make matters worse.

"I blame my knee," Lepov said quite seriously. "It hurt so bad I spilled my drink while I was trying to find a comfortable position for my leg. And when I moved it the wrong way the pain shocked me so bad I dropped my cigarette."

"You're not only a clumsy fool," Lilly put a hand to his cheek and pulled it slowly across his sandpaper stubble, "but you're a lousy detective, remember?"

"How could I forget that? Not only lousy, but unwanted," he added.

"If she's gonna kiss you, I think I'll go downstairs. I suppose it's my duty to see if anyone's still alive in that burning car."

MacNally shut the door and stood in the hall for a moment, thinking about Reno's words. What had he meant about Lilly's father? Maybe it was best to let the answers die with Reno.

109

Helen had not expected the attack until it hit her with full force. She was in the elevator, waiting for it to open. At the last moment, before the doors hissed and slid apart, she knew it would happen. In that last, vaporous moment in time, she saw the hallway, saw how empty it would be, and she saw that brutal, sadistic man waiting for her. With flushed face and sweating palms, she tried franticly to breathe, to take one full sweet breath of air. She only managed to take in a shallow breath as the doors slammed into their pocket grooves leaving her exposed to the empty hallway.

It didn't matter that no one was there to throw her against the wall. It didn't matter that she was silently and utterly alone. It made little difference that she had only imagined the apparition that had once been her attacker. The panic attack that seized control of her was all too real. She barely had the strength to take a step forward and block the elevator doors from coming back together.

But she had enough strength to recognize that she had been attacked by her own fear. And as much as she despised herself for giving into that fear she knew that she would be able to claw her way out of it. And she knew that the most effective way to do it was to focus on what was true.

The truth was that her attacker had been arrested and was safely locked up behind bars. The truth was that extra security had been added at her building since the attack. The truth was that no matter how strong her memory of the attack, it was over. She had to move on. She had to put the attack in the past.

The truth was she was still frightened beyond all reason.

She walked the length of the hall for what seemed like an hour, maybe even two hours. By the time she had reached her door she had found a shallow but reasonable cycle of breathing. She was proud of this fact until she heard the elevator doors slide open. She was still trying to enter the code into her door lock and she briefly forgot the number.

Panic had not completely overcome her and she was able to recognize Dr. Haupt as he stepped out into the hall. He saw her standing at her door and she saw relief in the place of his ordinarily stoic expression. Something was wrong.

"Dr. Haupt?" She left her questions unasked, waiting for him to explain why he had followed her home.

"Helen, let's go inside." He watched her finish entering her code then stepped in front of her to open the door. "Wait here. I want to make sure no one is inside."

That didn't help her anxiety. She reached out a hand and grabbed the door, preventing it from opening.

"Who would be here, Dr. Haupt? What is going on?"

He hesitated; it was obvious he didn't want to answer her.

"Please, tell me." She looked him in the eye and willed him to speak. His silence was more disturbing than anything he might say.

"After I look in your apartment, Helen."

"I'll look with you." She had no intention of standing alone in that hallway.

"Alright." He pushed open the door.

She kept as close as she could. They moved through the whole of the apartment turning on lights and opening doors. She had no idea what they would have done if they had found anyone. The apartment was empty.

"I believe I should take you to a hotel tonight." Dr. Haupt said this as she lowered herself onto the couch and tried to relax.

"I think you'd better tell me what happened."

"Lt. MacNally called me a short time ago. The man who attacked you, Shaw Parks, is no longer in police custody. He has escaped. The police are searching for him. The Lieutenant asked that I look after you, and that we both find a safe place for the night. They are unable to provide us any additional protection."

Helen closed her eyes and tried to find that shallow but reasonable cycle of breathing. It proved to be too elusive. As much as she wanted to get out of her apartment — the images of that attack were too fresh in those rooms — she could not bring herself to go back out into that hallway. She was not sure Dr. Haupt would understand.

"Please," she asked him, almost pleading with him, "can't we stay here? We can keep the door locked. There is no way for anyone to get in. We can make sure of that."

If he were embarrassed at all by the thought of staying in her apartment for the rest of the night, Dr. Haupt did not allow her to know it. He merely nodded, agreeing that her idea might be for the best.

"I had thought it would be too painful for you to stay here. But you are the best judge of that. If it does not disturb you, we will stay. As you have said, we will not allow anyone through that door."

"Thank you," she said. He smiled at her, and Helen thought she caught a glimpse of embarrassment—or at least uncertainty—in his manner. She almost smiled as Julia's words came back to her. *You think he found some cute little accountant and they're crunching numbers right now?* Helen knew she must never let Dr. Haupt know what she was thinking. "You've been exceedingly thoughtful, Dr. Haupt."

"It is nothing."

"But it is." She stopped short. How did one person tell another she had never expected this level of tenderness from him? How could she explain that she was surprised by his compassion and loyalty? Why had she ever misjudged him? From the first day they had met, he had been honorable, considerate, conscientious and guileless. How could she have discounted his humanity?

"Helen?" He waited until their eyes met before continuing. "I would like to ask you a question, if the news of Shaw Parks has not troubled you inordinately."

"No, no. I'm fine. Go ahead." She could not tell what he was leading up to, but she could see that he was in great earnest.

"I will, of course, need you to help me finish our report over the next two days. I know, I said I could do it myself. I was only being— what is the right word?—bravado? I was only putting on a brave front. I did not want you to worry. I wanted you to relax. But that is not the point of what I am saying. After the report is submitted, I will be returning to Earth; to Baltimore."

Helen was caught off guard by his statement and more so by her reaction to it. She had known he would eventually go back but she had not expected to feel such pain.

"I do not want to put you in a difficult position, Helen. And I do not want to do anything that would interfere with your career. However, I hope you might consider what I am about to propose. You do not need to give me an answer at this moment, but I do hope you will...how is it your friend Julia would have said it? *Chew it?*"

"Chew *on* it," a bittersweet laugh accompanied her correction. It was certainly something Julia would have said.

"I like the way you handle yourself, Miss Segal. I like working with you. You are a reliable woman which gives you great value. I want you to be my assistant in Baltimore. There is much work that needs to be done and you would be an important part of that."

Helen could not stop the tear from spilling down her cheek. She wiped it away but not before he noticed it.

"Helen, what's wrong? I did not think it would be inappropriate to ask you to join me." He was clearly nonplussed; an expression she had never seen him wear so plainly.

"Nothing's wrong, Dr. Haupt. Nothing at all." And that was true. But how could she make him understand what had brought that tear to the surface? How could he ever know that she had given up on ever getting out of the Lazaretto? That she had given up on being wanted by anyone for anything ever again. Was she really wanted? Was it possible? She could not believe it. Not when she thought of the stigma that would haunt her. Could he even understand the stigma that she would carry for the rest of her life? And if he did come to understand it, would he still want her to work with him?

"If there is nothing wrong," he said, trying his best to work out the logic of her response, "then why do you cry?"

"I'm not so sure you will really want me to work with you. It would be an honor to work with you, don't misunderstand me, but obstacles will prevent my joining you. People who have worked in the Lazaretto are not welcome on other worlds. There is too much myth and paranoia to overcome. It would interfere with your work. As for the tears, well, they surprise me too. You see, Dr. Haupt, I wasn't aware of how much I wanted to leave the Lazaretto until you suggested I go to Earth. It was terribly sweet of you to offer me the position. Only, I'm sure you will think better of it before you depart."

"Helen," he tucked his chin into his chest as if he were bracing himself for an argument, "There can be no obstacle. When we have cleared through the quarantine zone, there will be no doubt that you are free of contagions. The Lazaretto system effective and no one need worry about you. I will personally see to it that no one treats you with any foolishness."

She almost believed him; a dangerous idea. The hope that she might actually find a life outside of the Lazaretto was too treacherous to allow it any kind of foothold in her heart. If she allowed herself to think that she could find another life beyond the dark and infected world of the quarantine she might begin to believe all kinds of dangerous ideas were possible. And for a single woman of her advanced age, some ideas were much too dangerous to start believing.

Helen knew she would never say no to Dr. Haupt. A small measure of guilt threatened to surface when she thought of Julia — buried under the bitter, jagged crust of the Lazaretto — and another tear fell. Once, she had allowed Julia to live for the both of them. Now, it was Helen's turn. She wondered if she really could do it. Wrapping herself in a soft cotton nightgown and sliding under the protective warmth of her grandmother's quilt, Helen knew she would have to try.

Despite her anxiety over the escape of Shaw Parks, she smiled. The idea of the stoic and proper Dr. Gerhard Haupt, guarding her while sitting on her living room couch as she lay only one room away from him in her nightgown, was too fun to contemplate. Julia would have had a field day.

110

The night lasted longer than any night Maria had ever spent in the clinic though she had only been there three hours. After Kjarsta had been taken away — he had fought so long to stay in his body that she could not cease to think of him and the body in separate terms — she remained alone in the empty room. It was only at Della's insistence that she prepared to go home. There was, after all, little more for her to do. For the first time in many months she felt as if she were only in the way. She was no longer needed.

She made her way down to the first floor, knowing full well that Karl had been alerted to her departure. She did not mind. She looked forward to his company; looked forward to the attention. It would help her stop thinking about Kjarsta.

She walked the length of the long hall that separated the lobby from the back entrance and found that Karl was not waiting for her. There were four or five people standing near the rear doors. She did not recognize any of them. They were part of the emergency staff that remained on the first floor and were the first contacts for any patient entering the clinic during off-hours. A silent yet palpable expectation hung in the air. Maria saw Karl appear at the security office door.

"Mrs. Duvalls?" His usual smile was missing. "Were you planning on leaving already?"

"Yes," Maria wished she had not come this way.

"If you'll wait a few minutes, we are about to receive a new patient, but once he is in, I can walk with you to the SubTransit station."

"I don't mean to be a bother," she said.

"You always say that, Mrs. Duvalls. And I always say it's no bother." he turned at the sound of a Medical Transit beyond the doors. "They're here. I'll only be a minute."

Maria watched as the little crowd of orderlies and nurses braved the cold, wet night to assist the ambulance drivers as they wheeled their patient through the doors. She could not see much of the patient; her view was blocked by the fast moving workers dressed in their stark-white uniforms. It shocked her to hear one of the doctor's say "poor bastard's still alive." The second doctor said "He'll wish he were dead. So will we. He will require constant care."

There was no moment of indecision; no time spent wondering what Georges would say. Maria knew she would do it.

Later — many weeks later — Maria would discover that her instant desire to care for the new patient had not meant that she had already forgotten Kjarsta. She found, in fact, that it was her deep and abiding love that she had developed for Kjarsta that enabled her to care for the man who rolled in through those double doors that night.

As the gurney carrying the man passed through to the clinic's emergency care unit, Maria tugged at Karl's sleeve as if she were a little girl trying to get her big brother's attention. Karl looked down at her.

"Did they say why he's here? What sickness he has?" Maria was worried she would sound like a child as well but she had a great and sudden desire to know everything about the new patient. "What did they mean he would wish he were dead?"

"Mrs. Duvalls," Karl looked awkwardly at her but avoided making eye contact, "I don't think he's sick from anything. He was brought here because we have the closest thing to a burn unit. Our equipment is not the most modern for that kind of thing, but the hospitals here do not even have equipment as good as ours."

"Burn unit?" she asked. She knew nothing about burn victims or the care of them. "Was he badly burned?"

"From what I could tell," he nodded, "he looked pretty bad. We do not have the technology needed to properly restore him. He is also permanently blinded. Honestly, we're not equipped for this like the home planets. And no one's going to allow him to be shipped out of here. Well, you know how that is."

Maria held back her tears. This new patient, like Kjarsta, would need someone like Maria. She determined to be someone he could depend on as he awoke to what could only be a nightmare of a life filled with terror, pain, and despair.

111

MacNally had been shocked at the paramedic's news of Reno's pulse. It was a horrific thought to be so badly burned and yet still alive. But MacNally hadn't been shocked enough that he couldn't think quickly on his feet. He made sure no one else was informed of Reno's condition. It had been good luck that they were so close to the *Terminal Clinique de Lazaretto* and that he had recently met its chief doctor. A few simple orders ensured that the burn victim was taken to the clinic and Dr. Duvalls made certain that no one would know his identity.

That had been the easy part, making Reno disappear. The harder part would be concealing the truth. They would never be able to hide Reno forever. Not when three people knew that truth. And either the doctor or the paramedic would eventually make a mistake that would point others to the truth. But that might not be for many years. And that was long enough; long enough to make sure that Reno was officially replaced.

MacNally never worried that he had made a mistake. He still believed what he had told Lepov; the Lazaretto did not need an investigation into what had happened. The Lazaretto was already a stained and filthy community that did not need to have its dirty laundry hung out for all to see. Few people cared enough about it; MacNally was one of those few. And no matter how foul it could be, the Lazaretto was the town he had sworn to protect.

And there was plenty for MacNally to do. Moments after he watched Reno's tortured body being taken away, a call came in about yet another dead body. A TransitCar driver had found a body down near the shipping zone. A body with no PDT. MacNally drove across Center City and wished Fenelli could join him.

MacNally took it as a matter of course that the body turned out to be Shaw Parks. The body was in pitiable condition. It was wretched enough that even MacNally couldn't gloat over the fact that Fenelli's killer was dead. It was simply a depressing end to a long and ghastly week.

It wasn't until he'd crawled mindlessly into bed with only an hour or two of night left that he remembered he should have called Gerhard Haupt with the news about Parks. It could wait. It would have to. MacNally was far too tired to talk on the phone.

As tired as he was he couldn't fall asleep right away. He kept hearing Arturo Fenelli's voice chiding him for some offensive comment, or maybe an encouraging word designed to cheer him out of a blue funk. No matter how he turned in the bed he couldn't make Fenelli's voice go away. MacNally finally came to the realization that he didn't want to. He didn't want that voice to stop. All too soon it would be gone forever. The one voice in the Lazaretto that had ever given him a chance. The one man that had ever wanted him as a partner. Why in God's name would he ever want to silence the voice of Arturo Fenelli? Sleep finally came, even as that voice continued to speak and speak and speak.

112

As the gray light of the Lazaretto morning tried to press the black night back into one corner of the horizon, Maria walked wearily up the stairs of the Trireme SubTransit station. Though there had been occasional fits of rain that night, there were only a few puddles scattered across the potholed Trireme Avenue. A few lights from the apartments above winked in the still, deep puddles as if they had been lit from within.

She had waited most of the night for word on the condition of the burn patient. He did not even have a name at that point; there had been no identification on him. She could not have gone home while still wondering if he would live or die. Georges had come and waited with her. She was surprised at his level of interest. One of the younger doctors handled the case.

When the young doctor—she was too tired to recall his name—finally stepped into the nurses' lounge and gave Georges a report on the man's condition, Maria was emotionally spent. She had been holding her breath, fearful of his report. No one had believed the man would live. Maria had so wanted to care for this poor soul. She could not understand it. She should have hoped with everyone else that he would be mercifully released from his ruined flesh. It was selfish to wish otherwise. And yet, despite this, she could not help herself. She wanted him to live so that she could be a light in his darkness.

Georges had shown no reaction when told the man would live. Maria had seen, however, the confusion on the young doctor's face. She understood. He had done what he had been trained to do and what his heart had always longed to do; he had saved the man's life. But the enormity of what he had done must have left him wondering exactly how compassionate his effort had really been. Maria wished she had known the young man enough to assure him he had done the right thing; to assure him that despite how it looked the soul inside that horrific body would still have a chance to find God's grace and love in his world of pain and terror. Somehow she would make that happen.

Maria shook as she thought of it. How could she make that happen? How could she have the audacity to think that she might be able to lift that man out of the misery he was sure to experience? Only God knew, she told herself. Only God knew if she was being arrogant or if she was doing what he had asked.

The margin of error in that was humbling. Disturbing. And as

Maria approached her building's entrance, she did not want to lie in bed, trapped with such a thought. The idea alone made sleep impossible. She did not have to think twice about it; she walked on past the entrance and headed out towards the park. The morning sky was already lighter, the night's chill would not last long. Tightening her coat around her little waist, she stepped into Terran Park. Georges would worry over her when he discovered where she had gone, but by then she might have found the peace she was seeking.

Cutting through the trees, Maria watched her thin shoes collect the rain that had been caught and held by the thin grass of the forest floor. She ought to have stayed on the path; more scolding from Georges. The trees above her were much like Georges, watching over her, standing silently by as if they might scold her whenever she might need it. As she walked beneath them, moving through a light morning mist, she imagined that the trees were moving and she was the one standing still. They were marching slowly past her, watching her and taking their measure of her. Would they find her wanting? Would they see she only wanted to do her best? It wasn't much, she knew that. But shouldn't that be enough?

The silent judges continued to parade around her until the last taciturn shadow faded from view. Fortunately, there been no verdict passed down. She was left alone with the hope that she might not be guilty of arrogance; that she might be following her heart down the right path.

She had come to the fountain of the four fauns.

Shrouded in a mist that was growing whiter as each minute of the morning slid by, the sound of the waters pouring forth from the fauns' pitchers was muffled. Maria could see the vague outline of her beloved fountain and knew that she had been right to come there despite the good soaking her shoes had endured. Already she could feel the peace that poured forth from those pitchers. Maria imagined that even the presence of the angry faun could not trouble her that morning.

As she came nearer to the fountain from the north side of it, the fog slowly relented, finally revealing the face of the smiling faun. It amazed Maria, after such a long night of sorrow, that the faun's smile should immediately put her in mind of Kjarsta. No matter that his long, cruel fight with a murderer's virus had finally come to a fatal end; she could only think of him as he had been the day he had spoken of his little truck. That mischievous smile of his was still contagious, here at the end of this desolate and exhausting night.

How had he done it? How had he managed to find anything to smile at as he grappled with death? She knew the answer though she did not want to say it even in the privacy of her heart. But she knew.

She knew that he had conjured up those moments of happiness for her sake. He knew what he had been doing. Knew that she had needed him as much as he had needed her.

Her heart briefly filled with joy and she almost laughed again at his little truck full of cabbages. And then, as she had known she would, her heart filled with tears and they began to flow as steadily as the waters flowing from the fountain. She did not fight it, nor did she wish it to last. She needed to cry; needed to allow the tears to purge her of her sorrow. But she also needed them to stop after a time. There would be more, at other times, and that would be both necessary and welcome. But she found that Kjarsta had taught her more than laughter. He had taught her strength and courage and she discovered a small reserve of that where it had never been before. When she thought of the burn patient lying unconscious in the clinic, she knew she was going to need great amounts of both.

At first, when she heard her name spoken softly, she thought she had imagined hearing it. The voice was weak and raspy like Kjarsta's had been near the end. But she knew she was not hearing a memory of Kjarsta. The voice was real. It called again.

"Maria?" Someone was sitting on one of the benches.

She could not see him clearly in the fog, which was now nearly white and had grown much thicker. But she could see his silhouette. He was sitting up; his head cocked to one side as if he were tired or his head too heavy to hold upright. As she stepped closer to him, the shadowy man spoke again.

"I was hoping you would come." His voice was stronger this time. He cleared his throat and tried again. "I hoped I would see you here."

Maria didn't recognize the voice. The fog obscured her vision and she could not see the man until she advanced close enough to nearly touch him.

It was William; the blond young man that had scared her so much only a short week ago. Now, William did not look so young. His eyes were blood-shot, his cheeks hollow. He no longer had the striking good looks of youth. If she had not known him in the recent past she might have guessed he was in his early sixties. His hair was thinner now, he trembled with a weakness reserved for those who have already lived a long, full life. Maria thought he looked brittle.

"I don't know," he said to her.

It sounded as if he were answering a question that she had asked. Perhaps he had read the question that surely must have been visible in her eyes. How could he have come to such a state?

"I'm some kind of sick." He spoke to her but his focus was lost to the surrounding haze.

Maria was now only a foot away from him. She could see that not only were his eyes blood-shot, but his skin was marred by dark, subcutaneous streaks of reds and blues. In many places, these streaks were smudged into bruises.

"I didn't do anything, you know." His eyes pleaded with her. He gripped her hand, clasping and pawing at her in desperation. "It's important. I didn't do those things."

She was supposed to know what he was talking about but his words were a mystery. She did not know what he was trying to say but she understood that he wanted her to know he was innocent.

"William, you're sick." Maria could not help but state what was so obvious to the both of them. She leaned in close and examined the flesh on his face as well as his hands. "I must get you to my husband's clinic. There's no time to waste."

He pulled back then; she could feel the nails on his hands as if she'd been stroked by the paw of a wild dog. He shook his head slowly, the effort obviously disorienting him.

"Don't be silly, William. You need help."

He sunk lower on the bench. His efforts to speak with her had drained him of energy and he was no longer able to hold himself up with any degree of control. Maria, long accustomed to aiding Kjarsta in his bed-ridden state, leaned forward and gently took hold of William, easing his descent as he slid down on the bench. She slipped a hand under his head and made sure he did not drop it hard against the wooden slats.

"Don't get me help," he whispered. She wasn't sure he had said anything and had to put her ear close to his lips as he said it again. "Don't get me help. They won't let me leave—"

Anything else he said was indecipherable. Maria was down on one knee now, her dark long coat soaking up the puddle beneath her. One hand still cradled his head. She could feel the cold wood against her skin and realized that William's body was cold. His head twisted awkwardly as she slowly pulled her hand free. Once it was out from under him, she tenderly rolled his head back until it was in a more natural position.

His eyes were closed, he was still breathing. All she could do was watch him. She had no personal phone with her, no way to get help. She did not know what to do but stay by his side. It was a pitiful choice; one that would do nothing for him in the end.

She reached into her jacket and withdrew a thin white handkerchief. The young man's breathing became ragged and she could see mucus running from a corner of his eye. Wiping him clean, she brushed his hair from his eyes with her other hand. He had been so young, but no more. No more.

The fog was lifting by the time she stood up. A cloud-soaked sky became visible high above them, running fast with air currents that did not reach down into the park. It might mean a break from the wet and turbulent season.

Maria took a few steps away from William, drawn towards the fountain by that incessant and dream-like sound of running water. She did not have to look up to know that the melancholy faun was watching her. Water stains in the deep grooves of the faun's face would be black after the wet night, highlighting its expression of grief. She would not look upon it. Not then. Not after a night like that. The night had bestowed enough sorrow on the Lazaretto. Or maybe it had been the other way around. It did not matter to Maria. It certainly wouldn't matter to the fauns.

Epilogue

Comic Joe's was nearly empty at ten o'clock in the morning. The bartender had finished serving coffee and pastries to the morning customers and now sat with his back against the great mirror reading a small book that demanded a great deal of focus. A lone Lazar sat in a booth near the front of the room, an empty coffee cup sat on the table.

It was Alpha Quadrant's lockdown day. Most of the people who wanted to leave the Lazaretto had already settled down into their quarantine quarters in Alpha. Nearly everyone had opted to get in early. There was no last rush to get inside. Strange rumors of a new and deadly virus had fed the usual paranoia until no one wanted to stick around unless it was absolutely necessary. And few people could think of any reason that might be absolutely necessary. Alpha was crowded; the barracks-like dormitories were the only places left to find a place for travelers to lay their heads. A brief public discussion was waged about what to do if Alpha actually ran out of room for people who wished to get out. This scenario was still in the theoretical stage but many believed it could become a reality.

The only other two customers at Comic Joe's were seated in a booth midway along the length of the bar on the opposite wall. The woman was Lilly Stewart; her companion, Gregor Lepov. They sipped bad coffees, avoiding conversation.

The front door opened as a tall, heavy man pushed into the room. He was wearing a stained raincoat with a hat pulled down over his eyes. He made straight for the couple in the booth. Tipping his hat at Lilly, he squeezed his bulk onto the bench beside Lepov.

"You missed breakfast, MacNally." Lepov scolded.

"Would you like some coffee?" asked Lilly.

"No coffee—I've tried it. And I didn't miss breakfast. I skipped it." MacNally looked down at Lepov's coffee and wrinkled his nose. "Maybe I'll try the coffee again." He called to the bartender and gestured for a cup. The bartender dropped his novel on the bar.

"Why'd you skip breakfast?" Lepov gestured for more coffee as well.

"Lynne Fenelli is settled into Alpha. We made sure she had a decent room in one of the hotels. She's going to stay with one of her kids for now. I get the feeling she may return to the Lazaretto. But that has more to do with the fact that Arturo was buried here. She's got a long way to go to get over this."

"And you?" Lilly prodded him.

"I'm fine," MacNally lied. Bluster and bravado were still two of his greater virtues. "They found some dumb kid straight out of college—from Arcobia of all places—who was willing to be my partner. God, it's like I'm teaching elementary school."

"Elementary, Watson!" Lepov barked.

"Who's Watson?" MacNally asked.

"Oh, some guy in a book. Lilly has me reading a book. She has this idea I need educating."

"You may have succeeded in getting his knee repaired, Lilly, but trust me, you're wasting your time trying to repair his brain. That damage is permanent. By the way, I saw Dr. Haupt at the hotel in Alpha a few minutes ago. He's heading back to Baltimore. He's taking that assistant back with him, too."

"The woman who'd been attacked?" Lilly had never met her.

"Yeah, a real good skirt." MacNally stared down Lilly's disapproving glare. "You know, that's a compliment where I come from."

"I hate to think about where you come from," Lilly dead-panned.

"You know," MacNally accepted his cup of coffee from the bartender and blew on it, "I do have some detective skills. And from what I could see, this wasn't the happiest table when I arrived. What's with you two?"

Neither Lilly nor Lepov answered him. They both shot looks at each other then began to pay overzealous attention to their coffees.

"Hold on," MacNally spoke sharply, "don't tell me Lilly's decided to stay behind. That's not gonna happen. I won't let her, okay Lepov?"

Lepov gave MacNally a wooden look but said nothing.

"It's not safe, Lilly." MacNally began to lecture her: "Even though we found Layne's body, we don't believe the virus died with him. So far, we haven't been able to isolate it on anyone. I won't let you stay. I can throw you out of here and that's exactly what I'm gonna do."

Lilly looked up at him and shook her head.

"No, what?" MacNally frowned.

"I'm not the one staying."

"The hell, you say!" MacNally spun on Lepov. "Don't tell me you think you're gonna stay."

"I think I'm gonna stay," Lepov said right on cue.

"That's funny. Very funny. Don't worry, Lilly, I'll throw him out. He won't stay. And what do you want to stay for anyway?"

Lepov shrugged his shoulders. Lilly rolled her eyes.

"Well?" MacNally was waiting for an answer.

"He's got a job—a client." The bitterness was evident in her tone.

"He's what?"

"I've been hired." Lepov sat up straighter and rolled his shoulders back. "I've been hired to investigate some stolen property. You know how little the Lazaretto Police Force is interested in the misfortunes of one of its citizens."

"Tell me he's joking," MacNally begged Lilly.

Lilly shook her head, a dry stare in her eyes.

"Well, do you want me to take you down there?" MacNally warned them how crowded Alpha Quadrant had become.

"I've got a room, Ed. Plenty of room." This last she added after looking over at Lepov.

"Traffic might get crazy. I'll pull my car up to the door and I'll get you there on time. Any bags?"

"No, they're already in my room."

"Okay, then." MacNally stood up and glanced over at the private detective. "Lepov, you're an idiot."

"Says the man who's lived in the Lazaretto for a hundred years." Lepov held out his hand and MacNally shook his hand with a sigh. "If you're gonna live here, you're gonna have to stop doing that. I'll be out front, Lilly."

Lilly told him she'd be right out and watched him leave through the front door. "Well, what a lucky break for you."

"How's that?" Lepov frowned.

"You don't even have to bother to accompany me to the gates. You can stay right here and get started with your new life in the Lazaretto."

"Lilly," Lepov lowered his voice and leaned in towards her, "I asked you to stay with me. I also told you why I was staying. I don't have anything to go back to there. Hell, by now Eudia Layne's probably ruined my name all over Bukovina."

"I know all of that."

"And you know I might have found a place where I'd be

wanted."

"You were already wanted. Do I have to spell it out to you? You really are as stupid as I first thought you were. I can't believe I was almost murdered because I stayed behind for you."

"I'm never gonna hear the end of that, am I?" Lepov could tell he was losing his temper and it was the last thing he wanted to do. "Lilly, this isn't permanent. You'll come back through here or I'll follow you after I finish this job. At any rate, we'll see each other eventually."

"I'll make damned sure we do." Lilly didn't want to argue either. She was still too eager to want this guy. But she was learning to handle it with more dignity. "And when I get back, you'd better not be buried out there in that rock pile. Take care of yourself."

She wanted to say more. But why? He knew she cared for him. She knew he cared for her. But they were both too stubborn to compromise. It was going to take a great deal of time and the eventual act of self-denial by one of them before they could ever end up together. That was, if the Lazaretto's newest virus didn't kill Lepov first.

Both of them had the same thought and neither wanted to mention it. It was too real a possibility. Lepov meant to ignore it. Lilly was terrified to acknowledge it. And so the subject passed on without ever reaching their lips.

"Ed's waiting," Lilly said. She could see his car sitting directly in front of the door.

"Don't look so sad, Lilly Stewart." Lepov set his coffee down and slid his hand over until it was covering one of hers. "I've got the funniest feeling we're going to get back together much quicker than you're going to want. As a matter of fact, you'd better enjoy the break from me while you can. Once we become permanent fixtures in each other's lives you're going to get good and tired of me."

"You're wrong, Gregor Lepov. I'm already getting good and tired of you. I simply don't want you to stay here and catch a virus."

"We've got to meet some place where it's more acceptable for people to touch each other. This paranoid little town isn't all that fun."

"I think I know a place." Lilly leaned across the table. "And when we get there, what exactly did you have in mind?"

"This." He leaned forward and kissed her.

She sat back and knew he'd done it again. That little-boy-charm was as dangerous as a virus. It was as contagious as one too.

"I'm gonna get away from you now." She slid out of the booth and left without looking back.

Lepov watched her slip through the door, her white ponytail

bouncing in rhythm to hurried steps. It was enough to make a man question every decision he'd ever made in his empty little life.

Lepov left Comic Joe's a short time later. He had nowhere to go. Of course, he'd lied about the job offer. Lilly had probably seen right through that. But it didn't matter. He had an idea that no matter how much she wanted him to join her, he was destined to be alone. Maybe MacNally was right. Maybe when all was said and done, he really was an idiot.

Gregor Lepov shrugged off his doubts and decided he sure as hell wasn't going to lose any sleep over it. After all, every forty days he had the chance to change his mind.

The End

About the Author:

Jason Phillip Reeser, having the spent the first half of his life traversing state lines in a nomadic life that covered ground from the snow-covered forests of Michigan to the sun-bleached sands of Florida, now lives and writes in Westlake, Louisiana. His ghost story anthology, *Cities of the Dead*, which Louisiana Poet Laureate Julie Kane called "a twist of Louisiana Gothic," is set in the cemeteries of New Orleans. He recently published *Room With Paris View*, a travel memoir with his wife, poet Jennifer Reeser. His short stories have appeared in such publications as *The Louisiana Review*, *Bewildering Stories*, and *Danse Macabre*. If you would like to contact him, send email to editor@rocketfirebooks.com. He welcomes comments and questions of any kind.

Visit his FaceBook page at:
FaceBook.com/Jason-Phillip-Reeser
Jason's blog, *Room With No View*, can be read at:
roomwithnoview.blogspot.com

Rocket Fire Books is a small publishing company. If you enjoyed this book, we would appreciate your willingness to mention it to friends who might also enjoy it. If you are active online, at sites like Facebook, Goodreads, Amazon, Shelfari, or similar sites, we ask that you remember us when reviewing and recommending titles. Look for us at rocketfirebooks.com, as well as our Facebook page:

Facebook.com/TheLazaretto.
Thank you in advance for your kindness.
RFB

**In New Orleans, Louisiana,
the dead refuse to be buried.**

Praise for Jason Phillip Reeser's
short story collection:

Cities of the Dead

"...a skilled and entertaining
Louisiana storyteller." *--Lake
Charles American Press*

"...powerful and compelling."
--Neal Connelly, author of *St.
Michael's Scales*

"Jason Phillip Reeser proves an expert guide to the necropoli of
New Orleans, where some of his thirteen tales from these moldering
crypts pay homage to the classic pulp magazines. Others, however,
engage deeper philosophical questions of morality and mortality, as
the dead try unsuccessfully to make their peace with one another and
with the living, who are equally incapable of breaking through the
time-worn yet timeless marble that separates two levels of being. As
one hapless soul concludes, 'Death was not going to be terribly
different from life.' "

R.S.Gwynn,
University Professor, Lamar University
Author of *The Narcissiad* and *The Drive-In*

from Saint James Infirmary Books

Turn the page for news on current and forthcoming
books from Rocket Fire Books.

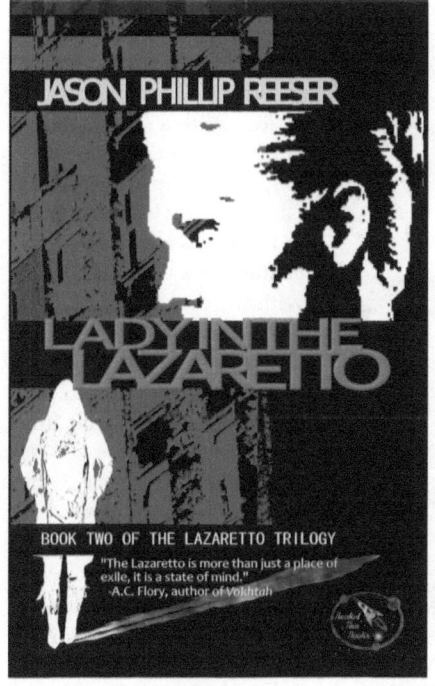

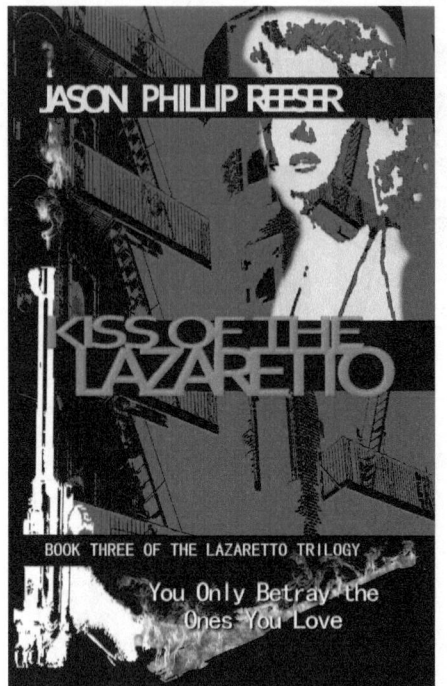

www.ingramcontent.com/pod-product-compliance
Lightning Source LLC
Chambersburg PA
CBHW020328180626
46812CB00001B/94